A WOUND LIKE LAPIS LAZULI

A WOUND LIKE LAPIS LAZULI

MELODY WIKLUND

Melody Wiklund

Illustrations by Melody Wiklund.
Cover design by Melody Wiklund.
Cover oil painting: *St. Rufina of Seville* by Francisco de Zurbaran, painted 1640.

First Printing, 2023

Contents

I

CHAPTER ONE

Most members of the painters' guild in Ferrar, capital city of Salandra, would have agreed that Ricardo Montero, who after all was only a jumped-up country dweller, had a little too much nerve, all of it gifted to him by King Alejandro. The king had given him this commodity along with several commissions over the years—most recently a painting of the most important members of his household, a group portrait into which Ricardo had audaciously inserted himself—a modest salary, and his own small studio in the royal palace. Who else could claim such honors?

Rumor had it that Ricardo did not properly appreciate the king's generosity, that he did not deserve it. And Ricardo was well aware that such gossip would only have been encouraged by how he was behaving today. Not that he was doing anything scandalous. It was only that the king was for the thousandth time late for one of their meetings, and Ricardo, expecting this would be the case, had invited Beatriz de Comete into the palace studio to model for a separate, non-royal project he was working on while he waited.

Beatriz was fortunately as unconcerned about this type of gossip as Ricardo himself, if not more so. She'd asked him if he was sure she should come in, but when he said "yes", hadn't questioned him further. Almost a noblewoman herself, she was at ease in grand surroundings, possibly more comfortable than Ricardo was at heart. On the other hand, she was not the best of models, as she kept on asking him questions or craning her neck trying to see what he was sketching, and her fidgeting was a serious impediment to the sketching process. When she moved her whole body, it ruined the pose entirely and he had to scold her back into place, but what was worse was when she changed the angle of an arm ever so slightly while he wasn't looking, leaving him mystified as to how he could have gotten the shape and position of it all wrong until he realized what she had done.

"Well, I'm no professional," she protested when he complained. "I mean, I'm sorry, Ricardo, but I'm trying my best. It's not as if you're paying me."

"Damn right I'm not." He almost asked if paying her would make her hold still, but then what if she said yes and actually did demand payment? His "modest salary" had been delayed for a couple weeks now and he was having a hard enough time making ends meet already. Until he finished this current commission, he couldn't afford anything unnecessary. Beatriz being willing to model for free was one of the main benefits of using her.

The other benefit was that she did actually have a suitable appearance for the commission. His subject was a diptych of anger and discipline. Anger, his patron had requested, was to be coarse and wild; discipline, on the other hand, was to be portrayed as the desirable virtue it was.

Beatriz was modeling for anger.

"Because you're a perfect model for vice," he had told her when he first made the request, and she had laughed. It was true they often quarreled, and he'd seen her lose her temper more than once. More than that, though, he wanted anger to look like a simple, rude farm girl, and while Beatriz had noble blood, she had a rather simple, honest face. Her complexion was slightly tanned, and her nose was a bit large too. She had a frank look to her, especially when you put her in an apron and a plain white headscarf, but she was still very pretty if you liked that kind of thing, and she had nice, fat arms that went well with an angry pose, though he hadn't yet decided whether she should cross them or put her hands on her hips.

He was on a variation of the second idea, with one of Beatriz's hands on her hip and the other fist raised, when the door opened and the king strode briskly in. The pose, of course, was instantly ruined, as Beatriz turned and dropped into a curtsey.

"Your majesty, forgive my presence. Ricardo had said that we might work a little on one of his projects before your appointment. Now that you are here, I pray you will excuse me..."

Beatriz was very comfortable in a palace and around other nobles, but King Alejandro was imposing enough to recall her to pronounced formality. He would have been enough for anyone. Not only was he the king, but he was a legend throughout Salandra—war hero, and famously blessed by a goddess.

He also was a man who liked to walk in on Ricardo unannounced to see how he would react. Ricardo had gotten pretty good at nonchalantly putting down his pencil and paper and turning to the king with a smile and a greeting, as if he were unaffected. He was not. Five years he'd been the king's favored artist, but he never quite got over that presence.

King Alejandro, however, waved Beatriz's excuses aside. "Stay a little longer. It's no imposition, and I know I've made poor Montero wait. But see, I've brought someone to introduce you to, Montero. This is Countess Leonor of Suelta, my dear cousin. You may have heard of her. And Leonor, this is Ricardo Montero, the best artist in the city, or the country for that matter. Perhaps in the world. And Beatriz de Comete, ward of Don Fernando de Comete."

The king's praise rested pleasantly on Ricardo's head, but the guest he was introducing was far more interesting. Countess Leonor de Suelta. Ricardo had heard of her before he even became a fixture at the court; she was well known once as the previous king's daughter, though now she lived on a country estate far from the capital and did not involve herself in matters of the court. He had more recently heard about her from King Alejandro, who had muttered about her planned visit to Ricardo a couple weeks ago, something about how he'd have to put away all the good cutlery and keep an extra guard on the garden. She was a woman of mystery, and Ricardo had been dying to catch a glimpse of her. And here she was.

She looked like Alejandro. There was a family resemblance in the shape of her nose, the height of her forehead. Her hair was golden brown like his too, and her eyes had a sharp look in them. Ricardo expected her voice to be likewise sharp—he expected scandal and intrigue to break forth when she spoke—but all she said was, "Enchanted, Montero."

"Equally."

"I admired your paintings in the hall."

She had to mean not the hall outside the studio door but the grand hall where Alejandro held parties and important gatherings, decorated as gaudily and thoroughly as a jewel box. Ricardo wasn't the greatest master featured on those walls, but he was perhaps the best of modern times. He liked to think highly of himself. Still, one could not admit to such things. He smiled politely. "His majesty is an excellent subject for any artist." It was the king's portrait, after all, that called the most attention to itself in the grand hall currently. "Still, that painting was from some years ago, when I first had the honor of serving the king. I believe I've improved a great deal since then. Soon I hope to replace it with a new piece."

Ricardo had gotten pretty good at nonchalantly putting down his pencil and paper and turning to the king with a smile and a greeting, as if he were unaffected.

"I heard your portrait of Alejandro's household was more recent."

"Oh, so it is! You noticed that one?"

"It was brought to my attention by Sir Grigio, who was showing me around. I see you do resemble your own portrait there. Though you look younger in person."

The tone was still polite, but Ricardo's face heated. He was almost thirty now, and even had his own apprentice, but people at court, especially women, did say he looked younger. They liked to tease him, flirt in ways he tried not to encourage, especially the older ones. Leonor was older and looked it, with a face beginning to show wear, but she was hardly old enough to smirk as she did on making that remark. It wouldn't have flustered him so much except that he'd tried his best to impart his image in that particular painting with gravitas, and had felt a little self consciously aware that in real life he couldn't pull that effect off. But no one had called him on that, not until now.

"Montero was a prodigy when I first met him," Alejandro said fondly. "Twenty years old, barely joined the guild, and already brilliant. Since then, all that talent has matured in my service and he has come into his own. And he is going to paint the ceiling of Marina's temple for me, as I told you."

"Madonna has thoughts on Marina's temple?" Ricardo asked.

"Oh, no, I have no insight on religion or on art," Leonor said. "I'm merely curious. Anything my esteemed cousin pours so much energy into must be an important project. And I've always admired his reverence. Indeed the whole country must."

Alejandro said, "How could I fail to revere Marina? She has always been my benefactress. Before I became a king, after all, how did I gain the love of the country and your father? Not through my good looks, however they may look in a portrait. But through my feats in battle, battle at sea, and there I may say I was more blessed by the goddess than talented. The waves and the weather always favored me.

"There was a time I encountered a trio of Fiterian vessels in open water—Fiterian water it was, back then, during the war. I on my little ship was outnumbered three to one, but I sailed closer, preparing to fire. Yet before I could even get in range, the sky darkened with clouds. It did not rain, but the sea grew rough—and rougher near the Fiterian ships than near me. Of a sudden, there was a crack of lightning, and the mast of the largest ship was felled—and blown onto another ship, too. Thus they were already entangled and damaged when I came near. I don't doubt I won that battle thanks to Marina, and many others besides. So I do honor her. It is only what she is owed."

"Though," he added with a roguish smile inappropriate to the subject, "I will admit I would worship her anyhow, for I do love her, my lady of the sea. My offering is scarcely sufficient—still, I'll admit it pleases me so far. The vault is higher than I had pictured! Not higher than the original plans, but I simply had not imagined it accurately. I plan to have Montero here paint it with images of Marina from the legends, though he has his own ideas about what images to use... but it will be a discussion. One cannot allow an artist too much leeway in a matter like this; he may have his ideas, but he's never been at sea, and I know Marina far better. I know what she'll like." He smiled fondly again.

Ricardo smiled peaceably. "Of course in the end I will follow your directions, your majesty. My own ideas I simply present in case you should find them useful."

"Oh, Montero, I meant no offense. I'm glad you have ideas—it means you're investing in this project as you should be. Though you're clearly still distracted with other matters," he added. "What's this you're working on here with Miss Comete?"

"Only a private commission, not very important. I promise that once work on the temple starts, I will drop all else, but I thought perhaps I would have some time for other work for now. This commission should only be a matter of a few weeks' work, I think, less if I paint wet on wet for some portions, and it will be months before the painting of the vault must begin in earnest. If your majesty has more important work for me..."

Alejandro waved an indulgent hand. "Ah, very well, you are forgiven. It is allowed! I know you can work quickly when you want to."

"If you end up having some free time," Leonor said, "I might consider commissioning something from you as well. To have my own portrait done by the king's artist would be an honor."

Ricardo pursed his lips and gave Leonor another once-over. She certainly looked royal, and painting her wouldn't have been unpleasant, and though her current outfit was out of style by a couple years and the fabric used in her dress was a dull green and not all that appealing, all that could be easily remedied. Out of the corner of his eye, though, he noted that the king did not look terribly pleased by the idea, and why would he be? Everyone knew Leonor de Suelta was the least favorite of his relations. They had been close once, rumor had it, but then Leonor's father had died and left Alejandro king, and Leonor had become surly and unmanageable. Alejandro had kindly arranged her marriage to a noble friend of his, the count of Suelta, but the count and Leonor hadn't gotten along, and then the count had died, and Leonor had remained in Suelta and become something of a recluse. These days, Alejandro hardly ever spoke of her, and when he did, it was more often with annoyance than affection.

Ricardo couldn't offer his services to someone his king disliked. He shrugged and said, "I beg your pardon, milady, but I'd heard you will only be in the capital for another month, and I don't think I'll have time for it after all. Perhaps at another time—or if you were to provide me with references of your husband. I heard he was a great man."

Leonor's expression soured.

"A great man indeed," Alejandro said. "Ah, but Montero is right, Leonor. It's not the season for him to pick up a new commission. Here's an idea—maybe if you bring Feli to the capital next time, Montero could paint a portrait of *him*."

Leonor's expression soured further.

Perhaps the most controversial thing about Leonor was that she was the mother of Alejandro's current heir apparent. Alejandro's wife had died three years ago, and their marriage had left him without any son of his own. This left Leonor's son, grandson of the previous king, next in the line of succession. Despite this, Leonor had refused multiple invitations to come live in the capital and bring the young Prince Felipe with her, or to simply send Felipe here by himself to live with his cousin once removed and learn a king's duties. She had never even brought Felipe to the capital for a visit.

There was always some excuse. Today she said, "I've offered my apologies for Feli's illness..."

"Oh, it's nothing, it's nothing. I would never blame you for worrying over your son." But the king did blame her, and his smile was bitter.

Yes, it was for the best if Ricardo never so much as sketched this woman. Best if he didn't even say much more to her, though he was curious, very curious, and although he did actually like the idea of drawing the young prince. Well, he might get a chance someday. To draw Leonor with her son—he wondered what that would be like. She'd make a very imposing royal mother, but she'd simply have to wear a better dress than this one. Something both regal and maternal, a difficult balance to strike. It would be an interesting concept to play with, but the politics of it were too delicate. Regretfully,

Ricardo abandoned the idea and focused instead on the present conversation.

King Alejandro wanted to rediscuss the composition of the vault's design. Ricardo was pushing for the edges of it to look like the seashore, filtering from a sandy color into blue and green, with depictions of various legendary figures higher up, perhaps conversing with each other. Alejandro, on the other hand, had little interest in the shore and thought the whole thing should be pure ocean. Sand, he said, was what land folk associated with Marina, but it was earth, not water, and besides, there was nothing grand about it. Ricardo argued that the temple was about "land folk's" associations as much as anything else. Its art was meant to evoke feelings and thoughts in those that visited and bring them into a certain state of mind. Depicting Marina truly and perfectly was not the point, and that would be impossible anyhow.

As he said this, he glanced over to see if Beatriz would object, given her penchant for realism and specificity, but at some point, she had quietly vanished, leaving Ricardo between the king and countess—one opinionated master and one quiet observer who occasionally would throw in a contrary remark with no real intent behind it, apparently just for the hell of it. It was a wearying conversation, and by the end Ricardo had been forced to concede several areas of his design concepts. At least he kept seaweed and shells, if not (much) sand. Otherwise, the king wanted blue and blue and blue. Ricardo had no idea how he was going to pay for it all. The price of ultramarine paint was through the figurative roof; to cover a literal ceiling in it would be ridiculously expensive. And while the king would probably claim he was willing to pay whatever necessary for good art, Ricardo knew from experience this was not exactly true. At the end of the day, it would be on Ricardo to figure out what could be done with the bare minimum of blue paint and a whole vault to cover...

Then again, maybe this piece would be different. There was Alejandro's devotion to Marina, after all. For her, perhaps he wouldn't skimp. Ricardo could hope.

"Ah, Montero, I've lost track of time again," Alejandro said with a sigh. "I was supposed to meet with the ambassador of Jukwald half an hour ago... Well, I hope he won't mind my being late. At least I can introduce him to a beautiful woman to make up for it."

Leonor took the hint, and trailed after Alejandro towards the door. She said to Ricardo, "Perhaps we'll meet again."

"Perhaps, if this busy, crowded capital allows," Ricardo said.

He had a sense that for all Alejandro had initially liked showing him off to Leonor, he'd become irritated by the end of the conversation, whether that was because of Leonor's disagreements or because of Ricardo's retorts, which had by the end become overly familiar. It would be better if they did not in fact meet again. But he smiled. Later on, he could complain about her to Alejandro, and balance would be restored.

* * *

The painting of "Anger" took even less time than Ricardo's estimate. It was only a week and a half before Ricardo was satisfied it was done. That made him wary. It was a small piece—the diptych altogether was meant to fit over a mantle, and each painting would be less than a foot wide—and he'd been working wet on wet, both factors which added to his speed, but he wondered if he had rushed the piece. With this in mind, he invited Beatriz back to his studio to take a look at it.

Ricardo's real studio was not at the king's palace. In fact, despite what the gossips said, that room was not entirely his at all—technically it could be used by any artist the king hired and was merely a convenient back room with enough space, decent lighting, and windows to let out the paint fumes. Ricardo's real studio was at his house, which again, was not really his house. Both his house and his studio he rented, as he could not yet afford to buy the property. Houses in the capital were terribly expensive.

It was not that grand a house, either. The first time Beatriz had come visiting, she'd been very unimpressed. Just as she was now unimpressed by his painting of Anger.

"That's it?"

"It might need a little more polish," Ricardo admitted. "I'm waiting for it to dry before I add a last few touches." And that could take days.

"Ricardo, it's not about polish. Look, the shape... I told you I'd be willing to stand for the painting as well as the sketches, didn't I?"

"And I told you it was unnecessary." He hadn't wanted her fidgeting to interfere with his process. "As you can see."

"Unnecessary." Beatriz gave the canvas a hard stare. "But it hardly ended up looking like me at all."

"It isn't a picture of you but a painting of Anger." Ricardo smirked. "How could I use such a lovely face—"

Beatriz swatted him.

"...at any rate, the client doesn't want anyone recognizable, I'm sure. He only asked that I might depict women, young and simple women. So, there you have it."

Beatriz sighed.

"What?"

"Young and simple women. Anger and Discipline. Your client has interesting taste. I'm sure he's paying you more than you've admitted to me, too." Beatriz gave him a judgmental look. "If he's asking for anger, he wants passion. If he's asking for simplicity, he wants crudity. Something solid and frank. Look at how you've painted this figure, Ricardo! The expression isn't bad, really, and even looks like me a bit, but there's not much below the collar, is there? Lots of cloth but you can barely make out the chest and legs."

"Of course you'd harp on that. Beatriz, I was commissioned to portray an emotion, not to focus on showing every curve of a woman's body."

Beatriz shook her head. She reached into a knapsack she had brought here with her, and offered Ricardo a small stack of papers, the whole stack of which was folded in half lengthwise. "Here. I thought things might turn out like this. Some practical help for you."

Ricardo unfolded the stack. His jaw clenched. "Beatriz."

"What?"

The papers were sketches, as he had expected, anatomical sketches. Of women's bodies. Nude. And done in a very flagrant style, plenty of attention lavished on legs and breasts. Not that Beatriz neglected stomachs or heads, arms or feet or hair—as always, she gave all the body its due—but one's eyes certainly did not end up fixed on the face, not with the poses she had chosen.

There were at least three different women in the sketches, though none Ricardo could identify as someone he knew. He knew they were different because one appeared to be old, judging by how the skin hung on her, especially around the neck, and one was fatter than the others by a good deal, and then one appeared fairly similar to his own painting—probably not Beatriz herself, though, since he had in fact altered her form when painting her.

"You need more practice on chests and legs. Everything a women's clothes cover, you're afraid to touch," Beatriz said matter of factly. "A good artist can't be squeamish..."

"Or pornographic, Beatriz."

Beatriz had a flair for detail. She'd paid particular attention to each woman's pubic hair, and to the veins on one woman's breast. There was also one sketch with two of the women together, one sitting on the other's bare lap, the other's arms wrapped around her. One arm just covered the nipples on the woman's breasts, and the covering up only made her nudity more evident.

Ricardo folded the sketches back in half. He looked up to find Beatriz's arms crossed and a typical challenging expression on her face.

"Sir, I am a woman. My asking women to bare themselves for me is hardly scandalous, nor is my drawing them in great detail. I understand that as a man and the king's own artist, it's different for you. That's why I thought I'd offer you some references, as a friend. You can thank me now."

Thank her. Ricardo wasn't sure which irritated him more: Beatriz's arrogance or her pretense at being offended. He sighed and shook his head. "Beatriz, this painting is already almost complete. I'm only working on fine details now, not reworking the poor woman's whole body. And I'm sure if I copied your little sketches—" The offended look that phrasing evoked was not faked at all. "—I could make my madonna of anger look just like whatever woman you called into your studio, but it might occur to you that is hardly the point of the painting. This is neither that woman, nor you, nor any woman in particular; it isn't meant to be a real woman at all. It's the painting of an ideal."

"Anger, hardly an ideal. Although..."

"A concept," Ricardo continued. "A higher truth, a state of being. This is meant to be not just an angry woman, but the human being, greater than the singular. She shouldn't look too concrete or too common. She shouldn't look like a person you could run into on the street. I'm conveying a concept through a body. Yes, it should look like a body, like a person—and I used you for that purpose—but the focus should, ultimately, be on the concept. If I mimic the specific too closely, in the end I only lose the general, the platonic form."

"Ideals," Beatriz scoffed. "I've heard that talk from you before, Montero, and what it comes down to is nonsense. Ideals don't exist except inasmuch as they affect the flesh, so how else are you meant to portray them? Specificity comes first. We human beings create the general in our own minds."

"Ah yes. I forget that you, the great Beatriz de Comete, believe in nothing at all."

"I believe in what I can see and taste and touch, which is a great deal. That is the only way anything can be understood, really. And on the rest, I'd be willing to be convinced. But you understand not even the physical—and you're planning on decorating a temple to Marina. That really worries me."

At this, Ricardo went a little beyond irritation. Placing Beatriz's papers on a table, he sat and faced her. "Worries you how?"

"I've seen some of your designs. Waves as soft as a ringlet of baby's hair, and women that looked like—that. Have you ever seen the real sea, Ricardo? Have you ever tasted the salt, or felt the force of a wave against your thighs?"

"Yes, I've been to the sea before. I've seen it. As for my sketches, they were sketches and un-detailed. They will be edited with the help of his majesty, who was a sea captain before he was king, and certainly knows more of Marina than you."

Beatriz shrugged. "Well, I'm sure your work will be up to his standard. After all, he's never found reason to criticize you. If he didn't think you up to the task, he wouldn't have chosen you in the first place."

"Quite," Ricardo said.

They stared angrily at each other for a while, then lapsed into conversation about other matters. Beatriz's recent work, for example. Another still-life, this one of fruits and vegetables. She wanted him to come look at it; he promised he would come see it soon. By the time she'd left, he'd calmed down for the most part. But his gorge rose again when he realized the sketches had been left behind on the table, even though he'd intended to demand she take them back with her.

He looked through them again, this time looking more closely. Beatriz did have a way of capturing the body. None of the sketches were actually suitable references for his painting, though, and he still felt she'd brought them over to taunt him. Nevertheless, it would be a waste to discard or burn them. He handed them over to his apprentice instead. "Here, take a look. Don't ogle them, but think about them scientifically, maybe copy them for practice. They're observation drawings of things we can't observe—a favor from Beatriz. Of course it's better to study the masters for such references, but these still aren't bad, and I know you struggle with the female body."

"Thank you, master."

"But don't ogle them," Ricardo repeated. He hastened away and back to his work, feeling a little embarrassed.

* * *

"She wore the snidest expression on her face the whole time," he said to a drinking companion later. "I really could slap her sometimes... but her brother would kill me if her father didn't. That damned Comete family. Sometime around twenty years ago their daughter—no, excuse me, ward—bastard, really—their bastard came up to the don and said 'Daddy dearest, I simply must learn how to paint' and the sap decided to let her, and I'm sure the whole artistic community of Salandra will eventually suffer for that evil day, perhaps for generations to come."

He was a little drunk already, and enjoying it even though it brought out his irascible side. At least he could relax this way. At the end of a long day, especially a day graced by a visit from Beatriz in the mood for debating, he often headed out to a local bar for wine and tapas. A local bar, or two or three if he found a friend in the mood for wandering. One thing the capital did not lack was bars! Bars and fountains, Ricardo thought tonight, as he had often thought before—that was what the capital had, was bars and fountains. But mostly bars.

This bar was the closest to Ricardo's humble home and therefore the most convenient. It did not have the best wine in the city, but it was not so bad either, and it cooked pig's ear with a combination of spices he could not quite place and had not seen matched at any other bar yet. Its bread was decent too, though not made by the bar itself but bought from a small bakery a street away. And its cheese was strong but not so strong as to upset the stomach of a man who had been working at a painting all day and had had only the tiniest lunch. For all these reasons, while Ricardo did not hold it to be the best bar in the city, and to his more sophisticated friends would not even admit it to be his favorite, it did hold a certain place in his heart and his wallet.

It was a good place to make new friends, too. Like this man, who called to the bartender to refill Ricardo's glass, and asked him, "Is she really that bad? Still, sir, at least she's not all that popular. I'd scarcely heard of her until today."

"That's a saving grace to be sure, but it's really good, her art, on a mechanical level at least. One can admit she knows how to draw or paint a body or a face or a tree or anything really... she can depict it so you would think it real. I swear I once saw her portrait of her father when I was coming around a corner and thought it was the old goat himself. But where's the soul in her work? She's more like a copyist, no invention or deeper truth, only gritty details and dull coloring and coarseness. Were I to listen to her, my paintings would be as soulless as... as paint!" He took a deep gulp of wine. "And the gall she had, coming to me with drawings of naked women as if she were trying to seduce me. Incredible."

His companion laughed. "I'd say she does show nerve."

"Nerve. Gods, what does she not show!"

"Well, we'll speak no more of her, eh? Clearly she makes your head ache."

"Indeed she does. I'll need another glass." He called the bartender back and, on reflection, asked for the bottle that he might pour for himself and save the man labor, to which request the bartender grinningly agreed. Ah, they understood him here... or at least understood he would pay, and liked him for that. He was not one to worm out of his debts, unlike some patrons he could mention.

"There must be finer women you encounter in your line of work."

"Oh, not so many. Apart from Beatriz de Comete, I can't say I've met many female artists. Judging by her, I may count my blessings! Of course, I am sometimes commissioned to paint a woman—I painted the late queen, may her soul rest in peace—but far more often I paint men."

"I heard the countess of Suelta asked you to paint her."

Ricardo frowned. "Oh, yes. Her."

It had been two weeks and he'd almost forgotten the incident.

He swallowed. "At least she wasn't too insistent about it. I hate having to turn down an insistent noble, especially a woman."

"Why didn't you want to paint her?"

Ricardo waved a hand. "Eh, politics. And I have enough on my plate right now. Forget it." There was something too curious in his companion's eyes. "The only client I need is the king anyway. Let's drink to his health."

"To the king's health," his companion echoed, and their glasses clinked together in celebration. His voice perhaps lacked conviction, and he drank less deeply than Ricardo, but Ricardo didn't notice it, for he was off in his own world, and would still be even hours later when, half-conscious, he allowed his new friend, who happened to be Countess Leonor's captain of the guard, to guide him out of the bar and down the street in the wrong direction, quietly further and further from home.

2

CHAPTER TWO

There were many artists that, if they had disappeared from the capital of Salandra one lonely evening, would hardly have caused much of a stir. Workman or apprentice artists came and went, sometimes stealthily or with little notice, upsetting few but their superiors; even master artists often went away on unexpected vacations, informing their clients that their commissions would be delayed. For the king's own artist to vanish, though, and without the slightest message left behind, whether on paper or by word of mouth... well, at least among artistic circles, this was a disturbing occurrence.

Plenty of people were convinced it was simply a case of irresponsibility. Of course, Ricardo Montero had never proved himself to be flighty before, but that simply meant an incident like this was overdue. His top rivals, in particular, had plenty to say about it: that they'd heard he was courting a woman of ill repute and maybe he'd run away with her now, that he'd been embezzling from the funds his majesty gave him for expenses and feared being found out, that he had a dread of painting the vault, doubtless a long and arduous task, and had run off to avoid it—that he had gotten in with bad company and met an accident...

Beatriz de Comete was unconvinced by most of these rumors. She knew Ricardo well enough, after all. He had no woman in his life that she knew of, and he hadn't shown any sign of plans to abscond the last time she had seen him. On the contrary, he'd been in the midst of his commissions on anger and self discipline, and very invested in the plans for painting the vault, and outraged at the merest slight to either. The last suggestion, that he had met some accident, seemed the most likely, and it worried her. She hoped it, too, would turn out to be incorrect.

She'd visited his studio when the first whisperings of Ricardo's absence had reached her, hoping they were only the typical nonsense of the city grapevine and Ricardo was still at home, busy at work and out of the public eye, or at worst sick and refusing company. Instead, she found only a cluster of anxious servants who hadn't seen their master in days. Ricardo's apprentice, Juan, was delegated to tell her the whole story.

"He was only going out for a drink and a light dinner, I swear. He even invited me along, but, well..."

Beatriz laughed. What apprentice would want to go drinking with his master, really? Especially after a long day working with Ricardo in the studio.

"Anyway, he didn't come back that night or the next day, and hasn't come back yet. He didn't take his clothes or any of his belongings. He still had everything set up to work on the painting of anger the next day. Something must have happened to him. He wouldn't just run off like that!"

Beatriz nodded. "I agree with you. It doesn't seem likely."

"We asked the city guard to look for him, or at least to keep an eye out. I don't know if they took it seriously. We had a messenger from the king—I was taken to report to the king myself, since

Montero was supposed to meet with him and had failed to do so—I told the king what had happened, but that was two whole days ago now, and nothing. He said he would see what could be done. I guess there's no higher up someone could go, but it's been three days now he's been missing. Miss Comete, we're all very worried. And my master wouldn't just run off without telling us. He's usually very careful about these things."

By the look on Juan's face, he was still worried that Beatriz wouldn't believe him. She assured him she did, and that she too was concerned. This did not make him relax any further, though, and only inspired him to ramble more. Most of his ramblings were about arrangements Ricardo had or hadn't left behind that he regarded as proof that Ricardo had not intended to absent himself, or about Ricardo's more or less conservative drinking habits. He did make one comment that Beatriz thought worth further consideration.

The king, he said, had seemed worried at Ricardo's disappearance as well, but oddly preoccupied. He had said at one point, shortly before dismissing Juan, "I wonder if this is her plan." Juan had not been bold enough to ask the king who he meant by "her", but found it highly suspicious. There were many who might conspire against Ricardo, he said to Beatriz, and a few of them were indeed women.

"Not that I suspect you, of course," he added.

"Of course not."

"Not that you don't fight with the master like cats and dogs, but you usually come to some sort of agreement. Or if not, at least you state your grievances up front. I don't think you two hold grudges against each other for long—you fight, you make up, you fight, you make up. Sure, you'd fought that day, but that was very normal, and you would have made up eventually. I'm sure if the master were here today you would be making up right now."

"Probably."

"Besides, what would you get from his disappearance? You've

gotten half your clients through his connections, and he always offers you guidance on your paintings. With him gone, you're a weaker artist and less esteemed in the public eye rather than more. No," Juan continued, oblivious to the insult in his words, "I'm sure it was either some insulted patron—you wouldn't believe how sensitive some of them are, or maybe you would, being an artist yourself, but I still think we have some of the worst clients in the city—or one of my master's rivals. Valdez, for example. There's a man who stands to profit. Not that he's any kind of brilliant but he'll swear the king would favor him if it weren't for my master sucking up to him with flattery and political maneuvering. Thinks he's the better artist, which is ridiculous..."

Juan had quite a number of theories. Some involving women who might be the mysterious "her" mentioned by the king, others involving men, others involving whole groups of people. Beatriz did her best to calm him down, and when it became apparent her efforts weren't really going anywhere, told him she'd let him know if she got any new information, carefully extracted herself from the conversation, and went home.

The situation worried her, and her worry only increased as days passed and Ricardo didn't reappear. But there was little she could do about it. She did feel a bit guilty over their last conversation. She'd called his art trash, basically, which she didn't really believe; she only thought he could be a bit more realistic and less focused on his precious "ideal forms". If that would be her goodbye to him... But no, she did not think he was gone forever. His body would have showed up by now, she told herself, and what she really meant was that she vaguely thought that if he were dead she would somehow know it by instinct.

She did not get further involved, but her curiosity and sympathy must have made an impression on Juan, for he showed up at her house a week and a half later with a letter in hand. A message he had received from the king. It was apparently a letter that had been sent out to many of the more esteemed artists in the city—those highest ranked by the painters guild, or simply those with good reputations or connections.

"An inquiry into your master's disappearance, then?" Beatriz asked. She frowned. "I doubt any of them know much, or would be willing to tell if they do—surely they would have come forward by now. Still, at least it shows some concern, I suppose."

"No," Juan said, shaking his head in disgust. "No, it's about the vault."

"The vault?"

"Read it."

"To whom it may concern,

"You may have heard of the unexpected and unexplained absence of the royal artist, Ricardo Montero. We have been looking into it with due diligence. However, as it may be that he will not return in a timely fashion, we are considering commissioning a different artist for the painting of the vault of the new temple to Marina. To that end, we wish to invite you to present your best efforts and make your case.

"If you wish to be chosen as the new painter of the temple vault, we are asking that you present us with a painting of Marina, depicted as you see her, preferably in accordance with tradition and proper decorum. We will accept these paintings in three months' time, and judge them to see what artist may be most suitable. If Montero returns before this time, you will be informed, though you may still make your case if you wish. However, if he does not, it would seem imprudent and indeed disrespectful to the goddess to delay progress on the temple further. An artist will be selected from those who present their work, and plans will be drawn up for the painting of the ceiling.

"Signed,

"His Majesty King Alejandro II de Ferrar."

Beatriz read the letter twice through, trying to understand it in a more charitable light than it probably deserved. Three months—well, one could see that as a reasonable amount of time, and the letter did allow for Ricardo's return. But it had been less than two weeks since his actual disappearance. Though a royal project, especially one involving religious matters, ought not to be delayed, and though it took some time for an artist to prepare a sample of their work, surely this announcement could have been put off a while longer.

"The king," Juan said bitterly, "has decided my master has abandoned him. Or is dead. How could he be so callous, when my master was so devoted to him? If my master is dead, his corpse is hardly cold."

"Ricardo Montero is not dead," Beatriz said, folding the letter. "Don't say such things, Juan. You despair as easily as the king does."

"Very well—if he is alive, how much worse! He may be in need of help, but all the king can think about is his damned temple. Imagine how happy all the artists receiving this letter must be, thinking that my master is dead or out of favor, out of their way for good. Valdez must be rubbing his hands together in delight. He must have already taken out his sketchbook and started working. If one of them is to blame for my master's disappearance, this will be their unjust reward—I could curse the king for this."

"The king's not to blame for Ricardo being gone." Or at least, so Beatriz assumed, though she supposed one could not discount any possibility. "But I agree, it's precipitate. It's..." Insensitive, offensive, and, as Juan said, exactly the bone to throw to Ricardo's rivals to make them rejoice even more at his absence. "Anyway, Juan, Ricardo will come back and this announcement will come to nothing. Don't worry too much over it."

"Oh, I won't worry in the slightest. And he will come back," Juan said. There was conviction in his voice, too; but there was equal conviction as he added, "However, I brought this letter to you in case he doesn't. In that case, you must win this competition. You must be the one to paint the vault of the temple."

"What?"

"I'm not good enough myself to win the commission. I've only been apprenticed to Montero for three years; if I were good enough, the king wouldn't even bother advertising like this. You, on the other hand, might be. Montero always says your paintings are brilliant. You focus too much on minute details and imperfections, and you use dull colors a lot of the time, and you misunderstand the philosophy of painting entirely," he allowed (a recitation of Ricardo's criticisms), "but you still have the talent to make most of those half-witted puff-chested bird-brained rivals of his quake in their boots. If my master doesn't come back, we mustn't let any of those assholes win by his absence either. So the one to win the commission must be you."

"Juan," Beatriz said, "I wasn't even sent a copy of this letter. The king, or whoever sent this out, doesn't even consider me an option."

"Of course not. You're only nominally a member of the guild; you're a woman of noble descent, and really only a dabbler. Why would you consider such an arduous task, and who would trust you with it? But if you can do it, and beat out these fucking bastards, at least my master could rest peacefully in his grave—or on his vacation in the country, or wherever he may be. Anyway he at least respects you, even if he doesn't always express it properly, and I know you had nothing to do with his disappearing. Miss Comete, say you'll at least try to win."

He looked so earnest that Beatriz couldn't help but feel for him. Still. Ricardo would return—why waste her time? Besides, she doubted she could win the commission if he didn't. The competition would be too stiff.

"I'll make some sketches and think about it," she said. "But really, Juan. I wouldn't worry yourself."

* * *

It was a strange letter, she thought—Juan had left it with her—and Juan's idea that she should take the opportunity presented was even stranger. Ricardo had been given the commission for a reason: Not only was he the king's favored artist, but his work had the proper gravitas and beauty for such a work. Beatriz had seen his sketches for the vault, and they didn't seem like the kind of design she would usually work with. Too many swirls to represent waves when waves didn't look like that in the slightest. The figures of people who would feature in the image had only been just outlined, but they had already looked majestic in a way Beatriz could only struggle to achieve.

She'd mocked Ricardo's ideas for the vault, but she didn't exactly have better ideas herself. She had a hard time picturing gods and goddesses and heroes in the abstract. For Marina, there were a couple old paintings she tended to picture that she had seen as a child. But they never quite hit the right note for her—she pictured, also, the sea. She had grown up by the seaside, at the Cometes' estate in the country. Her home had not been near a comfortable beach nor a convenient harbor, but near a set of cliffs with only the merest strip of sand at the bottom. On some nicer days, lured by the sound of the tide and its blue and white beauty, she had climbed down a precarious route to touch the waves, and even on those days the water had slapped her, rough salt against bare legs, like a playful bully. On worse days she had sometimes sat at the top of the cliff and looked down at waves that hurled themselves at the rocks as if they wanted to climb right up and eat her.

It would be hard to depict that kind of masterfulness in human form, especially when painting a woman, especially in a way that the temple priests and the king himself would find acceptable. After all, Alejandro was known for seeing Marina as his benefactor. He would want her to be beautiful and kind, surely; Beatriz thought it would be hard to paint the sea goddess that way.

...but the challenge of painting Marina did have its appeal.

And Juan was right, wasn't he? Those vulture rivals of Ricardo's could not be allowed to win this competition. If she had the slightest chance of beating them...

Well, it was all ridiculous.

Still, two days later she went out for a walk down to the temple. It was not a difficult trip or a long one. In a port city, it was traditional to have any temple to Marina be close to the harbor if not directly on it, but the capital of Salandra was land-bound in the center of Salandra itself, so the king in turn had decided to put the temple near the center of the city so that it was easy to get to from any neighborhood at all. It had been a controversial decision, given that the land it was on had previously been part of the nearby market district, but no one had kicked up too much of a fuss; it was the king's command, so in the end it was reluctantly obeyed, and merchants moved their shops and stalls elsewhere, compensated for the inconvenience with royally miniscule fees.

The temple was not quite built. Its skeleton structure was all in place, and the walls were built of strong stone, but the back half was still in progress, and in the front, the door had not been installed yet. There were sculptors still working on chiseling designs around the doorway, designs of waves and mer-folk and other sea creatures, and doubtless the door itself would be even more intricate. These things took time.

Inside, the vault would already be erected—one could see its dome from outside, now complete. But the temple was still too unfinished to allow for painting it, both inside and out. Sculpting came before painting, and architecture before sculpting. This was why the king had given three months before the vault would need to be painted, before Ricardo would need to return. But then time would be up.

Knowing this, and thinking of Juan's suggestion, Beatriz was unable to simply take in the temple as an incomplete work, a masterpiece in progress. She had to look at it as two things simultaneously: A clock ticking down, and a work that perhaps she might take on herself. A possible commission.

An odd way to find oneself looking at a monarch's pride and joy.

She let herself look at it objectively, presumptuously, as if the project were already hers. With what could she cover the ceiling of such a temple as this? Her own paintings were often dark—would that be suitable for a vault? There would be some solemnity in filling in empty places with dark, tumultuous waves. The sea she had known in childhood. Then for the rest, she would choose one of those legends the king wanted depicted—one or two or three at most, not as many as he wanted crowded in. Save the rest for the walls. One painting, perhaps, of one of the famous captains Marina had favored, painted meeting with Marina, or in battle with Marina standing behind the ship or perched on the ship's prow, looking down at the crew. Solemn, yes. A temple was made for awe.

And what would Marina look like? Commanding, yet kind. Beatriz searched her memory for women who might serve as proper models. Lady de Comete, her foster mother, would not be suitable. While she had a commanding personality, it was of the practical kind, and she did not have a commanding face—it was too soft and round, like Beatriz's own, causing some to say they saw a nonexistent family resemblance. Marina's face would need a strong jaw, Beatriz thought, and eyes like sapphires. But she still struggled to picture it. Surely, though, she could find a good model once she got started, if she looked hard enough.

As she mulled it over, she walked away from the temple, not

thinking too hard about where she was going. She came to an abrupt stop in front of a fountain. The splashing broke her concentration.

She looked at the water.

She didn't pray much. While she believed in the gods, she found it hard to believe they listened to mortal attempts at communication, unless those mortals were kings or queens or maybe priests. Now, though, felt like a time for praying if any. Surely Marina would have some sort of stake in how her temple was constructed. So Beatriz moved her lips, barely letting breath escape them in her whisper: "Marina, if you want me to paint your temple instead of Ricardo... isn't it a bit harsh on him? He intended to do the best job he could."

The fountain babbled at her uncaringly. It mocked hubris, she thought, but whose—Ricardo's, his faith in his secure position as the king's favorite, or hers, imagining she might be meant to take this job meant to be his?

"Fine," she muttered, "but if you do want me to paint this temple, you'll have to make it a bit clearer. And you'll also have to help me win. Otherwise..."

A hand fell on her shoulder and she whirled around to face a grinning woman. It took a moment for Beatriz to recognize her—Baroness Anthona de Mestos, of course, and accompanied by her typical handmaid, who was carrying a basket of groceries—but when she did, she dropped into a curtsey, feeling her face heat up. To be caught talking to herself in the middle of a plaza, how embarrassing.

"Beatriz de Comete, as I live! You don't know, child, how hard I've been looking for you. I've been meaning to talk with you for ages, but every party I go to, every gathering, it seems you're never there, even when I've been told ahead of time you'd be there."

Beatriz glanced at the woman's maid, for surely this had to be an exaggeration. The maid, however, looked mildly annoyed, and at Beatriz, not at her mistress, so Beatriz assumed it was in fact true. Why would the baroness of Mestos be looking so hard for her, though? The baron of Mestos was friends with her father, but Beatriz didn't go about in public all that much (except in artistic circles) so she and Anthona had never spoken to each other much. Still, she made a courteous reply, begging pardon for her absence and claiming the call of the muse had distracted her from social affairs for a while recently. "But if you wished to speak with me, you could have come calling, you know. I'm sure Don Fernando would welcome the visit."

Anthona smiled apologetically. "I'm sure you're right. But still, I'm so fortunate to have run into you. Walk with me for a bit—would you like to grab something to eat? I'm just about in the mood for some chocolate, perhaps with a pastry. You'll join me, won't you?"

Like this, Beatriz found herself dragged into a chocolateria. The maid settled respectfully a few steps away from their table, and Anthona ordered enough chocolate for two. Then she leaned forward and introduced the real reason she'd accosted Beatriz in the street: "I hadn't heard that you had any particular plans for this summer."

"Well, I suppose I'm not planning on going anywhere," Beatriz said. "Don Fernando and Luis will be staying in the city, and our estate would be rather boring alone."

"Oh, yes, it is dreadfully boring to be out in the country alone," Anthona agreed. "That's why I wondered if I might impose on you—my own family isn't greatly looking forward to the summer, as we're going back to our own estate. I know Jorge finds you charming, and I've always wanted to get to know you better. Lady Gelvira and I are close, after all, and I really should be better acquainted with her ward. Would you care to spend a month or two with us? It might not be as lively as the city, but we have our own local entertainments—festivals, and there is of course the ocean right nearby. And after all the city in the summer is not always so riveting either. Might I entice you?"

Beatriz said, "It sounds lovely of course. But I do have some small plans for the summer, if not for traveling. You may have heard his majesty has announced a competition to see what artist will paint the vault of the temple to Marina. I intend to paint a portrait of Marina in order to enter."

"An artistic competition! Well, well. We had heard you dabble." Anthona smiled simperingly, clearly casting about for some reply to this unexpected objection. "Well, but one can paint anywhere, right? And what better place to paint Marina than by the sea? Do say you'll join us, then."

Beatriz paused.

The offer was anything but tempting. She could see Anthona's motives quite clearly; they were one of the reasons she rarely went about in the social circles of nobility. The Comete family was not high ranked, as nobles went in Salandra, but it was wealthy. Their land housed a profitable mine, and contained as well quite an active port town. And Beatriz, while not formally recognized as Don Fernando's daughter, and ineligible to inherit the majority of his wealth or title (that would go to Luis, and she was content with that), would still have a large dowry, doubtless, and a smaller inheritance when Don Fernando died. As for Mestos, its port was inactive—most of its commerce came from people visiting to enjoy the waters, but that was hardly a rare commodity. There were rumors about the baron and baroness being low on money, and about their son, too lavish a spender for them to afford. A gambler at times, and a womanizer with expensive taste. Rumor had it his parents were getting desperate to marry him off, to a woman respectable but not too respectable to put up with him, and preferably a woman with money. And Beatriz had money, and she came from a good family, but she was a bastard with poor prospects when it came to marriage.

Of course she could see what Anthona was doing, and it was neither enticing nor flattering to her in the least.

However. Beatriz wasn't superstitious, but sometimes oddities caught her attention. Anthona had been looking for her for weeks, she said, and hadn't managed to make this offer until today, finding her at the very minute Beatriz had prayed to Marina for guidance. And Mestos was by the sea; Anthona told no lies there.

She felt a fool to say this was a message from a goddess, but wouldn't she be more of a fool to reject an answer this direct?

"All right," she said. "I'll talk to Don Fernando, and perhaps I'll come. I have no solid plans for the summer, after all."

* * *

"No," Luis said flatly.

"I was asking Don Fernando, not you," Beatriz said. She looked past him. "And what do you say, then?"

Don Fernando cleared his throat and looked at his wife. Lady Gelvira said, "The baroness is a good woman. I've meant to be more in touch with her—the past couple years it seems that Mestos family's always busy."

"Lady Anthona isn't the issue here and we all know it," Luis said. "Beatriz can't run off and spend a summer in the company of Jorge de Mestos. He's a terror."

Beatriz had sometimes thought her life would be easier with a less respectable brother. Oh, Luis was understanding about Beatriz's art, about her lack of desire to marry, about any number of things he could have been pushy about. Her whole family was probably more understanding than she deserved. But Luis was still horribly protective of both her safety and her reputation. Of all her awful habits, he criticized most how often she ran around without a maid or any other escort, since this habit jeopardized both. He had also once come close to challenging a man to a duel over an insult to Beatriz's chastity. Beatriz had had to soothe him and beg him to be reasonable. The insult had been accurate, and Luis had known that to begin with, but that didn't matter to him. Beatriz was his sister, his older sister by a year but still his sister, and he would defend her to the unreasonable death.

"Jorge is just a boy like many others," she said now. "Harmless."

"A boy! He's a man by several years, though it's true he still acts like a boy, with how he drinks and all the women he..." Luis squinted at Beatriz. "You aren't actually interested in him, are you?"

"I've made it twenty-seven years without throwing myself at any man," Beatriz said drily. "If I were to break now, it wouldn't be for Jorge de Mestos of all people."

"He's succeeded in strange pursuits before, if the rumors are right."

"I'm not his type of prey.Men have courted me before, you may remember, and I've somehow managed to turn them down. I've been propositioned by worse than Jorge, too."

"What? Who was it?"

Beatriz flapped a dismissive hand. She turned back to the don. "Lady Anthona is generous, and I haven't left the city in so long. Besides, they say the sea view at Mestos is excellent. If I'm to win this competition, I'll need that sort of inspiration."

Don Fernando was always indulgent of Beatriz's wishes. Unlike Luis, he wasn't that respectable at all. He said to Jorge, "Beatriz can take care of herself. And Mestos is hardly a den of sin. Lady Anthona's a fine woman, and her husband's a fine man. As for that son of theirs, eh. If he tries to make any trouble, he'll see how the Comete family deals with an offense."

"And you'll take a maid with you," Lady de Comete cut in. "Won't you, Beatriz?"

Beatriz pursed her lips. She didn't really want to, but it would be better, she supposed, than accepting a personal maid of Anthona's, who would probably sing Jorge's praises at her and report back on all her actions to Anthona. "Certainly. Does that satisfy you, Luis?"

Luis was not satisfied, but they talked him around eventually. The turning point was Beatriz saying how staying in the city, she was feeling more and more worried about Ricardo, and leaving would do her some good. If it would give her peace of mind, he said, then fine, Mestos was acceptable. Though he still thought a visit back to the Comete estate would be just as good in all areas.

Beatriz was happy when he gave way (not that he could have stopped her, but she hated when he was upset), but her method was perhaps a bit dishonest. She was not at all sure Mestos would grant her any peace of mind. How could she stop worrying about Ricardo when this whole contest was based on his disappearance? And beyond that, there was the fact that she wanted to go partly because she felt Lady Anthona's request had been a message from Marina. If she were to say that, she doubted any of her family would have reacted well. They were not overly religious, the Comete family. Neither Luis nor Don Fernando nor Lady de Comete would have liked the idea of a real sign from a goddess. It was not as comfortable as the simplicity of a commission to paint a temple, which they did approve of—as artistic projects went, this one was high profile and worthy in subject, and involved the king's own patronage. Marina, they had little opinion on, but when it came to Beatriz's career, Don Fernando in particular had always hoped she'd make a name for herself as she dreamed. In that area, with this project, they would support her as much as they were able.

Of course, Beatriz herself still very much hoped Ricardo would come back and take the temple back again. Except for the small worm of artistic attachment that had started to squirm in her gut, that had decided this job was going to be hers by hook or by crook.

3

CHAPTER THREE

Whether Ricardo would have appreciated others making an attempt on his commission was something of a moot point. Ordinarily he would have had a strong opinion on the matter, certainly. For now, however, he had a whole catalog of other things to stew over. The temple vault was nowhere near the top of the list.

Of course, as Ricardo told himself over and over again, he had himself to blame for the situation. He'd been careless. Drinking with a stranger, pouring out his thoughts freely even upon private matters, and getting so drunk that he'd not thought it strange when the man led him down unfamiliar streets: it had all been very stupid. But how could he have known he'd be targeted? There was no one in the capital with enmity against him but his rivals, who were vicious in their own petty ways but would hardly go as far as kidnapping. He had no powerful enemies, or so he'd thought at the time.

He'd blacked out in a stable the stranger had led him to, as near as he could remember. The night was all a bit of a blur. The next thing he knew, he was waking up to the jolting rhythm of wagon wheels, unkind to a pounding headache. Where... what...

And something scratched at his wrists and ankles when he moved, trying to stretch out. He groaned, trying to find a comfortable position. The only bright side was a dark side—there was a blanket over his body, including his head, and from what he could tell it was blocking out a lot of sunlight which would not have been kind to his hangover.

"Juan?" he muttered.

No one responded.

Still dizzy and not entirely sober, he'd fallen back into a light sleep, waking now and then at being jostled against other items in the cart. There was a chest of some sort, that was the biggest thing, but also a couple of smaller boxes, and a length of rope. Half-asleep, he felt the oddest thing about his situation to be a lack of hay. When he was young he used to sneak into hay wagons and hide under the stacks. You could catch a ride that way, at least until the farmer caught you. He felt that he was hiding from someone now but couldn't remember who or why. And there wasn't any hay, no hay at all.

It was only after a good long while—maybe half an hour or maybe a couple hours even, hard to tell half asleep—after a thousand bumps in the road and a few muffled overheard conversations and a whole lot of confused pondering about the lack of hay—that Ricardo realized the source of discomfort on his wrists and ankles was rope. He'd been bound hand and foot, and he was in a strange cart with no memory of how he got there. This realization demanded some action.

"Hello," he called out. "Excuse me. Who's out there? What are you doing? What-what is this?" He kicked at the bottom of the cart too, though he doubted that would be heard over the rattling of the wagon. His voice was a bit raspy too, as his throat was almost as sore as his head, and he wondered if that would be heard either. After a couple minutes, however, the wagon slowed to a stop, and the blanket was lifted off his head, exposing his eyes to sunlight. He winced, groaned, and then slowly processed the face he was seeing, the face of the stranger who'd been drinking with him at the bar last night. What had been the man's name… It had started with a D. Oh, right, Diego.

"Diego," he said, "What the hell is this? Get me out of these ropes and this damn wagon. Gods, what time is it?"

"Almost noon," the man said. "And I'd prefer you call me Captain Alban. Not that I didn't enjoy drinking with you, but I wouldn't say we're on first-name terms, Montero."

"I really don't care," Ricardo said. "Fine, Captain. Am I under arrest, then? This is a fine way to go about it. If the king hears…"

"You're not under arrest. I'm kidnapping you," Captain Alban said far too calmly. "As for the king, I don't really care what he'd have to say about it. I'm part of the guard of the countess of Suelta. As you mentioned last night, we don't get along well with the king."

"You're what?" Ricardo almost yelled, but his voice was too raspy and didn't carry well. Captain Alban sympathetically offered him a flask of watered-down wine.

"Should curb your thirst and take the edge off too. Hair of the dog, though it's only wine. You really did a lot of drinking last night."

"Which you encouraged," Ricardo said, after a short drink, "because you wanted me drunk, so you could fucking… kidnap me."

"It was the countess's orders. Nothing personal; I'm sure it's only to spite the king. She'll probably give you back when her temper cools, or she thinks the king's fretted for long enough. Maybe in a year or two," Captain Alban said optimistically. "But don't worry. We'll take good care of you in the meantime."

He gave Ricardo more to drink, which Ricardo accepted. It

stopped him from saying anything thoughtless or just screaming at this man that he and his countess were both clearly insane and would never get away with this. Both points were true, but they were far from the city, and alone. There was no need for Ricardo to antagonize him, not yet. He had the look of a decent fighter by his build and posture, and he had to be clever if he'd gotten Ricardo this far without anyone noticing. "Where are we?"

"On the road to Suelta. We should be able to make it in three days, if we keep up the pace. Speaking of which, we really should keep going soon. You'll keep quiet here in the back, won't you?"

It occurred to Ricardo now that the blanket over his body had not been placed there to ward off his hangover pangs, but rather to hide him from view. They had to still be close enough to the capital, or at least far enough from the countess's territory, that Captain Alban was worried about their being caught by law enforcement or other meddlers. He offered a queasy smile. "It's not so comfortable back here in the wagon. Perhaps I could ride up front with you."

"I'm not driving the wagon," Captain Alban said. "I'm riding alongside. We don't have enough horses to accommodate you too—I'm sorry."

"Then I could walk. I could keep pace easily enough. We haven't been going so fast, have we?"

Captain Alban eyed him. "If you think you're being clever right now, you must think I'm an idiot. I'll ask you again: Can you keep quiet, or should I gag you to make certain?"

Ricardo said, "I can keep quiet."

It was a lie, of course.

The first time he heard the sound of someone coming close to the wagon—a group of passersby, though more he couldn't discern—he screamed for help as loud as his lungs and slightly soothed throat would allow, thrashing to add to the noise and call more attention. The cart, regardless, did not slow down. There was some quiet conversation that he could hear—not the specifics, but that the passersby were hesitant and Captain Alban's voice was authoritative if not quite frightening. Then a farewell, and then nothing more.

The cart stopped sometime later and Captain Alban lifted the covering. He told Ricardo, "A group of poor farmers isn't about to fight a man with a sword just because you scream at them. You've given them a good story to tell, though, I suppose, the next time they're at a tavern."

The mention of a tavern only reminded Ricardo of the captain's treacherous pretense at friendship the night before. He scowled. "What did you tell them?"

"That you were a raving drunk and not to worry themselves."

"You must feel pleased with yourself."

"Not particularly. But don't worry, I'm not mad at you either. Honestly, I didn't expect much better. Thought I'd give you a chance, but..." He shrugged. "I'm sorry, but I can't trust you further. Not everyone on the road is as easily taken care of as that pack."

After that, he insisted on gagging Ricardo after all, stuffing a handkerchief in his mouth and then tying it in with a rag. It took Ricardo a while to get used to the sensation; for a while he was constantly choking, convinced that any moment he would stop being able to breathe. He had to calm himself and work on regulating his breathing. The day's journey grew a bit easier after that, though it had its moments of frustration when he heard travelers on the road and had to judge whether or not it was worth it to try to get their attention. Was the group big or strong enough to be able to rescue him? Did they sound like they would care? Several times he made an attempt to call for help, but his voice was stifled and whatever noises he made thrashing around must not have carried far—the wagon made enough noise to drown them out in its creaking and rattling, and it never stopped to chat with anyone on the road. His efforts bore him nothing but a bruised hip.

They made camp in the evening, a little ways off the road. The horses tied to a tree, and a small tent for everyone to sleep in. The man driving the cart introduced himself as Sancho. He was apparently a servant, not a soldier, for he was put in charge of feeding the horses, setting up a tent, and making a simple dinner. Ricardo hadn't realized, beneath all the panic and the pain of first his hangover and then being banged about in the wagon all day, how hungry he'd gotten—he felt grateful for the food and then angry at his own gratitude. It wasn't that good, the food, really just bread and beans, and if he was starving then it was his captors' fault for not feeding him earlier.

After dinner, Sancho and Captain Alban slept in shifts, while Ricardo struggled to sleep at all. At least he was allowed to sleep without a gag in, though his hands and legs were still tied and he had a hard time getting comfortable.

The day after passed much the same at first, except that Sancho had become friendly with Ricardo overnight and therefore gave a little more thought to his comfort. Perhaps he and Captain Alban felt more relaxed, too, now that they were farther from the capital. At any rate, he put a shirt under Ricardo's head in the cart to cushion it, and talked Captain Alban into pausing for a nice, long lunch break, during which Ricardo's legs were even untied so he could stretch them and walk around a bit. "Lying still for too long isn't good for a body," he told them both as he untied Ricardo's legs. "You get cramps, chafing, distemper..."

"Now it sounds like you're talking about a dog," Ricardo muttered.

Sancho sent him a reproving look.

Ricardo forced himself to smile and mend his manners. "Thank you for untying me. I do appreciate it."

"Of course. We're similar type folks in the end, aren't we? Both serving our own noble leader as best we can, even if Alejandro's a rat."

He dared to speak of the king so rudely! Even the countess hadn't dared to do as much to Alejandro's face, but apparently she encouraged disrespect when he wasn't around. Ricardo's already low opinion of her plummeted more with every hour of his capture. She was worse than disgraced or rude or low; she was a coward, striking only when there was no chance of retaliation. He'd thought she at least had a certain dignity about her when they first met, but these, her people, filled him with repulsion. He hated them, especially Sancho, who watched him with a curious and kindly gaze as he ate. Captain Alban he hated too, in a bitter, wary sort of way, but Sancho, who indeed seemed to view him as a dog that just needed some additional training on how to behave, evoked in him a visceral hatred he'd rarely felt before. He thought perhaps the last time he'd felt it had been when he'd just returned from visiting the late queen's secluded wing of the palace to paint her, and one of the ladies of the court had asked him how she was doing, and when he lied and said she was doing well, had tittered. Hid it behind her hand, of course, but tittered. He'd felt a similar sort of hatred then, but on the queen's behalf, and even then not as strongly as he hated Sancho right now.

Seething in this way, Ricardo bided his time, waited until Captain Alban was distracted for a moment, and made a break for it. He dropped his bread and bolted down the road in the direction from which they had come.

He hadn't made it far before Captain Alban had caught up and tackled him. They landed hard on the dirt. Ricardo made the most of his freed legs, twisting them around the captain's and flipping their positions so that he was on top. He couldn't keep the pin, though—his hands were still tied, though in front of him, and useless for wrestling. Captain Alban surged up. Ricardo smashed their heads together, and for a moment stunned his opponent. But he stunned himself as well, and Captain Alban's recovery time was quicker. He punched Ricardo in the face, then in the gut, once, twice, and a third time before Ricardo backed off him and cried out his surrender.

He was dragged back to where Sancho was still sitting and calmly eating bread and cheese. Captain Alban shoved him down into a seated position, then turned to Sancho and twisted his ear. "Soft idiot. See if I listen to you again on how to treat prisoners."

"Well, you caught him, didn't you?" Sancho protested. "And now he's had some exercise for the day, too, like I suggested, so don't look at me like that. Anyways it's all settled. And while you were busy, I've poured you both some wine, so sit down and we can all eat together. Let's be friends, shall we?"

"We're not friends," Ricardo said. He could have added a great deal to that statement, all about how they were ruffian kidnappers from Suelta, which was basically the middle of nowhere, while he was a civilized and morally principled artist from the capital who had never and would never kidnap anyone in his life—but he was out of breath. Still, he thought his declaration unambiguous. But Sancho somehow managed to misinterpret it, for he patted Ricardo's arm and offered him the wine again, cheer undiminished.

* * *

The trip to Suelta took only a few days. Less time than Ricardo might have estimated had he been asked at the capital (Suelta's countess so isolated herself that her county seemed like it should be a remote wasteland) but an interminable amount considering his circumstances. When they at last arrived he felt half relieved and half filled with dread. On the one hand, he didn't enjoy lying in the bottom of a cart with his hands and legs tied, bumping and thumping all the way. On the other hand, what awaited him in Suelta was still uncertain, and the unknown might well turn out to be far worse than an uncomfortable road trip. Captain Alban had made this kidnapping sound more like a prank than anything else, and Countess Leonor had no reason to be cruel to Ricardo, but on the other hand, he wasn't best impressed by Leonor's sanity at this point, and as far as pranks went this one was cruel enough already. Who knew what her intentions might be?

Whatever Leonor had in mind, however, she was not in Suelta at the moment, but still back in the capital. Captain Alban had gotten around to explaining that to Ricardo too. She still had obligations to fulfill, visits to make out of courtesy. Besides, if she left Ferrar at the same time as Ricardo mysteriously disappeared, it might make people suspicious.

This meant that at the moment, Suelta was governed not by its real mistress but by her ten-year-old son: the Prince Felipe.

The prince was too young to do much in the way of governing, but he understood power well enough—at least, he was very good at lording it over people. He was a brat.

He greeted Ricardo, the captain, and Sancho at the door to the countess's manor.

"Captain, you aren't supposed to be home before Mother. What are you doing here? Who's he?"

"The countess told me to fetch him here, your highness. He's the king's favorite painter," the captain had explained. "The countess thought he'd make a nice addition to the household, I guess."

Felipe had frowned. "He doesn't look that nice. Or very... painter-ly."

Ricardo was, at that moment, trying to kick Captain Alban in the shins, without very much success. He was also aware that he looked less than presentable, since he'd gotten into a few more tussles with the captain in the past couple days, and had a bruise on one cheek, mussed hair, and dirty clothes as a result. Whatever "painter-ly" was, the prince was no doubt right that Ricardo was not it, not at the moment.

"Wear of travel," the captain offered. "Also, he wasn't exactly amenable to coming. We're still trying to persuade him about that, Suelta's merits and all. Please be understanding."

At that, Felipe laughed. He patted the still-struggling Ricardo on the arm and said, "All right, he can have the guest room in the East Wing. Unless Mother said otherwise."

"She wasn't particular."

Felipe was still grinning as Ricardo was hauled away, and he was smiling and laughing every time Ricardo saw him after that over the next couple weeks, which was nearly every day—he must have been lacking other amusements. Apparently, Ricardo being kidnapped and dragged out here was the funniest thing to happen in Suelta in Felipe's memory—the funniest thing ever, Felipe had assured him, unbothered by his annoyance.

"I have a life in the capital," Ricardo told him. "I have clients—friends who will be worried—this is not a joke, no matter what your mother means by it. It's not a joke to uproot someone's life!"

Felipe indignantly and mendaciously told him, "You don't have to get so mad. I'm not laughing at you. It's funny because the king will be so angry about it—just think of his face!"

"So I'm just a trinket to be stolen from the king, is that it?" Ricardo asked. Seeing Felipe shrug carelessly, he said, "You should take that more seriously, by the way. The king won't find this as funny as you do."

"That's the point," Felipe said. "Anyway, don't be stupid. Mother will have thought it all through. Don't worry too much either—I'm sure you'll be fine. Mother will take care of it." This was his vague reassurance to all of Ricardo's worries, from his concerns about whether Leonor eventually intended to murder him to his irritation at not having any painting supplies to work with. Leonor would take care of it all when she showed up—but what exactly that would mean, he of course did not clarify.

Ricardo could only wait.

4

CHAPTER FOUR

Beatriz's impulsive choice to go to Mestos took a while to put into action. First there choosing a maid, which Lady Gelvira commandeered. The eventual selection was a maid a couple years younger than Beatriz, Inez, who had been with the family for a few years. Beatriz happily agreed because Inez was fairly useful, and was comfortable with Beatriz but did not see her as someone who required either coddling or scolding, unlike some of the older maids of the household.

Beatriz also had to inform some people that she would be out of the city, noble acquaintances and regular clients and patrons. The one conversation of this sort she took seriously was her conversation with Juan, for she realized that if she vanished without telling him anything, he might think she had fallen to the same mysterious fate as Ricardo—or at least, if he heard she'd gone on vacation, he might assume she'd given up on winning the commission for the temple vault. Which would be unfair, since in fact she was taking the task more and more seriously.

"I'm going to the seaside to paint Marina," she told Juan. "Otherwise, I wouldn't be going at all."

Juan looked only half convinced. "Why do you need to go to the sea to paint a woman's figure? You've seen the sea before—if you need it in the background, you can imagine it well enough."

"Painting from memory is a fool's game," Beatriz said sharply; it was yet another old disagreement between her and Ricardo. "At that point you're basically making it up. Anyhow, there's no reason I need to stay in the capital to do it either, is there? I'm not much use here whether your master returns or no."

"You might be of use," Juan said. "If one of his rivals causes trouble, for example. If Valdez starts more rumors."

"I couldn't help much with that. That circle barely acknowledges me, as you know."

Juan hmphed.

The truth of it, Beatriz suspected, was that Juan, along with all of the Montero household, was getting more and more worried the longer Ricardo was gone. Their master was absent; some of the servants had already given notice, assuming they would not receive pay any time soon, and those who had stayed on still had an eye on the door. Juan in particular was in a tricky position. What would he do if Ricardo didn't return? Take up a new apprenticeship with one of those rival artists he loathed even more than Ricardo did? Go back home to his village? Life must have seemed indeed precarious to Juan, and here was one of his few allies leaving the city. Even if Beatriz couldn't help Juan or the absent Ricardo a whit, still better for her to be here than elsewhere. Better to keep friends close when enemies were looming ever nearer.

From that point of view, her leaving on holiday did seem heartless, she supposed. She hesitated. She didn't doubt her reasons, but how to explain them. "The truth is, I... I think it's very important I paint in Mestos. You see..."

Juan raised her eyebrows when she paused. "Yes, miss?"

But to say she thought Marina had told her to do so would sound incredible. Beatriz didn't know Juan's religious beliefs, whether he would believe Marina had sent her this quiet message or no. Either way, though, a superstition or a religious concern would not matter to him; to him the painting of the temple was about Ricardo, not the sea goddess. She shrugged. "Doubtless your master would disapprove, but I have a hard time painting without a source of inspiration near at hand. So for a sea goddess, I must be near the sea. Don't worry. I'll be back in a month or so, and I'm sure your master will be too."

"As you've said it, keep your word." Juan's tone was joking, but he didn't quite pull it off. "Paint a masterpiece, then. I suppose each artist's process is different."

All inferior to Montero's, his expression said, but at least he had the courtesy not to voice it.

Then there was the trip to Mestos itself (but that was pretty quick, only a couple days of travel) and all the bustle of unpacking and the baroness proudly showing off every square inch of the estate that she could drag Beatriz to on foot. And she'd show her the village later, she told her, and more of the beach, and the fields... Beatriz acquiesced because she was too tired from travel to really argue and because it was only polite, but she was relieved when she could make her way up to the guest room prepared for her and flop down on her bed.

"How long can I nap?" she asked Inez, who was quietly hovering.

"Not long, miss. There's dinner in another two hours and you'll have to freshen up before it, and you know you're never quick waking."

Beatriz sighed. "I suppose I shouldn't sleep at all then."

"Take an hour. I'll make sure to wake you up."

But Beatriz stayed awake. Instead of sleeping she washed her face and neck of sweat and changed into a dress more suitable for the evening. She spent the rest of the time mostly staring out the window. This window didn't have a sea view, but her makeshift studio (for the baroness had shown her where that would be, too) had quite a nice one. Was that fortuitous? Maybe she was being stupid about all of this, and there was nothing of destiny or divine intervention in any recent events, far less in the arrangement of her rooms. In any case, the view out of her bedroom window wasn't bad either. She could look into the garden, as carefully trimmed and arranged as if it were the king's.

As she looked, she saw some movement behind a tree some distance away. She squinted, trying to see what it was. Then a figure emerged. It was a man's figure, she thought, but as it came nearer, she thought perhaps it was a woman, but it was hard to tell with the gathering dusk. Were those separate legs, or the shape of a skirt? Hard to say, and the figure was tall for a woman but seemed a bit curved for a man. Only with the shadows it was hard to make out the shape clearly anyhow. The one thing Beatriz could tell plainly, despite a small cap on the figure's head, was that it had long, startling red hair. She strained to make out more detail, but within moments it had walked behind a hedge and was gone from her view.

Huh.

She watched for a while, but the figure did not return. The only other person she saw was Jorge, who came slowly walking through the garden just as Inez began to remind her that it was almost dinnertime, and she still had to fix her hair.

So she turned from the window and submitted to Inez's preparations.

Although she'd been prepared for some hubbub around dinner, it was still more of an event than she expected. Baroness Anthona was in high spirits, having finagled a wealthy guest from a good family out of the capital. She had invited some notable locals, including the town mayor and some well-to-do merchants, and she had seated Beatriz next to Jorge, and she spent much of the dinner telling anecdotes about Jorge and looking at Beatriz for her reactions. Beatriz tried her best to smile or laugh at most of them, or look fittingly touched at the stories that were clearly supposed to stand as examples of Jorge's virtues.

Perhaps the one upside of all this was that it gave Beatriz ample time to gauge Jorge's reactions, both to the stories and to his mother's clear machinations at putting him and Beatriz together. He did not seem very happy about any of it. Not that he was rude to Beatriz, though he was a little distant when he spoke to her, and his attention sometimes strayed from the table entirely—no, he was still mostly polite. But the stories made him obviously uncomfortable, and his lack of effort in even talking to Beatriz made one thing clear: whatever schemes Anthona had at capturing a rich bastard girl for her dowry, they were hers alone.

That might make Beatriz's time here a little easier, if all went well. Unless it just made Anthona try harder.

Dinner was heavier fare than was typical with Beatriz's family, but it finished with a light dessert, and Beatriz was hopeful she might be dismissed and finally get the sleep she had been craving. This, however, was not to be. Anthona, in her whirl of gloating enthusiasm, had planned entertainment for her fine guest. Music, she said, and dancing, and hopefully to Beatriz's taste. "Though we cannot of course match the pleasures of the capital."

"Well, I was not brought up in the capital, but on Don Fernando's estate. Not so dissimilar a place to here, and certainly not known for its fine music or dancing. I'll take in whatever you have to offer as a simple rube, and hope to be sufficiently cultured to appreciate it," Beatriz said, "and that I prove a worthy audience for your effort."

Anthona grinned. "Oh, dear, you are far too humble—still, I

hope what we have will please you." With that, she called out for the musicians to enter, and so they did.

At least Anthona had thought better than to drag out all the musicians in the town. Rather, there were only three here: one with a lute, one with a pipe, and one with a drum. They played well in harmony, and though indeed Beatriz did not consider them all that technically impressive, their music was merry and made her smile. Had they been street players, or at a party in the capital, she might have been thinking how much coin to give them when they were done as a sign of appreciation; since they had been brought in specifically to amuse her, hired by the baroness, she felt it would be taken as rudeness, as if she were paying for a gift. So instead she merely sat back and enjoyed.

It was as they began playing a third song that the dancer came in.

Beatriz recognized her instantly. It was the figure she had spotted in the garden. Up close, she still felt confused for a minute: the dancer was wearing a man's outfit, with leggings, breeches, and a tunic, rather than a skirt. But the tunic was arranged so that the dancer's womanly breasts were quite obvious, even emphasized, and the dancer wore garishly bright makeup as well. The rouge on her lips was just a hint darker than the scarlet of her hair.

Her outfit and makeup were vulgar, but her dancing was less so. She danced a lively jig with a bright smile on her face—a smile that Beatriz thought to be directed towards her, for their eyes met more than once, and there seemed to be some meaning in her gaze. Then the music shifted, and the dancer ceased dancing and instead began to sing. She was a little out of breath, but her voice was still steady and melodious.

"My love, her hair is gold as corn
Her blush as warm as breaking dawn
Her skin like bark on a pale birch tree
Her eyes blue as Marina's sea..."

As she sang, she advanced further into the room, close to the table, gaze now solidly fastened on Beatriz, and only the tiniest smile on her face. As if she were speaking of me, Beatriz thought. Well, as a literal description it was poetic tripe, and not in the least accurate. But the mention of Marina caught her attention. That, and the look of mystery in the woman's eyes.

Those eyes were as blue as the sea, in fact. Or close. Perhaps they were a bit too green—Beatriz was still not close enough to her to see all that clearly. But either way, they held both allure and command, and were entirely intriguing.

When the song at last finished, and the dancer swept a rather feminine curtsey, Beatriz applauded enthusiastically. Jorge next to her did too, and he shot her and the dancer a grin, though he looked... tired? Stressed? Perhaps he was picking up on the mixed reactions of those at the table. Most of the other guests were clapping with a bit less energy, but a few were staring at the dancer with silent censure. To Beatriz's surprise, Anthona herself was one of those not applauding, and there was quite a disgruntled expression on her face. Maybe she had expected the dancer she hired to perform in more appropriate dress, or maybe she thought the serenade to Beatriz directly a bit too forward, especially coming from a woman. And now, maybe she thought Beatriz would be offended. Beatriz cleared her throat. "You have great talent here in Mestos," she said to the baroness.

Anthona smiled sourly. "I'm glad you think so, my dear."

"What's your name?" Beatriz asked the dancer, adding, irrelevantly, "You have such a lovely voice, I'm jealous."

"Vulpa," the dancer said. "My name's Vulpa."

Fox, for the red hair. Probably not her real name, then. But if she'd given it to herself, she'd chosen something fitting for a brash coquette. Her voice was quiet and demure now, though, and she was standing very still, as if all her boldness had been used up in the dance. Of course perhaps it really all had been an act. One's persona in a performance was not necessarily the same as one's real nature. Once Beatriz had been commissioned to paint quite a dark scene—the suicide of a pair of lovers—and after seeing it, quite a few of her acquaintances had thought her morbid and been very concerned. She had explained to them a few times over that her paintings did not necessarily reflect her state of mind, but it had little effect, until sometime later she completed an innocuous still life of some flowers, and then they had all decided she was quite all right again, which had been equally ridiculous. Art told you a little about a person's nature, but not everything, and not clearly; a person's art would only tell you riddles about them, and there could certainly be answers, but hard to discern. And so perhaps the audacity of Vulpa's smile had really been only an act. Still, it had been a lovely performance, and Beatriz said so again, adding, "I hope I will see you perform again during my visit."

Anthona began, "Oh, I hardly think—"

Vulpa interrupted her. "Thank you, Miss Comete. I'm honored by your interest. Of course we are all so pleased to have you here. For you, I could give no less than my best."

She put a light emphasis on the word "pleased", but on every word, her voice had a sort of purr to it now. No, Beatriz thought, she'd been right after all. This woman was a flirt, and a confident one, as she seemed to give no thought to Anthona's apparent displeasure.

Impulsively, Beatriz said, "You may have heard I am a painter."

"Yes, miss."

"You have a very singular appearance, you know, with your bright hair and your height." Vulpa was as tall as Beatriz had estimated out the window earlier and perhaps even a bit taller when she stood straight and proud. (Nice posture, that.) "If you wouldn't mind, I think I'd like to paint you. Would you be willing to model for me?"

Vulpa blinked. She glanced at Jorge, then at Anthona. Then, looking back at Beatriz, she squared her shoulders and said, "Certainly, I'd be flattered. When would you want me?"

"Oh, in a couple days, maybe. I have to set up the studio to my liking, I think, before I ever begin my sketches. I'm working on a portrait of Marina, by the way," Beatriz said. "You have a good air of command about you, and you have just the eyes for it. But I will have to think through the pose, too. Yes, a couple days will be fine. How can I reach you?"

Vulpa gave her an address to which a note might be delivered. Business concluded, she headed away with a last bow to the table in general. Beatriz sent another smile to Anthona, assuring her again that nothing here had offended her proprieties. Yet even though Beatriz acted so warmly, and had even complimented Vulpa and asked her to model, Anthona's annoyance must have remained, for she abruptly declared she was exhausted and would be heading to bed, and wished all guests a good night. And so dinner was over.

Beatriz worried, as she headed up to her room, that she might have handled that entire situation wrongly. Had Anthona heard some of the more scandalous rumors about her and her affinity for beautiful women, especially tall ones? They weren't all that common in the capital, partly because Luis did his best to quash them, but they did spring up now and again, and when they did, they nearly always mentioned the type of models she used. Anthona was desperate for a bride for her dear, hopelessly unrespectable son—a small stain on Beatriz's reputation might have been more encouraging to her than not, but that didn't mean she would appreciate seeing Beatriz's predilections in action at the dinner table.

As it turned out, however, Anthona's annoyance had another source, which Beatriz learned from Inez later that night, Inez having enjoyed a good gossiping session with the household's maids.

The baroness hadn't been scandalized at Vulpa's outfit, dance, or song; rather, she had been infuriated that Vulpa had dared to show up at the manor at all. For Vulpa was not just a local dancer, but Jorge's most recent mistress.

"Really?" Beatriz asked.

"Really. He'd been keeping her in the manor until recently. Then Anthona kicked her out just a couple days ago so you wouldn't see her or know about her. He's been belligerent about it, but who would guess that he'd arrange for her to appear in front of you tonight?"

"Hm," Beatriz said. "I wonder did he arrange it, or did she make her own way in?"

"No, it was definitely the young master! He had asked the baroness if he might be in charge of tonight's entertainment, and she agreed because he seemed to be showing some interest in you that way. And now Vulpa appears, mocking both his mother and you."

"Mocking me? But she said nothing of her claim on Jorge, nor was she particularly rude."

"No, but the way she courted you, like a parody of how the baroness wants Jorge to court you—of course it was mockery of the whole situation. The butler thinks she's angry at Jorge as well and was making fun of him too. He might be right. She really did seem very angry, after all."

"Did she? I thought she seemed very self-controlled," Beatriz said. "Then again, I've never been all that observant. Of colors and forms, of course, but no head for these stupid tangles. It's a good thing I brought you along, Inez. But if only I'd known all this sooner... now I've asked her to model for me, but imagine how uncomfortable she must be with it all. She probably only have accepted out of pride, or maybe because she was mad—well, honestly I don't know why she would accept. I guess it's an excuse for her to come to the manor that Anthona can't refute. How stupid of me to get involved in all this! But she seemed so interesting."

"Interesting, no doubt," Inez said. "But just draw her or paint her, Miss Comete. No need to worry about all these rural intrigues, is there? It would be an insult for her to show up if the young master were really courting you, but you don't want his attentions anyhow, so as long as he keeps his distance, he can have a hundred mistresses and it's no business of ours."

"Sensible." Beatriz yawned. "Enough scandal, then. I need my rest if I'm to set up the studio tomorrow." And after all, her business here was to paint Marina, not to court anyone: not pretty dissipated lordlings, and certainly not angry, mysterious, red-haired dancers.

5

CHAPTER FIVE

Ricardo had acquired something of a daily schedule, if not a particularly interesting one.

He was given a small meal in the morning and evening, and a heartier meal in the early afternoon. Servants took away his dirty clothes at night while he slept, and deposited clean clothes in his room. During the day, he was left largely to his own devices, but he had at least been given a sketchbook and some charcoal because the household was generally aware he was an artist. When he complained that this was hardly the end-all be-all of artistic supplies, he was met with general indifference, and the response that it would be seen to when Countess Leonor returned. Now it had been a week and a half, and said countess still hadn't arrived. But apart from the lack of amusements and the general confinement and all, he was treated fairly well—indeed, the servants and Felipe as well had informed him that he was as well fed and clothed as anyone in the castle was, so he could grudgingly admit they were doing their humble best to treat him as their guest. This simply did not make up for the fact that he was, in fact, not a guest but a prisoner.

Felipe had no respect for his griping. "You get bored so easily," he said. "We got you the sketchbook, didn't we? And some books. Stop complaining. You're an adult, aren't you?"

"I have been locked in a room for ten days," Ricardo said, "and at this rate it seems I'll be left here till I go mad. I'm sure that will amuse you too."

"Don't be stupid. Mother will be back pretty soon. She sent a message. Anyway, it hasn't been ten days, it's only been nine. You arrived in the afternoon, and it's only afternoon now. Nine days," Felipe said. "Just draw some more. But why do you keep drawing fountains?"

He'd taken it as his right to snoop around in Ricardo's sketches. And Ricardo had been drawing fountains, among other things, because...

Because he was thinking about the capital, its roads, its architecture, its familiar sights. It was a habit of his to sketch the fountains from time to time. He could do it by heart, now, as easily as he could draw himself or Juan or Beatriz. (Though Beatriz would always claim his drawings from memory didn't look a thing like her, but that was what she said about all his drawings.)

"Boring," Felipe said. "You should draw me." He perched on Ricardo's bed. "Should I sit or stand? I guess I should stand. I am a prince."

"You are a brat," Ricardo said under his breath. But he didn't repeat it when Felipe asked him what he'd said, and began to sketch the boy instead. It was at least a small challenge, to draw a child (children had such undefined features, so hard to draw convincingly) and to draw a prince, a task requiring a certain gravity. How did one capture the solemn dignity of royalty when drawing such an impudent creature as this hellion? But he'd imposed dignity on unlikely subjects before, though maybe never any as obnoxious as this one. The boy standing did help. If he'd been holding something regal, perhaps a horse-whip or a small sword or a book, it might have been even better. But at least he'd schooled his features with some level of seriousness. He couldn't draw a picture of a prince grinning. That wouldn't be right.

"Hm," Felipe said when he was mostly done. "It does look like me! Thanks." With that, he went rushing out of the room, sketch in hand. Ricardo, who had wanted to put on a couple finishing touches, made to run after him and take it back, but was stopped by a guard at the door.

* * *

The room Ricardo had been stashed in had a window, and not even a barred one, though it was too high up for him to seriously consider climbing out of it. It looked out towards the front gate of the manor, and out it, Ricardo could see Countess Leonor's arrival when it finally occurred. She had far more of a company with her than Ricardo, including several guards, a small flock of servants, and multiple coaches. Ricardo felt oddly defensive staring down at this party as it rode up to the manor, thinking about how underwhelmed Felipe must have been by Ricardo's arrival a couple weeks ago when he had been expecting all this fanfare. Not that that had been Ricardo's fault.

In all the bustle, though, Ricardo could barely glimpse Leonor. He thought he spotted her chatting with Felipe, but the window really was high and the servants really were crowding around and telling one woman from another was difficult from a bird's eye view. Eventually he gave up. He retreated from the window and sat on his bed and waited, wondering how his circumstances would now change.

Despite himself, despite knowing the high-handed ways of nobles, he'd imagined Leonor would deal with him within a day of her return. After all, she'd taken the time to have him kidnapped, using the very captain of her guard. After all, he'd been doing nothing for weeks now but waiting for her. However, Leonor didn't do so. All Ricardo got that day was yet another visit from Felipe, who in the wake of his mother's return was incandescently gleeful and far too energetic.

"She has much better stories about the capital than you," he told Ricardo. "Then again, I suppose you won't have been invited to all the places and the parties..."

"I've lived in the capital for eight years," Ricardo said shortly. "I've been almost everywhere, seen almost everything. I just don't indulge you."

Felipe scoffed. "I doubt you've been everywhere. Mom is a countess, so she's been places you haven't. She had dinner with the king himself. Three times."

"I've certainly had dinner with the king, if with anyone," Ricardo said. "I'm his favorite artist." He could remember several pleasant dinners, in fact, where they discussed art and literature and philosophy and religion all in a stream. Ricardo was not well-tutored in philosophy, being honest, or in literature, but he made a good show of it, and of course Alejandro's thoughts were always enlightening.

"Well, that's different," Felipe said.

"Your mother and the king don't get along well, you know. Three dinners in a month of visiting the capital specifically to pay her respects to him, and she his cousin. It's barely anything."

"Mom was busy with other things," Felipe said. "We have a lot of friends and relatives in the capital. She has to visit all of them. Even the king can't get too much of her time."

"Oh? Tell me about these friends."

"Well, there's Lady Julieta Ruiz. That's probably my mom's best friend in the capital. She's a very rich and smart lady, and she's the sister of the Minister of Finance."

Ricardo frowned. He could vaguely remember the Ruiz family. They weren't very active in court, but they did show up now and again. The lady Julieta was a stern and forbidding woman, so he talked to her as little as possible. "Interesting."

Felipe named a couple other names, two nobles and a merchant Ricardo had never heard of, and then ran out. But, he declared, he couldn't remember all the names of his mother's friends and relatives in the capital because there were too many of them, and anyway his mother had all kinds of adventures at the capital and all kinds of connections, and Ricardo was only jeering because he was jealous.

He left a bit quicker than usual, and did not sit for Ricardo at all. Whether he was uncomfortable or simply excited and restless would have been hard for Ricardo to say. A couple weeks weren't really enough to get to know a boy well.

When the next day passed with no word from Leonor again, Ricardo's restlessness also grew. Felipe didn't even come by that day, but fortunately, Captain Alban popped in shortly before dinner, when it was already dark outside and Ricardo had despaired of anything at all happening until at least tomorrow.

"Here," he said, "I brought you a pantxineta. Cook's made all kinds of desserts to celebrate Leonor's return. Of course, after her time with fancy capital food, she barely notices." He shook his head wryly.

Ricardo accepted the pastry and took a huge bite of it. He regretted this when the captain immediately smiled and said, "Feel any better now? Felipe said you were grouching again," and his mouth was too full of cream to answer with even a modicum of dignity. He chewed furiously and gulped down the bite as quickly as possible.

"It's not being grouchy when—"

"I know, I know," Captain Alban said quickly. He had forced the smile away, but it was still quivering at the edge of his lips, ready to return at any moment. "You have good reason to be anxious, I understand, although we've assured you that the countess means you no harm. Now she's back and you're more nervous than ever. It's perfectly understandable."

"I'm not nervous," Ricardo said immediately. "Why should I be, when all my days are nothing but boredom? And why should I be afraid of cheap thugs like you and your damn countess? She's the coward, refusing to face me day after day like this."

"So you're not nervous," Captain Alban concluded, "but rather: grouchy."

Ricardo glared at him.

Captain Alban patted his shoulder. "Listen, the countess isn't deliberately making you wait. There are a great many things for her to deal with. She was absent for a month. She has a county to run, you know."

"Oh, how heavy a crown," Ricardo muttered. "How hard her life must be."

"I can get you a meeting with her if you want one, but you will have to be less rude. Promise me."

Ricardo took another bite of the pantxineta and sullenly chewed it. He really did want to see Leonor, even though the prospect worried him. On the other hand, promising to behave himself felt like giving up his moral high ground—or no, perhaps it was the best way of keeping it? Well, practically speaking, he had no intention to go out of his way to anger Leonor anyhow. If he could just cajole her enough that she would soften and give up whatever she had against him, perhaps he could make her see reason. Perhaps he could make her let him go. So it would be better to be polite, really, and he had plenty of experience sucking up to infuriating nobles. It just annoyed him to have to give his word on the matter. Felt like binding himself further when he was already trapped and thoroughly screwed.

Captain Alban apparently took his silence as agreement anyway, because he went on: "Tomorrow Countess Leonor is holding an appeals court. Anyone who wishes to bring a case to her, however small or large, may do so. Usually it would only last a couple hours—most of this business is handled by the magistrate or town authorities—but it's been a while, and the cases have built up, so it's likely to take all day. You probably wish to make your own sort of appeal to her, don't you? Well, it would be fitting for me to take you there, and perhaps Leonor will see you and remember to speak with you. Of course you can't make your case so publicly, but it will do you good to be out and about, seeing how we govern around here, and if Leonor sees you in court waiting for her she'll probably be amused, and that will put her in a good mood. She's easier to deal with in a good mood, trust me."

"Last time I trusted you, you got me drunk and kidnapped me."

"Still not over that?"

"Should I be?"

Captain Alban shrugged. "Do you want to try to appeal tomorrow or not?"

"I'll go," Ricardo said, "but if she won't speak with me, I may well make my case like anyone else. She's made me her subject by force, after all, and as her subject I have a right."

"You will behave yourself," Captain Alban said pointedly.

He stared at Ricardo, and Ricardo stared back. Then a maid arrived with Ricardo's actual dinner, which was heartier than the pastry if less interesting, and Captain Alban excused himself, leaving Ricardo to consider how to conduct himself on the following day.

* * *

The appeals court was held in what Ricardo supposed was the biggest hall in the manor. In fact, he suspected it had been initially designed for dances and banquets and generally happier affairs than this, for the figures sculpted into the pillars wore gay expressions and rich, flowing outfits, and were surrounded by curling flourishes of marble. It was actually quite lovely, the architecture here, and Ricardo made a mental note of certain aspects he might imitate in his own work, though in a different medium.

Captain Alban hadn't managed to fetch him at the very beginning of today's session, so there were already a large number of people gathered in the hall. It was full, but not crammed. Fortunately, Ricardo saw that many people stood in clusters, so it was apparent not each of them had their own case to discuss, or allotting them a single day still wouldn't have been nearly enough to hear them all. In fact, a couple clusters were even glaring at each other, which suggested their cases might be related. Of course, this also added to some of the tension in the hall, which quite clashed with the festive décor—there was a good deal of grumbling, too, as well as the glaring, and Ricardo got the sense things could have been much louder and perhaps even come to blows between a few angry appealers if not for a number of guards stationed around the hall and for the fact that the day's work had already begun, and a case was already being heard. The case was a boring one involving how much tax needed to be paid on a large estate. The estate owner was making a strong case for less, and he had a lawyer with him to help, but the countess, sitting at the head of a hall, did not seem to be impressed so far.

Leonor.

Had she grown a couple inches since Ricardo had seen her last? She was sitting down, actually, on a chair that was only not a throne because of the heavy table in front of it that diminished its effect. The chair was a bit tall, but she was still sitting, and yet the way she dominated the room—silencing loud mutters with a glance, nodding brusquely at the appellant, never interrupting but always having her say when and how she wanted it—made her presence feel much larger, as if she were looming. No, Ricardo told himself practically after a moment, it wasn't that, or it wasn't only that. He was an artist, and whatever Beatriz might say about him, he really did notice anatomy and posture. In the capital, he now realized, Leonor had been hunching a little, drawing her shoulders in. But in her own house, head of her own county court, her shoulders were back, her spine straight, and her head held high.

She didn't quite intimidate Ricardo, not yet. But he adjusted some of his plans from the night before. He would have to act even more confident and charming than he had thought if he wanted to soften her. This was not a woman who would be easily influenced.

When they first entered the hall, Leonor spared a glance at Captain Alban, and gestured with her chin to the side. At this signal, the captain pulled Ricardo off to wait with him, leaning against the wall, in a spot that gave them a good view of the whole room, countess and supplicants and all.

"I like to keep an eye out in case there's trouble," he told Ricardo. "Have to stay alert. You might enjoy yourself more than me, actually be able to follow the proceedings. I can't focus on such things."

Ricardo doubted he'd find any of these cases amusing judging by this first one, but he nodded, and as Captain Alban had said, he did find he paid more attention to the actual cases going on than his distracted companion.

The second case brought before Leonor was a criminal case. A man named Gelmiro Abascal had been caught stealing a sheep from one of his neighbors, one Esteban Ochoa, and it was now believed he'd done this before given that Ochoa had lost several sheep recently. Previously he had blamed wolves, but now he believed it had all been theft. Of course Abascal denied it—said this was his first offense and he'd done it only to feed his family. He was an old man, and his son had become a no-good drunkard, and now there was only him to provide for his daughter-in-law and his grandson and granddaughter. And times were hard, lately, so hard. He'd tried to steal just one sheep, and he'd been caught, so no harm had been done, really. Could not Countess Leonor offer him mercy?

Leonor sighed.

To Ochoa, she said, "What evidence do we have that Don Gelmiro committed these earlier thefts?"

"The day before the last one disappeared—this was a month ago now, countess—he'd been hanging around the area. Chatted with one of the shepherds, even, and offered him a drink. Of course he wanted to get my boy drunk and steal the sheep right then and there. None of my men drink while they're working, though, not the hard stuff Abascal carries around in that flask of his, so he said no, but I guess Abascal must have come back later that night and stolen a sheep anyway—only one shepherd stays out at night, and it's hard for him to cover the whole field at once..."

"Mm. I see. And the previous thefts?"

The other sheep had gone missing months and months ago. At the time there had been a rash of missing animals in the area, and a couple alleged wolf sightings. This was the reason Ochoa had assumed his sheep had been taken by wolves rather than by any human. That being the case, he hadn't looked too hard into the disappearances (he'd noted a little blood one time, but no other clues), and had a hard time remembering anything that would point to Abascal now. And it was too late to go back and investigate at this point.

"Mm," Leonor said again. "I see."

Ochoa wrung his hands. "Please, countess, even if I have no evidence for the other incidents, the last time, Abascal was caught red-handed. I saw him, two of my shepherds saw him, and even he isn't shameless enough to deny it. My sheep are my livelihood; this is a serious crime, and I hope you will treat it as such."

Theft of livestock was indeed a serious crime in Salandra, on a similar level to poaching large game. In Ricardo's youth in the country, he had seen a couple similar cases tried. The usual punishment was death or near to it, depending on the magnitude of the theft—one man had been given a hundred lashes in Ricardo's town and had survived it, but he had been very sick afterwards and certainly come near death. That had been over a goat, which was less serious than a horse or cow, for example, but perhaps on a similar level to a sheep. Ricardo didn't personally think stealing a sheep warranted death. As for Leonor's opinion...

Leonor turned to Abascal. "Don Gelmiro, this story has disturbed me greatly. The Abascal family is a noble one, and in this region used to be among the most eminent. How have you managed to drop so low as this?"

"Countess, I've already said it. Much as I regret the necessity that brought me to theft, it was indeed necessity. I have mouths to feed at home, four of them, and what must be done must be done."

"You used to be a knight when you were young, and now you've become a criminal."

"Shameful indeed, but I still beg your mercy."

Leonor sighed. "Considering your past service to the nation, and that there is only evidence of one sheep having been stolen—and unsuccessfully—I can offer a certain degree of leniency. But I will not pardon you. You will be given twenty lashes, and if you offend again, punishment will be more severe. As for those mouths you have to feed, you will send your grandson and granddaughter here within the week to serve and learn in my household. The house of Abascal will need rehabilitation if it is not to collapse in this generation. And get your son to reform, don. Nobles should set a better example for the people of Suelta."

Ochoa, outraged at how light a punishment this was, complained at length, but Leonor ignored him and eventually he was removed from the hall by some guards along with Abascal and a number of others who had come to testify in favor of one supplicant or the other. Court moved on to judging an assault accusation, which Leonor punished more harshly, and after that, an argument between two families over which one had the right to plant in a certain field, which went on for far longer than it had any right to, and which ended with neither party satisfied.

The appeals went on for hours. Ricardo tried, after the first couple, to discern any unifying principles in how Leonor dealt with the appellants. There were a couple, maybe. She had no patience with rich middle-class complainers. The poor and the noble both she showed more sympathy. She favored women over men, Ricardo thought, but there were few women in court that day so it was hard to say for sure. And she favored the old over the young.

How was she likely to favor a well-to-do commoner painter, young and male, then? Ricardo didn't much like his odds. Then again, he already knew she didn't regard him much by how high-handedly she'd kidnapped him in the first place.

When it was a little past noon, and a wearying case had drawn to its close, Leonor called for a break so that everyone could sit down, eat some lunch, perhaps talk over their case if they had not been called up yet, and generally rest. She herself headed out of the hall by a door in the back, and she must have given Captain Alban some subtle signal, for he immediately grabbed Ricardo's arm and followed her.

She was already a ways ahead of them, striding purposefully down the hall, and they had to hurry to catch up. When they did, Ricardo saw that they had come to a small dining room, where some food had already been set out, but only enough for one. Leonor sat down and gestured for Ricardo and the captain to do the same. "I'll have more brought in," she said. "Aldonca should be here in a minute, I'm sure, to check how I'm enjoying things. In the meantime," she said to Ricardo, "I hope you'll forgive my lack of hospitality."

"I'm sure I'm the one who should be begging your pardon,

madonna," Ricardo said. "How could a humble painter like myself dare to judge you?"

Leonor's gaze sharpened. "Oh? Why are you begging my pardon?"

"I'd like to ask you that first. How have I offended you? I admit I was impolite when we first met..."

"Oh, it was nothing you said," Leonor said, a little too quickly.

"I see. Then why have you brought me here?"

Leonor poured herself a cup of wine. "You understand, it's not really because of you at all. I simply have some differences with my cousin, the king, and as he will never redress them, I sometimes must take vengeance in my own small ways. Your absence should trouble him a great deal. After all, right now he cares about that damn temple of his more than anything in the world. What will he do, minus his great painter to work on the ceiling?"

Ricardo had to swallow a comment on Leonor casually cursing the temple. Years in Alejandro's service—in genteel company in general, but especially the devoutly religious king's—had taught him to speak of Marina, her works and her worship, with only the greatest respect. But scolding wasn't going to help him here. He had told himself he had to be courteous, even ingratiating. He smiled. "Madonna, you overestimate my value to the king. The disappearance of a single painter won't trouble him much."

"Won't it, though? The temple is his pride and joy, and you are one of the people closest to him in the capital. That bastard hardly allows anyone close, even nobles, but you seem to be an exception. He's fond of you, and you're useful. I think it will bother him a lot."

Ricardo took pride in his connection to Alejandro, and he did think, at least on good days when he dared to, that if he was not precisely Alejandro's friend he was at least something like a confidant. When others mentioned it, largely to schmooze or to flatter him, he always felt a flutter of smugness in his chest, no matter how sincere the flatterer really was.

Today he felt that small flutter again, but ruthlessly quashed it. This was no time to ruminate over royal connections. This was a time to minimize his own importance to a spiteful woman's enemy. "Madonna, a painter is a painter, a commoner a commoner, and a king a king. Hurting me will hardly cut him deeply."

"I won't hurt you," Leonor said placatingly. "Don't worry yourself. I'm well aware that you are only Alejandro's tool, not Alejandro himself. Have you been treated badly here? I gave orders for you to be treated like a guest, and you will be in the future as well."

"Your hospitality has been sufficient, but..."

Ricardo was interrupted by the arrival of a maid, who worriedly looked at him and Captain Alban and told Leonor she would be back with more food. Leonor told her to bring some sweets as well as more soup and bread and some more cups for the wine. She hurried off, and Leonor gestured for Ricardo to continue, but his train of thought had been broken, and he struggled to regain it and to tell if it was even worth regaining. The conversation thus far was going nowhere fast.

"I pray," he began again, "that you will consider my situation here. It is not a matter of hospitality—Suelta does seem fine." Not that he'd seen a bit of it beyond the road and his room at the manor. "But I have business to conduct in the capital, a household to consider, an apprentice and various patrons, not only the king. And the temple is my own project as well as the king's, and it is dedicated to Marina herself, making it a concern of a goddess and all her worshippers in the city. Surely you can understand why such work should not be delayed."

"The temple is a construct of Alejandro's ego," Leonor said. "Gods, you've seen the way he looks when he talks about it, and you still think it's—well, you've bought into his bullshit, so I suppose that can't be helped. But no, I'm afraid I can't see why it's so very important that it be finished immediately. I'll release you eventually, of course. I'm not so cruel as to keep you here forever. But Alejandro can certainly sweat for a while and learn something about patience, and how it is not to get every little thing he wants."

"Madonna..."

Leonor raised a hand. Her manner was judicial again. Ricardo, the petitioner, had not made a very successful plea. "I can see this will be hard on you as a painter. Rest assured, I do not expect you to give up your art during your time here. We will get you whatever supplies you need to do your work. Make me a list, and I'll have it seen to. And Suelta may not be the capital, but it has its own beauty to inspire you if you give it a chance."

I may not be the king, her face said, *but you will still respect me and know your place.* At least, that's what Ricardo thought. Beauty, though. That was suggestive.

Retreating, or at least changing his angle of attack, he said, "Very well. I'm sure Suelta does have much to inspire me. Perhaps I could even paint its countess."

Leonor leaned back, frowning. "I thought you had no interest in painting me."

He had been right. He had offended her in their first meeting after all. "Oh no, madonna, I only had no time. I think you'd make quite an interesting subject. And now, there is little but time on my hands." Due to Leonor's own interference.

Leonor huffed. "Perhaps, but I am now home, and have little free time myself. A countess has duties."

"But you could spare a little time," Ricardo wheedled. If he could convince Leonor to let him paint her, he was sure he could win her over and talk her into letting him go before the painting was even complete. It would take strategic effort, but he could manage it. "Of course my talents are limited, so I understand if you are no longer interested, but I do have a certain knack for capturing people at their very best. I could show you at your most beautiful, the lovely countess of Suelta, gracious mother of our crown prince."

"You'd make me look maternal?" Leonor looked amused and a little skeptical.

Admittedly she wasn't very maternal. Too intimidating for that —well, depending on the mother. But Ricardo couldn't exactly say he would paint her as a domineering judge, as he had seen her today. "You are right, madonna," he said. "No, I would paint you fair and full of vivacity. Youthful, if you wish—many ladies prefer..."

"Paint me younger?"

"I am not saying you look old," Ricardo said quickly. Leonor was only in her late thirties, after all. "Only that I could paint you with all the joy of younger days, when you did not have all these many cares and duties." Surely that would satisfy a woman who didn't want to be painted as a mother.

But Leonor's source of offense was not what Ricardo had guessed. "My younger days. Montero, have you not heard what they were like? Is my story no longer spread about the capital as it once was? I suppose it's been too many years now, and it would get boring to keep on talking about it. Really a dead subject, I am."

"I don't listen to gossip," Ricardo lied, as the gossip he had heard about Leonor began to stir to life in his mind. Oh, damn. He'd forgotten...

"I suppose you didn't hear, then, that my younger days were not what you would call happy. My father dead when I was eighteen, my mother when I was twenty. Myself banished to this county you despise—oh, no, Montero, I can tell you do despise it, for all you've been polite—myself married to a man I didn't know, forced to bear his child and live in his household, be his wife for years before he died. Myself a widow at twenty-eight. Is that what you would like to paint, Montero?"

Ricardo swallowed. "I did not mean to offend you."

"You do not offend me," Leonor said. "But you don't understand me either. Why would I want you to paint me? Choose another subject. I hear still lives are still favored at court."

They weren't, actually.

"Or paint Marina, if you really have Alejandro's religious fervor. But not me." Leonor stood. "I'm done eating, I think. Duty calls."

She'd only eaten half her food, though she'd finished a glass and a half of wine. Ricardo and Captain Alban were left with the half-empty plate and bottle until the maid arrived to offer them meals of their own. She was distressed to see Leonor had left, but Captain Alban soothed her worries, telling her that the countess had enjoyed the lunch greatly, but had business to attend to. Today she had a very busy schedule, after all, too busy even for the typical break of an hour or two after lunch. Ricardo and the captain could still enjoy the food, and certainly would, eh?

They did eat, but they ate in silence, and neither really enjoyed it. When they were done, Captain Alban said, abruptly, "Cheer up. She isn't mad at you, you know. And she said you should be well treated, so you will be."

Ricardo thought Captain Alban might be right about this. Leonor was a proud woman; she would disdain to abuse a commoner over a matter like this. But saying she wasn't mad at him.... If he hadn't already known Captain Alban for a liar, Ricardo certainly would have known now.

6

CHAPTER SIX

"I see you came in women's clothing, this time," Beatriz remarked when Vulpa showed up at the studio. It had been a few days since Beatriz's arrival now, and things were more or less set up according to her preferences: table and chair, easel with a stool, canvas and other larger supplies in a corner. Only one day since Beatriz had sent a note to Vulpa's house, which she now knew, courtesy of Inez's grapevine, was actually rented by Jorge, another grievance of his mother's. Learning more of this kind of gossip over the past few days had made Beatriz doubt Vulpa would actually come model for her at all, never mind this soon. Either Vulpa really wanted an excuse to be at the manor (a covert rendezvous?) or she had some other reason to find Beatriz's request a matter worth urgency.

To be fair, it might have just been the money. Beatriz had said in her note that she was willing to pay a standard hourly wage to anyone who modeled for her—and she'd offered better than standard in this case. She was set on having Vulpa sit for her painting of Marina, and she'd been ready to offer a high incentive for the purpose. Well, whatever reason Vulpa had, here she was, and in a saucy red gown that cut low at the collar and high at the hem.

"Your letter didn't specify clothing," Vulpa said. "I hope this is suitable. Or will I have to run home and change?" She lifted her eyebrows.

"Well, honestly," Beatriz said, "I was thinking it might be better if I could draw you nude. Then..."

But she did not finish her sentence, because Vulpa gave her a look of such affront that she was forced to pause.

Vulpa said, "Naked."

"Yes. For the painting itself, I will probably have Marina either naked or in traditional garb. For reference before I make that decision, it would be good to have a few sketches of you nude. To see what it would look like."

"Miss Comete," Vulpa said, after a moment of consideration, "I was given to believe by your letter that you were sincerely looking for help and offering decent employment."

"I am."

"I am not a whore," Vulpa said. "Whatever rumors you may have heard about me, I am a dancer only, and I was not given to believe that this painting was going to be erotic. You can find someone else if that is why you wanted me."

She was already angling her body towards the door, hands clenched at her sides. Beatriz quickly moved between her and the door, speaking pacifying words. "Please, I did not mean to insult you with my request. It is very common in my trade to use nude models."

"I had not heard such practice was common." Vulpa was still glaring. (Such spirit in her! Yes, Beatriz thought she would make an admirable goddess.) "Not with women, anyway. Not with respectable artists."

"Well... no, not exactly common, perhaps," Beatriz admitted, "not in Salandra, but in Fiteria, for example, all the best modern artists see nothing wrong with it. The old masters, too, have such realistic paintings of the naked body—male or female—that one cannot doubt they painted from observation. And in the capital, most artists use nude models at times when painting men. Less so with women, but I am a woman, so I don't see anything improper about it."

Vulpa's fists were no longer clenched, but she crossed her arms. Still, there was something settling about the gesture. People didn't cross their arms when they were about to storm out, but when they had a point they wanted to argue, and Beatriz didn't mind arguing if she didn't lose her model entirely. She listened politely as Vulpa said, "I'm afraid this is not the capital. I'm not interested in modeling naked."

There were other women in the area that Beatriz could ask to model for her, even now. In the capital, she was used to getting exactly what she asked for in matters like this. Sometimes she did use whores, but more often she could get maids or other working women in want of a little extra money. She was known as a decent artist, if an eccentric female one, and usually the women who worked for her were happy to do so. That was what she expected from a model. That was what she should be seeking now, too, especially for as important a project as this. But precisely because it was important, she felt that it was necessary she do this right, the way she wanted to, and she wanted Vulpa. (Wanted her in more ways than one—was honestly very curious about her, rumors only whetting further curiosity—but as a model, yes, that was a start. That mattered.) She would be flexible if she had to be.

"All right," she said. "Today I'll try drawing you in this dress in a couple different poses. If I decide to use you as my model for this project, I'll have to get a hold of a more traditional dress, something more suitable for Marina. But that's for another day."

Vulpa warily nodded. "Then how do you want me to pose?"

"We could start with a simple, imposing stance. Standing with your hands on your hips, maybe? Yes, I think that would do for the first pose. Like that is good," Beatriz said as Vulpa moved into position. "Now just try to hold as still as possible. You can talk if you want, for now. I won't be focusing on your face for this one."

She took out her sketchbook and deliberated for a moment over whether to use charcoal or a pencil. A pencil, she decided. She wanted more precise line-work.

Later she would wonder what might have happened if she had chosen charcoal. Something similar, probably. Marina would find a way. Still, it all felt eerily predestined when she looked back on it. One of those things that made her wonder how far the goddess's interference went, how much one could ever control one's own life.

But it was only a split-second decision at the time. She chose the pencil. She sketched Vulpa briskly, not lingering unduly on either face or curves, focusing on the overall structure of her body (taller than average though not giant, probably big-boned, thick-wristed but without highly muscular arms) as well as the way her dress fell over it. The dress would be different when—if—she modeled for the painting, but some things would remain the same, and Beatriz was always fascinated by the way fabric folded and draped, and the fabric of this dress was bright but light, and it rumpled a little on the shoulders and skirt...

Vulpa was a good model. She sat very still and didn't talk very much, though she did respond to Beatriz's distracted ramblings about lighting and possible compositions for the piece with neutral comments—"We could close the shades" or "That doesn't sound very typical for a religious painting", comments like that. Quiet, but her presence was still companionable in a way, and not too awkward or self-conscious. Beatriz had a funny feeling that Vulpa was observing her almost as intently as she was observing Vulpa. What conclusions she was drawing remained to be seen.

She finished the first sketch and asked if Vulpa might sit down for another study. For this one, she thought she would indeed close the drapes and light a lamp on the table, just to change up the lighting a bit, make it more direct and less diffused. Lighting could change so much in the presentation of any object, let alone a body or a face. Today it shifted Vulpa's appearance from casual if a bit flamboyant to almost mystical. And what remained mundane, Beatriz could shift mystical in her interpretation if she wanted to... though she was hesitant to stray far from what she saw, even in an initial sketch, perhaps especially in an initial sketch. Once you started making things up, it grew harder and harder to recapture the brilliance of a real, true impression. The particular beauty of Vulpa would be something tricky to catch already. She would have to try to be exacting about it.

As she began to outline the shape of Vulpa's body, she noticed her pencil had gotten dull with all the shading of the first sketch. "Hold on," she said to Vulpa—pointlessly, as Vulpa had been perfectly patient so far, but like her talking about light, she felt the need to vocalize her process. "I'm going to need to sharpen this." She rummaged in her supplies for a moment and brought out a small knife.

The pencil was not in the mood to be sharpened. When she first attacked it, the tip broke. Cursing, she worked at peeling the wood back further, bracing the pencil hard against her hand.

Maybe she pressed too hard, or maybe the pencil was just poorly made, because with just the slightest extra pressure, the wood snapped. The knife skidded down and gashed her left palm. She let out a little cry.

"Miss Comete?" Vulpa was at her side in a minute, startling her. After half an hour of stillness, it was strange to see the woman move so fast. Stranger still to have her grabbing her hand (by the wrist, then uncurling the fingers) to reveal the injury. A hiss of sympathy. "Oh, that looks bad."

"I was pressing hard on the knife," Beatriz said. She pulled her arm away and cradled it close to her chest. "You'd better go fetch Inez. That's my maid. She knows something of how to treat injuries."

"There's a midwife in town who might know more. She's who I usually go to when I have difficulties; Jorge trusts her absolutely. She's reputable," Vulpa added. "The baron and baroness rely on her too."

"It's not that serious. And I don't want to wait for someone to fetch her. Just find Inez. I'm sure she's either in my room or off in the kitchens unless she wandered off—you know your way around the manor, right? Or I suppose I can find her myself." Though she was likely to get waylaid if she did so, given that she was conspicuously bleeding and also the manor's honored guest. She didn't want to have to deal with any hysterics over her injury, and she didn't want this to get back to Baroness Anthona before it had been dealt with and she could confidently say she was completely fine.

Vulpa bit her lip and then sighed. "How about I take care of it? You should have someone else look later, but I know a little about these sorts of things. My mother's an herbalist; I learned about injuries and sicknesses growing up. I didn't bring my supplies with me, but if I run down to the kitchen, I can find the basics and be back in just a minute. And if Inez is there, I'll bring her back too and maybe she can handle it."

"All right," Beatriz agreed.

"Keep your hand elevated until I get back. But level," Vulpa commanded, and then she was gone in a swish of blood-red skirts.

Beatriz sat down on her stool and waited impatiently for Vulpa's return. Her hand hurt. The initial gashing had been awful, of course, but it almost hurt worse now. She wasn't sure how much treatment would even help with that, but sitting with her hand held up, arm braced at the elbow, trying very hard to keep the palm still enough that she wouldn't bleed too much, was complete torture. She was aware of the role reversal—now she was the one who had to sit still and quiet and wait for Vulpa to complete her task. It was ironic and a little funny but she didn't like it. Ricardo always called her an awful model in that area. She really had no idea why he kept on using her, when his paintings never even looked like her in the end. Probably just because they were friends.

Vulpa was back soon, with four items on a tray. The first was a pitcher of water. This she used to wash Beatriz's hand of blood and splinters. The second was a towel to dry the hand off. The third was a pot of honey.

"I have actual ointment at home," she said as she poured some of the honey out onto her fingers, "but honey is the main ingredient, at least in my recipe, so it will do in a pinch. This should prevent infection and inflammation. Hopefully it will ease your pain a little too, though that may take time."

She smeared the honey over Beatriz's wound, and then used the fourth object, a roll of bandages, a length of which she cut off with the very knife that had hurt Beatriz in the first place (though she cleaned the knife of blood and wood fragments first). She wrapped the bandage three times around Beatriz's hand and fastened it with a couple pins she took out of her own hair. This done, she examined her work one last time and nodded in approval. "It should hold. Just remember to change the bandage every day until it heals. Hopefully that won't be too long, and it won't get infected. I'd go to see the midwife if you have any problems, though. Jorge could give you instructions on where to find her, or the baroness. Or anyone, I suppose."

Beatriz nodded. "Thank you. You're talented in many areas, it seems. Medicine and dance."

She wrapped the bandage three times around Beatriz's hand and fastened it with a couple pins she took out of her own hair.

"My mother wanted me to be an herbalist when I grew up." Vulpa shrugged. "Maybe when I grow old I'll follow that trade. But I love dancing."

"And I love to watch you dance, as I'm sure many do," Beatriz said.

They smiled at each other. She felt that she ought to say something more, but wasn't sure quite what. In the end she must have hesitated for too long, because Vulpa announced she had to return the supplies to the kitchen but would be right back, and she scurried off, leaving Beatriz alone again, though in quite a different mood. A clean bandage was a much nicer thing to be left with than a ripped open palm, and the honey really did seem to be doing something for the pain.

She picked up the fragments of the pencil which had fallen to the floor, and placed them on the table next to her sketches. They were nice sketches, she still thought. Vulpa looked nice in them, though it wasn't exactly hard to draw Vulpa so she looked nice. Did she look a goddess, though? Beatriz touched the completed sketch lightly, and her hand twinged. She snatched it back against her chest. Honey wasn't an instant cure, after all—she'd have to be very careful and baby the hand for a few days until it got better.

When Vulpa returned a second time, Beatriz reluctantly told her that she thought she'd done about all the drawing she could do for the day. "I'd still love to draw you again, but my hand... it's not the one I use for drawing, but you kind of do use both. And I'm afraid I've lost my concentration."

Vulpa accepted this with a smile. "You stabbed your hand. Go have a rest or take a walk to get some fresh air. Better not to keep on working."

"Well, it wasn't serious. But yes, I think I'm done. Perhaps you could come back tomorrow? Unless you're busy."

"Tomorrow would be fine. I'm not at all occupied lately."

Right, because her primary patron was Jorge, and she'd been

kicked out of the manor and effectively banned from seeing him and was therefore at odd ends and probably with a shaky revenue stream. Largely because of Beatriz. Beatriz smiled, did her best to hide a wince, and said, "Tomorrow, then, at the same time. I'll look forward to it."

* * *

So it was that she planned to meet and draw Vulpa in the afternoon, but her morning was mostly free, apart from eating with the baron and baroness and Jorge and listening to them all express concern over her recent injury. Anthona made some suggestions about how she might spend her day: she and the baron were going out riding with a friend, might Beatriz join? Oh, well if her hand was bothering her too much for riding, she could at least join them for some entertainment after dinner tonight. There would be music again, though no... dancing. (A sour look crossed Anthona's face.) So, she would be working on art this afternoon? Miss Comete certainly was diligent! Well, until then, she might enjoy walking in the gardens, as the air this morning was still quite cool and nice.

Oh yes, and there was also a letter. A letter had arrived for Beatriz this morning from the capital, from a sender with whom Anthona was unfamiliar. A man.

"A good friend?" Anthona raised her eyebrows suggestively.

Beatriz, who had accepted the envelope handed to her by one of the maids, smiled slightly at the writing. She would have recognized it without the sender's name. It was a nervous smile, though; why was Juan writing to her when she had only been gone for a week? "A friend of a friend," she answered absently. "I expect it's something to do with this competition of the king's. Probably wouldn't interest you much."

Anthona agreed with a mix of socialite fluttering and clear relief that it was not a love letter to the woman she was trying to set up with her son. It would have amused Beatriz if she were not distracted by concern over the letter's actual contents. She took her leave and, following Anthona's advice, went out to the garden to read it.

"Dear Beatriz de Comete,

"Things are mostly the same as they were when you left. My master has still not returned, nor has he sent any word of where he might be or why. I've written to his family, and they have not heard from him either, nor have his friends from our village. My worries continue to grow, but as you told me to remain calm and persevere, I will endeavor to do so, and will not allow those worries to dominate this letter. You have already done enough for me and my master, and I do not want to burden you any further with unnecessary rambling.

"Valdez has been talking a lot all around town. He has not yet admitted to intending to compete for the temple ceiling; I think he thinks it beneath him to appear to snatch at the opportunity as soon as it comes up, especially to snatch at a commission that rightfully belongs to my master. He has, however, spoken slightingly of my master's absence, and said that he thinks it will 'serve Montero right' if he does lose the commission or even the king's favor entirely, because 'one ought not to behave so carelessly, being a painter in royal service.' He says my master thinks himself above his station, better than other painters, a high artist like the old masters rather than an honest craftsman. I have not heard any of this directly from his mouth, probably because he knows I would not stand to hear it and is too cowardly to face my fists. But talk travels, and I do not doubt he has said all these things I have heard secondhand and worse.

"That is only Valdez, who is more insulting than outwardly ambitious. Other artists might talk less boldly about my master, but have already begun their work on a portrait of Marina. 'If Montero doesn't care so much for the commission,' they justify themselves, 'it might as well go to someone who will put more effort into it, who wants it more.' These and other justifications I have heard whenever I venture into the company of capital artists or even their apprentices, who are quick to defend their masters. Valdez is still the most likely to win the king's favor out of all of these

artists, but if he really does disdain the competition, disdain to take my master's 'leavings', then they will grab the commission immediately.

"I do not say these things to worry you more, for as I said, I do not wish to burden you. I only wish to express my hope that you are, as you said when we last spoke, at work on the portrait of Marina. These petty, spiteful, beastly and conniving painters in the capital must be brought down, and I trust only you to do it. I have begun my own attempt at a portrait—I hope you will not see this as me despairing of my master's return, for it is only a way to occupy the time, and perhaps a last resort—but I am only an apprentice, no master. You must be the one to win the day, and I am convinced that you can, if you will only put all your heart and soul into it. Pity my master, or hate these wretched rivals of his, or at least pity me,

"Your servant,

"Juan Rojo."

"So you don't wish to burden me with your worries, Juan," Beatriz murmured as she folded the letter back up. Yet his letter had done little but that. She supposed she shouldn't be too judgmental of him. For a man as stressed as he had been when she left the capital, he'd kept the letter admirably brief. Still, she didn't appreciate his distrust that she'd actually come out to Mestos with the intention of working on the portrait. She'd already started on it, after all, and she'd only been out here for one week.

A single week. And yet, that did make it a month since Ricardo's disappearance.

Where on earth was he?

"You seem troubled, Miss Comete. Did your letter contain bad news?"

She looked up from the bench she had settled on to see Jorge standing over her, a solicitous expression on his face. She forced a smile. "Nothing new. I believe I mentioned over dinner the other day that I'm trying my hand at winning a commission from the king."

"Oh, yes. I remember."

It had been discussed at as great a length as the baroness's patience for such matters had allowed. "Well, the only reason the commission is open is because Ricardo Montero has gone missing. You've heard of Montero?"

"I've heard him spoken of in the capital, during my visits."

"Well, he's still missing. And it's not much like him." Beatriz sighed. "Frankly I'd much rather know where he is than win this commission."

Her hand twinged as she spoke, and she let out a little gasp. As if it were calling her out for lying. No, that was true, wasn't it? She really was worried about Ricardo. As for the temple vault, it did appeal to her, the idea of painting such a lasting and prestigious monument, the technical challenges and the glory it might win her, but in the end there was no guarantee she could win this competition in the first place, and painting a ceiling was a hard task, and she had no great experience with religious subjects—if she could give it all up...

Her hand twinged again.

"You're friends with Montero then? I suppose artistic circles are small in the capital."

"Small enough. Though I know Ricardo better than I know most professional artists in the capital. Artistic circles, as you say, can be a bit exclusive, and many don't consider me serious enough about painting as a profession. But Ricardo..."

She wasn't sure Ricardo believed she took painting as seriously as she did. She'd told him once how she felt about painting—how it made her feel more alive, more joyful, how she felt it added meaning to her existence—and he'd sighed and told her that was exactly what marked her as an amateur. "You paint because it's fun," he'd said.

"Fun!" she'd protested. "That's a very light word for it." She felt he'd ignored all that she'd said to him.

"Painting is fun, at its best. But at the end of the day, it's not what brings you food, and it's not something you have to devote all your time to. I'm not slighting your art. I'm only saying you are not a professional. If I were you, I'd be happy about that. But it's no reason to act superior either."

"I don't act superior."

"Oh, Beatriz. You really can be such a little liar."

Now she bit her lip. How did she describe Ricardo, how he and she related to each other so easily, so happily, even though at times they barely got along at all? She'd never been able to understand their friendship all that well herself. Only that they did not resent each other or judge each other for standing out among others in the capital, only that they enjoyed debating and didn't hold back out of courtesy but were able at the end of the day to make up after their arguments, only that she looked at Ricardo sometimes and knew that for all his high and mighty condescending words, he loved painting as much as she did, and they both could understand it as both craft and art. Only that they liked each other.

"Ricardo and I have known each other for a few years," she settled on saying to Jorge. "We have a lot of mutual respect. We admire each other's art greatly, and sometimes we help each other out. I'm really trying to help him out now, in a way, though I suppose it doesn't seem like that from the outside."

Jorge hummed. He sat down on the bench next to Beatriz, though a respectful distance apart from her still. It was a long bench. "It must be hard for you, being apart from such a close friend. I have noticed you seem distracted." He met her eyes solemnly. "I hope my mother does not bother you too much with her fussing. Please do not feel any pressure to be... more social than you are comfortable with. Such demands might be difficult for you, especially with this intimate friend of yours missing..."

It was thoughtful of him to say such a thing, but his tone was insinuating. A laugh escaped Beatriz's lips as she realized what he meant; she coughed to cover it up with dignity. "Sir, I'm sorry, but I think you've misunderstood. Though it is kind of you, and I am worried about my friend, Ricardo and I have no interest in each other beyond that."

"Ah," Jorge leaned back. "I'm sorry, I didn't mean to imply..."

"You have no need to worry, though. I have no interest in you, either. Indeed I hope you and Vulpa will be quite happy with each other, and I feel rather bad if my presence here in Mestos has disturbed the two of you."

At this, Jorge outright blushed. It was a funny look on him, as he was usually quite composed. "Rumors seem to spread quite fast in this manor. My mother will combust if she knows you've heard about it."

"By all means don't tell her."

"I'm sorry if..."

"What should you apologize for? If anyone, I should apologize. I should have known my coming here could put you in a difficult position."

Jorge shrugged. "My mother already disapproved of our relationship. It's more that she asked you here as an excuse to get rid of Vulpa. She would have found another if inviting you failed. Of course, we do genuinely appreciate your visiting—it's a delight and an honor to have such a distinguished guest." This last part was clearly belated courtesy. Ha.

"Well, I do enjoy being here." She returned the courtesy if only to relieve his embarrassment. "It must be hard for you, though, to deal with such difficulties coming between you and the woman you love."

"Ah... Vulpa..." Jorge sighed. "Well, it is hard. But of course I can see that my mother means well; she only wants me to be more respectable. And Vulpa and I—well, we aren't as serious as all that. We aren't exactly star-crossed lovers."

"Oh—oh, of course, I suppose."

"We enjoy each other's company. I suppose in time we will have to part ways, but I hope it will not be quite yet."

"I see. Yes, well... good luck."

"Thank you."

After an awkward moment, Jorge stood and moved on, leaving Beatriz sitting with the letter and a puzzled expression. No, that did make sense, of course. Vulpa was Jorge's mistress, and the latest in a string if even the capital gossip was to be believed. No need to romanticize it. It was only that, having met Vulpa, having seen her beauty and intensity and even her kindness, it was so hard to think that a man could have all that and be less than utterly in love with her.

"Well," she said to herself, "he's said to be foolish in life and love, so it should be no surprise. Doubtless Vulpa will find better someday." Though perhaps not wealthier; indeed being the mistress of such a man was a cozy position, and it would be too bad for Vulpa if Jorge broke their relationship off. If only Beatriz could avoid precipitating such a situation—well, she would try her best, and be as polite and generous as possible with Vulpa in the meantime.

With this, she came up with many things she wanted to say to Vulpa that afternoon, and various half-formed ideas about perhaps paying Vulpa more than her current reasonable wage for modeling, and other ideas, more artistic, about what poses would best suit the portrait and what clothes she would have to procure for it. But in the end, all of these thoughts led nowhere, for while Beatriz waited all afternoon in the studio, Vulpa never showed up.

She sent Inez to Vulpa's house with a message after a couple hours. Inez returned with a report that the door had not been answered. She had slipped the message under the door, but had no reply to give.

"Damn," Beatriz said. She stared at her sketchbook. The hour was late. "Another day wasted. Juan would kill me if he knew. Well, she'll come tomorrow if she got the message. Then back to work."

That night she dreamed that she was on a ship sailing the ocean. Staring out over the waves, she had the unnerving feeling that someone was watching her, and she kept looking back over her shoulder.

"You look," a voice said (or was it a voice? Or merely a thought), "but you see nothing. Look closer, Beatriz."

Beatriz squinted at the waves, but the sunlight dazzled her eyes.

The voice in her ear was almost a laugh. "Look better, Beatriz."

She stared and stared until the dream faded and she saw nothing at all.

7

CHAPTER SEVEN

The countess Leonor was as good as her word, Ricardo discovered. He was asked only the day after the appeals court for a list of needed painting supplies by one of the servants. He battled conflicting impulses—one to ask for extravagantly expensive supplies, as Leonor was surely the one who would be paying for it all, and the other to ask for only the bare essentials as cheap as possible, so that his request would be seen as reasonable and would therefore be fulfilled, as he did get restless without anything to do. In the end he took a middle road. There was no need to make his captivity less of a burden on Leonor, since she was the one who had created the situation in the first place, but on the other hand, he didn't want to test her temper. He'd seen a glimpse of it already, gleaming through her control at lunch the other day. And he really did want the supplies, as he was currently as bored as he was anxious and outraged over his current state.

Pigments (the most expensive request he had) were given to him after only a couple days, and he assumed the delay was because they were not so easy to get a hold of in Suelta. Medium was given to him at the same time. Canvas and wood to frame it were brought to him even earlier, but he was not allowed to nail the frame together or cut the canvas to size himself, or even to nail the canvas to the board. All this would have required giving him tools that apparently were too dangerous to trust him with. Well, it wasn't as though Ricardo actually enjoyed stretching canvas—he couldn't imagine anyone did—but it still irritated him. He'd hardly been planning on hitting someone over the head with a hammer, stabbing them with a nail, and making a run for it.

Though maybe he should have been. He hadn't made any real escape attempts since arriving in Suelta, given the number of guards and other servants Leonor had scattered about the estate, but he'd have to give it a go at some point if he ever wanted to get out of this godsforsaken place and back to the capital where he belonged. He just didn't have a good plan for it yet, hadn't seen a convenient moment.

It had occurred to him, of course, even when asking for painting supplies, that starting a painting was not a great step towards escape. Oils dried slowly, and paintings in general were hard to transport in good condition. It was enough to make him hesitate, when he had his canvas and supplies and all was ready, to begin a painting at all. He told himself, however, that he might as well. If an opportunity presented itself for escape, he would not feel obliged to pack up his painting if it were not in traveling condition, but would promptly and heartlessly abandon it as he had trashed many drafts and ill-conceived projects over the years. In fact, it might even be useful to work on a project, as it would keep him fresh and alert rather than languishing and dull, and might convince his captors that he had settled into captivity with no intention of going anywhere soon, so that he might catch them off guard when he did make his escape in the end.

With this in mind, it was probably for the best that he really didn't have any interesting subject in mind for the painting. With Leonor crossed off the list of possibilities, he briefly considered finding another human model, but quickly rejected the idea. Maybe Leonor would order a servant to model for him, but the servants here all were very awkward around him, half-curious and half-pitying this strange pet of their mistress's. Captain Alban still visited him often, but he was even more infuriating. And he'd drawn sketches of Felipe, finding the subject of a future king enticing, but for a longer project, Felipe was too flighty and obnoxious to sit for long periods of time; Ricardo would have put up with that kind of behavior for a commission, but in his free time, he preferred to work with models he actually liked.

All this meant that ultimately, he begrudgingly followed Leonor's casual suggestion, and settled in to work on a still-life.

It had been a while since Ricardo last painted a still life. With the king's favor shining on him, when he wasn't at work on royal commissions there were other patrons practically waiting in line for him to get around to them, and none of them wanted a painting of a nice vase of flowers or a bowl full of spoons. In fact, the last time he'd had time for any prolonged effort of that kind had been—if he was remembering correctly—the autumn before last. Juan had only been his apprentice for a year then, and Ricardo had set him to work on a still life for practice in colors and shading, especially colors. Then Beatriz had come over and somehow harassed him into working on his own piece from the same set-up. "We can all do our own piece and compare how they come out," she had said. "It'll be fun, and educational for Juan."

Ricardo was pretty sure she'd just been in a competitive mood, a suspicion that solidified when the actual pieces were done and Beatriz went on and on, in front of Juan, about how Ricardo's work was less crisp than hers, less detailed—"but of course he does have a way with highlights and smooth contours, I can never compare in that area," she added with a beatific smile. Ricardo had been embarrassed, and Juan had been somewhat offended on his behalf, but the painting itself had been fun. It was a pity it was only early summer now, and not autumn. There had been some excellent veiny vegetables to use on that occasion, and brightly colored fruits as well. Summer had its own fruits, of course, and flowers, but flowers were less to Ricardo's taste, and Suelta wasn't exactly known for having orchards and vineyards, as its agriculture was more focused on grain. Or maybe Ricardo was simply missing home, and thinking about past paintings was leaving him picky. Grouchy.

Whichever the case, Ricardo cast aside his homesickness and decided on a still life with no plants at all in it. This did not mean he would be unambitious, regardless of the frustrated, lackadaisical mood he was in. Countess Leonor had told him he would be given any supplies he required, and even mentioned still lifes as an option. It didn't take much creativity to interpret these words beyond the basic needs of paint and medium and canvas and brushes.

"Stones," he said to the servant apparently delegated to taking his requests. "Interesting stones, preferably large ones. A metal pitcher, silver if possible. And cloth. Silk or velvet, not cheap cotton. Embroidered, and brightly colored."

The servant frowned but nodded, and the next day Ricardo was presented with several large stones, mostly gray but one a gleaming, pearly white, a pitcher that did appear to be fine silver, and a length of crimson velvet cloth with a texture that almost seemed to shiver when Ricardo ran a finger over it. Ricardo didn't offer any thanks, but he did tell the servant it was quite adequate, and the servant nodded and said that he would be happy to help with anything else Ricardo needed in the future.

Ricardo took his time setting up the arrangement. *Here's an area I can best you, Beatriz,* he thought to himself. *You'd probably just throw it together and say it looked more natural that way.* He cared about composition far too much for that. The positioning of the stones around the vase had to look even and mostly balanced, but not so symmetrical as to be trite. And when he crumpled the velvet, left it disheveled underneath the vase and stones both, rising up in folds behind it as well, it might have looked rumpled and messy, but in reality, he thought through every fold and crease, imagining their appearance on the canvas as he set them into place.

And when it was done, he set himself to painting.

He was two days into the effort, and still laying down flat color on the canvas to indicate general shapes, when Leonor showed up, taking a belated interest in what her captive artist might be up to.

"I thought you might be commissioning a new tunic for yourself next, with that velvet you asked for," she said, looking over his arrangement, "but now I see you're putting it to an artistic use after all."

"I'm not so extravagant as to order new clothing from you," Ricardo said flatly. He'd been given clothes already, and already resented wearing things provided by his captor. If he were to get fancier outfits, it would only make him feel more like a caged bird than he already did—and with the amused way Leonor was looking at him, that feeling was already increasing by the second.

"It would be more practical, don't you think? Better than ordering that much velvet just to let it sit around."

"The velvet will be returned to you when my painting is done, and you may put it to any use you wish," Ricardo said. "In the meantime, I am painting it. Velvet has a unique texture, very interesting to paint."

"Your painting doesn't seem very textured."

"It is not complete." Not even close.

"I suppose not," Leonor said skeptically. "Very well. We'll see how it progresses."

Ricardo assumed this meant she would return in a couple days to see how far he'd gotten with the piece, but it became clear, when she settled down in an extra chair in a corner of the room, that in fact she meant to stay and watch him paint and see how the painting would progress right now.

Well, in a sense that was probably good, right? His initial plan to paint her had been premised on the concept that spending more time with Leonor would make her sympathize with him and eventually decide to release him. Yes, good. Only her gaze prickled at his spine as he turned back to the canvas and got to work. He made an effort to show focus, diligence, in his efforts, care and attention paid to the mixing of colors and to the outlines he was laying down. Occasionally he made a remark about his work, and Leonor would give him a laconic response. Not a whole lot of interaction, and if he tried to engage her in further conversation, asking her about herself —whether she had any petitioners left or had settled the business that had piled up in her absence, for example—her answers only got shorter.

The first remark that she made of her own initiative is, "This bores you, doesn't it?"

"It's not exactly a high-profile commission. But it's still something to do."

"You don't enjoy it. You get distracted, and when you do focus, you still aren't having a good time."

That was because Leonor was here, not because of the painting itself. She made him nervous, self conscious. He thought she would have made him feel that way even if she weren't his captor. She had such sharp eyes, such a commanding presence. He would still have wanted to make a good impression, have fought not to cringe or bridle under her scrutiny.

"You could have painted Felipe," Leonor said, "if you didn't really want to do a still life. I would have told him to sit for you. He likes you, anyway."

"I could never waste the time of our country's heir that way."

"Meaning you don't want to."

Ricardo demurred and did not respond.

Leonor tilted her head. (Her hair, which was spun up in a complicated twist, tilted as well.) "If you would rather not paint my family, very well—I know, though you won't admit it and I won't force you, that you'd rather not paint me either, really. But still lives clearly don't interest you. Why don't you paint yourself again? Like you did in that painting of the king's household. That was a good piece, and you were especially good in it."

There was a twitch of warmth in Ricardo at that. He tried his best to hide it.

That painting—ah, for all the gossip it had caused in artistic circles, for all the people who had called him arrogant for it, he had a soft spot for it, and he thought it would likely always occupy a fond place in his portfolio, in his memories.

* * *

It had been a major commission, to start with.

Of course, Ricardo had done more personal work for Alejandro in the past. Painting Alejandro's wife, in particular, who rarely received visitors, whom Alejandro protected in a way some called caring and others jealous (and some, "embarrassed", but Ricardo didn't listen to that kind of gossip). Painting Alejandro himself. A couple religious pieces too, which to another king might have been simply requisite piety to maintain reputation but to Alejandro were vital signs of his reverence and worship.

This commission was quite a challenge, though, and unique in multiple ways. That many people in one painting, all in detail and meant to be recognizable, would have been a major undertaking in itself, but then there were the identities of the people in question.

They were all nobles and all important people to Alejandro and to the court, but they had many of them never been painted before, as their opinions on art varied. Steward, chamberlain, master of the horse, treasurer, and so on and so forth... hell, the treasurer had been known to express disapproval of how much Alejandro paid Ricardo in the past (which in turn infuriated Ricardo—the Salandran court already paid its artists less than would have been typical in many other countries), and was unlikely to appreciate Ricardo painting him. Ricardo wondered if he'd be able to muster a smile or even a neutral expression while modeling, or if Ricardo would have to paint him with a grimace of annoyance. Well, perhaps viewers would take that as a sign of proper severity.

Ricardo would have to find time for each subject in his schedule. Tricky to coordinate around the pace of courtly activities; trickier in winter, when there was a flood of events and parties throughout the city to attract the sociable, while crabbier spirits hated to even venture out into the cold for actual business affairs. It would be impossible to get all eight men Alejandro had selected to model at the same time for him—Ricardo doubted it could be accomplished even by royal command. So he would have to find opportunities to sketch each of them separately, work out their positions in the composition separately, paint each separately, but make it all work together. Not impossible, done that way, but still quite a task.

Alejandro hummed and nodded the day that Ricardo showed him his basic sketch of the piece's composition. He had yet to bring a single one of the men in for a modeling session, yet to start on the actual piece or even studies for the piece, but he was getting the concept down, he thought, pretty well, getting an idea of how to position each man to best show their appearance, including height and typical fashion choices, and their role in Alejandro's household—more important members towards the center, less important on the fringes, but with all in full view so that none would be insulted.

As he explained his reasoning to Alejandro, Alejandro seemed to take it all in and really be listening, far more carefully than Ricardo, a mere artist, had any right to expect. But then Alejandro had always been that way. He would even come in and watch Ricardo at work many days, and his gaze had never unnerved Ricardo the way Leonor's did, never felt judging or piercing even though he was a king, just... attentive. Somehow sharp and relaxed at the same time. He took in all Ricardo did, all Ricardo said, all Ricardo was, and ultimately accorded the majority of it with fond approval. When he did have critique to offer, it was never harsh or petulant but direct and reasonable. And usually, once he'd explained himself, Ricardo would agree he was in the right.

He would have been a great patron to work for even were he not the king.

Today, Alejandro pursed his lips when Ricardo had finished, and said, "It's a little too balanced."

Ricardo looked at his sketch. Yes, maybe. He'd done his best to vary positioning enough not to make the piece feel staid, but it was true that the sides of the painting mirrored each other very closely. "Any suggestions, your majesty?" Most clients he would never ask such a thing, not trusting to their taste; the king, he always would.

A smile bloomed on the king's face. "I've been thinking—eight's a boring number, and these eight in particular are boring men. Should we make it nine? We could put the ninth seated in the middle, or a little off to the side, in front. Perhaps in front of our dear treasurer."

Alejandro didn't always like the treasurer either, even though he was a very sensible and useful man. Ricardo had often heard his complaints. It would be like him to enjoy poking at the treasurer's pride, but what tool would he be using for the poking? "Who would the ninth be, then, your majesty?"

The smile widened. Alejandro's eyes twinkled. "Why not the court painter?"

Ricardo stilled. "Your majesty, I'm flattered but I'm hardly as important as your—your steward, or master of the hunt..."

"Not to the court at large, perhaps. Many of them have hardly met you. But your art will be part of this court's legacy; it is vital in its own way. And from day to day, I'm sure I spend more time with you than with the master of the hunt. As a member of my household, you're very significant."

By that argument, Ricardo should have been painting Alejandro's personal attendants and bodyguards. Perhaps he would have to do that someday, but today he couldn't bring himself to make an objection. It didn't matter whether Alejandro was teasing—whether he simply wanted to mess with the treasurer—or if he was sincere. He was still telling Ricardo to put himself in a piece depicting the most important people in Alejandro's household, arguably in his life.

Ricardo could not refuse him. He tried his best to paint himself as a serious man, an industrious artist, someone worthy of the king's regard. According to Leonor, he'd ended up painting someone who didn't look entirely like he did in real life. But Alejandro had smiled at it and said Ricardo did a good job. "And see? It really did do wonders for the composition."

Improved the composition, and upped Ricardo's notoriety. But no matter how many rivals accused Ricardo of arrogance, to his face or behind his back, Ricardo never mentioned that the king had ordered Ricardo's presence in the painting. It was a boast that sat more comfortably in his chest and stomach than coming out of his mouth. To vocalize it would even have felt petty.

* * *

Certainly, Ricardo was hardly going to tell Leonor about it, even though it would have made for a good retort, pointing out that he had done it on the command of a king she hated, pointing out that he was not so proud as to want to paint himself all the time. Instead he said, "Generally I find myself a boring subject", which was true. Frankly, he'd grown tired of self-portraits in his days as an apprentice, when he'd had to do far too many of them. (This hadn't prevented him from passing similar torture down to Juan, to whom he'd assigned three self-portraits so far.)

Leonor said, "We could make it more interesting. Give me back the velvet, and I can have some clothes made for you after all. You weren't in a great amount of finery in your last portrait."

He hadn't been, instead choosing a simple black outfit that lent him gravity without too much pretension. But wearing better clothes would hardly make a self-portrait less tiresome. He said as much: "I'd still have the same face and body, so it would still feel much the same. As for the velvet, I can paint it well enough as-is, laid out on the table—it's far too hot this time of year to wear it anyway."

Leonor hmphed. "Suit yourself, but don't tell me you aren't bored. I'm not fooled."

Ricardo wanted to ask her why she thought she knew him well enough to read his moods after such a brief and conflicted acquaintanceship, but he bit his lip and stayed silent. Leonor wasn't Beatriz to be teased and bickered with, nor was she the king, a patron with patience. She was a thunderstorm. There was no reason to poke at her. Even if a part of him wanted to see what she would look like losing her temper—wanted to drag her into really showing that spiteful side of her that kept him locked up here, wanted, more than that, to somehow understand this strange woman beyond what she was willing to reveal—even so, he knew that such a display would ultimately be much to his detriment.

"I'm honored by your concern," he said. "But in truth, there is no reason for it. This occupies me as well as anything might, locked up in this room."

Leonor leaned back. "I've been thinking about that, too. You really shouldn't be stuck in here all the time. I'll see to it that you can get out and about more in the future. Would you like to go riding with Felipe, perhaps? He'll be going out with Captain Alban tomorrow."

"No, thank you," Ricardo said. "I wouldn't want to intrude." Going for a horseback ride would be an excellent opportunity for an escape attempt, in any other company. With Captain Alban along, it just sounded like an opportunity for annoyance.

Leonor gave him a long look. "Well, perhaps just a walk, then. I'll have it arranged."

Again, the countess was as good as her word. (Ricardo might have admired her honesty or generosity, were it not for the fact that she of course was always the one setting the limits on her own offers.) The next day, Sancho came by Ricardo's room and informed him that he'd come to take Ricardo for a walk, and could bring him anywhere he wished—inside the limits of Leonor's estate, of course. And in the company of a guard Ricardo hadn't met before, who hovered outside Ricardo's room as he slipped on a pair of boots before heading out alongside the two.

Sancho was in a cheerful mood (though to be fair, Ricardo had never seen him in anything but a cheerful mood, and wasn't sure what it would look like). As they walked down the hall and then down the stairs, heading out to the courtyard, he talked and talked and talked. Had Ricardo enjoyed dinner last night? Sancho had thought the stew very good, but had worried there wouldn't be enough leftovers that Ricardo would get any. Oh, he got a good-sized helping—well, that was good to hear. Perhaps they saved some out for him early in the evening, or sent it up beforehand? Ricardo didn't know. Oh well, Sancho might ask the kitchen girls now, as he was getting a little curious. There was one girl there in particular, a Chabela, who Sancho was particular friends with. Not in that way, Montero, although maybe someday, if you know what I mean. Actually Sancho had hopes to impress her with his performance in the long run at the Festival of Sektos.

"Oh, the Festival of Sektos? Is that coming up soon?" Ricardo asked.

"Yes. Just two weeks away, now."

"I hadn't thought we were that far into the summer," Ricardo mused. The Festival of Sektos was in the early summer, actually, but he hadn't thought it was summer yet at all. He was losing track of time, and he didn't like it.

On the other hand, Sancho's enthusiastic description of how each and every event of the festival was being arranged, and which ones he intended to attend or join, was less annoying than his usual chatter, perhaps because it didn't revolve around Leonor or Captain Alban or Ricardo himself. Ricardo even allowed Sancho to convince him to take a look at some of his friends' training in the back courtyard, behind the manor, for the upcoming festival's wrestling matches, though this was as much because he wanted a look at the estate's layout than out of any interest in these friends' possible talents.

Wrestling was one of the most exciting events of any Festival of Sektos, and one of the most central, Sektos being a war god and wrestling being one of the festival's few truly warlike events. Not that endurance or speed were not important for a warrior—the races held for the festival were also respected—and of course, the fire and the sacrifices made at the end of the festival were supposed to be the real high point. But it was common opinion that a war god really smiled more on those contests that involved actual violence, and wrestling was foremost among them. Some cities would have fencing matches as well, or contests of archery, but those still tended to be less violent, as the arrows would only be shot at targets, and the fencing matches generally ended at first blood—not exactly visceral.

Ricardo enjoyed watching wrestling himself. He even had partaken from time to time, as a youth in the country, before his station as the king's painter had made such activities unsuitable for him. His was a position with too much dignity to wrestle with the peasants of the city, but too little for him to join in the matches of the younger and more restless noblemen. So he'd relinquished participation in these games without too much regret. Still, it was fun to watch, and he supposed Sancho's friends might be descent wrestlers. After all, they were Leonor's guards according to what he said, and if Captain Alban was a good example, then Leonor had some tough and unscrupulous guards in her employ indeed.

So his hopes were high when Sancho introduced the friends to him: Benito, Diego, and Nicolas. But after watching Benito fight Diego and then Nicolas in frankly slow succession, these hopes of his were sinking.

"They really intend to compete in the wrestling competition?" he asked Sancho.

"Oh, yes. You don't think they're good?" Sancho asked. His lips twitched slightly.

"How long have they been training?"

"Well, wrestling isn't one of the guards' usual exercises. They've been at work on it for the past week and a half. Feel free to give them pointers, but I doubt they'll listen, except maybe Benito. I've been trying to tell Nicolas to work on his stance for the past week."

"So you know something of wrestling then. But you only plan to run."

"I know what an observer can know. Myself, I'm not one for violence." Sancho shrugged. "May Sektos pardon me, I don't like blood much. Chabela makes fun of me sometimes when I visit the kitchen and they've had to butcher a chicken in there, or a goat. I just think we should get our meat from the butcher shop in town, you know? And they do most of the time, but sometimes we get live animals as gifts, or the countess has a particular hankering for something the butcher can't provide. She's a woman of strong ideas, the countess. When she has a craving for something..."

"Are these the only guards of Leonor's that plan to wrestle at all this year?" Ricardo said. Partly because he was curious, partly just because he had no desire to listen to Sancho ramble about Leonor's culinary taste.

The guard accompanying Sancho and Ricardo said, "No. But you know how it is. Not everyone wants to train together—besides, we have different shifts. It would do Diego a deal of good to fight against Carlos Puig, for example, but Carlos has the night watch and sleeps through most of the day. Anyhow, those two don't get along well. Oh well. Perhaps they'll meet in the actual matches. It would be very fun to watch that match-up."

Sancho, taking up the ball, went on for a while about the talents of Carlos Puig, while Ricardo only half listened. Diego and Nicolas's fight was coming to a conclusion, with Diego barely winning against Nicolas. He grinned in triumph when Nicolas finally admitted defeat, and he and Nicolas walked over to talk to Sancho, to brag a little about how they were improving, having finally noticed he was there.

"Hey," Sancho said, "how would the two of you like to fight my friend Montero here? I know you've all been curious about him. He's been bored lately, and he's not a bad fighter. Back when we were on the road, he gave Captain Alban a couple nasty bruises. One on the face, even. Right here." He touched the right side of his forehead. "How about it? Captain Alban beat him, and the captain will be in the competition this year, so I've heard. So to win the competition, properly you should be able to defeat Montero too."

Ricardo gave Sancho a look, which Sancho returned with bland amusement. Nicolas, having been just beaten, was hesitant. He said, "Eh… well, of course we shouldn't begrudge a guest a match…"

But Diego, fresh off two victories, promptly said, "Certainly I'll give it a go. Let's see how they fight in the capital, then." He strode back to the space where he and Nicolas had been wrestling; there was a circle, slightly smudged now, drawn in the dirt.

Ricardo's fighting style had developed solely in his days before capital life and wouldn't tell Diego shit about that, if he really wanted to know. He shook his head and walked over to the ring. Sancho had exaggerated how well Ricardo had fared against Captain Alban, and made him sound like more of a fighting personality than he really was, but he was right that lately he'd been bored out of his mind. And not just bored either—frustrated.

A chance to tackle someone and grind them into the dirt was exactly what he needed.

Diego was half decent, certainly better than the other two, but he'd been tired out, and Ricardo had noticed that a lot of his success with Nicolas and Benito had been built on brute strength. Accordingly, when Diego lunged at him, he ducked at the last moment, and tripped the man to the ground, immediately following up with a pin. The match was over in seconds.

Diego got up again with a red face, but he forced a laugh, and said to Sancho, "He's not bad. I went too easy on him. Next time I'll have a better idea of what his skill level is."

Benito came forward now and, to Ricardo's surprise, asked if he might be interested in fighting a loser. "I'm not as good as Diego, but how will I get better if I don't get toppled enough?" was how he put it. "If you don't mind doing me the favor."

Ricardo didn't mind. He actually found Benito to be more of a challenge, as he was less tired out and a bit more tactical than Diego. He had just beaten him down for a second time when he heard the sound of applause. As Sancho and the guard and the others had not been applauding thus far, too intent and perhaps too lazy to bother, it surprised him. When he looked up, he discovered that the applause was coming from a more authoritative source. Countess Leonor had appeared on the scene.

He stood up slowly. Would she take offense to him downing one of her guards? No, she looked like she'd enjoyed watching it. When had she shown up?

"Montero, you have hidden talents," she called out to him. "All I'd heard those hands could do was paint! Well, I suppose Captain Alban did complain, but I supposed he was complaining for the sake of it."

Ricardo couldn't imagine Captain Alban whining, but did not say so. He bowed slightly. "I'm glad you were entertained."

"Do you plan to join the competition on the Festival of Sektos?"

"I'm a prisoner here. I can't imagine it would be appropriate."

"I'll put you in the list," Leonor said with a smile. "There, that will be something to keep you busy apart from your still-life."

Ricardo had no real objection, so he agreed, although he felt a bit like he'd been herded into something without really thinking it through. Later, though, when he was alone again in his room, it occurred to him that if he could attend the Festival of Sektos, no matter the degree of his participation, it could only be a good thing. For what better opportunity to escape than the hustle and bustle of a festival?

8

CHAPTER EIGHT

Despite her mixed motives for taking on the enterprise, Beatriz found herself as consumed by the idea of painting Marina as she ever had been by a project taken on of her own desiring. Unfortunately, passion didn't always smooth the way in art, and she also found that she had seldom been as frustrated.

After failing to contact Vulpa for days on end, she'd had Inez ask around in town, see who else might be interested in modeling, but no one struck her as having the right look. If she could only be professional about this, she could probably just pick someone tall and strong looking and have at it. Dark hair would be best, probably—a redhead had been an odd choice in the first place. But ever since she'd accepted this challenge, she'd found herself acting superstitious. *I'd know*, she thought. *If it was the right person I'd know.* She hadn't found anyone right yet.

She'd tried to just go at it without a model, the way she knew Ricardo did sometimes. She knew human anatomy as well as he did, after all, maybe better. The sketch onto the canvas went all right, but then she'd started painting, and it all went wrong over and over again. Brushes snapped in her hands. The medium would mix perfectly well with the pigment, and then on the canvas it would become watery and translucent and run off the canvas onto the floor. She'd never seen paint act that way before. It gave her chills when she stopped to think about it, but when she was focused, trying so hard to just get the painting right, it mostly just gave her a headache.

Work-related frustration wasn't all that was bothering her either. There was still the injury on her left hand. She'd thought it would have cleanly healed by now, but sometimes pain still shot through her hand and wrist when she strained herself, and the cut itself looked strange beneath the bandages. It should have been just a bit lighter than the rest of her palm by now, or perhaps still a bit red or brown if it were going to refuse to heal, but instead it had turned a crusty purple. Almost the color of bluebells, with the scab rippled like the pattern on a shell. She'd had the midwife Vulpa had recommended look at it, and the woman had shaken her head and given her some ointment.

"What's the matter with it?" she'd asked. But the woman hadn't answered, only hmphed. It occurred to Beatriz that she might simply not know and be too proud to say.

So there was her hand still hurting her, the stress of work, and then there were her dreams, which sometimes she could remember and sometimes she couldn't... All in all, Beatriz's little seaside vacation was draining her a little more every hour. Had Don Fernando, or worse, Luis, known the state she was in, they would have summoned her home immediately and ordered her to get some rest; she could only imagine their outrage. Even Lady de Comete would have tutted and told her this was what came of obsessing too much over one of her "little painting projects", and probably summoned her home too—the only difference would have been that Don Fernando and Luis would have blamed Lady Anthona for not taking proper care of Beatriz, while Lady de Comete might well have apologized to Lady Anthona for Beatriz's poor manners as a guest.

For Beatriz truly was a very poor guest, and growing worse by the day. She was still trying, at least, to eat meals with her hosts, and to go for walks with Lady Anthona in the evening and partake in what amusements were suggested. But she was aware that her participation in all these activities was peremptory, and, doubtless to Lady Anthona's despair, that she was not spending much time at all with Jorge—who, to be fair, spent much of his own time who-knew-where, nowhere to be found by Lady Anthona's best and Beatriz's most lackluster efforts.

Then one day he breezed in to lunch with a grin on his face, a slew of apologies towards his mother, and a surprising amount of interest towards Beatriz. He even asked her if he might sit in on her painting efforts that afternoon and keep her company—would that be too forward?

Lady Anthona's eyes went wide with delight. Until now she could only have seen Beatriz's artistic focus as a rival, and here her son was unexpectedly exploiting it. Beatriz had never seen her look prouder, and so, despite not really wanting a spectator, she reluctantly agreed that Jorge might sit in if he wished. "I'll be starting up again in a couple hours. I can't promise it will be very interesting, though. I'm currently still working on laying down the underpainting, and it's been slow going thus far."

Jorge smiled graciously. "Oh, I'm sure I'll find it much more interesting than you say. What's familiar to you, after all, will be new to me. I know very little about the process of painting."

So, so.

But when he came down to her studio later with a wicked smirk on his face, he didn't so much as glance at the canvas. (Which was just as well. It was another day of watery paint dripping down to the bottom of the canvas and then to the floor. Very depressing.) Instead, he handed her an unsealed envelope and sat down on a stool with his chin in one hand and his eyebrows raised.

"A letter for me?" Beatriz asked.

"Yes. Specially delivered by me, your humble messenger."

"What, you intercepted the mail today?"

"It didn't come in the mail," Jorge said. "This is a note from Vulpa. Her apologies, mostly, I think. I was tasked with delivering it—thought it best not to hand it to you over lunch, given what Mother would probably think."

"She'd probably think you were giving me a love note," Beatriz suggested, "not that you were smuggling something from your..."

"Exactly. Think of the cost. Not that I'd hate to give you a love note."

"Don't worry. I'm not offended. But it's good to hear from Vulpa. I've been trying to reach her for ages. Thanks."

Beatriz opened the envelope and pulled out a piece of paper that had been folded in half and was a bit crinkled. The envelope had been a bit crinkled too—Jorge must have been carrying it around in his pocket for a while. The writing on the page, however, was neat and easily legible, written in delicate, careful ink.

"Dear Miss Comete,

"I beg your forgiveness for not having met with you or even written to you these past couple of weeks. This forced separation is not mine by design. When I went to meet with you at our last appointment, I was stopped by certain members of the household who have never liked me much; they said her ladyship the baroness had forbidden me to set foot on the premises. Since then I have tried to send word to you, but I believe my messages have been intercepted. So I've been reduced to sending Jorge. I'm sure you have heard or guessed before now, but he and I are well acquainted. I hope you won't be offended by my using him for this.

"Things being as they stand, I doubt I'm a convenient choice of model

for your painting. I only wanted to write to you since I had left you with no word of why. However, if you do still want to paint me, or wish to talk to me for some other reason, meet me at the beach behind the manor early tomorrow afternoon, when the sun is high and everyone is at home resting. Come alone if you can—there is no strict reason for secrecy, but I don't believe the baroness thinks much of our associating with each other. If you cannot come, I will not be offended, given that I failed to arrive when we last arranged to meet.

"Yours truly,

"Vulpa."

Beatriz reread the ending of the letter, and then folded it back up and put it back in the envelope. "Should I burn it?" she asked Jorge.

"What? Why? Was it that offensive?"

"I'm wondering what might happen if someone got ahold of it. The gossip in this house..."

"Oh, just throw it out then. Burning it surely isn't necessary."

"Perhaps I'll throw it into the sea tomorrow. She asks me to meet her then, you know."

"Oh? Do you think you'll go?"

Beatriz looked at Jorge. Beyond the smirk, he seemed a little uncomfortable. Was it simply discomfort at the woman his mother was trying to set him up with being acquainted with his mistress, or did he suspect Beatriz's motives? No one so far—not even Inez—seemed to have noticed that Beatriz's interest in Vulpa went beyond the ordinary. No one had called her out on her fascination at Vulpa's dancing, her curiosity in Vulpa as a person. But Jorge, who frequented the dirtier parts of the capital, surely had heard the dirtier rumors about his peers. Would he suspect that Beatriz had fallen for his woman? Did he want her to attend this rendezvous on the beach, or would he prefer she stay away?

Oh well. Propriety might dictate that Beatriz not steal the mistress of her host, but Jorge had been an absentee host if anything, and besides, Beatriz might enjoy Vulpa's company and the sight of Vulpa's figure, but it clearly wasn't going anywhere. "Certainly I'll go," she said to Jorge. "I quite like Vulpa, after all. It's a pity I haven't been able to see more of her."

If Jorge disliked this, it didn't show. He nodded. "Good, then. Well, I hope you two women have fun. I won't be seeing Vulpa myself for a couple days—the call of duty. Mother had a great deal to say to me at lunch today after you'd left. But I won't bore you with the details. Like I said, have fun."

With that, he left. Whatever his comments on the call of duty, Beatriz got the sense he was heading down to town, perhaps to a bar or to visit with friends other than Vulpa. Interest in her painting—pssh. She'd known that was too good to be true.

But her heart was light. Even looking at her wet and anguished canvas, on which the soppy medium had almost eradicated traces of the initial sketch without providing any worthwhile color, she couldn't help but smile. Enough with this interlude of imagination. If Vulpa would model for her—and Beatriz thought that with proper persuasion, and some discreet arrangements, she surely would—Beatriz could cast this rotten draft aside and start anew. Paint a better painting.

She'd finally be able to read one of Juan's too-frequent letters without a feeling of guilt!

She went to bed easy at heart. But her dreams were as turbulent as they always were lately. Again she stood on the deck of a ship, but the ship was sinking. There was no storm overhead, but it was sinking fast, too fast to bail. And there was no one else there on the ship with her to bail even if that were a hope. The ship was sinking, and she was alone.

"Marina," she cried out. "Marina! I know—I know it's you."

A rustle that could as easily have been a laugh as a sigh, or just the wind.

"I'm looking for you. I'm trying my best to paint you. Why are you angry with me? Please."

"Stop trying."

The voice could have come from anywhere. It fit like one of Beatriz's own thoughts. "Do you not want me to paint you, then? I don't understand."

"Playing games, making things up. Stop trying to create me and look."

Beatriz stared at the water rising up on the deck now. "I can't... I can't..."

She could look, but what exactly was she supposed to see?

* * *

She left the manor quietly the next afternoon, bringing with her a sketchbook and a stick of charcoal. She was feeling hopeful, though not hopeful enough to drag along a freshly stretched canvas or anything so ambitious. That might come in time. But she felt a longing to draw Vulpa again, even if it didn't lead anywhere pertinent to her Marina project. She just wanted to shade the ripples and curves of the woman's hair, trace the turns of her body. However this meeting went, she doubted Vulpa would deny her that much.

Her heart beat a little faster when she spotted Vulpa on the beach. She was standing on the sand barefoot—the portion of the sand still wet from the receding waves, else it would have been painfully hot for a woman not even wearing sandals as Beatriz did. She was wearing a cream colored dress, just a bit lighter than the dry sand. On seeing Beatriz she waved, and Beatriz found herself running down to meet her. She stopped a couple feet away, stumbling to a halt, a little out of breath. It felt anticlimactic—rightly a run like that should have ended with her pulling Vulpa into her arms, but of course she could do no such thing with a woman she hardly knew. "Miss Comete, I didn't think you'd come."

"Why wouldn't I come? You wrote to me."

"Well, I'm only a... model, after all. And it's hot out." Vulpa shrugged. "I thought I'd probably spend a couple hours walking along the beach and go home when I was sure you weren't coming. It wouldn't really have hurt my pride."

"Well, you're my model, and I've been trying to get a hold of you for ages. You won't quit on me, will you? If it's just that you can't get into the manor, I'm sure we can work something out."

"I don't want you arguing with the baroness over me. It's far too dramatic, and I doubt it would work. The baroness doesn't like me in the least. And Baron Gaspar really just goes with whatever she says. The whole household does."

"Hm. Well, if you can't come into the manor, I'll simply have to come to you. You have your residence not so far from the manor, don't you? How much would you mind the smell of oil paint in one of your rooms? If it would be too much of a bother, I suppose I could just make sketches for reference, but ideally I like my models to sit for me through much of the painting as well."

"You'd transplant your studio to my house, just for me?" Vulpa looked a bit flattered for a moment. Then she shook her head. "Please, Miss Comete. That would really be too much trouble."

"Then I'll just sketch you. You'll at least let me sketch you?"

"Of course."

"Sit down, then."

"Now?" Vulpa was a little taken aback.

"No time like the present."

"I suppose you're right."

Vulpa didn't sit; she knelt, folding her dress neatly beneath her to get as little sand on it as possible. Not so much like a sea goddess when she was acting prim, Beatriz thought. Indeed not like the Vulpa Beatriz knew so far, but then, Beatriz didn't know her all that much yet. And what did Beatriz really know of Marina either? Even in this pose, Vulpa still had dignity, and there was still in her eyes that barely restrained wildness. Beatriz doubted she'd use this sketch for her painting, but maybe. Goddesses were supposed to have poise, after all. It might work. She opened up her sketchbook, set her charcoal to the paper...

And gasped as a painful twinge ran straight from her palm up her arm, even to the shoulder. The charcoal fell out of her fingers, the sketchbook out of her other hand as she clutched at her arm, letting out a sob. Vulpa was up and beside her in a minute. "Miss Comete? Did you hurt yourself again?"

"It's the cut on my hand again," Beatriz said, biting back more sobs. The pain was fading in her arm, leaving only soreness, but her hand was still pulsing with a hot, unclean ache. "I don't—I don't know that it's healing right. The midwife had her doubts, but she couldn't give me any real advice. I have some ointment she gave me back in my room at the manor. I've been applying it regularly."

"If a little cut like that is still hurting you this much, that ointment's not doing you any good." Vulpa pulled her arm. "Come. We'll go back to my place, and I'll look at it. At worst, I can change the bandages. But maybe I'll have a better idea of what's wrong with it than the midwife. She's usually competent, but she has her blind spots. It must be some rare breed of infection. Come on."

Vulpa's place, as it turned out, was very close by, probably why she was offering—and probably why she chose this meeting spot in the first place, when Beatriz came to think of it. It was a small cottage but well furnished and cared for; Vulpa told her that Jorge sent a maid around now and again to help with cleaning. "I wish he wouldn't," she added. "It's nothing I couldn't do on my own, and mostly everyone from the manor hates me. Well, the kitchen doesn't, but it's not like he sends me the cook. I wish," she said with a laugh.

She sat Beatriz down at the table in the dining room, told her to hold still, and went off to fetch her medical supplies. When she returned, she took careful hold of Beatriz's hand. "Oh," she said.

"Oh?"

"It's hot. Your hand. Hotter than... earlier, your arm wasn't hot. Here, let me..." She checked Beatriz's forehead with the back of her own hand. "You don't have a fever. This is strange."

With a frown on her face, she unwrapped the bandage layer by layer. When finally the last of the bandage was removed, they both stared uneasily at Beatriz's palm. "Sektos," Vulpa whispered.

The line where the cut had been was no longer a blue-purple. That had seemed strange, but still within the realm of natural injury. Instead, it had turned a pure and glistening blue, somewhere between the shades of sea and sky.

Beatriz swallowed. Then she processed what Vulpa had said. "Sektos? Why Sektos?"

"What?"

"What has my hand to do with Sektos? That didn't sound like an idle curse. Why him?"

"Oh, I'm sorry, Miss Comete. I'm not usually superstitious. It's just that his festival's coming up soon, and Jorge and I have been talking about it, and it all muddles the mind. I've just never seen anything like this before—but I'm sure there's a natural reason, just one I..."

"I'm not so sure of that," Beatriz interrupted. "But it's not Sektos. It is most certainly Marina."

Vulpa picked Beatriz's hand up, cradling the back of it with both of her own hands. "Ah. Marina is who you're painting, after all. Miss Comete, I'm no priestess nor serious devotee of any god, and I'm no expert to give you advice, but are you sure this commission of yours is a good idea? Perhaps it would be better to abandon it."

Pain lanced through Beatriz's arm even more violently than

before. Her hand jerked wildly in Vulpa's suddenly firm grip, and a shriek ripped its way out of her throat.

Vulpa's hand was on her arm steadying her. "It's all right, it's all right. Just an idea. I'm just a dancer and sometimes a medic, I don't know Marina's will and wouldn't presume to speak for her. It's all right. Calm down."

Beatriz took a deep breath. Her arm was shaking.

"We'll put on more ointment," Vulpa said, "my mixture this time. And redo the bandages. That's all I know about this kind of matter. I'm sure your painting will be lovely when it's done."

"Ointment," Beatriz said. "Yes, that would be good."

She held her shaking hand as still as she could while Vulpa massaged cream onto it. It would have been quite nice, she thought, for Vulpa to touch her, to hold her hand so intimately, had she been able to properly appreciate it. Even now, Vulpa's closeness made her heart beat faster, her head swim a little. But pain already made her nauseous, and the mix of sensations was not very pleasant. Still. It was a little nice.

"It might not be the time to speak of this now," Vulpa said quietly, "but... would you mind finding another model for your work?"

Beatriz felt a strange heat rise in her, now. But it was no divine influence causing it, only her own mortification. "Of course," she said. "When else would we speak of it? It's what I came here to discuss, after all. Of course if you don't want to model for me, that's fine. I know my requesting it in the first place was a little..."

"No, no, it was fine," Vulpa said hurriedly. "I misunderstood you, at first, but once I understood, I was quite flattered. I really would love to have you paint me. But I might not be the best subject."

"You would make the perfect subject," Beatriz said. "You have a unique figure, and your hair is breathtaking."

Vulpa laughed. It was a breathy, hollow sound. "Ah, my hair. Yes, it's very nice, isn't it? Men like anything different. But it's not real, you know, not my real hair."

"A wig?"

"No, well, it is my own hair, but I dyed it. A few years ago, when I first started dancing. Men think it's exotic—it really helped my popularity. But it's not my real hair. Anyone could have it, with the application of the right herbs. Not so unique."

"But very you," Beatriz said. "And very lovely." Her hand twinged again, and she winced.

"I'm flattered," Vulpa said, "but there are many beautiful women in Mestos, you know—models with much purer beauty than I, better suited to a goddess—and anyhow, if you think about it, I'm not really a practical option, am I? Such a walk for you to come here, and the baroness will be outraged if she hears about even this meeting."

Beatriz wanted to say, *to hell with the baroness, to hell with all gossipers*—but of course Vulpa was only making respectable, practical, reasonable excuses as cover for a far wilder yet more compelling reason for flight: Marina had her eye on this painting, and she did not favor Vulpa as a model. So far, she had only lashed out against Beatriz for her poor taste, but if Beatriz pushed things, if Vulpa did not withdraw herself from consideration, who knew what might occur? No, it was not worth the risk. So Beatriz sighed and only said, "You're right, of course. Very well. But perhaps I will still see you around? Mestos is not such a large town."

"Not so large, no. Sometimes it feels horribly small," Vulpa said, "especially to an outsider. We may meet again."

"I hope we will."

"I hope so too. I will have Jorge tell you if I am performing again, if you want—though lately, it seems there's never any call for me to perform in public."

"Tell me. I would love to see you dance again."

"You're so nice." Vulpa smiled. "And I would love to dance for you."

The pain in Beatriz's head and body had subsided. Now if her pulse was racing in her ears, there was only one reason for it. With her uninjured hand, she boldly squeezed Vulpa's. "Thank you for your kindness today."

"It's nothing. Will you stay for dinner, maybe? Or, not dinner, but an early snack?"

They ate bread and drank wine together, and Beatriz thought that when they parted, they parted friends. No more than friends—she kept in mind still that this was Jorge's mistress, and that besides, her business in this province was not philandering. But still on warm and friendly terms, and the warmth of it held in Beatriz until she had walked halfway back to the manor. Only then did it begin to fade. It was all very well for her and Vulpa to hope they'd meet again, to call Mestos a small town, but they no longer had any excuse for meeting, and Beatriz was busy, and making Jorge pass notes was awkward and even a little risqué. And more importantly, Beatriz's purpose today had not been a friendly encounter. She was supposed to be finding the solution to the troubles facing her painting, and all that had happened today was that they had gotten worse.

Her hand wasn't hurting right now, so there was that, at least. But that might not last for long. And still no satisfactory model! And still no idea what Marina wanted from her—only an impression of her anger, which was terrifying but not exactly communicative beyond the negative!

No more painting for today, she decided. On the morrow she would face it again, would struggle with it again. But tonight she would give up and let it be. She had no answers.

For all that, her sleep was strangely peaceful.

9

CHAPTER NINE

The Festival of Sektos came fast. Ricardo had thought that he would have plenty of time to prepare for the wrestling competition over the next two weeks. But there were not quite two weeks remaining, and despite Leonor's promise that Ricardo would be allowed out of his room from now on, he was not able to train every day. The closer the festival came, the busier everyone in the manor was. No one had time to chaperone a painter's martial training.

Celebrating the god of battle was less of an event in Suelta—a town in the middle of nowhere, with the only local soldiers being Leonor's guard—than, say, in the capital, or near the border where there were still garrisons located even if Salandra was not currently at war. However, Sektos remained an important god, and even a small town like Suelta had a number of fervent veterans, besides which, it was the best excuse for merrymaking that the summer offered. So it was going to be quite a festival, and the preparations had everyone scampering this way and that—and therefore there was little time for anyone to be escorting Ricardo on walks or supervising him while he practiced wrestling with Nicolas, Benito, and Diego. In the end he only managed four more training sessions, and if either he or the other three improved, he couldn't have said he noticed it.

Despite that, he anticipated the festival's approach fiercely. He still thought it might be the best opportunity for him to attempt an escape, as it would get him off Leonor's estate at the very least, and probably into a bustling crowd. And even if that failed, he would at least get the chance to wrestle and possibly punch someone. (The rules of the wrestling matches at Suelta were apparently loose and allowed a certain amount of hitting as well as grappling.)

He was excited enough that he couldn't fall asleep for hours the night before the actual date, and when he was roused before dawn by Sancho and one of the maids who often brought him breakfast, he had a hard time heaving himself out of bed.

Sancho ruthlessly manhandled him upright, saying, "If you need help getting dressed, I'm here for you. But you need to get going. Leonor wants you down at the town gates for the start of the long run, and she told me to get you. And I need to be there early myself, since I'm competing."

He muttered some complaint under his breath that Ricardo wasn't quite awake enough to catch. Doubtless he was annoyed at this arrangement. Well, Ricardo was too—why he had to be constantly around Sancho of all people, he really didn't know. And he didn't like being summoned so peremptorily this early in the morning. "Leonor this, Leonor that. Get out. I can dress myself."

"Fine, we can wait outside. You should wear something light but not too plain—a nice shirt at least. I know you're wrestling, but you'll take the shirt off for that, so no need to worry about it."

"I've been to festivals before, Sancho. I know how things are done. Get out."

He had actually thought through what he would wear a few days in advance. In the wardrobe Leonor had gifted him was a very nice cream-colored shirt with a small amount of red embroidery around the collar and buttons, which would be a little bit festive without calling attention to itself. It was light, too, which was a major selling point. The Festival of Sektos always stank of sweat along with the smoke of bonfires and the smell of food, but still, there was no reason to sweat more than you had to. For his pants, he would simply wear the pair he'd had on when he was first kidnapped. They'd been practical pants to begin with, meant for days at work in the studio and lightly smeared with paint here and there, and days on the road bumping up and down in a cart and fighting Captain Alban in the dirt had worn them further. As such they would be far better for wrestling than a new pair. Despite their worn state, they were an attractive shade of brown that paired well with the shirt, so he thought it was not a bad outfit, if not something he would have worn at such festivities in the capital, where, as court painter and something akin to courtier, appearances were crucial.

He dressed quickly and called Sancho back as he jammed on his boots. "Let's go."

Sancho grinned, clearly relieved Ricardo hadn't taken too long. "Yes, let's go! You must be excited, Ricardo. Best spectacle you've seen in months, I'm sure, and you've barely seen the outside of your room in weeks."

"Barely," Ricardo said drily.

His excitement was not heightened by Sancho's chattering as they walked out of the manor and out into the festival. But it did give him a surge just to leave the estate grounds and head into town, and more of one to see the number of people who were already in town setting up booths before daybreak. The festival looked like it would be as busy an event as he had hoped.

Of course, as yet it was not very crowded, and he was still accompanied by Sancho and a guard. It was not yet the moment to slip away. But it would come—he could taste it in the air, hope interwoven with the morning dew. And already he was getting one advantage: the long run started at the town gates and headed out into the countryside before looping back around, so Ricardo was being taken all the way through town, getting a stronger grasp on its geography than he'd had when he was first dragged around the outskirts to Leonor's manor about a month ago.

The town gates were both the busiest location he'd seen thus far and the farthest from Leonor's manor, but when he got there it would have been a very poor moment to slip away. For one, while arrangements were busy, they also were very orderly. The runners were all lined up—close to two dozen of them—and all eyes were on them and on the road they would be racing down. The landscape beyond was clear, road cutting through fields of wheat that had been recently harvested and so was not particularly high, and a couple fields that were lying fallow and currently infested with brilliant poppies and bluebells. The town gates were at the top of a slope, moreover, allowing an even better vantage point. Excellent for spectators of a race. Terrible for a fugitive.

For another thing, the moment Ricardo arrived on site, he was met by Countess Leonor.

"You arrive with the sun," she said, pointing at the horizon. And indeed, light was just beginning to peek through the distant trees that marked the end of the wheat field.

"The race will start soon, then," Ricardo said. The long run always started at dawn.

"Indeed. You're late."

"I'm on time. You almost made Sancho late, though. He wouldn't have forgiven me."

"It would have been my fault," Leonor said graciously (and Ricardo silently agreed with her). "I'm sure he wouldn't have held a grudge."

No more talking after that. Leonor guided Ricardo over to the front of the crowd, where they could get the best view of all. A few final runners joined the lineup, Sancho included. A rope was held in front of them all, at approximately waist height, which had them all standing in a very close line but also told them it was not time to run yet. At a signal from a judge, the rope was dropped on both ends at once, and the runners headed out immediately, some at a jog, others, perhaps foolishly, beginning with a sprint.

After a few minutes, most of the spectators were gone. Some were heading to other places along the route of the race, others to other events. Leonor stayed until the first runner hit the woods, and then she turned to Ricardo and said, "It will be more than an hour before anyone returns. Come, the soldiers in town are doing a demonstration in the town square soon. Captain Alban says it's what kicks off the day, even though the long run really does. But I suppose it's more of a spectacle."

* * *

The morning passed in a swirl of chaos. The soldiers—both guards actively serving Leonor and older veterans—did indeed put on a fine display of marching and various sword and spear exercises, but out of consideration for the older soldiers, they were kept brief. Still, they were impressive. Then there were the street stalls, selling food and drink, candy and toys and souvenirs. More selling weaponry than would be common at any other festival, but a lot of those weapons were flimsy, more symbolic than meant for real use.

Leonor bought Ricardo a small folding knife, and laughed when he told her that she shouldn't be providing a captive with a weapon, especially one currently accompanying her. "If you murder me, it will be my own fault. I accept it," she said, and again Ricardo silently agreed. It was a good knife though. He could use it to cut canvas in the future, perhaps, or to sharpen pencils or trim brushes. He folded it up and tucked it away in a pants pocket.

There were official contests—more races, some weight-lifting, some pole-vaulting—and some less official contests too, games staged at booths that anyone could enter for a price. Enough at any time to cause a ruckus. Ricardo trailed Leonor as she stopped by event after event, booth after booth. Sometimes they were accompanied by Felipe as well, but he would linger at contests after they left or run off to talk to a friend, while Ricardo was forced always to stay close to Leonor, part of her entourage, always on the move. It was all a little overwhelming.

Then at a little past noon, most events of the festival drew to a halt for lunch. Large tents had been set up in a field on the outskirts of town, with tables and pots of food brought for the event, enough to put the stalls, with their jars of wine and pastries and fruits, to shame. Leonor had apparently paid for most of this fare, as it was her responsibility as countess and head of the festival. There was ham, cheese, fish, all you would expect from any festival, but to honor Sektos, there was also a lot of hard bread made to resemble army rations, and a spicy pudding made primarily of rice and pigs' blood. Ricardo had never liked the hard tack, but he did enjoy blood pudding, and ate a full three helpings. Leonor, on the other hand, seemed to like neither traditional food, and preferred to honor Sektos's bloodlust more metaphorically by downing a full bottle of red wine. It was good wine, too—Ricardo had a taste of it himself, but the wrestling matches would be in the early afternoon, so he was careful not to drink deeply. Better not to fight intoxicated.

Full, he sat back and looked at the people around him. More people than he'd seen in ages. They swarmed the booth giving out food, squeezed in at the tables, mingled voices loud as thunder. Suelta's people out in force. "I should have brought my sketchbook today," he said to himself.

Unexpectedly, Leonor responded: "You should have. Perhaps you could draw the sights from memory tomorrow. All this could make for a fine painting."

Shit. Ricardo hoped he hadn't just committed to something. As impressive a scene as all these festivities made, crowd scenes had never been his forte, especially not depictions of commoners on holiday. Such things were growing in popularity, from what he'd heard. Paintings of crowded bars or of men and women at work in the fields, or indeed festivals. But he'd never tried his hand at them, nor did he particularly want to—the colors and the hubbub would be fun to sketch, but torture for a finished, formalized piece.

He had no desire to explain his taste in projects to Leonor, however, and somewhat feared she would critique them, as she seemed to enjoy doing, so he borrowed a line from Beatriz's book. "Working from memory is a fool's game." She always looked superior when she said something like that. He tried to put on a similar demeanor.

Leonor said, "I suppose I wouldn't know. I'm no artist. Oh well. A pity." She took another long gulp from her wineglass, set it down empty, and signaled a server to bring her another bottle, as the current bottle had run out. "I will have to preserve these sights and sounds in my memory instead. But that is how it always is anyhow, isn't it? A painting is nothing. They painted my father many times. He is still dead."

To this, Ricardo had no response, but fortunately, Leonor did not seem to require one. The server had come over with another bottle of wine, and she took it and inspected it critically, as if the sheen of the glass would tell her all the details of its quality. Then she poured herself another glass and took a sip. "It's hot today," she remarked.

It really was hot. The Festival of Sektos always fell in the beginning of the summer's true heat, when tempers were just beginning to boil over but the late summer's lethargy had not yet set in. And right now was the day's hottest point. Ricardo sighed. Soon it would be time for the wrestling matches, he told himself. By then it would be a bit cooler, and he would also be able to take his shirt off. That would be a nice change. At this rate, a good wrestle really might be all he got out of the day. All day long, Leonor had insisted he trail along after her as she flitted from event to event, putting in official appearances and occasionally serving as one of the judges. And Leonor, in turn, was trailed by a couple guards at all times. No opportunity for escape had turned up so far, and while Ricardo refused to give up hope yet, he was getting discouraged.

* * *

He finally shook off Leonor when it came time for the wrestling matches, but only because he was hustled into the group of contestants. They were gathered at the side of a bare field that was divided into sixteen small squares where the individual matches would be held.

There were a number of women wrestling as well as men, and for the preliminary matches they were paired up against each other. The first sixteen matches had ten male matches and six female. Ricardo overheard the gossip of who was favored: There was one very strong guard named Antonio among the men, and a buff farmer named Dario, while among the women, the favorite was Fidelia, who happened to be Dario's daughter and who was nearly as large as he was. None of these were people Ricardo thought he was likely to fare well against, but fortunately, his first round was against none of the three, but just a scraggly youth who had never entered before, who introduced himself as David.

In preparation, Ricardo stripped off his shirt, boots, and socks, and left the knife he'd been given along with them, figuring it might too easily slip out of his pocket. He went to stand at the edge of the square he'd been assigned to and stared David down. Tall. Skinny. Light on his feet, not too firm a stance—though to be fair they were not competing yet, so that might change. A light stance could be an advantage if you were agile and a bit bouncy, but more often it was a detriment. Ricardo could take advantage of that.

When the match started, he darted forward. Better, usually, to be the defender than the aggressor. But David looked like the nervous sort, and Ricardo didn't want to give him time to get his nerves together. Better to startle him. And David did flinch back, which made him stumble. Ricardo wrapped a leg around the back of his leg, tripping him. For just a moment David salvaged the situation, grabbing Ricardo's shoulders and trying to both regain his balance and shake Ricardo's. But Ricardo grabbed his arms, one by the elbow and the other by the shoulder, pulled one and pushed the other, and the twist sent David sprawling. Ricardo pinned him pretty easily after that, and though he was squirmy, the five-count of the judge was short—intentionally so, to bring a quick end to these preliminary matches. And so Ricardo was declared the winner.

Mostly the crowd spectating did not react to this announcement, as they were watching other matches with more prestigious or talented competitors, but there was a little clapping, and Ricardo heard a familiar female voice call out, "Well done!"

He didn't need Leonor's approval.

He felt a swell of pride regardless.

The next couple rounds, he sat out, as the preliminaries finished. Then, the second round of preliminaries. This time Ricardo was placed in a ring that was close in front of the judges' pavilion. He gave them all a long look, trying to pay some attention to the judges other than Leonor. A couple older men, one younger, no other women. Leonor stood out among them like a rooster among hens, bright yellow dress against more soberly colored suits, and shining equally in authority. Next to her sat Felipe—he'd been off with some young friends for most of the festival, only occasionally joining Leonor and Ricardo, but apparently the wrestling matches warranted his full attention and so he had taken his proud place as

Mestos's young master, and was watching intently, on the edge of his seat. He and Leonor both offered Ricardo a smile. He ignored them and turned to his opponent.

His luck at having an obviously weak match-up had not carried through to this round. He was now going against a man named Pedro, about the same height as him but slightly heavier. A guard, too, judging by his haircut, and better trained than Benito or Diego or Nicolas judging by his stance. Ricardo took a deep breath. He wouldn't be rushing this one.

They squared off against each other cautiously. Even when the announcer called for the fighting to start, they didn't move immediately. For almost a whole minute, they circled each other. Sometimes Pedro would make a quick move, and Ricardo would dart backwards or to the side. Sometimes Ricardo would step closer, and Pedro in turn would step away. They examined each other, took each other's measure.

Pedro tossed a taunt in Ricardo's direction. "Afraid to face a fighting man, painter?"

Ricardo's lips tightened.

"Don't try too hard to hit me," Pedro continued lazily. "You might hurt your fingers."

"And you afraid to face a painter," Ricardo responded, "but you call yourself a guard. Best watch yourself."

Pedro smiled at that, and Ricardo smiled back, but kept his eyes on Pedro's hands.

Neither was really invested in the argument either way. Words were words: they were a good weapon if you could get your opponent into an incautious temper, but otherwise they meant nothing. What mattered were blows, but none came yet, only feints and dodges, Ricardo and Pedro's bodies mirroring each other and reacting as if in dance.

At last Pedro moved a bit quicker than Ricardo expected, lunged a bit farther, and managed to grab Ricardo's arm. In a fast tangle of motion that Ricardo had a hard time unpiecing later, he snagged Ricardo's ankle with his own foot and knocked him forward in a full-body tackle. Ricardo struggled to push him off, but the weight was working in Pedro's favor now, and he sat solidly on Ricardo's stomach, keeping him well-pinned. The count for the second round was a bit longer than the first, lasting seven seconds rather than five, but two extra seconds was nothing like enough for Ricardo to dislodge him. After the long lead-in, Pedro had ended the match with embarrassing ease.

There was more applause after this match than Ricardo's first. Probably because Pedro was more popular than either Ricard or David had been. He was a gracious winner, at least. He got off Ricardo with a laugh, gave the crowd a wave, and cheerfully helped Ricardo to his feet. "Ah, that was fun! For a painter you've good reflexes. Let's get you something to drink, you look pretty roughed up."

Ricardo felt the reference to his appearance was a little too self-congratulatory on Pedro's part, but he couldn't hold it against the man, whose good mood was clearly not the least malicious. They both wandered off to the side of the field together to join some other guards, all Pedro's friends and all jubilantly predicting he could win the next round as well. Both he and Pedro were offered wineskins, and he took a long swig as Pedro had suggested. He was pretty sweaty after all. Pedro pounded his back and said, "Next year, little painter. Next year."

Ricardo was barely smaller than Pedro and truly hoped to be gone by next year, but he smiled and said, "You won't beat me again."

"Ha, that's the spirit. Drink up. Sektos is in the both of us today. Pray to him on my behalf, friend—my next round's against Dario."

All Pedro's friends immediately chimed in to say Dario was no big deal—this was Pedro's year, he could beat even Antonio or

Fidelia!—but Ricardo could not participate in this ritual reassurance, as he was distracted by the sight of Leonor hovering a short distance away. She beckoned Ricardo with a jerk of her chin, and reluctantly, he got up and separated from the group to join her.

He expected she would drag him back to the pavilion, but instead she led him away from the main crowd, off to the outskirts, where they stood alone.

"So, Montero? You enjoyed the matches?"

"Yes, madonna. Thank you for entering me." Ricardo kept his eyes lowered. There was too large a grin on Leonor's face, and he didn't appreciate her smugness in the face of his early defeat. Sure, she had some competent guards. They could beat up a mere painter. Was that really something to be so proud of?

She was conciliatory. "You did well. You handled that first boy tidily. And against Pedro, well..."

"He handled me tidily," Ricardo said drily.

"Not for a while, he didn't. Smart to keep out of his reach. The two of you were fun to watch."

"I imagine it is fun to see me get knocked over. Did you imagine I was Alejandro?"

He couldn't help but look up for her reaction to that. She grimaced. "No, no, that's not what I meant. You weren't bad. It was good watching you, anyways. I enjoyed it. You were good. Beautiful."

The last word came out a little breathy, and Ricardo squinted, noticing now that she was red-faced, that her words stumbled just a little. Drunk. All that "good red wine" must have gotten to her. Now he saw the grin on her face was more foolish than spiteful. He sighed. "Thank you, madonna. Now, if you're done..."

Her hand reached out, clumsy, and grabbed his shoulder. Squeezed it. She was no grappler, but she still had a strong grip. Of course, he had no desire to wrestle her. He looked at her and raised his eyebrows. She smiled, and leaned in, and kissed him on the lips.

Her breath on his was thick and alcoholic and heavy. Her lips were softer than he would have imagined from the rigid way she always held herself. For just a moment he stood there, heart racing. He had never put his shirt back on after wrestling. Her hand on his shoulder touched bare, sweaty skin; and then she reached up a second hand to touch his chest, and it nestled itself in his chest hair.

His pulse was pounding. Her tongue was slipping into his mouth. His eyes were open, staring at her, and then darting past her to see a few guards on the outskirts of the crowd watching them, leering at them.

It was their eyes that spurred him to action at last, made him push her off and step back. Her hands clung to him for a moment before letting go. "Montero," she murmured.

His face was hot, and it was neither from exertion nor from the sun still beating down on activity better relegated to evenings behind closed doors. "You should go back to your pavilion," he said. "The next round is beginning soon."

She closed her mouth and nodded. "Yes, you're right. I'm..."

But what she was, she hesitated to say, and before she could finish her sentence, Ricardo walked away.

Part of him expected her to follow him. He was halfway down a street before he realized she hadn't. He paused next to a fruit stand and took deep breaths. Humiliating, he thought. It had been humiliating. He'd never felt so horribly on display. Thank goodness they hadn't been visible to the pavilion or the full crowd from where they'd been standing, but they hadn't been exactly concealed either. Had those guards been laughing at them? Had they thought Ricardo ridiculous, or Leonor? Why was it that the latter possibility angered him almost as much as the former?

On second thought, he wasn't even sure they had been laughing. He'd been too stunned at the moment to process much of anything except that Leonor was kissing him in front of a crowd. Leonor, a countess, and a countess who had kidnapped him, a condescending bitch of a woman who on second thought had often complimented his appearance and talents before, whose attitude towards him he'd perhaps misread ever since meeting her.

He ran a hand through sweaty hair. The woman running the fruit stall said, "Grapes, dear?"

"No, thank you."

"An orange?"

"No, thank you."

"Wine, then?"

"Wine is the last thing I need," he said curtly, and at last the woman took the hint and huffily turned away to another customer.

He scanned the people walking by in the street. No guards here. No one he'd seen watching him at the wrestling matches, actually. No one had followed him. He was alone.

Alone, still a little aroused, and very confused.

Alone, on the loose with no supervision, for the first time in months.

Where had the town gates been, again?

10

CHAPTER TEN

The night before the Festival of Sektos, Anthona had told Beatriz, "You've been working so hard. No need to get up for the long run, or any of the races if you don't want to. Sleep in, get some rest, and come down to town and join us in the festivities when you can. I promise we'll be easy to find—I stay wherever things are busiest!" (Despite this, she gave Beatriz her full itinerary of festival plans with unsubtle hints as to which she expected Beatriz to attend along with her.)

Beatriz did not sleep in. Not much. She tried to, but woke early in the morning as she had been lately, and out of habit, went down to the kitchen, grabbed some bread and a little fruit, and then headed to the studio.

There she came to a halt at the door and stood looking over at her canvas. It was a new canvas, actually. She'd given up on the last one she'd been using, as it had become a sodden mess after days and weeks of slapping paint onto it to no avail. This new canvas had only been in use for a couple days. Under the thin, watery, still-wet oil paint, you could see the gesso still. She'd laid it down more roughly than last time, impatient to get back to the real work, and as a result it was thicker, less uniform in texture, full of bumps and cracks.

Despite that, it was her object of devotion.

She cleared her throat. "I don't think I can work today," she said apologetically. "It's the Festival of Sektos. Sektos is your brother, so perhaps you can understand. I do need to show the proper respect. I can't just work straight through."

Having made her excuses, she tore herself away from the studio door, and, finishing her bread along the way, she headed out to town.

* * *

Anthona had done a lot of humble bragging about how the Festival of Sektos was celebrated in Mestos in the days leading up to the event. In the end, it was more or less what Beatriz might have expected from a coastal town. A fair number of men from the navy, some more invested than others, participated in the various marches and contests, and some citizens were very enthusiastic, but mostly it was just a lot of revelry. Beatriz tried to enjoy it, of course —some years she enjoyed this festival quite a lot, and she considered it a proper show of reverence at the least—but throughout the entire thing, her mind kept wandering back to her studio. Despite herself, despite knowing her attendance here was both a religious practice and a show of respect and appreciation toward her hosts, she couldn't help but feel she was wasting her time. She should be painting right now. Every moment she didn't spend painting lately felt worthless to her, frivolous. Of course, she tried to hide the sentiment, but she could tell she wasn't entirely succeeding; it made her poor company, and she wondered that Anthona hadn't attempted to send her back to the capital yet. She really had to be desperate to marry Jorge off.

This evening, in particular, she was approaching this goal by trying to get Beatriz and Jorge to dance together in the dancing that had begun in the town square now that the festival's more official events were over. Beatriz had agreed to dance with Jorge—she didn't dislike him, after all, and refusing Anthona was a hard thing to do—but the man of the hour had yet to show up. He'd wandered off shortly before the closing ritual and had been missing ever since.

"Well, I'm sure he'll be here soon," Anthona said after Beatriz had sat out three dances. She looked at Beatriz anxiously, scanning for signs of impatience. "You can dance with someone else in the meantime if you want—or, you could join in the dance of the virgins for now..."

"I'm a bit old for that," Beatriz said politely, which was true. Also not pure enough, but that wasn't something she could bring up with a woman like the countess. "But don't worry about me. I'm tired. It's been a long day. I'm fine just sitting here, really."

She absolutely wasn't, but it certainly wasn't due to a lack of Jorge. Despite this, she did feel a little relieved when Jorge emerged through the crowd to join them. He kissed his mother's hand, all apologues. "I got separated from you—there was a man who wanted to talk..."

"Well, you might have gotten back before now," Anthona said peevishly. "Beatriz has been waiting all this time for you."

Jorge grinned and held out a hand. "Forgive me, Beatriz. Will you dance with me? Of course after leaving you stranded I hardly deserve it."

Beatriz accepted with a brief, courteous nod. Dancing would be better than sitting around, anyway. So they joined the swirling crowd of dancers, making up two parts of a four-person set. Then the next song that the musicians played was a slow waltz, breaking the four-person sets into partners. Beatriz couldn't help but glance over at Anthona to check if she'd wandered over to their stand

and told them what to play, but she was still sitting where she was before, so Beatriz let the notion go.

Well, it wasn't a sufferance to slow dance either, though it was more boring. Jorge grimaced and said, "Sorry about all this."

"No, the festival's been lovely. Nothing to apologize for."

"I probably shouldn't have abandoned you with my mother. I know she can be pushy."

Beatriz grinned. "But you had good reason. How's Vulpa?"

"Vulpa? Fine, good. Oh, you mean—no, I haven't seen her today. I think she had plans to stay home."

"Stay home? For the festival?"

"She might check out some of the stalls. But lately she's been so reclusive. Of course I couldn't go to an event like this with her anyway; it wouldn't look good. She didn't really want to go alone. I hope she changed her mind and at least watched one or two of the contests, or got herself some pudding."

"Oh, yes. I'd hope so. Couldn't you..." Beatriz trailed off, went into a spin, and let the matter go. How Vulpa and Jorge conducted themselves was surely none of her business.

* * *

The festival wound down with a ritual sacrifice at the local temple of Sektos. Fewer people attended this final event than most others, out of necessity—it was not a very large temple, not the one in Mestos—and out of a lack of interest, since most people considered the festival more as a holiday than as the religious practice it was supposed to be. Lady Anthona and Jorge attended, and so of course Beatriz did as well. She might have anyway. Lately she'd been feeling... spiritual felt like the wrong word for it. Anxious.

When a goat and a cow had been killed, and all that was left was a lot of chanting, she stepped aside from the temple's main chamber, off to one of its smaller chapels that was still open to the public. There she knelt before a statue and prayed.

"Sektos, you are not a god I have ever offered much worship, nor do you have much reason to hear me. I am no warrior. I am a lady, a painter—to some, an outrage. Nevertheless, I am here at your temple."

The statue's silence felt like a kinder response than many of her prayers had been offered lately. Emboldened, she said, "I can't ask you for guidance in my own life. None of it is in your domain. I would like to ask you to protect and guide my friend Ricardo Montero. He is not a warrior either, but he's been missing for so long, I fear he's met with violence. Some might assume you would favor an aggressor, but I know you have pity on the oppressed and those who fall as war's victims. Perhaps you can extend that compassion to my friend. If he is faced with violence, grant him courage and strength, and some measure of protection. I danced in the square today, one of those dances held in your honor. I left my work to come and observe your worship. For that, even if I am not your devotee, I pray you will hear and answer me."

11

CHAPTER ELEVEN

Running away was now for Ricardo a more serious object than it had been when he first considered the opportunity the previous week. Not only because the opportunity was now before him. Leonor had kissed him, and he had pushed her away and run from her. People with power didn't take rejection well; when the festival was over, Leonor would be out for blood. He already knew she had a spiteful personality.

Maybe Ricardo should have let her continue kissing him, kissed her back, returned to the pavilion with her. She was beautiful, objectively—he'd always thought she would make an interesting painting—and he could admit he felt drawn to her from time to time, in a certain oppressive sort of way. He could have given into that attraction. But that might have been a pitfall in itself. Leonor had been drunk; she would probably regret kissing him when she was sober, and if he had encouraged her, tried to charm her, she might well have taken vengeance for that later anyway.

There hadn't been a correct way to react. Now all he could do was try to get the hell out of Suelta before Leonor sobered up or the guards realized he was missing.

He didn't know the geography of the town that well, but he'd gotten a rough idea of it based on his wanderings at Leonor's side today. (How much of the day had she spent thinking about kissing him? No, it had probably been a momentary impulse and soon regretted, and it was better not to think about that anyway. But, looking back, he'd certainly noticed her staring, today and previously, all those days she visited him in his makeshift studio...) He knew more or less how to take the town's main road to the gate, and how to follow it the other direction—back towards Leonor's manor.

To go back towards Leonor's manor would be as much as to admit defeat, not to mention it would take him further from his eventual goal, the capital. On the other hand, while the races were done for the day, there were still guards at the gate, especially today of all days, keeping an eye on who came and went. Not to mention how swarmed the roads were in general. To take that path, he'd also have to go back past the wrestling grounds, and there he would surely be spotted by some of the guards, if not by Leonor herself.

He would wait, he decided, until the festival died down and the guards and Leonor had gone back to the manor. Then it would be safe to go, when the roads were empty. And maybe he wouldn't even take the main road out. There was a wall around the town, but it wasn't high everywhere, and surely he could find some broken-down corner where it could be easily scaled. In the evening, maybe, when the guards had gone back to Leonor's manor and were no longer wandering and merrymaking all over town, he might be able to get away without notice.

His chest tightened as he came to the decision. Perhaps if he had been willing to think closely enough about it, he would have realized it was a bad idea, setting out on empty roads as a fugitive, waiting until there was no crowd to cover for him. But right now he was tired and the crowd overwhelmed him, and the thought of passing Leonor right now, meeting her gaze and seeing what she now thought of him—if she still wanted him—was too much for him to face. He headed off the main road to a quieter spot and curled up behind a shrub to take a brief nap. It hid him from view without casting him in shadow, which was good. The day was hot, but cool in the shade, and Ricardo was still shirtless.

It was intended to be a short nap. But when he woke, the sky was already dark beyond dusk. The road was not as busy as it had been earlier, sure enough. Of course it was not entirely quiet—the Festival of Sektos was a big deal, and many would celebrate into the night. But a certain number of people had already drained out of the town, back off to their farms or neighboring villages, and others had gone home to their separate dinners or private family rituals. Those left on the streets were stragglers, merchants beginning to disassemble their makeshift stalls, revelers who had yet to get so drunk they fell down and so were still stumbling here and there, grinning and singing or looking for a fight in Sektos's name.

Ricardo stretched and considered whether it was a good time to go yet or not. It would be easier to avoid all notice when it had gotten even darker out, and when there were less people on the street. But sitting beside the road doing nothing was also bound to draw attention eventually, and he was getting restless. He would move now, he decided. Sektos could smile on his escape or frown on him; he would take his chances either way.

He moved through the street covertly, shoulders a little huddled, head down. Not a soul was paying any attention to him, but he felt an obvious outsider. At least he blended in well—plain brown pants, shirt still missing, he matched dozens of other sweaty, grinning men thronging through the street. If Leonor was looking for him, if the guards were to describe him, they'd have a hard time naming any distinguishing traits.

All was fine as he walked through the center of town, but as he neared the outskirts, a hand fell on his shoulder. He turned and saw that it was one of Leonor's men, one he recognized from the manor.

"Montero. The festival's over now." The man's tone was politely commanding. "The countess is looking for you back at the manor. It's time to go home."

Ricardo nodded and made as if to follow the man, then darted in the other direction.

He didn't look back to see if he was being followed, knowing his only hope would be speed. But he wasn't fast enough. He was brought to the ground in a full-body tackle that knocked the breath out of him. Another wrestling match, he thought—but he hadn't been able to beat a guard earlier either, and this time his opponent was taking it more seriously. Well, he was too. He tried a dirty shot, kneeing the man in the groin, but missed and only got his inner thigh and a slight wince. Then he tried to headbutt him—it had sort of worked on Captain Alban, once—but again didn't hit. The guard, in turn punched him in the face, and his head cracked against the ground. This part of the town was paved with cobblestone, not just dirt, and the impact stunned him for a moment. He pushed himself up dizzily. The guard had gotten off him, and seemed to be waiting for some retaliation. Ricardo had to get up, had to hit him back, but his balance was off...

The guard was calling out, and in a minute another had joined him. It was Nicolas, Ricardo's former opponent. Not a good fighter in the least, but two against one didn't need to be very good. Together they hauled Ricardo to his feet and dragged him, one holding each of his arms, back down the road towards Leonor's manor.

"Bastards!" Ricardo fumed. "Fucking cowards! If either of you faced me alone, you'd be dead."

Neither of them responded to him no matter how much he yelled. The first guard looked tired and bored, while Nicolas's lips were pressed tight together. Ricardo hoped he felt ashamed at treating a friend this way. It was more likely he was holding back some diatribe in response to Ricardo's own taunts, feeling it would not be professional.

It was not a pleasant walk back in the slightest.

* * *

When they entered the main hall, they were greeted by a sobered up Leonor.

"Montero," she exclaimed, and then, to the guards, voice like a lash, "You hurt him!"

Perhaps it should have relieved Ricardo to see her angry on his behalf. At least that meant she probably wouldn't avenge herself on him for that rejected kiss after all. Overall, though, the hypocrisy of it infuriated him. "Madonna, why scold the man for following your orders? You told him to bring me back and here I am. Give him a commendation, for Sektos's sake."

"I said to find you, not to hurt you."

"Well, what did you expect? I'd just come running back to you gladly? Your captain had to hit me a bit too, when he dragged me here in the first place. What do you expect?" Ricardo repeated. He wiped a little dried blood off his face—it probably looked worse than it was, and it made him feel pathetically self-conscious. "Now we've all enjoyed the Feast of Sektos sufficiently. I'd like to go to bed."

He was impudent enough to turn towards the hall where he knew his room was located, but Leonor blocked his way. "Montero, I need to speak with you."

"What about, then?" If she propositioned him in front of the guard, he wasn't sure what he would do. Maybe slap her. He was in the mood for it.

"I wanted to apologize. Today I've... I acted inappropriately towards you. Now you've been hurt, too. You must forgive me,

Montero. I was not myself. I promise I won't do such things again, and I'll..."

"I don't want promises," Ricardo cut her off. "It's inappropriate to hold me prisoner here in the first place."

She wilted slightly.

"If you don't intend to make that right," he said, "then don't apologize to me to salve your own self-righteousness."

She bit her lip.

Her hesitance cut through his anger to something deeper; the desperate hope he'd felt earlier in the day. "You should let me go, madonna. Why should you keep me here? I'm no use to you. What grudge do you have against the king so large that you have to spite him like this?"

"A grudge larger than you can imagine."

"Then explain it to me! Or don't—why would I care—but let me go."

"I can't," Leonor said. Her hands clenched in her skirts. "Don't ask me to."

Ricardo could feel a smile growing on his face in a sarcastic snarl of teeth. "All right then. Don't ask me to forgive you either."

He slept surprisingly well that night. Perhaps it was because despite his nap he was still exhausted. Or Sektos's mercy on the defeated warrior.

12

CHAPTER TWELVE

It had been three days since the Festival of Sektos.

The night was late.

Probably into the morning hours, but Beatriz was still up in her studio with a lamp desperately trying to illuminate the room well enough for her to squint the vague shapes on her canvas into meaning. All evening and all night she'd been trying to make her watery paint resolve into a semi-human figure at least (forget details, quality, dignity—at least a basic shape, please, at least a shape she could have doodled at the age of five), with little success. And all evening and night it had been raining out. At first just sprinkling, but now truly pouring, with rumbling thunder and an occasional lightning flash.

The rain was loud, but over its rolling and rattling, Beatriz could still hear an argument happening down the hall. Anthona and Jorge were both in a temper. Apparently they had decided tonight of all nights was the time to hash out their differences and have the fight that had been brewing between them ever since Beatriz's arrival.

"...with that minx! Coming in after midnight drunk! I sometimes wonder why I haven't just given up on you entirely—clearly you have no sense of propriety, no idea what would appeal to a respectable woman—you'll just throw your life away on—no, that's too decisive for you, you'll just drink and fritter your life away and be surprised when there's nothing left of it. Well, when that day comes, don't blame me for it! What I've done for you, the patience I've had, the efforts I've made, are more than many a woman would make for such a wretched rogue of a son."

"I didn't ask you to! I didn't ask you to send me a line of your decent, respectable women—a new one every summer, just like those friends of mine you're always complaining about. None you even know beyond reputation or an evening's conversation, but I'm such a lost cause you'll just throw anyone at me, isn't that it? I wish you would give up on me! I swear to Ahava if I knew how to make you I would do it in a damned second!"

Beatriz closed her eyes. Blackness, for a moment. But it wasn't restful. Even the blackness of her own eyelids swam before her, and the rain and the yelling still pressed against her ears. Yet she could sit here, sit here and do nothing. She wanted to stop painting. She wanted to stop trying to paint a work that was so clearly beyond her—a work that Marina herself appeared to oppose.

Time crawled and raced in a blur of meaningless effort. It had been a week since Beatriz's last meeting with Vulpa. As Beatriz had expected, no reason for them to meet had presented itself. Nor had any explanation or cure for the affliction of Beatriz's hand. She still liked to pretend it was really just infected, just like she pretended, day after day in this studio, that the medium was simply poorly made (even when she replaced it with new) or that the canvas had issues (even after she stretched another two canvases). Maybe tomorrow she would pretend it was the pigment. She could afford to replace it all, even the lapis lazuli blue, if it would buy her another day of pretending there was nothing deeper at work here, if she could keep living in a world she could at least understand…

(She wished she'd never thought at the fountain in the capital that Marina had spoken to her. Then it would be easier to ignore her dreams.)

A crash of shattering pottery and a masculine yelp. Beatriz opened her tired eyes and forced herself to her feet. It was not her business to intervene between mother and son, but she still felt some vague sense of responsibility. If she hadn't indulged Anthona in coming here, maybe this fight wouldn't have happened. More likely Anthona would have dragged some other poor woman out here, but maybe not. She felt a responsibility towards Jorge, pressured to love her when he could not; a responsibility to Anthona, who thought Beatriz was her son's hope when she was nothing like. She reluctantly walked out of the studio and down the hall.

She found Anthona and Jorge at a corner of the hall, as if they had just left the parlor but never quite managed to go where they were headed. The shards of pottery on the ground seemed to have come from a vase Beatriz remembered having stood by the side of the hall as decoration. The two fell silent as she approached; Beatriz crouched and began picking up the shards.

She didn't know what to say to them. Only that it was late, and the summer was hot, and it was raining out, and why did they need to fight, now or ever but particularly now? Anthona spoke before she could. "Please don't trouble yourself, Miss Comete. A maid will have it cleaned up by morning."

"I should take responsibility," Beatriz said.

"What? What for?"

Beatriz shook her head. "Jorge," she said, "you should get to bed, shouldn't you? It's late."

He was looking at her strangely. She didn't think it was because he was drunk. She didn't think he looked as drunk as Anthona's accusations had made him sound, as his own yelling back had made him sound. "It's all right. I was talking to my mother."

"It's late," Beatriz said again, softly. "Go to bed, and talk in the morning when you're less tired. Maybe things will make more sense." She rubbed her eyes. How wise she sounded. But sleeping had not made her world make more sense, not lately. Every day she woke to more and more confusion.

Jorge was nodding, turning, leaving; good; and Anthona was touching her shoulder, pulling her up. "You should go to bed too, Miss Comete. I hadn't realized you were up."

Inez had said the same earlier. She'd tried to stick around the studio, encouraging Beatriz to give up for the evening. Beatriz had been forced to send her away. "Thank you," she told Anthona now, "but I can't yet. I need to..." Beatriz shook her head in frustration. "My painting hasn't progressed in days. I need to make some sort of progress."

"That painting has been driving you to distraction lately." Anthona didn't approve. "Perhaps you should put it aside for a few days, try to get a little more fresh air. And tonight..."

"A few days!" The thought of that made Beatriz almost want to weep. Anthona of course could not understand how very important this task was, how very urgent it was. It could hardly wait a few hours.

But she didn't want to fight, not after she'd just stepped in to end an argument. She took a deep breath. "I'd better just clean things up, and then tomorrow..."

A noise came from down the hall—a crack of thunder combined with something else, a noise of shattering and breaking. Beatriz gasped and hurried down the hall back to the studio, Anthona close behind her. *My painting*, she thought. *My painting, my painting, it's trying to get my painting...*

She burst into the studio to see the window had broken and

rain had flooded into the room. Torrential as it was, it had already dampened the floor of almost the whole room. The canvas, she had expected, would be even wetter than she had left it, but when her eyes focused on it, the situation was worse. The sogged cloth now had a ragged hole in the middle, splitting it apart—not a rip, though it was very big, but a burn, and the room smelled of lightning.

The room smelled of lightning, and was filled with a pale blue light.

"Miss Comete," Anthona said. Her voice was high, quieter than usual. "I'm—what are you holding?"

Beatriz, who was holding nothing—she'd dropped the shards of pottery in the hall as she ran, thoughts of cleaning cast far aside—turned in confusion. When Anthona gasped, she looked down at her hands and saw that the left one, despite the bandage, was emitting the cold light that filled the room. Oh. She hadn't realized—the blue in the room had felt natural to her, when everything else was so strange and yet so clearly Marina's doing.

She cleared her throat. It seemed wrong to frighten Anthona over these things, which were her own troubles, but how to soothe her? "It's all right." As she spoke she unwrapped the bandage, which was already wet from the rain still gusting into the room (it felt like the wind bent itself to her, the rain itself snatched at her, but that didn't matter, not among the rest of this, didn't matter at all in comparison). "It's just the cut I got a few days ago, you remember. Well, a couple weeks ago now. But it's fine. It doesn't hurt." This was true. She was surprised to realize it was true.

Hand unwrapped, she held it up to show Anthona. The light from it was so much brighter than the glistening from before. All still turquoise. *Lovely*, she thought. *So much lovelier than my painting—my mess of a painting. Just as well it was destroyed.* But her heart still panged. All that wasted effort.

"It's fine," she repeated, because Anthona was still staring at her.

Anthona said, "You're cursed."

She didn't say it bitterly or even rudely, only shocked and still. Beatriz found she had no way to argue against the statement, either. She would have liked to interpret the mark as Marina's favor—she had thought Marina was speaking to her at the fountain in the capital, thought she had heard Marina in her dreams—but when she looked at the facts, she knew Marina's favor did not in fact sit with her. If she was marked, she was cursed.

She nodded.

Anthona looked around the ruin of a room, then gathered herself together. "Miss Comete, you should go to bed for tonight. But I think perhaps it would be best if you left our manor as soon as possible. So close to the sea, we cannot take Marina lightly, nor should you, and I don't think this place has been as useful to your art as you thought it might be."

And she hadn't been doing Jorge any good either, Beatriz mentally added. But all Anthona had said was true. "You're quite right. I'll leave."

"Very well then. I'm sorry about all of this. We'll see you off well tomorrow. Good night."

Beatriz was left standing in the studio alone, rain still blowing against the floor, the broken canvas, her skin. But there was nothing left for her here, nor in Mestos at all. She went into the hall and headed to the foyer, then out the door into the rain.

So convenient to have a manor located so close to the ocean. She followed the same path she had used to meet Vulpa last week. Of course the beach was abandoned at night, and in this weather the waves were rough, no longer lovely or welcoming. No, but they called to her regardless. *Come to me. See me.*

She was not going to run away. Not from the painting, which she had promised to Juan, which she owed to Ricardo, which she had determined on for her own pride. Not from Marina, who scolded her and slapped her but still spoke to her, which was more from a god than any human had the right to expect. Not from the storm, and not from the ocean. She walked down wet sand into the waves, and was so wet already that she barely felt the difference when her feet first touched the water. She could feel the waves when they hit her legs, though, cold and stinging through her skirt. The first one hit only her ankles, the second her knees, the third her thighs. Each wave pulled her in as it drew back, and she followed.

Let's talk, Marina.

The world was made of water, of blue and of stinging darkness when the waves washed over her head, forcing her eyes closed. But she did not feel any burning in her throat as her consciousness faded away, nor any fear. The goddess might do as she liked, and Beatriz would stand by her judgment. And if she chose to kill Beatriz, well, in her domain, with an artist who had the audacity to try to draw her, that was only her right.

But Beatriz somehow thought her choice would be different.

Let's talk, Marina.

13

CHAPTER THIRTEEN

Ricardo didn't see Leonor for a number of days after the Festival of Sektos. This did not mean he passed his time in solitude; Felipe came to visit him as regularly as ever and more so out of kind concern because, as he said, "Mother said you weren't feeling well."

"Did she?" Ricardo asked.

He was working on the shine of light on the side of a metal pitcher. His velvety still-life. He'd thought he would abandon this painting when he fled for the capital and it hadn't bothered him much as it was progressing slowly, causing him more than the usual frustration. Despite that, he felt a workman's satisfaction that he was able to continue with it, and today at least the work was going well.

Felipe grinned. "Yes, but she also said you weren't sick, so I thought you were probably just being grouchy again."

"I'm not being grouchy," Ricardo said. "I'm not sick either. Your mother and I had a disagreement at the Festival of Sektos, but I'd hardly hold a grudge against a lady. Of course your mother may be angry at me, still."

Felipe hummed knowledgeably. At least he didn't try to argue that Ricardo really was holding a grudge. Instead he said, "People fight a lot on Sektos's Feast Day. That's the way he likes it. But he doesn't really get anything out of people grouching around afterwards."

Ricardo personally thought—not that he disbelieved in Sektos or anything—that the number of fights at a typical Festival of Sektos had more to do with the heat, the wine, and the competitions, maybe even the music, than with any divine intervention. It was still a fair point. But it was also true that Ricardo wasn't holding a grudge against Leonor. Not fuming or brooding about it, anyway. There was no point in a commoner holding a grudge against a noblewoman who held him completely in her power; certainly no point in his remaining outraged at an inappropriate advance. It would do him no good and her no harm. So he was staying calm and waiting to see how things would play out, and pointedly not thinking about the festival or any of the events that had followed. Waiting to see what Leonor intended to do with him, as he had been all along—waiting because she made him, with this damned avoidance of hers. There was a slight hint of irritation in his voice as he told Felipe, "Well, you can ask your mother about it. She probably knows best."

"You really are grumpy!" Felipe was delighted.

"Don't be ridiculous."

"Don't be grumpy. I'll talk to Mother about it and I'm sure she'll forgive you for whatever it was. In the meantime, you should come outside and cheer up. You can ride horses with me and Captain Alban."

"No thank you. I wouldn't put the captain to the trouble."

"You just don't want to come."

"I have work to do," Ricardo said. He wanted to finish this

pitcher. He'd moved the velvet so that some of it draped just over one side of it, obscuring the shape. How was he to maintain a sense of its form without showing it in its entirety? It was an interesting challenge; self-imposed, but all the more reason he couldn't abandon it.

Felipe pouted and whined, but Ricardo remained firm. He stayed in and continued his painting. He wondered if Leonor would visit that afternoon.

She didn't, so he painted. That day and the next and the next.

Leonor's presence previously had distracted him from his work, her gaze on his back burning him, making it hard for him to focus. Now as he worked, he found her gaze came back into his mind as surely as if she were still there overseeing his progress. He would glance back and be startled when her chair, which he'd pushed off to an unobtrusive corner now, was still empty. Was she playing games with him, or had he ceased to be interesting?

He'd begun putting the kiss in context, thinking that had the situation been different, perhaps it might not have been quite so unacceptable. There had been various women at court who had flirted with him and even tried to kiss him now and then. A couple noblemen had also made insinuations. He'd rejected all of them without consequence; as the king's own painter he had no need to curry favor elsewhere, and he'd found everyone who approached him in such a way quite unattractive. But he hadn't been terribly outraged either. Presuming one could do as one wished with commoners was simply how nobles acted, especially potential patrons. If Leonor had been his patron and acted this way towards him...

Well, it still would have been no good, of course. He'd always avoided that sort of patronage—if he had to suck up to patrons he preferred to stroke their pride rather than their lust.

Well, maybe if they'd just met at the palace then, and she'd tried to flirt with him in a less aggressive manner while she was in the capital. No, no, of course that could have led nowhere. She was still on bad terms with the king, and rumors traveled too quickly in the capital for Ricardo to afford that sort of thing.

Why was he trying to find some situation where he would have let her kiss him? She might have been beautiful, but so were many women with far better morals. Leonor was his captor, and even if he sometimes found himself intrigued by her, there was something chilling about her as well. Ricardo doubted any affair with her could lead anywhere good—not just for him, either. People talked about her husband, who had died young. Said she'd been bad luck to him, or worse.

Ricardo's luck was already bad enough.

* * *

Maybe Felipe did go talk to Leonor about the temper she was in; maybe he forgot. Either way, it had been almost two weeks since the festival when Leonor finally came to visit Ricardo again.

Ricardo was almost finished with the still life by then. All that was left was the background, the wall and the table on which the objects sat. The arrangement himself he counted as done. If the texture of the velvet was still imperfect, if one of the stones looked a little too even, he had decided to let it go. The colors were satisfactory at least: yes, the dark red of his fabric was a bit richer than the red of the real cloth, and the metal pitcher a bit shinier, but what was wrong with that? Painting was about ostentation. This was the sort of still life that, despite its lack of flowers and fruits, would easily sell at court. Maybe not to Alejandro, who had to be picky what he hung up in the palace where everyone took his décor choices to be deeply meaningful and symbolic, but to some other patron. And he might have shown it to Alejandro first, for the sake of seeing him smile and say, "Ah, good to see you're keeping busy. Do you think you could put some rocks like those in your painting of the vault? Perhaps a bit smoother—erosion wears away stones' rough edges..."

It was really a pity the king was miles away and Ricardo had no noble to present it to except Leonor, and no desire for any piece of his to hang on *her* wall.

"It's coming along well," Leonor said. "You really are very good, Montero." She shook her head. "Feli told me you were sulking, but of course you were only working. I might have known."

"Your son always believes I'm sulking." Ricardo shook his head. "This piece will be done within a week, I think." And that if he continued working slowly.

What will you work on then? might have been a good question to ask him. Then he could make up some sort of plan, to paint a landscape based on studies of the garden or perhaps to paint Felipe after all if he could make the boy sit still. Anything to fill the time. She didn't ask, though. Perhaps she was aware, as Ricardo was, that this painting being almost done was not just the completion of a project but the measure of a length of time, of how long Ricardo had been stuck here. And that as it was completed, Ricardo's patience might begin to fray.

What she said when she spoke again was, "I have been thinking about some of the things I said to you, the last time we spoke. I think we probably both said some things we regret. I was too extreme."

"I could never dare to accuse you of such a thing, madonna."

Leonor laughed. "Well... it wasn't my finest day, overall. Perhaps I haven't been at my finest since meeting you, Montero. And certainly your impression of me—well, however it is, I surely deserve it. But I still regret it. You're interesting, and... well, I wish we could have some more understanding between us."

"That is kind, but I doubt I am capable of understanding one such as yourself."

Leonor sighed. "Perhaps. Still... I'd like to make some amends.

And I think we should really talk." She clasped her hands together. "Tomorrow morning, I will be riding with a few guards up the mountain. There is a place I often visit—the view isn't bad for an artist. You can come with me, and we can converse. Or you can stay in if you want. I won't force you."

Ricardo forced himself not to snort. "You're too kind."

Such a small freedom to have! Yet he felt all too aware, the next morning, when the guards came to fetch him for the excursion, that he would have been furious if he had not been given the choice. It would have been more of Leonor's insolence, her summoning him here and there according to her whim. Given the option to go or stay, however, he found he liked the idea of a ride with Leonor. There would be fresh air, at least, and if the conversation sounded a little menacing, it would still only be words. And there would be the view. Rugged mountains were usually, in his opinion, better at a distance (he preferred the streets and fountains and architecture of a city), but it might be interesting to try painting such a landscape for a change. If he would be stuck here long enough to start another painting, he needed at least some sort of inspiration.

* * *

The view wasn't bad.

Ricardo had expected Leonor might haul him off to the top of the mountain, but instead they stopped a little more than halfway up. She told the guards to wait at the path and led him to a clearing a small distance away. She hadn't lied that it would be picturesque. She'd chosen a clearing next to a cliff, with a view of countless trees from above, and more mountains off in the distance. Ricardo wasn't sure it was the kind of thing he would paint, but it was nice. And quiet.

Leonor walked right over to stand by the cliff's edge. It was surprising to Ricardo that she felt safe being here with him without the guards. He could easily have pushed her over the cliff, given

She'd chosen a clearing next to a cliff, with a view of countless trees from above, and more mountains off in the distance.

the inclination—well, perhaps not easily, as she was not a weak woman, but with enough desperation he could probably manage it. It seemed to him she was showing a level of trust that he wasn't sure he wanted to be given.

"I was thinking about what I said to you," Leonor said. "That I could never explain my hatred for Alejandro, and you would never understand anyhow. Perhaps I was wrong to say that. In general it's not something I talk about, and few have tried to understand me, beyond my most trusted friends and subordinates; few even believe some of the things I say, or think they matter. But perhaps it doesn't matter if you believe me or understand me. Since I've pulled you into this feud, I might as well explain it to you. You deserve that much. If you can't understand my anger, very well. But I'll explain a little of it."

Ricardo felt himself stiffening as Leonor spoke. Truthfully, he had expected the conversation Leonor had mentioned to be more apologies, or perhaps another attempt at seduction. Yet even the latter did not scare him as much as this. Understanding Leonor's anger—well, of course he wanted to. But she had refused him explanation and he had accepted that. Better not to understand the ways of nobles, after all, their illogical feuds and fancies. The only one he'd ever tried to understand deeply—apart from Beatriz, but she hardly counted as a noble—was King Alejandro, to the extent that he'd been willing to share himself. And even then, he'd only ever tried to understand Alejandro's love of art, of his goddess, of his people. Or his shallow annoyances at advisors and various courtiers. He'd never tried to dredge the depths of Alejandro's heart or inquired into his past. It was too dangerous. And with Leonor, his king's enemy, it could only be more-so.

But he'd asked for this. So he did not complain as she began to tell him the story, nor try to stop her or protest even as it morphed from a simple recounting of history to something far more complicated.

* * *

Leonor had been in her teens when Alejandro began gaining a reputation. She was old enough that the nobles at court had begun to call her a lovely young woman, in a flattering, condescending, speculative sort of way. She couldn't take such compliments seriously, as they clearly were intended more for her father than for her. Prince Alejandro, on the other hand, was praised sincerely by all and sundry. Every day it seemed there were more stories coming home about his achievements in battle against Fiteria. Not only was he an excellent tactician, but he had the practical skills required for sea warfare as well. And when Fiteria finally agreed to a truce, it was Alejandro they asked to deal with them, even though he of course needed to get all terms and conditions approved by Leonor's father. And Leonor's father agreed to their request.

The treaty was favorable to Salandra; Alejandro was then known for his powers as a statesman as well as a warrior. Leonor's father called him back to the capital, to be rewarded for his heroic actions and to help with matters of state. He was family, after all—close family—and Leonor's father was getting old with no male heir. It was about time for him to begin to delegate, to teach his heir presumptive something of how to rule not only as a general but as a king.

Alejandro had taken to it like a fish to water.

The capital had loved him, too. The country had loved him. There had already been talk of a possible golden age when he was king. Leonor had always disapproved of that kind of talk, in a vague sort of way, because it dismissed the golden age they already had under her father. Hadn't he been king when they won the war? Wasn't he king now, in an age of prosperity? Prince Alejandro couldn't take credit for everything.

He did not have authority over everything, either. There were a few areas where Leonor's father would hear him out and then politely (or impolitely) ignore him—sometimes in dealing with particularly irascible nobles, for example. And also on the subject of Leonor's marriage.

She was growing older, after all. Those at court who called her a young woman were no longer teasing a mere girl but stating the truth. She was a young princess, too, and very eligible as a result. A powerful political tool.

Her father's idea had been that she should marry one of the princes of Cherno. Alejandro had been vehemently opposed, on the grounds that Cherno could not be given that sort of influence over Salandra, especially since Leonor's son, if she had one, would be the new heir to the throne. But when her father asked Alejandro for a better suggestion, Alejandro dithered, saying that Leonor was still so young, why should she be married off so soon? His dear cousin would surely prefer to wait a while, and the question of who would be a good match for her could be pondered over at leisure.

"Considerate," those at court would say, "far too considerate. The man dotes on his cousin. But it's a little much, isn't it? It's a woman's way to be married early, especially for one of noble blood. The prince is so against her marrying, it makes you wonder.. what type of doting this really is."

It was the first time gossip at court was not kind to Alejandro. Not that it was altogether vicious. Leonor and Alejandro were cousins, not siblings—a marriage between them would not have been unthinkable—but there was still a hint of scandal that only increased the longer Alejandro and Leonor's father argued over the issue. Leonor at the time felt annoyed by it all. From the time she was a girl she had known she would marry for her father's purposes, not for love, and this was something she readily accepted. She did not care overly much whom she married, as long as it was no one she hated, but to have it dragged out like this was ridiculous and was giving her a bad name. As for the rumors that Alejandro was in love with her, she knew very well how false they were. Alejandro, except in the presence of her father, paid her very little attention, less than even the average courtier.

It all might have upset Leonor more if not for her mother, who was very comforting about the whole matter. "Arranging a marriage does take time and should be thought through carefully. Your cousin isn't wrong about that," she would say. "He is a bit inflexible, but I'm sure he has his reasons. Your marriage—a good marriage—will come in time. And at the end of the day, your father and I will be the one to pick your husband, not Alejandro or the court. We are your parents, after all, and your father is still king. Don't worry over it too much."

She should have been right.

But that winter, Leonor's father fell ill. It was a strange sickness, not one that was going around nor one that Leonor's father was typically victim to—he was a very healthy man, apart from occasional fits of dizziness. He began to feel exhausted all the time, to suffer from strange pains in his head and stomach and then all over his body. More and more business of state was handed over to Alejandro. Alejandro, who also insisted on being responsible for Leonor's father's care as he grew sicker and sicker, who chose the doctors allowed to see him and checked every medicine prescribed, allowing some and vetoing others. Alejandro, who when Leonor's father died shortly before the arrival of spring, would be crowned within a couple of days, to the joy of all the nation (which hardly mourned Leonor's father's passing at all).

* * *

"Mostly, no one suspected Alejandro of anything," Leonor said. "He was a revered war hero and politician at that point. Even if he had killed my father in front of a crowd, I don't know if anyone would have condemned him. As it was, my suspicions and my mother's suspicions looked paranoid. But we were hardly allowed to see my father once he got past a certain point in his illness, past the point of protesting. Some of the doctors Alejandro turned away were very reputable, very trustworthy, doctors who had served our family before. The doctors he did use were those who had served him in the army or had other obligations to him."

Ricardo, who had been trying to listen with full respect, could no longer hold his silence. "Madonna..."

"To be clear, I still have no evidence that Alejandro poisoned my father," Leonor said. "Only that the way he conducted himself was strange, as was my father's illness to begin with. And that if my father had lived even another year probably would have married, and very well might have had a son. Alejandro would have no longer had a chance at inheriting the throne."

Politically, it did make sense. Ricardo could even begrudgingly admit the theory wasn't entirely out of character for the king. Alejandro had always had a strong conviction in his own right to the throne, in his own glory; and he was not very merciful to political adversaries, one reason among many that his court fawned over his every whim. But to take down a rebellious or presumptuous baron was one thing—to kill a king, and to kill his own uncle, was another. And murder was different from legal execution. It was too underhanded for the man Ricardo knew. And, too, if all of this had been because of the possibility of Leonor producing a new heir, "Why wouldn't he kill you, then? It would be less dangerous than killing a king."

Leonor shook her head with a twisted smile. Apparently even in the midst of such a grim story she could still be amused. "I thought so too back then. Alejandro didn't care much for me, but he loved my father in his own way; I thought he should have killed me if anyone. But Alejandro is a practical man. If he poisoned me the same way, I'm sure my father would have picked up on it and he would have had to face the consequences, while my mother and I did not have enough power to stop him as things were. And, too, he was ambitious. Perhaps he simply could not wait to ascend the throne."

"Still, Alejandro has always respected divine right—"

"His own divine right, certainly! When has he shown such respect for anyone else?"

Ricardo hadn't known Alejandro before he was king. How was he supposed to answer such a question? It was true Alejandro never showed much respect towards the kings of other countries, but how could he—he firmly believed Salandra was the greatest and most blessed country in the world, and so all other kings were still, in his views, lower than he was. "But the king was his uncle," he protested. "Alejandro cares about his family. He would never harm a family member."

Leonor snorted. "In any case. I was not completely convinced of Alejandro's guilt at first, but as time passed I became more so, if only because of how he treated my mother and me. He avoided us in the weeks after his coronation, and within a month he had arranged my marriage to the count of Suelta. I was sent to live here with him, and my mother with me. Conveniently out of the way. Every argument he had made about my being too young or marriages needing careful contemplation was plainly a lie.

"I hated my husband. He was not a cruel man, but he was Alejandro's man to the bone. There passed not a conversation between us when Alejandro was not brought up, even though he was aware that Alejandro and I were not on good terms at that time. And I knew he corresponded with Alejandro regularly, and reported on everything I said and did. Suelta was like a prison.

"My mother took it worse than I did, though. She used to speak only to me and a few others about her suspicions of Alejandro. But in Suelta, she began to rant to anyone who would listen about how she and I and Father had been wronged. To me, especially, but I had grown tired of listening. Even though I felt the same as she did, what could I do about it? I pushed her away for that reason, as did most others. She began to take long walks and rides here in the mountains by herself, solitude being her only comfort. Then one day she didn't come back, and guards were sent out to find her. They found her body at the bottom of her cliff. She must have fallen from here, or somewhere around here. I've never been able to decide if it was an accident or if she jumped or if she was pushed."

Leonor took a deep breath and let it out in a sigh. She turned away from the beautiful view to look at Ricardo. "And that is why I hate Alejandro."

Ricardo... nodded.

What else was he supposed to do?

"It's not that he married me off, to be clear. My husband never treated me badly, and he died so soon after we married that I hardly had a chance to complain. But my father and my mother both died because of him. It's not something I can forgive." She clenched her fists. "If I were a brave or strong person, I would kill him, I suppose. But he is the king, and I... I have Suelta and a son, and I've never been willing to risk it. Maybe I don't hate him enough." She shook her head. "So time goes on, and Alejandro is king and I am here, and sometimes I have to hurt him, to remind him that what he did still matters. I should not have involved you in my revenge, of course, but... petty revenge is not enough. With every year, I find it more unbearable how he lives so happily over my parents' bodies!"

Her body was shaking. Ricardo tentatively touched her shoulder. "Leonor," he said, and she threw her arms around him and gripped him in a tight, desperate hug.

She began to cry, and Ricardo couldn't help but hold her. In his mind, distantly, he was thinking over her story—wondering how much to believe, how much was skewed—but her body was feverishly hot in his arms, and trembling, and smaller than it looked in its elegant dress yet still very solid. Maybe he would argue this over with her another day, but not now. Today, he would not argue with one thing she had said, but treat it as if it were all truth. He told himself Alejandro would understand if he were here. Maybe they were distant, but after all she was still his cousin. Alejandro would have forgiven Ricardo if, for the moment, he put forth no argument in his favor.

14

CHAPTER FOURTEEN

Beatriz slept in blue.

The world was steeped in it. It was not monochrome; there were variations of shade and color throughout. Sometimes it seemed to her that everything was so dark as to be almost black, a world roiling in indigo and navy. Sometimes it was terribly light, the color of the sky or of some woman's pale eyes. Mostly it was somewhere in between, a blue that mingled with hints of green, and it washed around Beatriz in gentle, dizzying waves. Speaking to her in whispers.

"Dear child, you really came to me! How brave. But it is not time for that, not yet—well, perhaps for a moment—do you like this, how it feels? Shall we go deeper?"

And the blue grew darker, and she was cold and water pressed around her body, but she did not mind.

A laugh bubbling around her.

"You are not ready to go deeper."

I am, she wanted to protest. *I am*. But she could not speak, could not open her mouth. And the tide was sweeping her in, sweeping her somewhere she knew not where.

"I must have servants on land, you know. Well... this is my own fault for pushing you too hard. But there now, you're open to me and I'll be open to you. Let me fill you. In the future, you need not come to the beach to find me. I will be in you wherever you are."

"Though to have you in my arms... Ah, Beatriz."

"But listen, it is not time for that yet. We have work to do."

The voice droned on and on. It came and went like waves. Like the waves that left her on the sand—like the waves that continued to wash over her vision, over her consciousness. There were hands on her. Hands too small, she thought, for the ocean, for the mighty Marina. Hands pressing on her chest, then tugging her, dragging her. Sometimes they pulled at her clothing or caressed her forehead. A couple times they tipped water into her mouth or draped wet cloth over her forehead. She craved water more than anything, for she felt abandoned out of it. She had to get up and go back to the sea, but she could not move, no more than if there were still water weighing down on her lifeless body.

But the voice still murmured to her, kind and encouraging.

"Beatriz, sweet child, sweet love. It is all right. You are not quite ready to serve me, but soon. In a couple days, we will begin. Really begin this time. Are you excited?"

Yes, yes, of course I am. I've been waiting so long. Don't leave me, Marina. Please.

A laugh.

"I will come back to you later. Now, wake up. Your lover has been crying."

* * *

Lover?

Crying?

The blue faded from Beatriz's vision only slowly, turning into the dark red of closed eyelids. Sleeping, of course she'd been sleeping. For how long? She forced her eyes to open, and now she could take in the room around her. It was not overwhelmingly bright, but light filtered in through a shaded window. Yellow light through that shade, not blue. Indeed, the room she was in was not very blue at all. The walls were wood paneling, the floor looked to be stone, and the blanket that covered her—for she was in bed—was a warm red. It occurred to her that she was hot, and her throat was dry. On a small table next to the bed—no, it was a small chest of drawers, but no matter—there was a cup of water, but her limbs were slow to obey her, and her hands were trapped under the blanket, and she could not reach.

She tried to speak, and at first could only let out a scratchy cough. Then she called out, cracking the silence of the room: "Hello? Is anyone there?"

No answer. Her call, though it had felt loud in the silence, had still been very quiet. Not feeling up to yelling for possibly no result, she wrestled her hands free of the blanket and slowly sat up. She noticed she was wearing a clean cream-colored shift that was a little too long in the sleeves, not one she owned. With a frown, she reached out for the water, but her hands were shaky and she knocked the cup to the floor, where it shattered.

The shattering cup made more noise than her yelling, and apparently was enough to summon her caretaker, for within moments she heard the noise of footsteps, and then the door opened, and there, radiant in a yellow dress and a quizzical expression, was Vulpa.

"Miss Comete!" She hurried over. "You're awake. How are you feeling?"

Frankly, with the dry throat and her shaky limbs and a mild headache she was beginning to notice, not amazing. But considering her last memory was of walking into the sea with only a vague hope she wouldn't drown, these complaints were hardly worth mentioning. "Good," she said. Full sentences seemed like a lot of effort. "Thirsty."

Vulpa glanced at the cup on the floor. Beatriz winced. "Sorry."

"It's fine. Not hard to replace such a thing. I'd better get you a new cup, and then I'll clean this up. At least you didn't spill on yourself." She smiled nervously at Beatriz. "Took me so long to dry you in the first place, and you've been sweating too."

"Sorry," Beatriz said. "Is this your bed?" It had to be her house, right?

"Yes. Don't worry about it. I'll explain, but just let me get you a drink. Sit tight." And she hurried off to do just that.

Beatriz reflected, in a tired, hollow way, that she was becoming far too used to watching Vulpa run off for medical supplies to see to her. Poor Vulpa, forced to take care of Beatriz time and time again. She wanted to protest to Vulpa that she wasn't usually this prone to accidents or sicknesses or having her life disturbed by divine intervention, but when Vulpa returned with water, she was quickly distracted. It felt cool and nice going down her throat. A memory flashed through her mind—"Have you been feeding me by hand, Vulpa?"

"I'm afraid I had to," Vulpa said, as if her meticulous care might somehow have caused Beatriz offense. "It's been almost a week now, and you haven't been lucid since I found you."

"Almost—how long has it been? When did you find me? How did you find me?"

"Five days and a little more, now, since I found you in the morning," Vulpa said. "I found you on the beach. Not the nice one we went to, either. One scattered with rocks. I go there now and again to gather clams. You were lying on the sand just above the water line. The tide had just gone out. You must have washed in—unless you remember otherwise."

"No," Beatriz said. "You're probably right. I... I'd gone wading at night, and got swept away." To say more than this felt too dramatic, though of course wading hardly summed up what she had done, what she had set out to do. She felt embarrassed to speak of her thoughts at the time, halfway between seeking a goddess and seeking death. What would Vulpa think if she told her that? Vulpa had a poor enough impression of her already.

"Wading," Vulpa said flatly.

"...yes."

"The night before I found you, it was pouring rain out. Not the best weather for it."

"I was in a strange mood," Beatriz said. It was true enough.

Vulpa took a deep breath. "Miss Comete, while I might not have an unstained reputation, I hope you know me well enough to find me trustworthy. When I found you, you were half-dead. I thought I would have to expel water from your chest and restart your breathing at first. It turned out I didn't have to, but you were in the water for a long time. Frankly, it's amazing you didn't drown."

Gently, very gently, she clasped Beatriz's hand. "I have not let anyone know about your presence here. I did not send word up to the manor; I did not tell even Jorge about finding you, or anyone in the village. Whatever happened to you, please trust me with the truth. You do not know me well, but I swear I'll help you in any way I can."

Beatriz's eyes widened. "You think..." She almost laughed, but ended up coughing instead. Vulpa stroked her hair soothingly. Her hair was clean, not a trace of saltwater in it. Vulpa must have washed it while she was delirious. Must have given Beatriz a bath, since her body didn't feel dirty or salt-saturated either.

The flush on her cheeks when she was done coughing was not entirely from lack of breath. She forced herself to focus, speak. "I promise you it had nothing to do with the baroness or the baron or anyone. I wasn't attacked or... driven into the sea, or whatever you're picturing."

Vulpa still looked skeptical. "You went wading."

"Well, maybe saying it had nothing to do with anyone is a little inaccurate. It had to do with this." Beatriz raised her hand, the one with the turquoise scar on it. There was no bandage hiding the scar anymore. Vulpa hadn't bothered to replace the bandage Beatriz had left in her studio. Her studio, not her studio anymore. Well, that hardly mattered. What work had she gotten done there anyway?

She wondered how Vulpa might react to her claim of divine interference; Vulpa took it calmly, though her eyes narrowed. "Marina, then."

"Yes. I think."

"Hm."

She did not question Beatriz further on the matter. Instead she asked if, since Beatriz had not been violently assaulted or thrown into the sea on purpose, Beatriz wanted her to contact the manor and let the baroness and Jorge know how she was doing after all, or perhaps go back there for her convalescence. Beatriz politely rejected the idea. She had, after all, been kicked out. "But can you find out if my maid Inez is still there, and bring her back here if she is? I should speak with her."

"Certainly. I think I heard she was leaving, though, and taking your things with her. Your disappearance caused a bit of a stir—there's been gossip."

Beatriz laughed. "I didn't expect to become infamous here, you know. Really I planned on hiding away in my studio and finishing a painting, nothing more than that."

"The fact that you were so 'reclusive' before disappearing is one of the things that makes people talk," Vulpa said with a smile. "Honestly I'm impressed you managed it—with how I heard the baroness was pressuring you, you still barely spent any time with Jorge! The poor woman."

Beatriz shook her head. Poor Anthona indeed. The woman had never intended to host a woman cursed or blessed by any goddess, only to match-make her son. Then again, she thought, it was hard to feel too much pity when you thought about how many girls Anthona had probably tried to push on Jorge in the same way, and how many she might still push on him in the future. She might have deserved a little shock.

Vulpa, on the other hand, deserved nothing of the kind. "Should I leave?" Beatriz asked abruptly.

"Should you... Well, if you want, though perhaps when you're a little bit better, if you take my advice. I know this house isn't..."

"Oh, it's a nice house. But it would be a pity to bring the wrath of a goddess down on it. I don't want to cause you trouble, Vulpa. Should I leave?"

Vulpa huffed. "If that's what you mean, then no. I don't think Marina's about to send a wave on the house for sheltering you."

"She broke Anthona's windows. Gave her a fit of hysteria."

"The baroness is not known for having strong nerves," Vulpa said. "I won't mind if a couple windows break."

"And if it's more than that?"

Vulpa hesitated, but said, "It won't be. You may be right that Marina has her eyes on you, but I doubt she's trying to kill you. You came out of the sea alive, after all. If Marina wanted you dead, you would have drowned."

"That's true," Beatriz allowed. "Very true." She sighed. "Well then, if you're offering, I'll stay until I'm fit for travel. I'd better write my family, though. If Inez has told them I'm missing, they'll be up in arms."

* * *

Being sick was boring.

Vulpa kept on insisting that Beatriz go back to bed, only allowing her to get up to eat meals and sometimes to sit in the parlor and talk with Vulpa or watch her practice her dancing. She had not seen Vulpa perform since their first meeting, and had almost forgotten that Vulpa's primary trade was this rather than modeling or healing the sick. Watching her practice was quite different from watching her perform in public. She would repeat a dance over and over, or pause partway through, even at the very beginning, and redo a move over and over again.

"Do you ever practice in men's clothing?" she asked. "Or is that only for performances? It seems like you would have to move differently than in a skirt," she added when Vulpa raised her eyebrows.

"Not many of my numbers require such clothing, so I do not wear it often."

"Ah," Beatriz said. Inez had probably been right that the crudeness of the dance had been meant as mockery, but now that they were friends she wouldn't call Vulpa out on it.

"You asked me about breeches when I first went to model for you, too," Vulpa said. "Did they make that big of an impression on you, Miss Comete?" Then, before Beatriz could deflect, she tapped her lips thoughtfully and said, "Then again, you told me you really would have preferred me naked, so I suppose it was my body overall that made the impression."

Beatriz flushed.

Vulpa had gotten comfortable teasing her now, it seemed. She didn't mind, though.

What bothered her more was all the time she was forced to spend in bed, or the time when Vulpa left the house and told her she should probably stay put and not go out if she didn't want to cause more gossip. Beatriz didn't care how the town of Mestos talked about her, but she did worry what might be said about Vulpa, having a cursed and recently missing woman hiding in her house, so she kept herself hidden. This worked well enough until one day she heard the front door opening and called out, "Hello, Vulpa. I'm not sleeping. Come in."

A pause. Then, "It's not Vulpa. Who's there?"

She didn't recognize the voice at first, though really she should have. But she got out of bed and threw a shawl over the nightgown Vulpa had lent her, and opened the door to see Jorge standing before her with an expression of bewilderment that morphed into surprise.

"Miss Comete! You?"

"Me," Beatriz said, stepping back a little. She should have known it would be him—what other man would casually wander into Vulpa's home while she was out, letting themselves in with a key without even knocking? But it was still disconcerting to see him after the way their last encounter had gone. "Hello, Jorge."

Jorge seemed to take her stepping back as an invitation to enter the room. He did so, sitting down on the bed and frowning at the ruffled sheets, the blanket she'd left thrown aside when she climbed out of bed. Evidence of her inhabitance. He forced his attention back to her, frown only deepening. "Where the hell have you been? You've been missing for days. Everyone's been going crazy looking for you—I mean, you ran off in the middle of a storm. Your brother showed up here—"

"Luis? Really?"

"Stormed in and yelled at everyone, said he'd have the whole town searched. All we could tell him was that you'd clearly parted of your own volition, and he wouldn't even believe us. Seemed to think we murdered you. By now he's probably back in the capital petitioning the king to have us all arrested."

"He won't," Beatriz said. "I wrote to my family—he must not have gotten the letter soon enough. But he was really here? Why didn't Vulpa tell me?"

"Why didn't—did Vulpa know where you were all along?"

"I've been here with her," Beatriz said, seeing no way around it at this point. Besides, Jorge was a good man and not likely to start trouble with Anthona or anyone. "She's been helping me regain my health. I almost drowned, that night I left, and I've been sick ever since. She's been very kind to me."

"Kind to you." The words sounded like a curse coming out of Jorge's mouth. "Is that so?"

"Did she not know Luis was here?"

"She's barely been up to the manor, and for a week she was refusing to see me, so no, it didn't come up. She wasn't around. She hasn't been around."

"She told me she kept up with what was going on. I thought she would have asked after me."

"We didn't discuss it at length," Jorge snapped. "I didn't know she was asking on your behalf. Why make her go doing spywork for you, anyhow? Why didn't you just come back to the manor and tell everyone you weren't dead?"

"I didn't want to cause any trouble."

"You've caused more trouble by avoiding it than you would have by just being straightforward."

Beatriz crossed her arms. "Jorge de Mestos, are you really going to scold me? Of all people, I wouldn't have expected it from you."

"I'm not—listen..."

He was still sputtering when Vulpa hurried through the bedroom door. "Jorge! You're here. I told you I would meet you this evening on the beach."

"I didn't want to wait until this evening. Is that a crime?"

"I wasn't home."

"No, I can see that. Is this why you've been keeping me out of the house all week? Meeting me here, there, and everywhere, anywhere but the house I got you with a proper bed? You've been reserving that bed for Beatriz de Comete instead?"

Vulpa crossed her arms, mirroring Beatriz. "Beatriz has been sick. Yes, I didn't want anything to disturb her. You wouldn't have had to go here, there, and everywhere, if you'd asked me back to your own house, though, would you?"

"You know why I can't have you at the manor anymore."

"And now you know why I couldn't have you over here. It's only been a week."

"Oh, more than a week."

"Not by much."

"I'm very sorry," Beatriz broke in. "I'm afraid it's all been my fault. Vulpa has only been trying to shelter me. Maybe she went overboard on my behalf, but you really can't blame her."

Jorge gave her a look. "Vulpa, can I speak with you privately?"

Vulpa stepped out the door. "Come out, then."

They shut the door behind them, but apparently Jorge couldn't be bothered to go to the parlor or the kitchen, because he began speaking in the hall right outside instead, where Beatriz could still clearly hear everything that was said.

"She's really been staying with you this whole time?"

"She's been sick."

"In our bed?"

"My bed, you may remember."

A huff. "You told me you weren't interested in her. You said she hadn't made any advances on you."

"What, are you saying I was lying now?"

"Am I supposed to believe the most infamous lesbian in Ferrar has been sleeping with you for a week but it's all been sisterly and chaste?"

"Shut up."

A silence.

Beatriz sat down on the bed, legs feeling wooden. That she might cause this kind of conflict with her presence hadn't even occurred to her. It was a worry that had left her after her and Vulpa's first modeling session. If anything, hadn't she been spending more time with Jorge? Dancing with him, meeting him in the studio? Yes, Vulpa was more her type by far, but she'd done her utmost not to show too much interest there. Was every attempt she'd made to avoid trouble in Mestos bound to be in vain?

"I haven't been sleeping with her," Vulpa said, her voice rough. Beatriz couldn't imagine what kind of expression she was making; Vulpa around her had only ever seemed worried or happy, not... whatever this was. "I've touched her, fine. She turned up half-dead on the beach and I had to nurse her. That's all I've been doing, nursing her. Would you rather I had left her there for dead? Would that make you happy?"

"I think we can both agree there's a lot of middle ground you felt no need to cover."

At this point, the two walked away, and the rest of their conversation was muffled, indistinct. They must have worked out their differences to some level of satisfaction, because Jorge dropped in to say goodbye to Beatriz before leaving, and he smiled when he did so, saying he was glad she was alive and well. Vulpa was preoccupied for the rest of the evening, though. Beatriz tried to apologize to her, but she angrily brushed this attempt aside, saying, "What I did for you was my own choice and I'm not ashamed of it. Jorge can be sensitive about it if he wants, but there's no reason for you to be sorry."

Very well. There was little else Beatriz could do.

* * *

She expected that after that, Jorge might come by the house now and then, but he still didn't, and Vulpa didn't go out to meet with him any more often than before. In fact, she seemed to go out less and less, spending more and more time at Beatriz's side. Beatriz should have felt guilty about this, but Vulpa was such pleasant company, and it was good not to be alone.

It was much better not to be alone.

When she was alone, with nothing to distract her, her mind would creep in perilous directions. More often than not, if she sat or lay still for too long, she would find her vision suffused in a blue haze, and hear the sound of waves in her ears. It didn't frighten her. Rather, she found it soothing, relaxing. But when the haze was broken by Vulpa's return, she would think logically of what it meant, and then she would feel afraid after all.

She felt that every time the blue called out to her, she would end up submerged a little deeper. And it was five days after she had first emerged from delirium that she wandered deep enough into the blue to once again here Marina's voice.

"You're well again now, child."

This was true. Beatriz quietly nodded.

"Are you ready then? You said you were willing to see me. You can run from me now, if you want."

This was not true. Beatriz was so dazed that she could barely think of anything but what the voice was saying; certainly she could never have mustered the will to run from the voice, try to leave it behind, even if she had wanted to or had any idea how. But she simply shook her head, and the voice laughed.

"Then look, and you will see."

It broke in front of her vision, blue into blue into blue into green-gold, rippling and crashing all about her. It was confused, yet sharper than anything she had ever known. Her hands moved with barely any effort on her part. She was painting, painting, painting. In the past she'd always fought to follow the admonition to look more at the subject than at the canvas; now she could not have looked at her own work had she wanted to. Marina was everything she could see or think of. Marina was everything she was, everything she could ever want to be.

Even when she blacked out, she felt the waves on her skin—not quite real but still heavy and wet, pulsing with a call for her to run down to the beach again and rejoin the ocean.

* * *

She woke up an hour before Vulpa got back, but in that hour, she hardly moved.

Vulpa gaped just as hard at the painting as her. "What—when... I didn't even know you had paint with you."

She didn't.

"I looked around. I think I was using the water you left beside my bed. And one of your makeup brushes." Beatriz looked up guiltily. "I'm sorry I ruined the sheet."

"Ruined." Vulpa let out a choked little laugh. "...I'm not sure that's the word for it."

Painting in water with a makeup brush on a sheet laid out on a bed, Beatriz had created the most beautiful painting she had either painted herself or set eyes on. It was primarily blue, but there were shades of yellow and green here and there, even specks of coral red. At first glance one could see no pattern in it aside from waves, but if you looked a little longer, you could grasp the outline of a woman. And if you looked a little longer, or a little closer, you might notice that the waves were not quite holding still on the paper, but rippled slightly as if moved by a current.

The paint was dry. Far drier than oil paint would have been after only an hour. But then, it had been painted in bare water, after all.

When Beatriz thought too hard about it, she found it hard to breathe. Felt like just a tool in Marina's hands, a helpless puppet...

But she had painted this. If she focused her memory, she could remember the individual strokes, though she'd barely been able to see or understand what she was doing. The masterpiece was Marina's; it was also hers.

"I must return to the capital," she said distantly. "This will be my entry in the king's contest."

It was not at all what one was intended to paint for such an assignment. It was no traditional depiction of the goddess, after all. But the king knew Marina and loved her. He would surely see her working here. Beatriz would win, not for her own glory or by her own efforts, not for Ricardo's sake or Juan's pleas, but for Marina and by her will. What would follow, Beatriz was not sure she wanted to think about.

Just painting, she told herself. *She must want you to paint the temple vault, though who knows why. Just painting. It was fine this time.*

Vulpa's eyes left the painting and settled on Beatriz's face. "Will you leave soon, then?"

"I should. I could stay one or two more days, maybe. But I think it's my time to return."

"When you go," Vulpa said carefully, "I would like to go with you."

"To the capital?"

"Yes. I've been thinking of going there for some time. They say there are some excellent bars and taverns there with amazing dancers. I could learn a lot. Who knows, I could even become famous." She smiled, flirtatious, joking, nervous.

"I'm sure you'd do well," Beatriz said, "but what about your work here?"

"What work? Every month I've danced less and less. All I do lately is private dances for Jorge. That's not business."

"What about Jorge, then?"

Vulpa's smile widened, tightened. "What *about* Jorge?"

Well, if that was how she felt, Beatriz certainly wouldn't push it. She'd felt Jorge didn't have the proper respect for Vulpa for some time.

"If you want to come to the capital, you are certainly welcome to come with me. I can recommend a good inn for you to stay at, and maybe introduce you to some people. I know a few entertainers. None quite like you, of course." She smiled. "No one is quite like you, Vulpa."

"So you've said before."

"I mean it. In all the world, there is no one. I'm sure you'll do well in the capital."

They began to talk about practicalities, traveling plans and the like. As they spoke, Beatriz slowly rolled up the sheet on which she'd done the painting. When the painting was fully hidden, she felt a bit steadier, though of course it still preyed on her mind, impossible to forget.

15

CHAPTER FIFTEEN

His still life complete, Ricardo set to work sketching what he remembered of the cliffside view. He hadn't actually had a chance to sketch while there, despite Leonor's promise to allow him the chance—an insincere promise, he now thought drily, as she'd spent the whole time talking to him and must have planned to do so all along. It was a strange thing to bother him, that small deception, but it did.

Painting from memory was not his favorite thing to do, but with a landscape it was more achievable than with a portrait. And he had more practice with it than a stickler for verisimilitude like Beatriz. So he could do a decent job of it. The grass and barren rocks of the clearing. The sweeping view below, trees and mountain in the distance. He could draw all of these things, but when he tried to draw the logs on which he and Leonor had sat, add them into the scene as he remembered them, he had a hard time leaving out Leonor's long, hard body, the expansive skirt she wore even on a difficult ride, the hair which she'd had tightly braided back so it wouldn't whip around in the wind. Leonor had expressly told him not to draw or paint her portrait, besides which this was a landscape, meant to be focused on a place and not a person. So he could hardly draw her in, but without her, the landscape felt off, askew. Leonor was the landscape; the landscape was Leonor.

Leonor was avoiding him again. Maybe Ricardo was learning something about her patterns: She would approach and then retreat, approach and then retreat. Each time she approached she would get a little bit closer, bare herself a little bit further. And then she would retreat. It was exhausting, this kind of courting dance with a woman he had no intention of courting or being courted by. Yet it enthralled him as perhaps it was meant to. It had been several days since he'd gone up the mountain with Leonor, several days since she'd cried in his arms after telling him wild stories of regicide and forced marriage, and he wanted to see her face again. He wanted to see if it would be hard and cold or if it would be crinkled and broken as it had been on the mountain. To see either version of her would hurt in its own way. Yet he longed to see her, if only to satisfy a restless, burning curiosity. Countess Leonor de Suelta, eccentric recluse, callous captor, remnant of a bitter child. He wanted to understand her.

When she came to see him at last, she was neither guarded nor as broken down as she had been when he saw her last. She looked worn, and he couldn't tell if it was seeing him that made her that way or if she'd simply spent a long day hearing petitions. For apparently that had been her day's business, hearing petitions—she told him this with a sigh, as if he should know how it was, as if they were long in the habit of gossiping about their daily work. And what had he been doing?

In answer, he showed her his sketch of the view from the cliff.

"Will you paint it?" she asked.

"I don't know. Maybe." *If I have the time*, he wanted to say, *before I manage to get out of here*, but it felt like saying that would be pushing his luck.

"I've looked at that view many times," she said. "Thinking of my mother. Of her, and my father, and Alejandro. It's a view with some significance to me." She paused. "You capture it well."

"I'd capture it better if I visited it again, perhaps. I had no chance to make any studies when I was there."

"There are some flaws I can see, as to accuracy, but you capture the feeling of it well. The space."

What feeling could there be in just a preliminary sketch? Ricardo hadn't been particularly trying to put any into the work at this stage. But of course Leonor would project onto any depiction of a place that held such meaning to her. He said, "I'm flattered you think so, madonna."

Leonor gave him a searching look. "You're back on your manners today, Ricardo."

"As I should be."

"Have you forgiven me?"

Ricardo swallowed. "Forgiven you for what?"

Leonor raised her eyebrows. "Montero."

"I've said before that such a lowly one as myself could never dare to hold a grudge against such a noble woman. What do you imagine to have offended me? Your lack of decorum the other day? Your lack of decorum at the festival? Or is it having brought me here in the first place—you want me to forgive you for that?"

"Any of those things, I suppose," Leonor said.

Ricardo shrugged. "Your decorum, or lack thereof, can hardly offend this coarse commoner."

Leonor tilted her head. "You still hate me."

She sounded surprised.

"I've explained already I do not."

"Sweet liar, Montero. It's no wonder all the women at court

adore you," Leonor said. "You could convince me too, with more effort. I thought, on the mountain, that you had forgiven me. I told you my story, like you asked. I explained myself. What more do you want?"

"I want my liberty."

Leonor flung out her hands impatiently. "I was looking for a real answer, Montero."

"I have no other answer for you, madonna. And it seems strange to me you should care about my opinion. I'm only a toy of Alejandro's, after all, that you stole to spite him. Why do you care about me at all? If anything, you should hate me."

"Don't be silly. I don't see you as Alejandro's, you know. Not really."

Ricardo took a deep breath and let it out. This conversation twisted here and there, and it seemed there was no way to get Leonor to listen to him or to make any sense. "If I'm not Alejandro's toy to you, then why did you steal me? Why keep me here? Madonna..." She was driving him crazy, but it wouldn't be diplomatic to say that.

Leonor looked away. She glanced at the sketch, which was lying on a table, then out the window. "Perhaps I haven't been fully honest with you."

"No?"

"It is humiliating. I can hardly be honest with myself." She bit her lip. "It's true I stole you out of spite, out of vengeance. I get angry that Alejandro has so many, many pretty things. He only has them because he stole the throne from my father first. Everything he has should rightfully be mine."

"Including me?"

"You—yes, especially you! Montero, when I first saw your art, your talent impressed me. Then I saw your self portrait, and I met you. You were handsome in your portrait, and more beautiful in person. Younger, more full of life. Why should you be his toady?

Why love him? Why should someone like you be his and not mine? It doesn't—it's not fair. I know it sounds childish to say that, but it's not. He's a murderer. Why should you be his?"

"I'm not..."

"The truth, though—yes, Montero, I'll tell you the full truth, like you've asked of me, I'll tell you—truthfully, I would have wanted you anyway, no matter whose you were. Even if you were no one's, even if you weren't even a talented artist. I would have wanted you no matter what. And that is why your opinion matters to me, and that is why, regardless, I can't let you go. I can't, Ricardo. Do you understand?"

She turned now to look at him, eyes blazing. Ricardo stepped back, instinctively. He'd riled her, not entirely on purpose but not entirely by accident either, having forgotten how much she sometimes frightened him.

"I understand," he said, because he did. How could he not, when she put it that frankly? Love, or lust, or some kind of unruly passion, flared out of her like a sacrificial flame. Any artist understood what passion was. Himself, he'd never felt desire with the sort of heat she described, but he understood the theory of it, had depicted it in his own art and seen it in the art of others. He understood it. "But I can't accept that, madonna."

Her jaw clenched. *A painting of anger, the vice*, he thought—just a private joke in his own head, not suitable for present or perhaps any company. "You will have to," she said.

"I am not yours. Even the king, I only belonged to as a contracted painter. You should not hold me captive, madonna. It won't satisfy you or endear you to me. I can't hold a grudge," he said, "against a noblewoman like yourself, but I could never dare to return your love either, madonna. It is futile to hope I might."

"Oh, I think you're daring enough," Leonor said bitterly. "You don't mind breaking my heart—humbly, diplomatically. Do the women at court who adore you know what a little bastard you are?"

She gave his sketch of the cliff view another long look.

Ricardo said, quietly, "I cannot return your feelings, nor can I release a grudge I cannot hold. But I don't hate you either. I haven't meant to break your heart. From what you told me the other day, you've lived a hard life. I feel sorry for you."

"Don't pity me," Leonor said. "It's what I meant, when I told you everything. But I shouldn't have done that. It was a waste of breath, and of both our time."

It had certainly been a waste of Ricardo's time, being dragged up a mountain ostensibly for art's sake and then not having a single moment to set pen to paper. Leonor, of course, meant something far harsher than his own stupid annoyance. But small grudges were stubborn, even against a woman so far above him he could not dare to touch her, against a woman who really could do anything with him she liked. Small annoyances persevered, regardless of the circumstances.

His small grudge, perhaps, had more strength than his greater grudge against Leonor for kidnapping him—more strength even than his loyalty to Alejandro against a treason-talking wretch—for both wavered when Leonor took one last look at him before departing. But when she was gone, these too settled into their old familiar places in his heart, and so his will remained immutable. If he had no power here in Mestos, his mind at least he still could rule.

16

CHAPTER SIXTEEN

Beatriz de Comete's return to the capital was not one that caused a huge splash immediately. After all, she was not the most loved or the most infamous member of Ferrar society, either among the noble class or among the artisans. Instead, her arrival had an impact in small pockets, with ripples that slowly went out here and there, accumulating force like rain sluicing down street gutters might gather water along the way.

* * *

Beatriz arrived at the Comete house in town at around midday, and Lady Gelvira was out visiting a friend, while Don Fernando was at the palace on business, meeting with a minister. So Luis was the only one home. He was sitting in the parlor in a chair that faced the window. Beatriz, smiling at the sight, walked in quietly and then loudly said, "I'm home."

Luis gave a start. He sprang up and gave her a good look over. "Beatriz! So you are. Home, I mean."

She was wearing none of the clothes she'd taken with her—no

outfit he'd ever seen her in, in fact, but a worn brown sleeveless dress over a cream-colored shirt. It was the type of outfit she might have worn to paint in, but there was no paint on it. Plain clothing with no paint stains on it was an incongruous look on her, and it was not all that concerned him. She looked as if she'd lost some weight out in Mestos, and there were shadows under her eyes that were not quite dark circles.

There was also another woman standing next to her, a red-haired woman who stood with her hands clasped behind her back and her feet pointed in, waiting to be acknowledged. But Luis couldn't be bothered with outsiders for the moment. He spread his arms and said, "Give me a hug."

Beatriz smiled and did so. She really had grown thinner, he thought as he gave her a squeeze, but she was back now, thank the gods, and that was good enough. If her health had been compromised, she would have the rest of the summer to recover. Starting now. "Inez," he called out over her shoulder. "Inez! Will someone fetch Inez? Beatriz is back."

"What do you want Inez for?" Beatriz asked, talking into his chest. "I don't have anything to be put away, you know, except a small bag. I think she brought back all the rest already."

"She did, and the story of you being missing. I almost dredged the sea by Mestos for you, you know. You should have sent us word earlier that you were all right. For that matter, you shouldn't have gone missing in the first place."

"Dredging the sea wouldn't have been a bad idea."

"What's that supposed to mean?"

"Oh, it's a long story."

"Save it, then. Here's what we'll do. Inez is going to look you over, and you're going to take a bath, and change clothes, and have something to eat and drink, and then you'll come back down here and tell me everything."

Beatriz laughed tiredly. "Luis, Luis, you're still a worrier. Slow down. Here, let me introduce you to my friend. And am I allowed to sit, or is even a moment's delay too much a deviance from your orders?"

Luis held Beatriz at an arm's length. "Sit down, of course. Oh, but not on Mother's white couch. Here, you can take my seat."

Lady Gelvira had heavily objected in the past when Beatriz sat on the same white couch and got it smeared with green and yellow paint. Right now Beatriz was cleaner than she often was straight out of the studio, but she was still dirty from the road, and Lady Gelvira was already annoyed by the tone of Beatriz's letter which had arrived a few days ago. It had said she was well and not to worry, but not included any details about where she was or why she had vanished. She was bound to have words with Beatriz sooner or later—probably today, probably as soon as she got back from her friend's house and found Beatriz had returned—and a dirty chair would only give her another remark to make about Beatriz's lack of responsibility.

Beatriz, still laughing, sat on the seat Luis had been sitting in instead, which was upholstered in sturdy brown leather that didn't show stains as easily. "That's better. Much better. If you knew the trip I had to get here, Luis, you'd know better than to hurry me. Here, Vulpa, come in. No need to hover. You can sit too—better stay off the couch, though, Luis is right. Luis, this is Vulpa. She's a dancer and something of an herbalist. I met her in Mestos, and now she's come to the city to seek her fortune. I thought she could stay with us until she finds work or a better place to stay; she was kind enough to host me for a while back in Mestos. Vulpa, this is Luis. He's the son of Don Fernando de Comete, and I consider him my younger brother."

The red-haired woman entered the room as Beatriz had bid her, and dropped Luis a courtesy. She didn't sit down, though, despite

Beatriz's urging. Standing, she was as tall as Luis. A friend—Luis had an idea of what that meant. He had the impulse to roll his eyes, but at the same time felt a little relieved. Had his sister's vanishing been caused only by one of her typical flirtations? His mother would give her a solid tongue lashing if that was the case, and his father would sigh, and he himself would be a little disgusted at Beatriz's thoughtlessness, but... better than some other possibilities.

Lady Anthona, when Luis stormed down to her manor in Mestos and interrogated her, had been disconcertingly vague. Beatriz had decided to leave. That was all she would say. They hadn't fought—no, she'd just thought it would be better if she left. She had been acting strangely. Mostly just focusing on her painting, not coming out of her studio very often. Not that unusual, probably, for an artist. And they'd decided it would be better—no, Beatriz herself had decided to leave. She couldn't say why she'd decided to leave that very night, taking nothing with her and heading off in directions unknown. She was very sorry, but there was nothing more she could say on the matter.

Her fists had been tightly clenched at her sides, and her face had been pale. Not in anger, in fear, and not because she was afraid of Luis, or she would surely not have been so steadfast in giving answers Luis was sure were lies. For Beatriz would never disappear without good cause. She could be capricious, but she was, at the end of the day, still mostly reliable.

He was angry then, speaking to Anthona, who refused to give him satisfactory answers. But he could admit, in private, that he would prefer to believe Beatriz unreliable than believe she had fallen into danger.

This Vulpa would have been an acceptable, harmless sort of danger. Luis said, "Welcome to Ferrar. I'm pleased to meet any friend of Beatriz's."

"I'm pleased to meet you as well, sir. Thank you."

"You'll have to see her dance," Beatriz said eagerly. "Luis, you'll love it. But she should have something to eat first."

"Then you should eat too, and clean yourself."

"Ah, we're back to that again." Beatriz abruptly stood. "All right, very well. I'll make myself presentable, and you get me and Vulpa some lunch. It better have some meat in it, understand? Walking wearies the bones. Give Vulpa proper sustenance. Oh, and Inez—" For Inez had arrived by now, and was hovering bright-eyed at the door. "—see that a bath is drawn for Vulpa, too. As for clothes, she's brought plenty of her own, so don't worry about that, but we both should freshen up. And tell Dina to prepare a guest room. She'll be staying at least a few days, maybe longer. I'll have to speak to Don Fernando about it."

Inez nodded, and Luis began to tell Beatriz that she didn't have to hurry, really, if she didn't want to, but she cut him off with a pat to his shoulder before walking decisively out the door. Vulpa gave Luis a curtsey that was barely more than a nod before following her.

Well, Beatriz was still Beatriz, no matter what trouble she'd gotten herself into out in Mestos.

By the time she was cleaned and changed and Vulpa was as well, not only was a sumptuous meal set out for them, but Don Fernando and Lady Gelvira had returned, and while they'd already eaten, they sat down at the table to watch Beatriz eat with the clear intention of questioning her.

Luis expected his mother to begin with some incisive criticism, but she instead asked Beatriz, "Did Lady Anthona do anything offensive?"

"No, milady."

"And Jorge? Did he?"

"No, he was fine. Kind."

"I've heard more and more about him over the past month. Perhaps I hadn't listened before, but there are rumors enough. If he made any advances on you that you found unwelcome, there are measures that can be taken," Lady Gelvira said. Voice calm and firm.

"Really he was fine. He hadn't the slightest interest in me, honestly—he was preoccupied with someone else. In fact, he avoided my company."

"Well, that's rude of him," Luis's father said. "If we'd known you'd be treated that way, I would have advised you not to go."

"Oh, don't be ridiculous. You know I didn't go down to Mestos to hunt a husband. I went there to paint."

"True," Luis said. He leaned back in his chair. Nothing Beatriz had said so far had explained her brief disappearance or the sickly look she had about her, which was what he was really worried about, but he'd let her get around to it slowly. "How did the painting go?"

Beatriz made as if to speak, then stopped. She bit her lip. And then she was laughing—just a chuckle at first, but it built into laughter that shook her body, nigh unto full blown hysteria. Seeing the murderously concerned look on Luis's face and the milder concern on those of his parents, she made a clear effort to stop, but the laughter just kept on going.

Don Fernando went over and rubbed Beatriz's shoulders. "There, girl. Take it easy now, all right? What's so funny, hm?

Beatriz clutched at her stomach and slowly steadied her breathing. "Ha—aaah. Yes. It's fine, really. I'm fine, don't worry about it. I just... I'm not sure whether to say my efforts at painting were a disaster or a wild success. Really there was a little bit of both—you can't imagine how many times I tried to sketch Vulpa, I really thought I had something there. Thought she might model for it." Another giggle bubbled up. Vulpa shifted uncomfortably as Luis glanced over at her. No, she looked like no Marina he would imagine. But was it really that funny?

Beatriz said, "Vulpa of all people really isn't like Marina at all, in retrospect. But I really thought... it's no wonder Marina stabbed me in the hand for that."

"Stabbed you in the hand?" Luis was out of his chair in a blink, but his father had already pulled Beatriz's hand out and was frowning at her palm. There was a line on it, a strange scar. It was hard to tell whether it was healed well or poorly; it was no color Luis had ever seen on an injury, not red or purple or brown, but an uncanny shade of light blue.

"...were you painting today?" his father asked. "You should be careful not to get paint in a wound. It will get infected for sure."

"No," Beatriz said. She sighed. At least her hysteria seemed to have subsided. "It's not paint. I've been... blessed I suppose is the word for it."

"Blessed?"

She settled back in her seat. "I've been wondering how much to tell you all about it. It seemed very private to me in the beginning. But Marina has no intention of my keeping it all a secret, so I suppose I won't. And to my family, at least, I should tell all of it." She took a deep breath. "We may as well start with my hand. That was the first sure sign I noted too."

* * *

Vulpa mostly liked the Comete household.

She'd felt skeptical when Beatriz said she might stay with them in the capital, and only reluctantly been coaxed into staying for a couple days before finding a suitable room at some inn or boarding house for herself. In her experience, nobles were mostly obnoxious. They came in varying shades, of course: Self important and dull, narcissistically perverted, self righteously disgusted, and occasionally even slick and pleasant but eventually tiresome. Jorge had been sometimes outright decent, but he'd been something of an exception. To no other nobleman would she have devoted more than a year of her life as she had to Jorge, not for any amount of money. It simply wouldn't have been worth the time and effort.

Beatriz was different, though.

Not that she wasn't self centered and cocky. Not that she wasn't a little bit perverted, even—she'd done nothing too forward, but Vulpa got flashes of interest from her, sometimes a look in her eyes, sometimes a spare comment, and sometimes just her receptivity to any form of companionship or entertainment Vulpa was willing to offer. But she had a passion for art that was bigger than herself, so much bigger that it dwarfed that cockiness that might otherwise have been annoying, so big that it could even draw Vulpa in, though she'd never had much interest in painting or sketching or indeed any form of non-performative art until now. And she could be humble, too, and compassionate, and her interest in Vulpa was as much genuine curiosity and gratitude as it was lust. Vulpa liked her for all these reasons.

That didn't mean she expected to like Beatriz's family. She'd liked Jorge well enough, after all, and his family, his household in general, had been utterly insufferable. Nobles were mostly awful, with only the rare standout exception.

The Comete family wasn't awful, though. Vulpa didn't think much of Don Fernando or Lady de Comete, the one being reticent, the other stern enough to remind Vulpa of her own mother and not in a good way, and neither of them being very interested in what exotic dancer Beatriz might have brought home with her. But disinterest was probably the best she could have hoped for from them given the circumstances—there were no accusations of Vulpa corrupting their ward and ruining her reputation, and no one named a date Vulpa would have to leave—indeed, they politely noted that they hoped she would enjoy their hospitality and find Ferrar as a city welcoming in general.

Luis was more personable and more intimidating at the same

time. He made a point of speaking to her for at least a few minutes whenever their paths crossed, and told her he would like to see her dance sometime, and that he appreciated her having taken care of Beatriz in Mestos. He also promised to introduce her to a few local innkeepers and bar owners who were looking to hire dancers, or to the managers of some local dancing troops if that was more what she'd prefer. Vulpa told him she wanted to have a look around the city and see what types of opportunities there were first: the best venues, the most bustling businesses. But it was a kind offer.

However, he also insisted on interrogating her about her past—how presumptuous!—and on how serious she was about her profession, and on her views on friendship, love, family, and a variety of other areas. And he made several pointed comments on how Beatriz seemed very fond of her, and he hoped their friendship would continue, but life could be precarious and he hoped she understood that Beatriz's generous nature did not mean she could be taken advantage of. How Vulpa would even attempt such a thing, she wasn't sure, apart from perhaps remaining at the Comete manor indefinitely, which she had no intention of doing, and which didn't actually seem to be his meaning given he'd made no suggestion that she leave anytime soon.

Then there were the Comete servants, who were very friendly and kind and also made Vulpa very uncomfortable. The servants in Mestos, when they'd run into her, had often given her arch looks and muttered things behind her back, but they'd never outright confronted her about being Jorge's mistress. The Comete servants, in contrast, meant no ill but had many many questions.

"So," a young housemaid asked her, after courteously changing her sheets and asking her whether she'd be wanting anything brought up to her in the mornings, breakfast in bed or a bowl of water for her face or any other amenities, "how far have you gone with Miss Beatriz?"

Vulpa was taken aback. "Ah," she said, hoping to dodge the issue, "we walked most of the way from Mestos, since we didn't have a horse and it would have been troublesome to hire one. She's very energetic."

The housemaid grinned. "Oh, yes. Miss Beatriz has a lot of energy on projects that interest her. But we all want to know, has she taken you to bed yet? Or maybe you've just kissed and done a little petting. Sometimes she goes slow like that."

"I think you've misunderstood," Vulpa said, trying to sound severe and forbidding like Lady Anthona might have at such an implication. "Beatriz and I are friends. She tried to paint me, and I took care of her when she was sick, but that's all."

The housemaid hummed and said, "Very sorry then, miss. Didn't mean to offend you. I'm sure it's none of my business."

She didn't seem convinced, though. And while other servants tended to be more discreet in their questioning, they still all made the assumptions. Would Miss Beatriz be staying in her room any nights, asked the housekeeper? Because if so, they would have to bring up some water and a few other things for her in the morning. No, no, Miss Vulpa, she didn't mean any offense, and of course they wouldn't be bringing up this subject with the don or the lady, but if Miss Beatriz would be staying, they hoped she knew there was no need to sneak around and make things more difficult for everyone. This was a small house; no use keeping secrets.

It was enough to make Vulpa wish she had secrets to keep. And wonder if Beatriz really might have an ulterior motive in asking her to stay here, and if so, when she might attempt to bring such intentions into fruition.

Beatriz, however, was... occupied. Or perhaps inaccessible might have been a better word for it. She'd promised Vulpa, as they made their way here from Mestos, that she would give Vulpa a tour of the city, show her all the best spots. But she spent her first day back from Mestos dealing with her family, the second day mostly in bed, and the third day visiting friends Vulpa didn't know. (She invited Vulpa along with her on these visits, but as they were largely artisans and of a circle Vulpa had no cause to mingle with, Vulpa politely declined.) After that, she shut herself up in her studio for the next couple of days. When Vulpa entered, she would find Beatriz staring off into space or sketching in charcoal on a paper already covered in thick, senseless lines. She would ask Beatriz to come for a walk with her—she'd already been around the city a bit on her own, but was still hoping for the tour—but Beatriz would say, "I'm afraid I can't today, Vulpa. Soon, perhaps. Today I can't."

Vulpa wanted to blame her, to say that Beatriz just didn't want to be around her. But when she left, if she looked back, she would glimpse Beatriz watching her leave with something like agony in her eyes.

One day she said, "All right, then. I'll stay with you today and watch you sketch." Though clearly her "sketching" was going nowhere.

Beatriz said, "All right."

Her hand stilled on the paper she'd been grinding charcoal dust into to no purpose, and for the two hours that they sat together, she did nothing but stare off into space and sometimes look over at Vulpa and say, "You're still there."

"Yes," Vulpa would say.

"I must be boring you."

"Well, a little. What are you doing?"

"Thinking." (Beatriz would close her eyes.) "Or trying to think, at least." No further elaboration.

The day after that, Vulpa went to Luis and said, "Sir, you had mentioned a while ago there were some people you might introduce me to."

"Oh, yes. There are a few."

"I think it would be good to work at one of the inns in town." There were theaters, too, and performing troops, and even an opera house. But Vulpa had looked into what kinds of performances they put on, and their style of dancing was different from what she preferred. More stiff and formal. Besides which, few of them offered steady work in the capital—many of the troops, for example, toured neighboring cities as well.

Luis raised his eyebrows as she explained her reasoning. "So you mean to obtain a permanent position here? You like our city?"

"I think so."

"Will you be staying with us too?" It was the first time he mentioned her staying here, and he said it with a smile on his face.

Vulpa hated to disappoint him, but, "No, I'll probably move out. Some of these inns offer free board to performers, or take it out of their pay. It's convenient, and I wouldn't be a burden on you any longer."

"It's no trouble to us if you stay. We can well afford a visitor."

"Still."

"Hm. Very well. Beatriz knows your intentions?"

"I'll tell her," Vulpa said, "of course. And I'll still be in the area. I hope we'll still see plenty of each other."

"Good, good. Well, it's probably for the best. Here, I'll give you a list of inns where I have connections, and perhaps you can tell me which of them interest you most."

She ended up taking a position at a place called the Inn of the Rising Moon. The innkeeper was, to Luis's face, very impressed by Luis's recommendation, as he was a generous patron here, but a bit surprised, as he'd never shown much interest in dancers before. "She's a friend of my sister's," Luis explained, and Vulpa immediately wished he hadn't for the knowing look that appeared in the innkeeper's eyes. The next day, when Vulpa showed up for work for the first time, he told her that he was impressed by her connections but that he hoped she would keep in mind that this establishment's clientele was primarily male. Vulpa said she would of course keep that in mind, and that this had been the case in other inns she'd worked at in the past, and it would be no problem, and he nodded with a frown on his face as if not entirely satisfied.

As for Beatriz, she told Vulpa she was very sorry Vulpa was leaving their hospitality so soon, and said she would visit the Inn of the Rising Moon as frequently as she could, and that the door of the Comete house would always be open to Vulpa. But Vulpa thought she seemed relieved by her departure. She gave Vulpa a hug before she left, and it was warm and soft and affectionate and regretful. She smelled less of oil paint lately due to her inaction, but the scent of it still lingered from her time spent in the studio. It was a scent that followed Vulpa down the road to the inn, and for many long nights afterwards, she would imagine she could smell it under the stench of alcohol and sweaty bodies at her work.

* * *

Perhaps the only other person who cared about Beatriz's return, at least at the time she first arrived, was Juan Rojo. He heard about it the day after her arrival, as she sent him a note via a servant.

"Dear Juan Rojo,

"I have returned to the city, so there's no need to send any further missives to Mestos. If you wish to communicate with me, you may send letters to the Comete manor, or you may come and visit yourself. Indeed, you may even summon me to the studio if there is a need, though I warn you that I have been out of sorts and my brother in particular would prefer me not to leave the house for a good while. I have been ill, but I am well enough now, so don't worry yourself about that. I have also finished a painting of Marina, which I will submit for the king's competition in due time. I expect I will win.

"If there has been news of your master, I would greatly like to hear it.

"Best regards,

"Beatriz de Comete."

Juan wrote back requesting Beatriz come visit him if possible. He'd been to the Comete house a couple times in her absence and not been given the warmest reception, and figured it better to keep his distance for a time. But he did want to see her. This painting of Marina—he had to see it. He was relieved, almost jubilant, to hear that Beatriz had managed to finish said painting. All her brief letters to him from Mestos had indicated she was struggling, with the subject but also with various other technical setbacks, ranging from a hand injury to supplies that had turned out to be faulty, especially her medium. He had worried that she would get discouraged and give up on the painting entirely, leaving him to challenge all his master's wicked rivals alone. She had promised she would try her very best to complete a painting of Marina, to compete and win the contest, but people didn't always keep their promises. Montero always said Beatriz was stubborn, but the next descriptor he would use for her was "willful"—and "willful" did not always mean "unchanging." It more meant that Beatriz could be intractable, and Juan had worried that if Beatriz were to drop the project, there would be nothing Juan could do to persuade her to pick it back up.

But she had finished a painting. That was good, very good. Of course, her confidence that she would win, stated so bluntly, did make Juan shake his head a little. He believed in Beatriz's abilities, and he did think she could beat out Montero's rivals more aptly than Juan himself or many another artist, but... no matter an artist's talent, winning was never a certainty. Especially when Beatriz's style was so, well, unique; genius, but not exactly to the tastes of a traditionalist king. Of course there was a possibility Beatriz had considered the king's preferences and tempered her usual style, but Juan couldn't quite trust she'd had the sense for that. Beatriz loved dark and dull colors, and, too, her devotion to realism often led her to harsh, unflattering portraits, or obscene nudity, angering artists, nobles, even models. It had driven Montero to cursing and drunkenness more than once, that and her blunt personality. Juan had wondered sometimes if Montero might be half in love with her, one reason he thought Beatriz the best candidate to avenge his master's honor—but he had to admit he was not sure of this theory, and if it were true he still hoped nothing would come of it. Beatriz was half-noble and a bit of a menace; surely not the right woman for his master.

Though, at this point, Montero could marry Beatriz with Juan's blessing, as long as he returned whole and hale.

None of this did Juan speak to Beatriz when she did come to visit him, except his concern that the style of her painting might not suit the king, which he considered to be practical and to the point. "For the king requested a traditional portrayal," he said, "though of course, we do need a painting that utilizes all your skill and your best inspiration. Still, I would like to see what you have. My master is the king's painter, his favorite. I can tell you whether what you have made would please the king or no at least as well as any other painter in Salandra, bar my master himself."

Beatriz gave him a look that was tired and amused and resigned. "I don't object to your looking. The painting will not be edited, however, no matter what you have to say. Not unless the goddess wills it."

It was another piece of ridiculousness, Juan thought, if not of Beatriz's usual type. Nevertheless he was happy he would at least be allowed a look at the painting, and so he made no retort. She took the painting out of her bag. She'd rolled it up and put it in a tube for travel, and when he drew it out, still rolled up, he saw she hadn't painted on proper canvas but on linen. He glanced at her questioningly, but she only gestured for him to unroll it and take a look.

The first thing that struck him about the painting was the sheer amount of color. Beatriz, a Comete whose father was willing to spoil her in her little hobbies, still rarely used too much blue pigment, perhaps wary less of monetary extravagance than of extravagance in expression, but here blue and green overwhelmed the eye. It was only when he had recovered from this first shock that he saw how the picture seemed to swim before him, how the style was in many ways so unlike Beatriz's usual—though there were still those crisp lines on little bits of rock and coral, except that he would look away from them for a minute and look back and they were not quite the same—

And the woman barely there at all, yet dominating once you saw her, commanding and cool.

"Miss Comete," he said, "what... what is this? This is not your work."

Beatriz's voice was the same as the look in her eyes, amused and tired. "I painted what I saw, the same as I always do. And what I saw was..." She trailed off and merely pointed at the painting.

Juan couldn't have said he left the Comete manor that day feeling more assured. *She will win*, he thought on the street as he walked away, *for the king cannot deny there is something unnatural about that painting. As he loves Marina, he cannot help but choose her*. But it was not a steadying thought. He'd wanted Beatriz to win for his master's sake, to beat out those bastard vultures who thought they could become the top artist in the capital while Montero was gone. Beatriz, his master's true rival, should have taught them their place by pure skill and superiority. This, whatever it was, was not that. This was something beyond him.

He wondered vaguely whether he should bother to present his own painting to the king as he'd planned. No, he could not withdraw—the king would see him and remember Montero, and that was important, that the king not forget Montero exist while he was gone. And Montero would want him to fight on his behalf. But if there had been the slightest chance of Juan winning, he knew well now that it had vanished. Beatriz had stolen it. Marina had stolen it.

He went home and did some more work on it regardless. Life went on, heedless of miracle or disaster. However the gods moved, there was still work to be done. Montero would want to see Juan had not been idle on his return.

* * *

The day arrived at last that the king allowed painters to enter the palace and show him their work that he might pick one of them to paint the temple vault. He sent out a letter to the same list of painters that had been informed of the challenge in the first place. Beatriz was informed of the date by Juan once again, and thankfully was allowed into the palace with all the others despite not having been on the list. It was not an invitation, merely an announcement; the king was open to any talent willing to take up the task. And after all, the palace staff knew Beatriz a little from her association with Ricardo. They had mixed opinions on her—some of the maids delighted in the genius of a woman while others thought her too stuck up and outspoken, and the butlers in particular had a good deal to say about her and Ricardo's relationship—but they still could acknowledge that she was, if not quite a noble and not quite a true artisan either, enough of each to warrant a certain level of respect.

So it was that Beatriz was one of the artists who were admitted to the king's parlor, where he waited a good hour to see who would arrive. There were four others. Juan, of course, and three older men, each of whom had a formidable reputation. Valdez, subject of Juan's hate, was there as he might have expected. The other two were named Ramos and Mendoza. Their names, and indeed their presence, would not matter in the end, but as they waited with their paintings in hand, they were all flush with a sense of importance at having been written to and summoned by the king himself, and drunk on the possibility that they might soon be assigned such an important commission as the ceiling of Marina's temple—that they might soon usurp the seat of the king's favorite artist, a seat, in their opinion, that Ricardo Montero had occupied for far too long.

King Alejandro waited until an hour before noon, to see if any more artists would show up. In the meantime he provided his guests with some light food and a little wine, and asked each questions about their recent work. He always did try to come across as a great patron of the arts, even though he was a bit fixated on Montero. At last he said, "Well, I suppose you are all who have answered my challenge. I thought there might be more of you, but no matter. Marina will pick who she picks; we are but her tools. And I have no doubt that the one she has picked will be among you, so we will wait no longer."

He turned first to Juan. "Rojo, you are my dear Montero's apprentice. He would have been the one to undertake this work, had circumstances not conspired against him as they did."

"Yes, your majesty," Juan said, keeping his eyes on the floor. "It is regrettable. My master would have been pleased to serve you in such an important task."

"He is one of my best servants. But perhaps not a good servant for Marina. I know he has little belief in the gods, though he has been known to paint them on occasion."

"He believes," Juan said, "it is only that... well, the opportunity has not arisen for him to do much religious work, and I know his reputation is more..."

"No matter, no matter," the king said complacently. "Even now, if he were to return with a painting today and compete, I'd wager he'd do exceedingly well. But no matter. Let me see what work you have brought here, since your master is absent. I know he's been at great pains to teach you all his craft."

Juan bowed. Hesitantly, he unwrapped his painting. The canvas was still on its frame, and he'd covered it in paper to bring it here. In it, Marina was depicted as a brunette woman, a classic beauty, sitting on a windowsill with a view of the sea out the window. Montero might have praised him for exploring background and foreground, developing two different spaces that depicted Marina in different ways. The king, however, was perfunctory. Marina was lovely, he said, and so was the sea. But there was still a critical look in his eye, and Juan knew that only courtesy—and respect for Juan's missing mentor—prevented him from saying the truth: that the woman looked like any other lovely woman, nothing divine about her, and that the sea, painted without a reference, was rote in execution, and the painting overall was the work of an apprentice, nothing more.

Then the king turned to Beatriz.

Perhaps his reasoning was thus: Neither Juan nor Beatriz had much of a reputation, but both were close to the missing Montero. So he'd show them some respect and look at their paintings first, but really he would see their work first in order to get it over and done with so he could look at the work of the remaining artists more seriously and make his choice between the three established masters.

If that was his intention—and indeed it seemed to be the expectation of the three masters present, at least—it was overturned as soon as Beatriz unwrapped her painting.

Blue and green and gold and little specks of red floated on the sheet. It was as she had painted it, yet it moved, and today, in the sight of King Alejandro de Ferrar, Marina's most ardent worshipper, the paint itself shone. Blue light emanated from the water in the painting, touching Alejandro's face like a caress. The king closed his eyes, then opened them again. Unable to help himself, he touched the painting. Beatriz noted that he touched it right next to the woman's face, unwilling to touch Marina herself but with a look of longing in his eyes the like of which Beatriz had never seen.

"Marina," he said. "Marina."

His voice was soft and hoarse.

And Beatriz could feel in herself a feeling rising up to answer him. She heard her own voice say, "You are greatly favored, Alejandro. You are loved."

His eyes shifted from the painting to Beatriz's face, then to the painting again, then back to Beatriz. Beatriz swallowed down the urge to say more—perhaps to cry. When the feeling of Marina's hand on her had subsided, she said, "Marina inspired me to paint this for you. She would like for me to paint her temple, as well."

Alejandro, king of Salandra, bowed to her. "So may it be, then. What a beautiful sign she has sent to me. Of course I will follow her will."

He looked at the other paintings before the three masters departed. Two of them he even bought. Of course there was no question of their getting the commission to paint the temple; that was understood.

Rumors spread across the city like wildfire: that Beatriz de Comete, ward of Don Fernando, half-noble bastard, audacious would-be artist, had either received an inspiration from Marina or pulled some devilish trickery on the king. Which story was believed depended on the credulity of the listener.

17

CHAPTER SEVENTEEN

Ricardo had expected that after their argument, Leonor would be keeping her distance again for a while, but instead she returned to her habit of sitting with him and watching him work. Sometimes she would just drop in for a couple minutes in a day. Other times she would spend whole hours watching him while he pretended not to be affected by her scrutiny. Often she would invite him on a walk, or come and join her and Felipe for a quiet dinner. Usually Ricardo refused her. Not always, but usually.

Leonor's moods varied. Some days she was cheerful, even flirtatious. Other days, grimly silent. Other days, prickly and restrained. And on the rare occasion—like today—actively irate.

They'd been exchanging pleasantries about the weather, which was still hot and miserable, when she abruptly said, "Why do you have so much faith in Alejandro?"

Ricardo blinked. "Pardon?"

"You still believe in him. I can tell. No matter what I say to you,

you still believe our gracious king is a gods-blessed hero, kind and good and perfect. Why?"

"It is surely not for me to judge whether a king is good or bad," Ricardo said.

"You clearly judge him to be good, so don't pretend you're neutral."

"King Alejandro has always been kind to me. He is a benevolent ruler and a strong adherent to his goddess. I understand why you hold your grudge, but myself I find your suspicions hard to believe from what I know of him. He is not a man that would commit murder. I cannot credit that."

"He was a warrior for many years before he became a politician," Leonor said. "I don't know why you find the concept of him as a killer startling when he clearly is one."

"Killing in war is one thing. To murder a family member is another. The former king got sick, madonna. Alejandro tried to get him the best care and failed. I'm sure it weighs on him that your father died, but that doesn't mean he killed him."

"My mother, too," Leonor insisted.

"You said when you first told me the story that even you weren't sure how your mother died. That it might have been an accident."

Since then she'd brought up her accusations a few more times, but never quite as aggressively as now, and she had yet to change her story or offer any actual evidence of her beliefs.

"What about his wife, then?"

Ricardo frowned. "The late Queen Mencia? She... died of illness as well. King Alejandro cannot be faulted for that."

He swallowed as Leonor gave him a hard look, wondering how much she knew of what went on in the capital. Even the inner circle at the palace did not know, for the most part, the truth of Queen Mencia's death. Leonor was a relative, though, and she seemed to have some sources of information or influence in the palace. But this was one of Alejandro's most closely guarded secrets. Leonor surely couldn't have learned it. It was only by a strange chance that Ricardo knew about it himself.

* * *

When Ricardo had first been given the task of painting the queen, Alejandro had taken him aside for a serious conversation. "Her majesty is a sensitive woman, and lately given to melancholy. That much I'm sure you've heard. No need to be ashamed of it—the court talks, of course, it must talk. That they still talk about Mencia shows a proper concern for and awareness of their queen." A bitter smile flashed across his face. "Oh, never mind all that. I know the truth, I know what they say. But listen: what matters is that Mencia really is sensitive, but she has a good heart. And she is queen of this nation. You must show her proper respect, and be patient if she gets angry or discouraged. I know it may be more difficult than some commissions I've given you, but you'll be well paid, and I assure you, even if she gets angry with you, it won't affect my opinion of you, so there's no need to be afraid of her moods. Only try to see the best in her. She is a good woman, if one is willing to see her in the right light."

Ricardo had said that of course he was excited at the chance to paint the queen and would accept any sort of attention from her as an honor, at which the king had shook his head and chuckled. In fact, Ricardo had approached the task of painting the queen with some trepidation, as the rumors about her were varied and not a one of them flattering.

But Queen Mencia had not turned out to be the sort of monster that many of the rumors had indicated. She did not yell or throw things at him any of the times he visited. Maybe it was because, as her personal servants murmured to him, the queen liked him. She was like Alejandro, if that was the case. Perhaps that was their only similarity.

What was the queen like, as he knew her? Quiet, distant. While he painted her, she was mostly still and silent, which made her a better model than many subjects he'd painted in the past. Sometimes she would try to make conversation for a moment, then lapse silent, and a look of furious embarrassment would fall over her face when he tried to get her talking again.

For Ricardo, the most noticeable sign of her illness—which was more an illness of mind and heart than of the body, though she did suffer from migraines and fatigue—was lethargy. Some days he would come to her wing of the palace and be informed that she hadn't gotten out of bed that day, and though he would sit down in her private parlor and wait while the maids tried to rouse her, he would end up leaving hours later with the queen still firmly ensconced in her bed. Another day she came out to model, but still wearing only her nightgown with a robe over it, hair barely brushed. She sat down on the same chair as usual and said, "You can work on my face, can't you, Montero? I don't have to get all dressed up for you to work on my face."

He'd already painted her face at that point, and had indeed been in the process of working on her clothing, on a grand, green-and-gold gown made of velvet and lace, a gorgeous piece the king had bought for her specifically for this portrait. But how could he say that to a queen who'd already forced herself out of bed for his sake? He told her yes, it was fine if she sat like this. For an hour he worked on the background while she stared off into space, until she got up and walked off, saying she was hungry.

"I shouldn't have bothered her," he said to one of the maids (one of the older ones, by the name of Ximena). "Perhaps in the future you shouldn't get her up if she's not in the mood..."

"No," Ximena said. "Keep coming according to the schedule, and we'll do our best to make sure she's available as well."

"My convenience is far less important than her majesty's."

"She was looking forward to this yesterday," Ximena said. "It put her in a good mood. If she's down today, she'd have been worse if you hadn't come. Only imagine how disappointing that would have been to her. No, Montero, you must keep coming, and never mind if she doesn't talk to you. She doesn't talk much at all, anyhow. But she's excited about this painting. And she doesn't get many visitors."

Ricardo agreed to continue as he'd done so far, figuring Ximena knew more about the queen's moods than he did. He doubted that the queen truly was excited about the painting, though. There was a reason he'd dared to fool her that day and only work on the background despite her modeling. She never walked over to look at the painting, even when he offered, never even asked how it was progressing or how close he was to done. How could it interest her in the slightest?

When he thought the painting was finished, with nothing left to add but the varnish, he at last suggested the queen take a look at it. Mencia slowly walked around the canvas to get an eyeful of the painting of herself. She didn't quite frown, but she bit her lip. Pale-faced, she turned to Ricardo. "Is that really what I look like? To you?"

Ricardo had painted a queen in full glory. The green and gold dress billowed and shone, but its shine was outdone by the gentle smile on Mencia's face in the portrait, and a certain ethereal glow in her eyes. (Ricardo had always been proud of how he painted eyes. Everyone seemed to like them, said his paintings came alive.)

"Yes, your majesty," Ricardo lied. In fact, Mencia rarely smiled for more than a moment, and when she did, the smile often was wan or, at best, surprised out of her by a moment of humor. But he thought that the painting sessions he'd had with her had been peaceful—he thought she had been patient and kind with him for the most part —and the painting had reflected that part of her personality, of his experience of her, if not her literal physical affect.

Mencia shook her head. "I don't look like that."

"Then I apologize for having failed to capture your majesty's grace and beauty."

"Montero! Certainly if you failed, it was not in that area. This—I look like some forest nymph, or an exotic bird. Not that it's ridiculous, but… I own a mirror. I know I've wasted away in here, and half the time I was posing for you I probably looked half-dead."

"Perhaps a little bored. But posing for me does bore most people."

"I wasn't bored," Mencia protested. "It wasn't that."

This time, Ricardo was pretty sure she was the one lying.

"Well," he said to smooth things over, "you didn't strike me as very bored either. What do you think, your majesty? If you want me to change the painting, I can change it." He could even paint over her whole face with a new expression, if she wanted to look more solemn. Hell, if he really had to, if she didn't like the brilliancy of the dress, he could get a new canvas, ask her to find something more staid to wear, and they could start the whole process over again. He wouldn't enjoy that, but he'd do it if he had to. The king was paying him a lot of money for this one—not that he'd given Ricardo the money yet, but the amount he'd promised was considerable.

"Don't change it," Mencia said immediately. "It's lovely." She bit her lip again. "Will this hang in the main hall, next to the portrait you did of Alejandro?" She'd seen that one. She'd told Ricardo this when they first met—that Alejandro had insisted she leave her wing of the palace to have a look at his portrait, and she'd thought it very nice. That had been a year ago.

"It's not up to me where it'll be hung, your majesty. But I think that would be a good place for it. Perhaps you could mention it to his majesty the king."

Mencia hummed noncommittally. Maybe she did, maybe she didn't. Ultimately that was where the painting was hung, but it might only have been a coincidence. It was the obvious place, after all.

Ricardo didn't get paid half what Alejandro had promised him, not immediately. He got a little more than a third, and then later another third, and he was promised that the rest of it would come eventually, but when it never did, he wasn't terribly surprised. Royal finances were slippery that way. It wasn't a sign that Alejandro didn't value Ricardo, not exactly, just that he knew that at the end of the day, Ricardo wouldn't get pushy over a small thing like some of his pay going missing—or if he did, he wouldn't be able to muster a small army over the matter like some of the dukes and counts were always threatening to over other types of royal debt. Ricardo understood Alejandro's priorities; they didn't offend him. And the task of painting the queen had not been unpleasant, so he considered the honor of having been allowed to meet with her as so few people did these days as part of his payment.

Mencia invited him back just once after the painting was done. For lunch. It was a quiet affair, with Ricardo doing the talking and Mencia not meeting his eyes more than twice the entire hour he was there. He thought, though, that she might ask him to come again. The prospect made him a little nervous, as it was not wholly proper for a single man, and a commoner at that, to meet with the queen of the nation, alone except for her maids. But it would feel even more formal and intimidating were Alejandro to be there, besides which, Alejandro and Mencia never ate together or did much of anything together, at least as far as Ricardo had gathered from court gossip. This left him on unsure footing: if the queen were to summon him again, was he to go or not? He decided he would have to consult with the king on the matter when it occurred, this being the most certain way of avoiding giving any offense.

The question never came up, though. A month passed, and then another, and Mencia did not summon Ricardo again. Then another month passed, and it was announced to the court that Queen Mencia had passed away—her heart had given out, it was said, after one of her bouts of illness.

The court mourned theatrically, wearing only black and gray for a few weeks. Only a few tasteless nobles failed to cancel parties or events scheduled during this time; it might be noted, however, that these few events were not lacking in attendance. Ricardo was not called in to court at all, and he might never have found out the truth about Mencia's death if he hadn't come down to the palace one day nonetheless, in order to fetch a couple jars of pigment he had left there before the period of mourning had set in.

He was walking down the hall, on the way out of the palace, and avoiding meeting anyone's eyes—the solemnity was stifling, but he was more afraid of how enraged he might feel to see hypocrisy in the mourning, afraid of how he might react—when a voice called out his name, and he turned to see Ximena. She was carrying a large bundle, much larger than the small bag he'd retrieved from his studio. She asked him if he might walk with her, since it seemed they were both heading out of the palace, and it was nice to walk with a friend. He complied because her voice sounded fragile, as if people she could call "friend" were few and far between.

As they walked, she made a few comments on how it was good to see him after such a long time. He said the same, said he regretted the circumstances, wished they could have met at another happy lunch or modeling session instead. She said, vehemently, "If only!"

Outside the palace gate, she plucked at his sleeve. "You must remember her well, Montero," she said. "She liked you a lot. Though I know you're the king's man, you have some softness to you."

"A man with proper respect for the king ought to respect the queen as well," Ricardo said. "There's no contradiction. Though I'll admit I did not only respect Queen Mencia. I had grown fond of her too."

"I know you had, I know you had," Ximena said. "Gods, it's awful. I…" She took in a sniffly breath. "I failed her. It's all my fault. I failed to make her majesty see the beauty of living, or offer her enough comfort to make it worthwhile. I thought, if we brought her enough good food and wine, brought her interesting books and pretty pictures and clothing, and if we cajoled her, sooner or later she'd come around. But it's no use. Life has to have more meaning than that, I suppose. But how could we have given that to her? I don't know."

"You could not have cured her sickness," Ricardo said carefully, already seeing that that wasn't what she meant, that there was something here he did not know.

"Of course you've only heard the official story," Ximena said. "But her majesty didn't die of any disease of the body. She cut her own throat." A shaky breath. "We found her soaked in blood, the knife still in her hand. We weren't attentive enough. None of us even know how she got the blade—well, that's one reason I'm leaving." She hefted her bundle a little higher in her grip. "Though I'd leave anyway. After serving her majesty, I don't think I could stay in this palace and serve anyone else."

Ricardo told her that it wasn't her fault, she couldn't blame herself. He could have been firmer, though, for he was too stunned at the thought of the pale, quiet queen covered in red blood to really think about anything else. She had never seemed violent in all the time he'd known her. Maybe violence against oneself required a different nature than violence against others, or maybe he simply never knew her that well. Probably it was both. He was a mere painter, after all; how much could he ever know of the life of royalty?

* * *

If Leonor knew the truth of how Queen Mencia died, Ricardo could see easily how she could misconstrue what had happened and claim murder. He held his breath, waiting to hear what she would say.

But Leonor only said, "They said my father died of sickness as well. I'm sure Alejandro had something to do with it anyhow—at least, he can't have been providing her proper medical care. One does not hear he spent much money on doctors for her. And she was shut up in her private branch of the palace for so long."

"That was her majesty's own choice."

"A choice he encouraged. He was embarrassed by her. It was bad enough she was from another country, married for alliance's sake, a foreign queen, but then she had the audacity to have mental issues as well. Not to mention she couldn't give him an heir, or even a daughter. Of course he'd shut her away, and then eventually decide to get rid of her. It's all of a pattern with his selfishness, his need to be the perfect king without a single spot on his reputation."

"You never knew the queen," Ricardo said. "You left the capital before Alejandro married her. Don't pretend you understand her story."

"I understand her story because it is like my own. You, who are too close..."

"I've always kept my proper distance from royal affairs. I am not the one blinded by proximity."

"You're not so nice this evening, Montero," Leonor said. "Do you have to get like this in defense of Alejandro, of all people? It's your worst quality—it would be fun seeing you feisty otherwise, but you have to pick him. Over and over again, always him. You were an ass the first time I met you, and that was because he was there too. You were showing off. It's obnoxious, Montero, it really is."

"Madonna may have whatever opinion she likes of me."

Leonor shook her head. "Do you think he cares about your loyalty? Do you think he cares about anyone, in his heart? Where do you think it will get you, loving him? It won't get you anywhere. Do you know what I heard today, Montero?"

"What did you hear?"

Leonor drummed her fingers. "A traveler from the capital was passing by. There are a few—mostly merchants—that will regularly stop by here and give me news. Good men. This one hears most of the gossip about Alejandro's little games and obsessions. Last year he told me about how much energy Alejandro was spending on his garden, and on the construction of the temple. Today he gave me an update on the temple again. The construction is almost finished, and work has begun on the ceiling, including on the vault. Another artist was found to replace you, and they've already begun painting it."

Ricardo blinked.

It was such an abrupt change of subject that he had a hard time taking it in. It had been ages since either he or Leonor had mentioned the temple. It had been in the back of his mind still—as a reason he needed to get back to the capital and Alejandro, as a project that was still in the brewing stage—but he hadn't seriously been worrying about it for months.

Months wouldn't be long enough to deter Alejandro, though, especially given that the construction of the temple wasn't even finished. "You're lying," he said.

"Lying! No, I'm not. Why would I bother?"

"Your man was mistaken, then. I'm sure he doesn't keep up with the news of the temple's construction, and when you asked him how it was going, he had to make something up or you wouldn't pay him for his news. I expect you do pay him?"

"The man heard about the vault being painted because there's been a phenomenon, apparently," Leonor said. "The artist they chose is some woman who sees visions of Marina, or so the king is claiming. It's generated a lot of gossip."

"A visionary? Who is she?"

"He didn't give me a name. You're right, he didn't think I would care about the subject. But he could tell me enough to know the king has dropped you. Why stay loyal to a man like that?"

"Your informant could be mistaken," Ricardo said automatically. "I know of no visionary painters in Ferrar, or even in Salandra. If he's right, there's still some explanation, surely. Alejandro always has his reasons. He is a king—I couldn't guess at them without even speaking to him."

"You still believe that."

"Of course I believe that."

"Even if he has abandoned you?"

"He hasn't abandoned me. If anything, it looks like I abandoned him, since you dragged me away from the capital without so much as a message left behind. I admit I wish he had waited for my return, but a king cannot always prioritize one subject."

"You are impossible." Leonor stood and began to pace. "What would it take, then, for you to admit your king is not perfect or all-benevolent? What would be enough?"

"I will always believe in Alejandro," Ricardo said. "He is my king."

"Go to him, then," Leonor said bitterly. "It's clear that's where you belong."

"Go to him?"

"I'm saying I'm letting you go, Montero."

Again, Ricardo was stunned. The first thing he could think of to say was, "Why?"

"What purpose does it serve to keep you here? I liked you but you'll never be able to tolerate me. As for the king, it's clear that keeping you here doesn't hurt him in the slightest, whatever you may like to think. Keeping you here does no good, and frankly, I'm sick of you, Montero. Go home. Get out of my sight."

She left before Ricardo could make any protest. He stood staring at the door for a moment, tongue-tied, and it occurred to him he shouldn't really want to protest anyway. She was giving him what he wanted. It was all just very sudden, and so very strange.

Hadn't she been in love with him?

He didn't understand it, didn't understand her. He told himself it didn't matter. The only reason he'd wanted to understand her in the first place was so he could figure out how to get her to release him. She was letting him go, and in the future they might perhaps never see each other again. There was no reason to obsess over the workings of her bitter, tangled mind anymore.

* * *

She offered him an escort back home. He politely declined.

"Very well," she said. "You're not my prisoner, after all. Go as you wish, where you wish. Safe travels, Montero."

That was her farewell. It was not especially warm. The servants expressed more regret at seeing him go, perhaps, particularly Sancho who helped him pack, talking him into keeping more of the clothes Leonor had given him than he would have of his own accord. Felipe also intercepted him on the way out the gate and said, "Have a good trip back!"

"Thank you," Ricardo said. "I hope to. The weather is good." The weather was broiling, but that was better than rain, for travel.

"Come back and visit sometime," Felipe suggested.

"Maybe," Ricardo said, "if I can." Certainly he wouldn't, but who would refuse a young prince in such strong terms? Besides, Felipe was a good boy (sometimes). There was no need to be too cruelly honest with him about what a miserable limbo this whole visit had been to him.

He left Felipe a gift, a small packet of the sketches he'd made of him in early days. Leonor he'd left a gift too—the almost-finished painting of the view from the cliff. He took the still-life, though, which was good enough he might even sell it off to one of the nobles in the capital, with a little luck. It was good work. That, and the clothes Leonor had given him—some of them, anyway—and the knife she'd bought him at the Festival of Sektos, which he'd lost that same day but had returned to him a couple of days later by a wary guard. He'd seemed to think Ricardo might take the knife and immediately attack him, attempting escape again. Ricardo hadn't, of course. In the end, he'd spent his whole captivity mostly very docile. It was embarrassing to think about that.

Well, that didn't matter anymore. He was free, and on his way back to the capital. Back to Alejandro. And, once he'd cleared up this matter of another artist painting the temple vault, back to his work.

18

CHAPTER EIGHTEEN

Beatriz's habits had become more regular now than they had been in the past. In the past, she often spent much of the day visiting friends and patrons. Her painting routine was inconsistent. She would schedule meetings with her models ahead of time, of course, but apart from that, she might paint all day or might only paint a little in the evening or the late morning. Sometimes her brother would pull her away from all her plans to go on some excursion; other times she would plan on going to Ricardo's studio just to drop by for a chat and accidentally involve herself in an hours-long debate about proper methods or even proper content of paintings—of portraiture, of religious works, even of still life pieces.

Had she been like Ricardo, working largely for a single patron, she would have needed to regulate her habits more. In fact, she would have needed to regulate her habits more had she relied on painting for a living at all, but given that she lived on her father's money in her father's house and only used the money she got out of painting for expenses she felt she couldn't bring to him or casual frivolities, there had never been a need for her to push herself to work hard when she didn't want to. Sometimes she would feel driven to work all day for weeks in a row, and other times she would go a month barely producing art at all. Such was her life, and if she sometimes felt a bit guilty that her output was not as consistent as that of many more respected and more serious artists, the guilt was still far too slight to rule her.

Now all of this was very different. She got up, ate, sometimes allowed herself a walk to exercise her body, and headed down to the temple. There she worked until a little after noon. Then she would eat lunch, take a brief nap, and get back to work until evening. Then home, dinner, and bed soon after.

There were, of course, interruptions to this schedule. Today, for example, Beatriz was surprised by a visit in the morning from a woman who often modeled for her, one Isabela, who urgently wished to speak with her.

"Milady, I wanted to ask if you would be needing a model again soon. It's been almost a year now, after all. Surely I can't be such a bad model that milady no longer considers me?"

Almost a year was an exaggeration, but Beatriz couldn't quite remember when she'd last employed Isabela so she didn't challenge the assertion. Her objection was more practical, unfortunately: "Of course you're a marvelous model, Isabela. I've always said so. But as it happens I'm not using any models just now at all."

"None at all? That's not like milady. You always say you need models for all your work to remain strictly accurate. Haven't you always said that to portray a woman or a man looking real, physically present, is the greatest form of beauty?"

"You paid more attention to my musings than I thought," Beatriz said—she'd always thought Isabela took her rambling about the pursuit of beauty and realism as half boastfulness and half flattery towards Isabela herself. Most of her models did, in fact.

"Little else to do when I'm sitting so still for you," Isabela retorted. "Well? You can't have suddenly changed your mind."

"No, no, I haven't changed my views. Strict observation is best, to paint as one sees. But you see I have no work presently except painting the vault of Marina's temple. You may have heard about that," Beatriz said, feeling a little awkward. In general everyone in the capital had heard about it, there had been so much gossip, but it still felt arrogant to assume someone had heard about your good fortune. "So—no portraits, no side projects for me. Only work, and work, and work..."

"I could pose for the temple then, couldn't I? I'm not saying I could be Marina, but one of her followers, perhaps, or a sea nymph, an undine. I'm quite thin enough for an undine, and I have the hair for it too." Isabela ran a hand through rippling locks. "I wouldn't go up on the scaffolding, but you must be making studies before you paint."

"I'm not using models for my work on the temple," Beatriz said.

"None at all?" Isabela was incredulous.

Beatriz swallowed. She could feel blue pressure building in the back of her skull. "None at all. Marina inspires me, and I draw and paint what she shows me. Models would only distract me from her vision."

Incredulity on Isabela's face was building to indignation. "Visions? You're telling me you paint from visions?"

This was not actually what Beatriz had said, but since it was accurate, she said, "As Marina grants them."

Isabela had little to say to this beyond a snort. And eventually, "Then I'll be interested to see your work when it is done." Not in a tone that suggested she expected to be impressed by Beatriz's results.

The pressure in Beatriz's head continued to build. It was almost anger, but she swallowed it down. It was fine for Marina to rage—she was a goddess—but Beatriz didn't snap at people just because they made vague insinuations at her. She felt rather bad for Isabela, who had to be badly off right now if she was actually seeking Beatriz out to ask for work. Usually Beatriz had to hunt her down and beg; usually, for that matter, if Isabela were to show up asking for work, Beatriz would have come up with something for her to do, even if it were something as simple as sitting for Beatriz to practice anatomy. Today all she could say was, "I'll write a letter of introduction to any other artist in the city, if you want. Just tell me who."

"And you think they'll care so much for a reference from you?"

Isabela had known Beatriz for long enough to know how little the other artists in the city respected her. But it was all Beatriz could offer. "I'm a bit of a phenomenon these days. It might help." Oh, there was another thing she could offer. "Or, if you want to borrow money..."

"I'm not that hard up." Isabela crossed her arms. "I'd like a reference for Valdez and de Sarmiento. One for each."

"I'll have the letters sent to your house tonight," Beatriz said. "It will take some time to write them, and I should have been at the temple some time ago. My apologies. I have to be going now."

Marina's voice was in her head all through her walk to the temple after that, scolding Beatriz for wasting her time with a useless wench when there was work to be done. Beatriz couldn't really ignore her, so she apologized in her head. A couple times she even broke into muttering apologies out loud, and the others on the street gave her odd looks, except for a few people who recognized her: Beatriz de Comete, formerly only infamous as a noble artisan and woman of scandal, now as well a madwoman regarded as almost a priestess. Those gave her even stranger looks, and when she looked back at them, they only continued to stare. Later they would say they sensed some deep meaning in her gaze, say they felt closer to the goddess in that moment than ever before in their lives. Beatriz was the one to look away, to cringe before their eyes.

Marina disapproved of this, of course. "You have nothing to be ashamed of if they marvel at you. You are mine, after all. Let them marvel."

Beatriz sighed.

She was tired, but the day had only begun and there was much work to do.

The workers greeted her at the temple with cheerful teasing, questioning where she'd been, why she was late today; was she slacking in her goddess's service? Ah, but surely the lady would never!—and they laughed, the title not disrespectful but not all that reverent either. At first some of them had been wary of her, having heard the story of her little miracle, the painting that moved and shone with Marina's unearthly light. After a while, though, they'd gotten used to her, and she became just another part of the building, another person on the team. They teased her as she struggled, as usual, to climb the scaffolding in a long skirt. She didn't think Marina would let her drop, but she wasn't really sure how much Marina's power would extend to gravity, and the height made her a little nervous every time. When she'd originally considered painting the temple's dome, she'd mostly thought about how in the future, people would stare up at her creation—not how in the present, she herself would have so far to look down...

And she was quite near the top of the dome. Not quite the peak of it yet, where Marina herself would be painted, but close. Near the edges of the dome she would later add undines and nymphs, traditional attendants of Marina, but currently, she was painting famous followers of Marina from various legends and historical anecdotes. The composition of the dome, where each follower was to be placed, had already been decided by Ricardo, and Beatriz was still following his plan in that area, though the actual painting—what each character looked like, the expressions and poses and physical features—

was guided by Marina's revelation, which came to her sometimes in little trickles and sometimes in forceful waves.

Today the man she was painting was Captain Soltenez. His story was well known to Beatriz, as was his traditional appearance. A man of medium height, well favored—golden hair and tanned skin, a single scar on his cheek. But as she worked, Marina murmured in her ear, blue voice thrumming like the waves, and both the story and the man became different.

Marina said, "Soltenez was a boy when I first met him. He lived too far inland to see me at first, so we met when he was ten years old. He was in an apprenticeship with a travelling minstrel—his training had just begun, then. We met in Mestos, just as I met you. He spent more time at the seaside with me than he spent singing with his master. His master beat him for it, but I always healed his welts quickly."

An image flickered in Beatriz's mind. She could see the boy walking naked into the seawater, undeterred by waves splashing against his legs and then, quickly, his chest—he was so short that he was soon swimming over his head. A land dweller, he should have been afraid of the sea, but he reveled in it. She felt herself in his body for a moment, or maybe his soul. Tossed and turned like a doll in the hands of a careless child, but rambunctious child that he was, he loved it. Songs he knew sometimes described Marina as rocking the sea like a cradle, but he wanted none of that. Marina could have dashed him against a sheer rock cliff, and he would only have loved her more for it—though Mestos had no cliffs, not near the water, only endless sand. Marina was not too harsh with him, either. And she pitied him. The blood from his master's whipping leaked into her water; he would reopen scabs with careless motion, and she would heal them, subtly close them back up again, trying not to sting him too badly with her salt.

"He could not stay in Mestos for long," Marina said. "His master was a traveler, after all—I respected that, for so are most of my devotees. He generally spent winters inland, but during the summer, whenever he was at a port city, he thrilled to the sea. He prayed to me whenever he swam; he was not a mindless worshipper, as most children, but very grave in that aspect. His apprenticeship lasted eight years. At the end of that time, I assumed he would become a sailor, but he decided to keep working with his master, now as partners. Even though that master had beaten him, and would drag him away from me for months at a time."

The frigidity of deep seawater crept over Beatriz, not the wrath of storms but the dread of drowning, deep below all human knowing, where sharks crept and bones shivered.

But he still came to visit you, she thought, or maybe whispered—she did not know if the words exited her mouth, they drowned along with all else.

"He told me I was his only love, but he still left me constantly. For two years, he continued to play with me like this. Then he killed his master."

Yes, the legends said this of Soltenez, that he had been a minstrel who killed his master and ran away to sea, and Marina granted him freedom.

Beatriz could see the scene now, a dark night, the two of them walking on a rocky coast. Soltenez liked to walk by the beach; his master laughed at him, called him a romantic. Tonight they got into an argument. Over money—Soltenez wanted more, since they were now supposedly equal partners in this business; his master thought the very notion of it funny, when he had seniority, when he'd taught Soltenez all he knew, when Soltenez had no leverage at all. The master laughed. Soltenez's face darkened. He hit his master only once, across the face—the instigation of a fight that also ended it. The rocks were wet and slippery. The master fell, and hit his head. He was dead within minutes.

Soltenez knew nothing about covering up a crime, hiding a body, running from the law. He did know he could stay in this town no longer. He could have returned to the route he and his master always followed, headed to the next city where they planned on singing. Instead, he found a ship looking for sailors, willing to take anyone. It was a pirate ship, of course—who else would be looking for boys with no experience and eyes filled with panic? They took him on; half their crew from their last journey was dead. They sailed within the week, and from then on, Soltenez was a pirate.

"People talk of how he killed men for me," Marina said.

"So they do," Beatriz agreed. She was on the hair now, golden hair, and focused on her brushwork—for once she could concentrate enough to see and feel the strokes. She'd been granted a limited amount of gold leaf by Ferrar, but she didn't have it with her just now—that would be added at the end. Here, in the highlights, it might be good to add a little. Using gold or jewels in her art always made her nervous—her family was rich, but not rich enough to justify that kind of extravagance in her work for the most part, and the same went for most of her clients—but she knew in this case it was justified. Marina was a goddess. She deserved the best. And this temple would stand a monument to her for all time. Once Beatriz had thought it would stand a monument to Beatriz's skill too, but on days like this, when Marina spoke to her, she hardly thought it just to call the work she did hers.

Marina sighed breathily in her ear. "He used to splash his decks down after a battle to clean the blood, and say he dedicated the blood to me. I accepted, of course. One must accept an offering in good faith. But how could I explain to him how little it meant to me? It meant much more to me that he was with me, always. Even in the winter, now, he stayed in port, and came to see me every day. During blizzards and hailstorms, he'd still go out to the pier to salute me! Those were glorious days. I knew he loved me."

And he sang, too. He never quite gave up his minstrel habits, though he learned and invented more sea chanties than he had ever known ballads of the land. Marina echoed his voice into Beatriz's ears now, how it changed over the years: at first soft and adolescent, later firmed by middle age, at last raspy and elderly. Still, he could carry a tune. Marina was not the goddess of music, but she still enjoyed it, just as she was not the goddess of painting or architecture but still relished in the creation of this temple.

"At last he had grown too old to sail," Marina said. "We both knew it. He was sick, very sick, and so old he was unlikely to get better. He made one final offering to me. He took his ship out from the harbor with a few trusted men, and set a fuse. Got off into a rowboat and sailed far enough away for safety. And it burned down. It was a ship he had been using for some years, and filled with all the wealth he had accumulated." Her voice was indulgent. "Timber and metal and cloth and spices—none of it meant anything to me, except that he offered it. When the ashes had all drifted down to the bottom, I sent a huge wave on his rowboat, and he and all three men he took with him drowned."

This startled Beatriz out of her trance. "Drowned?"

That was right, though, wasn't it? In every version of the legend of Soltenez, he returned in death to the sea. Came home to his mistress.

A happy ending, in most.

"I couldn't have let him die by inches, could I? What sort of lover would I have been, to let him go like that?"

Beatriz swallowed. "If he wanted to die, wouldn't he have stayed on the ship when it burned? And to kill both his men too..."

But a tightness pressed at her chest, and she stopped talking, hearing the roar of water. She forced herself to breathe. For just a moment she could feel Marina's presence crush down on her in warning, and then it released, and with it, the blue that had clouded her vision fled.

Before her, the completed work. She had painted Soltenez over a couple days, outlining and mapping in colors in days before, so she ought to have known what it would look like. But all the details and niceties had been today, and he looked utterly unfamiliar. His tunic, for example, was made in a style she was not familiar with. And his face had a specificity to it: His nose was a little more hooked than she would have made it from her imaginings, his eyes a little smaller, his mouth a little poutier, his chin a little sharper. His muscles were about as she had left him, but his hands were oddly chapped-looking and the veins bulged. His hair was golden as the tales had it, but all a tangle, as if infected by seawater.

This was how Marina saw Soltenez, in his long-ago life. And despite her story of his passionate love, he was not smiling. There was distance in his eyes.

Beatriz wanted to touch, but she wasn't stupid enough to smudge good work, even if the work wasn't really hers. She cleaned her brushes out and rolled them up in a piece of cloth, then put them and her cases of pigments in the sack she carried down on her back. Eased her way slowly back down the scaffolding, trying to keep her legs from shaking, her hands from sweating. Her poor aching body was unsteady enough—the angle of painting the dome hurt her back, her shoulders, and her arms, and drops of paint would fall off the dome and onto her clothes and skin, even her face, so that she inhaled the fumes even more than usual, acquiring headaches that she would notice no more while Marina talked to her than she noticed the men working down below. As they became small when seen from above, so did she herself become small when viewed through the eyes of a goddess... perhaps it was that, and not just the height of the scaffolding, that made her body shake as she descended.

A hand steadied her arm on the last step, and when she turned to thank whatever workman had paused at his task to help her, she found herself facing King Alejandro.

She rather gaped at him, but still with more composure than the way he looked at her. If a few faces on the street had "marveled" at the goddess's chosen painter, the king drank in the sight of her with a fervor that was halfway between worshipful wonderment and vulgar ogling. Beatriz, sweaty and achey and smudged here and there with paint, felt no fitting object for either.

She bowed. "Your majesty."

"No, do not bow to me. No priestess of Marina should do so."

"I am no priestess."

"No, you are something closer. You are her representative in a more intimate way. All the more reason you must not bow to me, nor call me 'your majesty'. I should bow to you, if anything."

It was horribly uncomfortable, the thought of that. He used to indulge her and tease her a little bit, when they used to meet, but certainly never show her this kind of respect. It was all for Marina's sake, but Beatriz hated it. "Please don't. I am in Marina's hands—myself I am nothing."

He nodded, admitting her words as truth, but looked at her with no less reverence. In a formal, ingratiating tone he asked her what she had been painting, and whether she thought this painting, like the painting of the sea, would shine and glow and move about when she was done. She told him she did not know, and gave him a brief version of the story of Captain Soltenez as she had seen it as she painted.

He said, "You say things that are in no version of the legend I have heard."

"Well, I'm only saying what I saw. That's how I paint—what I see—and so I must speak plainly as well."

Now he smiled and there was a ghost of his old familiarity for a moment. "Ah yes, the lover of realism now paints the goddess herself as she is. Poor Montero argued so vehemently for idealization, but he could never have pictured the wonders you create."

A pang of worry and a little guilt, like Beatriz always felt when Ricardo came up. Where on earth was he? It had been ages now, and still he was gone. Poor Montero indeed, and poor desperate Juan... he came to visit the temple from time to time to look at her work, but had much less to say about it than he might have said in the past. Indeed he seemed almost afraid to speak frankly to her about painting, or even about his master. She coaxed talk of Ricardo out of him when she could; when Marina was not buzzing at the back of her head telling her that all conversation was a waste of time.

All conversation except with the king, apparently, for Marina never discouraged time spent with him. Indeed Beatriz had a sense that Marina was pleased with his visit, and pleased with the attention he paid Beatriz. She felt an urge—quite unnatural—to say kind things to him, not flattery like you gave a king but condescending praise and approval like you gave a child—and then, too, sometimes she felt an odd urge to reach out and pat him on the head, or kiss him on the cheek, or even kiss him on the lips... that last urge she liked least of all. It was perhaps more natural than the other urges, for while she in moments of boredom might consider the possibility of kissing many people, she had never before fantasized about patting the king on the head and telling him he was a good boy. But it still was not her own desire—her own desire was engaged firmly elsewhere at the moment.

She had not yet gone to see Vulpa perform at her new workplace, even though Vulpa had sent her a few invitations to do so, and even dropped by the Comete house a couple of evenings ago just to tell Beatriz she was thinking of her. Whenever she considered going down to see Vulpa there, or perhaps meeting with her between painting sessions for lunch, she got the sense that Marina disapproved, considered the prospect as a waste of valuable time and energy. She might have had the boldness to chase down Vulpa anyways—her energy and time was her own to waste—but the idea of putting Vulpa between herself and a goddess's possessiveness did not strike her as wise.

She would have made a poor friend right now anyway, distracted and exhausted as she was, and an even worse lover. So. She kept away, sending only perfunctory responses to Vulpa's notes and speaking to her, when she visited, in no great depth. But her heart remained firmly stuck. And so, at least for the moment, she had no intention of throwing herself at the king, no matter how longingly he looked at her, and no matter how Marina meddled with her emotions. Some things were still off limits.

So she talked formally with him, and eventually managed to get herself away, home to eat a big lunch and take a nap. And afterwards she knew she would return to the temple and work for a few more hours, sketching the outline of the next figure she would be painting. Her life had such a simple pattern now, after all. A divine pattern. Who would be so ungrateful as to defy it?

19

CHAPTER NINETEEN

Ricardo had known that the capital wouldn't sit still waiting for him to get back, holding their breaths until his return. Nevertheless, when he returned to his own house to find most of his servants had left to seek employment elsewhere, it was still a shock. He had no cook anymore, and no maids, and no butler. Not that he had a whole fleet of servants to begin with, but to have none at all was something else.

He would have felt more disheartened, of course, if his apprentice hadn't shown up shortly after his arrival. He looked at Ricardo with wide eyes, let out a yell of greeting, and immediately pulled him into a tight hug. It was all much more informal than Juan would have acted towards him in the past, but at the moment Ricardo found it very welcome.

"Master, master, master," Juan babbled. "You've come back! Where did you go? Did someone—did something happen to you? Everyone said you were probably dead, but of course I knew you couldn't be. There wasn't a body, after all, and you wouldn't just go die."

Ricardo patted Juan on the back and considered what to say to him. On the trip back to the capital he had thought over what excuses to make for his absence. Leonor had not asked him to lie for her, nor could she do anything about it if he chose to tell everyone the truth, but he had no particular desire to incriminate her. So he'd decided to tell the general public that he'd been called away to help an old friend out with some difficulties, and gotten sick while visiting—and leave it vague, say the matter had been delicate. He knew the excuse would work well enough for most of the city (or if they didn't believe him or wanted to elaborate on his story, it would give them enough fodder to come up with their own theories and leave him alone), but Juan was a different matter. It had doubtless been hard on him to have his master vanish without explanation, and making it sound like Ricardo had just forgotten to say where he was going would only infuriate the poor boy. On the other hand, he couldn't tell Juan the truth; he was too much of a gossip and would never be able to keep his mouth shut about it.

He said, "I'm afraid I can't explain to you where I've been, Juan. You'll have to forgive me. I've returned now, though, and we'll say I was called away on urgent business."

"Why can't you explain?" Juan said fiercely. "Are you in danger? If you are, I can help."

"No danger now. I was in a bit of trouble, it's true, but now it's over. Only it's better not to talk about it."

Juan's jaw clenched; his effort to restrain his curiosity was visible. Ricardo decided to help him out with a distraction: "How have things been while I was gone? I see the servants all deserted you. I hope you haven't been having any issues with money—you know my purse is open to you in cases of emergency, and it should have been enough, but if it really looked like I was gone for good, I expect a few lenders came calling. Not too much trouble, I hope?"

"Oh, no, master, nothing too bad. I paid off one of them—Master

Estrada—and the others agreed to wait. That didn't worry me any. And I'm sure we can get the maids to come back, and probably the butler. You're a better master to serve than most in town."

"Mm." Ricardo wasn't so sure about that. "We can start working on that tomorrow, perhaps. A cook is the most urgent need. I'm starving, but I suppose we'll have to head down to a bar rather than cook for ourselves."

"I could make something."

Ricardo shook his head with a wry smile. Juan was a terrible cook, as he knew from experience—Ricardo himself was better, but he was weary from travel, and preferred not to go to the hassle of cooking for tonight. So they set out together for the bar Ricardo had been kidnapped from. It was, after all, still the closest to his house and the most convenient.

Juan had a lot to say about that bar and Ricardo's disappearance, actually. "I'm not sure we should still patronize them, master. Mostly I haven't been. I kept on asking the bartenders there, and the owner, what had happened to you—I knew you'd gone there, it was the last place I knew you'd gone—and they were very unhelpful. All they would say is that you'd been fine when you left, and then half of them claimed you'd left with a friend so you must have gotten home safely, and wouldn't even listen to me when I said you plainly hadn't. Who did you leave with that night? I never did get a clear description from them. An old man, a young man, a strong man, a skinny man... one of them even said you'd been with a woman. There were a lot of rumors you'd run off with a woman, actually. I didn't listen to them, of course. Rubbish. You never pay any attention to women, master."

"You make it sound like I hate women."

"No, not that, of course you don't. You're very close with Beatriz de Comete, and you show all the proper respect to women at court.

But you know the kind of talk I mean. You should have heard the things some people said about you."

"I'll probably still hear them. A lot of questions, too." He wasn't looking forward to it.

"Valdez was especially obnoxious. Ramos and de Mendoza, too. Those three were hoping you were gone for good—I don't think they cared if it was a woman that got you away or if someone hit you over the head in a dark alley or what have you. They just want you out of the way so they can sink their claws into the king and pry out some royal commissions. Same as they've ever been. They were particularly eyeing the temple vault. Well, at least that's well out of their grasp now."

"It wasn't one of them, then," Ricardo said, "who stole the commission?"

"Oh, you hadn't heard what happened there?" Juan said.

"No."

"It was Beatriz de Comete. In the end, the king had no choice but to choose her. Her painting was out of this world—I've never seen anything like it. Now the king has taken possession of it and hung it in private. You should ask him if he'll show it to you, though. He probably would."

Ricardo was stuck on the first sentence of this reply, however. The matter of how gorgeous and unnatural Beatriz's painting had been was of no interest to him, nor did he care what had befallen it. He was too shocked by the fact that Beatriz had been chosen as his replacement. Had someone asked him, he would not have been able to say which was more shocking: That she had attempted to win the commission in the first place, or that she, a woman and a decidedly nontraditional artist, had been the king's selection. The latter was mostly baffling, but the former felt like a betrayal. "Why was Beatriz even an option?" he asked Juan. "Alejandro barely knows her."

Juan explained: There had been a contest. Alejandro had made it open to the public, though he'd only informed a select few artists about it personally. Juan had been the one to approach Beatriz about it. "I asked her to ward off the vultures while you were gone, protect your position and your reputation. She agreed. I didn't expect she would succeed as thoroughly as she did, though. Now everyone says she's Marina's chosen painter, not the king's—people say she's been devoted to Marina her whole life, even, which you know and I know isn't true at all. I mean, she only joined the contest for your sake after I talked her into it. But somehow she's become... different. It's hard to explain. You'll know what I mean when you see her art. I know you say that you cannot generally judge a person by their art alone, or know their mental state, but in this case I think you'll see she's been nothing like herself. Some people say she's divinely overshadowed; in my opinion it's practically as if she were possessed. Though of course I know little enough of religion, master, you know I'm not that educated."

"Beatriz only joined for my sake, you say?" Ricardo raised his eyebrows. "Is that so?"

It was an odd notion. When had Beatriz ever put forth much effort into helping him with anything? Of course, she did some odd modeling for him, and sometimes came over and helped to tutor Juan. He always got the sense she did both jobs more for the fun of it and the boost to her ego than from any altruistic motive, though.

She was his friend, of course. He could begrudgingly admit that there were few things in life he enjoyed more than sitting down in the studio with Beatriz and a bottle of wine and nothing to do for a couple hours but talk and talk and talk: debating about artistic theories, trash talking bad clients and rival painters, praising mutual friends. But while their conversations could get deeply philosophical, their relationship was in other ways oddly impersonal. They rarely spoke about their families, never about their deeper worries or insecurities. Beatriz was a friend that Ricardo could spend a good time with—a friend he thought could understand him—but she was no devoted companion. When Ricardo told Beatriz about rumors spread against him, blows to his reputation, she would wince and shake her head, but she hardly went out and harangued his detractors to defend him. Juan had perhaps formed an overly romantic view of their relationship: Beatriz would not embark on a lengthy and arduous project simply for Ricardo's sake.

There were, of course, reasons she might do it for her own. Beatriz had a poor reputation among the painters of Ferrar, worse than Ricardo's. Ricardo was envied, but Beatriz was largely derided. She acted like it didn't sting her, but Ricardo knew it did sometimes. If she could get a royal commission, an important royal commission, it would be a huge feather in her cap, and the best imaginable defense against those in the capital who liked to say she was simply a pampered, capricious hobbyist. The glory of painting what would be the largest and most elegantly designed temple in the city would be enough to tempt anyone.

Juan said, "Well, I told her that of all people, Miss Comete at least could have had nothing to do with your disappearance. And you respect her. I couldn't bear the thought of you coming home to find Valdez painting the ceiling of the temple, encroaching on your territory like a common thief. He would have loved that."

"It's something I would expect of Valdez and his sort," Ricardo said sharply. "Not of Beatriz."

Juan said, "Are you angry, master?"

Ricardo took a deep breath.

Anger was a vice, he reminded himself. And the principle reason it was a flaw—as he saw it—was that it made you act like a fool. Juan had conducted himself as he thought best in Ricardo's absence. He'd been more loyal than anyone else in Ricardo's life, apparently. Ricardo couldn't snap at him just because he'd basically despaired of Ricardo's return and handed off his most valuable commission to an outsider.

No, no. That wasn't fair. Juan hadn't been the one to give the commission to Beatriz anyway. That had been Alejandro's doing, and royalty would do as they wished, and it was pointless questioning it. And Juan had meant well.

"I am only thinking," Ricardo said, carefully, "that it may have been kind of Beatriz to take an interest in one of my projects while I was missing, but now that I am returned, we will have to see if she is willing to hand it back again. After all, I spent months designing that ceiling, and the king would surely have preferred me to paint it if I hadn't been otherwise occupied. I'm here now, so we will see if Beatriz is willing to step down."

He gave Juan a look. Juan of all people might be expected to agree immediately. Juan of all people had awaited his return, while others had assumed he was gone forever and proceeded accordingly. But Juan now was biting his lip. "Master… I don't know. I told you, she's changed since you've seen her last. And she's very involved in painting the vault now." Then, almost hopefully, "Perhaps you could ask the king about it. He would have the final say, after all."

"Of course, I will talk to the king about it," Ricardo said. "But I should talk to Beatriz first. It's only artistic courtesy, after all."

"Right. Good."

"I'll go visit her tonight."

"Tonight! No, no, master. You should eat and get some rest first. No need to tire yourself out yet when you've just returned."

Noting that Juan admitted the conversation was unlikely to be an easy one, Ricardo allowed himself to be persuaded.

They had arrived at the bar, and now they sat down and gave their orders to the waiter, who recognized Ricardo and exclaimed that it was good to see Master Montero back in the city again.

Ricardo smiled and apologized. "I'm sure my disappearance has caused you a lot of trouble."

"Oh no, none at all. Not that we haven't missed you."

"But you must have had to deal with many awkward questions."

"I'll accept that apology from young master Juan here! He did come around a few times. But I know young folk worry, and persistence isn't a bad thing as long as you have some brains to go with it."

"The king's men must have come too, I expect."

"Not that I remember. But maybe I wasn't on shift at the time. I'm not here every day."

* * *

Ricardo ate and drank a great deal that evening. Drank more than he ate, feeling uncomfortable in a city that was his home and felt right now like foreign territory. He had a mild hangover in the morning, and so he headed out to see Beatriz de Comete later than he had planned, a couple hours before noon.

He went to find her at the Cometes' city house, and discovered she was not there, had left some time ago. It was an awkward encounter; the Comete family had never been on warm terms with Ricardo. No one there disliked him, exactly, but as a friend to Beatriz who was both lower in station and male, he evoked a certain wariness in them all. He suspected they advised Beatriz not to be as close with him as she was—she never brought up any such matter, but it was in the way they all looked at him, especially Luis de Comete.

Luis was one of those little brothers who acted as if he owned his older sister, perhaps because in childhood he had looked up to her so much, perhaps because, Beatriz not being an actual daughter of the Comete family, he could not help but cling to her, as if afraid she would run off and be someone else's sister instead. Perhaps Ricardo's. That was how he always seemed to Ricardo: jealous and reproving despite a veneer of politeness. Don Fernando and Lady de Comete, in contrast, were merely condescending in the manner of nobles who knew of Ricardo's art and did not find it terribly impressive, an attitude he was more used to. Today he didn't actually meet with any of these three—apparently they were all out—but only with the butler, who informed him that Miss Beatriz was down at the temple of Marina, working on the vault.

"She's had to work on it day and night ever since the king chose her for the project," he informed Ricardo. "Exhausting work for her, too, and hard on a woman's nerves, not that hers have ever been weak. Ah, well—someone had to do it, anyway, since you went missing, sir." His tone implied no apology, but rather a remonstrance on Ricardo for having been so inconsiderate as to force his mistress's hand.

Ricardo gritted his teeth and headed down to the temple. The weather was cooler that morning than it had been most of the summer, and walking briskly, he found himself full of vigor. He was ready for the conversation even Juan had found intimidating, ready to confront Beatriz and demand an explanation for her behavior. He was ready for anything, in fact, by the time he arrived at the temple, at which point his brisk walk slowed a little.

It would have been possible, perhaps, for a less feeling man to stride into the temple at full speed, but Ricardo, despite not being all that reverent towards gods and goddesses, had too much respect for art and architecture not to pause and admire the progress which had been made even in the few months of his absence. He didn't really want to be impressed by the temple, but he couldn't help but feel a little impressed anyway; he'd felt impressed every time he'd visited this place. Just the construction was a marvel. The high arches and thick pillars, all of stone, intimidated through size alone; then there were the small sculpted sea creatures and designs laid into the stone in certain areas. The door was bound to be the most sculpted and decorated piece of the construction work, but it had not arrived yet—the woodworker was doing his work at his own pace, and after all he could afford to, as the temple would not be open to the public for perhaps another year or two as yet.

As for the paintings on the ceiling...

Well.

Ricardo squinted up.

Not a whole lot had been done yet on the vault. Only a few people were depicted. Ricardo stared up at them, squinting, trying to get a really good look even though they were so high above him. They were in Beatriz's style even though Juan had claimed they would be so different—still a certain frank harshness about the characters, not particularly suited to a temple in his opinion. The features were very specific and a little atypical for tradition. For example, Soltenez looked older, softer, and less brutal than a pirate captain would generally be portrayed, but one could not say Beatriz was trying to soften her characters because she had painted an oracle known for gentle wisdom as very fat and a little bit grumpy looking. Strange choices, but if Beatriz expected Ricardo would call her a visionary just because she had painted traditional figures in non-traditional ways, her expectations would be sadly disappointed. He saw nothing supernatural about any of this yet.

Beatriz was there, at the top of the scaffolding, working on another painting that was not far enough along yet for him to tell what it was. He could barely tell it was her, lying with her head slightly elevated and arm outstretched, staring up at the ceiling. Her smock looked like one he'd seen her in before, though, and he could glimpse her dark hair, neatly tied back. He called up, "Beatriz! Beatriz de Comete!"

The figure above did not react, did not even glance downwards. Ricardo called up again, and again. "Beatriz! It's Ricardo de Montero! Beatriz!"

It couldn't have been that he wasn't loud enough. His voice echoed against the stone walls and the dome as if he were in a cavern, or perhaps an orchestral hall. The temple was designed purposefully to carry sound well, so that all worshippers could hear what was said during ceremonies. Of course, worshippers would rarely be so high up, but Ricardo was pretty sure his voice was carrying throughout the space, not just near him. The other workers were giving him annoyed or curious looks, even one who was up a ladder working on a window. Only Beatriz remained obliviously focused on her art.

Ricardo cursed under his breath; even the curse carried further than he would have liked it to, still eliciting no reaction from the painter above. Was Beatriz going to carry on some oracular act with him? He would have thought hearing his voice, and his name, would have been enough to snap her out of even a real trance, after he'd been missing for so long, after what she'd dared to steal from him. She should have sat up and stared down in fright. Instead, she hadn't noticed his presence at all.

He would have to make it impossible for her to ignore him. With this in mind, he approached the scaffolding, intending to climb up and get in Beatriz's face. He had only laid a hand on it, though, when the heavy hand of another lay on his shoulder. He turned to see a couple of the workmen had come over, and one stout and muscular man now pulled him away from the structure. "No one's allowed to touch the scaffolding except for Miss Comete, except for necessity," the man said. "You'll have to wait for her to come down, sir. She should be down in an hour, by her usual schedule."

"An hour?" Ricardo said. "Call this a necessity. I've been missing for months; Miss Comete would want to see me. I'm going up to her."

The workers glanced at each other, and the stout one, who perhaps was in charge, said, "I'm afraid that doesn't qualify as a necessity. Miss Comete gets many visitors, sir. Anyone can talk to her as long as they're polite, but you have to wait for her to be done with what she's doing. Right now she's communing with the goddess and cannot be disturbed."

Bullshit. But no matter how Ricardo argued, the workers would not be moved—and two of them were now standing quite literally between him and the scaffolding. It felt like forever, but probably was actually less than an hour, that he spent bickering with them before he heard some rustling and creaking above, and looked up to see that Beatriz had put down her paints and begun her descent back to ground level.

"Beatriz!" he called out, and this time she looked down at him and did visibly start.

"Ricardo?" she said, in a voice that wouldn't have carried elsewhere. Then: "Ricardo, is that you?"

"Of course it's me. Beatriz, get down here and tell these men to stop bothering me."

"I'll be right down! Hold on."

She climbed fast, faster than perhaps was cautious, but Ricardo wasn't about to tell her to slow down. When she was a few feet from the ground, she hopped the rest of the way, shoved the men in front of her aside, and grabbed Ricardo, pulling him into a hug.

It was not the reception he had expected.

"Ricardo, you're back! Where have you been? Have you seen Juan yet? He must be so relieved. You can't imagine..." She trailed off, probably noticing he had yet to hug her back, and stepped away. "Oh, have these guys been bothering you? It's all right," she told the workmen, who were still clustered around them. "Ricardo's a friend. He's the artist who was originally supposed to do the ceiling—didn't you ever meet him?"

"He does look a little familiar," one of the men admitted.

Another asked, "You're sure you're fine with him?"

"Of course I'm sure. We've known each other for years. Actually, never mind. Ricardo, let's get out of here. There's a nice bar a short walk away. Maybe you know it already—Towering Sign?"

Ricardo had been there once or twice. He was not much in the mood to go there again, or really to go anywhere with Beatriz. He followed her out, but in the street, he sat decisively down on the side of the first fountain they came to. He was not going to have it out with Beatriz in a crowded bar. In the middle of a public square wasn't ideal, but it was still better.

Beatriz paused in front of the fountain, a peculiar expression on her face. "You'd rather sit?"

Ricardo patted the bench next to him. Beatriz sat.

He took a breath and was about to speak when Beatriz said again, "Where have you been, Ricardo? Everything's been very strange since you've been gone. You really can't imagine it."

"A friend of mine was having some trouble, so I went to help him out for a time. Personal matters. I got sick while visiting him, and couldn't come back for a while."

"Oh. Is that so?"

"Yes."

Beatriz huffed and looked away. "I suppose you can lie to me, Ricardo. I'm glad you're back."

It was so infuriatingly typical of her to call him out. Oddly it made Ricardo relax slightly, made his irritation towards her ease. Beatriz was impossible, but maybe they could still understand each other. "Juan told me that he asked you to compete for this commission on my behalf."

"Yes, he did. He was very distraught. I hope you aren't offended by my having taken over."

"I understand the position you were in." He really didn't, actually, but he could be polite. "As far as I could see, you haven't gotten too far into the project yet. I will be speaking to the king about my taking over from here."

Beatriz was still looking away, not at Ricardo. Now she stiffened. "Ricardo, I'm afraid things have changed while you were gone."

"Yes, I can tell that."

"I can't give the ceiling project to you. Neither can the king. I'd love..." She winced. Turned around to meet his eyes and said, "I'm sure you would do a great job, but I'm the one Marina has chosen for this project. Neither I nor the king can unmake her choice."

"Marina?" Ricardo raised his eyebrows. "I had heard something about you playing at priestess now, Beatriz. Is that what this is? You're going to make that claim to me as well?"

"Not a priestess. Just... Marina began speaking to me some months ago, in Mestos. It's a long story, but now I work for her. Do her work. Am guided by her. Ricardo, I can't turn away from what she asks of me."

"Really. You can look me in the eyes and say you've been chosen by a goddess. Unbelievable. Beatriz, you've always been arrogant, but I used to think you were at least honest and had too much honor for a cheap hoax like this."

The fountain behind Ricardo had been misting his back slightly, dampening his shirt. As he spoke, the spray suddenly intensified, splashing him—he jumped up with a curse. Beatriz stood too, nervously glancing at the fountain. She took a deep breath. "Ricardo, it's not wise to insult Marina."

"Who's insulting Marina? I'm insulting you."

"Denying my relationship with Marina insults her as well."

"Enough. I don't want to hear this. I used to respect you."

"I'm not lying. I know it's unbelievable, but please, Ricardo. You do know me better than that. Can't you—you believe in the gods, I know. You've painted them enough. You told me once that you could feel connected to them through painting, through looking at the paintings done of them in the past and reading the works of great authors. Is this about you only believing in concepts again? Can you not believe in a goddess who interacts with reality? Is it too crude for you? I'm not lying. It's not my fault if you don't have eyes to see or the capacity to believe."

"Shut up." Ricardo's fists clenched. "It seems we can't have an honest conversation. In that case, there's no point in talking. I only had one purpose in coming here: to warn you I will be taking my commission back. If you think you can usurp me, you are greatly mistaken about my position in the king's regard. You're not even a legitimate artist, Beatriz, just like you aren't a legitimate noble. No one in the capital thinks so. Enjoy your day in the sun while you can. I will paint over every last one of your ugly scribbles."

20

CHAPTER TWENTY

When Ricardo reported the morning's encounter—Beatriz's ignoring him at first, and then her refusal to give up the commission—to Juan, Juan was completely unsurprised. Sympathetic, but unsurprised.

"I thought it might turn out that way. She's been different ever since returning from Mestos. Marina has her in her grasp—you should have seen the painting she did for the king's competition. The waves on it actually moved. It certainly wasn't natural."

Ricardo rubbed his forehead. He didn't want to deal with explaining the concept of optical illusions to his apprentice right now. He would have thought Juan knew better than to be so easily deceived.

"The way she's been acting isn't natural either. You saw for yourself. When she's involved in her work now, there's no breaking her away from it. She's dead to the world. It's not like the way you get when you're really absorbed in a project, or the way she usually gets when we all paint together. It's wrong."

"You've seen her at work on the ceiling? You've been to visit her?"

"Of course. I've been keeping a close eye on all this temple business. Had to, while you were gone. Besides, she's a friend. One of the only ones who was willing to stand by you while you were missing. I've been worried about her."

A friend? Ricardo sighed. "Are you going to support her claim to paint the ceiling?"

"No, of course not. It's clearly not good for her anyway. Besides, it's your project. But with Marina's involvement..."

"I doubt it's truly Marina at work here."

Juan bit his lip. "Master..."

The subject of Beatriz and of Marina was left un-dredged between them, however, because at this moment there was a loud pounding on the front door, at which sound Ricardo realized there had been a quieter knock earlier that they'd both been too wrapped up in conversation to notice. (That, and he was used to his butler handling such things. He was really missing having a staff.)

When they answered the door, it was a messenger from the king, carrying a summons—Ricardo's presence was requested at the palace that evening. The king, said the messenger, had been happy to hear of his return to the city and was eager to see him.

* * *

Ricardo hadn't been planning on seeing Alejandro quite yet.

Within the next week, certainly. He hadn't intended on procrastinating either. But he'd wanted a little longer to plan out what he wanted to say to him, both regarding his absence and regarding the temple vault. In a couple days, he'd been planning on sending a note asking when the king might want to see him, or on showing up at the palace at a time when Alejandro was usually free and asking for an audience. Or perhaps he could have just gone in to his studio and pretended like he'd never left, waited for the king to hear he'd come in and acted casual when Alejandro came down to the studio to see him. At least he'd thought he would be the one to establish first contact, not Alejandro. Being rushed like this made him nervous. Alejandro wanted to see him now, right away—why? What did he have to say to him? And how had he even heard Ricardo was back?

...well, the latter maybe wasn't a huge question. If word hadn't spread from the amount of animated talking Juan had been doing at the bar last night, it still could have gotten out from those workers at the temple—Alejandro was the one who paid their wages, after all, though technically they were employed by the temple itself and the city's priests of Marina.

Or Beatriz might have told him directly. Who knew how close those two were now? She'd said it herself; Ricardo had no idea what had gone on in his absence, but it was clearly a tangled mess.

For now, he had no time to speculate. Only to prepare himself for a meeting with royalty. Something he was used to, but it had been months. He had a minor crisis over what to wear, going through both his usual summer wardrobe and the clothes Leonor had given him, before settling on an outfit he'd worn many times in the royal studio over the past couple years, a dark brown vest and a plain cream shirt that was a little paint-stained. One stain on the sleeve cuff was lapis lazuli blue, a disgraceful waste of expensive pigment. It had frustrated him at the time, and Alejandro had laughed at him and told him not to worry so much about small expenses as they would be provided for. That had annoyed Ricardo in turn, as it had been one of those months when Alejandro was very late on paying him for his last commission, but he let it go, admitted that it was nice to have a rich patron who at least took care of supplies.

It was not an outfit for a formal audience, but a formal audience was not what Ricardo wanted to have. He wanted Alejandro to remember Ricardo was his man, had served him for years. To remember that Ricardo had always been his loyal servant, and deserved loyalty in return.

He made the trip down to the royal palace with his heart clenching every step of the way. At the gate, he was welcomed in by a guard and led to the royal garden.

The guard stayed at the gate, leaving Ricardo to seek out Alejandro for himself, which took several minutes. He found him standing in the section of the garden that was clustered with fruit trees. He'd walked in a ways, making him unseeable from the gate. Ricardo couldn't help but think he might have stood somewhere more visible or perhaps called out when he heard Ricardo entering and walking around. He must have known it was Ricardo; the royal gardens were off limits this time of day to any but the king and certain nobles who had been given special permission—and even those nobles rarely came here, knowing the king liked his privacy.

He smiled when Ricardo came into his view, though, and turned away from the tree whose oranges he'd been critically eyeing. "Montero, here at last."

"Your majesty." Ricardo bowed.

The sight of Alejandro was, after all Ricardo's worrying, underwhelming. Maybe it was exposure to Leonor, but he had somehow expected Alejandro to be taller or simply more imposing (more billowing skirts, perhaps?) than he was. Funny how fast one could begin to misremember another's appearance. Ricardo had even painted Alejandro before—perhaps the most prestigious commission of his life, apart from the temple ceiling—and yet his figure now seemed unfamiliar.

"How do you like the flowers?" Alejandro asked. "The geraniums are wilting lately, but the gardener tells me they'll be back in full force before fall comes. The carnations are doing well, though. You missed the first round of them, but I like this second batch better, I think. There are some pink and orange ones that are the color of the sunset. When the sun sets tonight, you should have a look and compare."

"Everything is beautiful, your majesty. Was there anything in particular you wanted me to look at?"

"In particular? No, not really."

"I'm merely wondering why you would invite me here and not simply meet me in the studio." Strolls in the garden with the king were usually reserved for higher ranking guests.

"Your studio would be a bit inconvenient at the moment. Since I heard you had returned to Ferrar, I ordered it cleaned. The cleaning should still be in progress."

"I appreciate your consideration, your majesty. It was unnecessary." Why would his studio need cleaning? He'd left it in good order, if he remembered correctly, and it wasn't like it had been in use all season. Or had it been? Had Beatriz de Comete usurped his studio as well?

Nonsense. He was getting paranoid. The king probably had just ordered the maids to give it a good dusting. A room not in use for months did get dusty, after all.

Alejandro waved off Ricardo's thanks with a smile. "At any rate, there's no need for you to get right down to work when you've only just gotten back. You should take some time to relax."

"That's thoughtful, your majesty, but I have no need of relaxation. Getting back to work is precisely what I would like to do. On that subject, I wanted to ask you about the status of the temple vault."

Alejandro's smile widened. His eyes sparkled. "I heard you went and looked at it today. Isn't it incredible, to see the goddess at work? I could not have imagined we would be so blessed, Montero. Marina's power shines through every stroke of Beatriz de Comete's brush; truly a celestial experience. Do you feel honored to see your outlines and designs put to such use? I myself feel light whenever I think about what part I have played in this project. Marina smiles on our work, honors us more than I could have dreamed."

The king's offensive was more aggressively positive than Ricardo had been prepared for. He seemed to feel no glimmer of doubt that Ricardo would be as happy about Beatriz having taken the project as he was. Ricardo took a deep breath. "Your majesty, while Beatriz is doing a good job, our initial plans were for me to paint the temple ceiling myself," he reminded him. "I feel that I understand its design and the philosophy behind our decisions better than anyone else could, given the many discussions we had on the matter. Perhaps I could take over the work from here. It is a difficult task for a woman, especially one of noble blood—hard on the neck and the back, and so prolonged a task..."

"You are kind, Montero, but there is no need to worry about that. Miss Comete is strengthened by the goddess. Her body is made of steel, and will well hold out." Alejandro paused. Put a hand on Ricardo's shoulder comfortingly. "I agree that you have great insight on the artistry of the temple, none greater. But it is Marina's will that Miss Comete work on this project, and her will that moves Miss Comete's hand. Who could understand this work better than Marina herself? I would never denigrate your abilities, Montero, but you are a human. Marina is divine."

Ricardo opened his mouth, then closed it. Alejandro's eyes were still on fire. In past years, Ricardo had always found this kind of religious fervor inspiring in his patron. Today, there was something terrible about it. Alejandro would not be moved—that much was clear. Ricardo would never convince him Beatriz was a fraud, not when he was this impassioned speaking about her work. And if Alejandro thought that it was Marina's will that Beatriz paint the temple vault, it would be impossible to stop him from following Marina's will, which he valued more than he valued his own life.

He was immoveable. And Ricardo wondered—dark parts of his mind stirring that he had tried to snuff out in Suelta—if this was how he had appeared before Leonor, all those years ago. He had considered it divine will that he become king, that much Ricardo knew. What would he have done to obtain the position? What would he have scrupled at? He would have been immoveable then, too, certain of the goal he set out to accomplish and unstoppable in the power he had already gained.

Had this inflexible side of him been what Mencia saw, too? Had it frightened her? When they married, did he set his invincible will on loving her or simply on making her his possession for the sake of the alliance, of his own glory? Had she ever looked into his eyes and seen an impossibility of getting through to him? Had he ever set his immoveable will on getting her out of the way?

These thoughts fluttered joltingly through Ricardo's mind all in an instant, not even fully realized before he forced them away and responded, lips numb, "Of course, I would never seek to rival a goddess." And he would never seek, never, to contradict a king.

"There will be other projects for you, Montero. I've been thinking about it. I always did regret that working on the temple ceiling would keep you busy for so long—there's always so much work I want you to do. I've been thinking it would be nice to gift a portrait to this new ambassador from Jukwald—you haven't met him yet, but he loves our Salandran art. Perhaps I could introduce you to him this week, and we could talk about it."

Ricardo was supposed to nod. He knew that. He was supposed to acquiesce, ask some follow-up questions about what the ambassador was like, what kind of art he appreciated, what sort of portrait the king was thinking of, size and style and so on. Instead, he found himself saying, "You haven't asked where I've been."

Alejandro raised his eyebrows. After a moment of silence he said, "Do you want me to ask?"

Ricardo hadn't wanted him to ask. He'd decided not to give Leonor's crimes away—she'd suffered enough in life without Alejandro going after her on Ricardo's behalf. He hadn't wanted to have to thrust away his patron's concern, or defend himself from criticism over leaving without giving Alejandro any warning or explanation. He hadn't wanted to have to stay silent, and equally hadn't wanted to lie. But he'd still expected Alejandro to ask. He'd braced himself for it, and now, without the inquiry, he felt bereft.

"Did you look for me?" he asked.

"I asked around. The local artists didn't know where you were, and your household had no idea either. I thought if you left without any kind of message, you probably didn't want people looking for you. I may be your king, Montero, but I've never wanted to put a leash on you. You can go where you want. I won't demand an explanation."

Ricardo stared at the ground, unable to meet Alejandro's sincere gaze. Hadn't he hated Leonor's controlling, possessive, presumptuous nature? If Alejandro was the opposite, that was surely a good thing. But hadn't he been worried at all? Had he really believed Ricardo would run out on him, on a project they'd been working on for ages—abandon him with no reason given? What kind of ingrate did he think Ricardo was?

And more than that... he swallowed. A couple months ago, when he was still unsure what Leonor would do with him, whether she would be kind or cruel, whether she would ever let him go or whether she would keep him prisoner forever, he'd had only one comfort. He'd told himself that the king had to be looking for him. His nerves hadn't settled much at that thought, knowing that Captain Alban had been subtle in sneaking Ricardo out of the city, knowing that Suelta was a good distance from the capital and its citizens were loyal and for the most part unlikely to blab. *Maybe*, his fears had whispered, *Alejandro will never find me. Maybe she's hidden me too well.* But he'd been sure that Alejandro at least would look.

Alejandro must have taken his silence for embarrassment at concealing a secret, for he continued, "Besides, I could never fault you in this case especially. It's my belief you were meant to leave for this time, so that Marina could put Beatriz forward. Were you not missing, I never would have looked for another artist to paint the temple ceiling. In the end, this is all the goddess's will."

Marina.

It came back to Marina again, and Alejandro's damned devotion. Ricardo had been missing, and Alejandro had only thought of his temple and his goddess, and not worried about Ricardo at all. Ricardo had told Leonor this would be so, told her he was only a painter and of no importance to a king, but he hadn't really believed it.

Ricardo trembled.

It wasn't his place to take offense at a king.

Even Leonor only resorted to acts of petty revenge behind his back—it wasn't Ricardo's place...

Alejandro smiled. "Don't worry about all that. Now, about the ambassador, I don't think you could meet him tomorrow but perhaps the day after. Would you be free, or are you still settling back in?"

Ricardo punched him.

The blow sent Alejandro reeling back, but only momentarily. In a flash, he was on Ricardo, hitting him back—hitting his face, his stomach, kicking his knees in a way that sent Ricardo stumbling down. Vicious in a way Ricardo had never thought he could be. He knew his king was a warrior, but he fought like a street fighter with a grudge. It was worse than anyone Ricardo had fought in Suelta; he hit harder and faster than Captain Alban. Captain Alban had only overwhelmed Ricardo, but Alejandro dizzied him. He was sprawled on the ground before he even realized what was happening, pain pulsing in his head, chest, stomach, legs, places he wasn't even sure had been hit. His ears were ringing. He thought Alejandro was saying something but he couldn't tell what.

Alejandro was over him. How had Ricardo thought he seemed

smaller just a few minutes ago? He was huge, looming over Ricardo, leaning in to grab Ricardo's chin, forcing him to look him in the eyes. Ricardo struck out at him, but he was flailing and only hit him in the side. You could still do damage, hitting someone in the side, if you went about it right. You could rupture a kidney. Ricardo wasn't going about it right. All he did was make Alejandro's eyes darken, and then his other hand was around Ricardo's throat, squeezing. He was going to strangle Ricardo. He was going to kill him. Him and his immoveable will—his arrogance, his belief in his own kingly version of divinity—he would kill Ricardo for his disrespect. Ricardo reached around in his pants pocket and found his knife, the knife Leonor had given him. Took it out.

He flicked the knife open and stabbed blindly at Alejandro's body leaning over him. He got lucky. The knife slid between ribs and found a home deep in Alejandro's chest.

Alejandro gasped. His grip on Ricardo faltered, and Ricardo wrenched himself away, scrambled to his feet. Coughed, regained his breath.

His head was still ringing.

Alejandro was gripping the knife where it went into him. It was a good, sharp knife. It had cut through a light jacket and shirt with no resistance, through skin just as easily. "Why?" he said, looking up at Ricardo. His voice was a croak. "Why? Montero."

Ricardo trembled. He crouched down awkwardly, off balance, to look at the bleeding wound. Alejandro did not strike out at him. The fight was over. "Your majesty..."

"I've treated you like family," Alejandro said. "Why? Why would you do this?"

He was beginning to slump; Ricardo grabbed him, held him up. There was so much blood on the grass. So much blood. A voice screamed, "Help! Help!" It was Ricardo's voice, and it was raspy from strangulation. But it was enough to summon the guards from the gate. There were three of them. Two knelt by the king, talking to each other, examining the wound. A third seized Ricardo and twisted his arm behind his back, cursing at him. It hurt. Ricardo should have been in too much shock to feel it, but it still did hurt.

It was growing late, but the sun had only just begun to set. It was a clear sky, but now it darkened—not with a sudden dusk, but with clouds.

Alejandro was still muttering. Ricardo couldn't tell what he was saying, but he imagined he might be asking Ricardo why—Ricardo still hadn't given an answer. Then the muttering quieted, and then stopped altogether.

Thunder cracked overhead, and it began to rain.

"Why?" he said, looking up at Ricardo. His voice was a croak.
"Why? Montero."

21

CHAPTER TWENTY-ONE

Beatriz was napping when it happened. Napping at the top of the scaffolding, which maybe wasn't the best place for it, but it had been a difficult day. The confrontation with Ricardo wasn't even the entirety of it. Marina was driving her hard that day and didn't care that it was already evening, had no patience for Beatriz wanting to go home and rest. She woke up in a swell of blue with her ears ringing even though there was no audible noise except the usual bustle of the construction workers below.

Marina was screaming. It didn't need to be audible to be deafening. Beatriz curled into a ball and clasped her arms around her head, trying to escape Marina's grief and anger, but it went on and on and on. She felt hands on her arms prying her out of the fetal position and looked up to see a concerned overseer staring at her. She had to look mad, or like she was experiencing some divine revelation. But she wasn't learning anything or seeing anything, not now, only shaking. By the time she'd been gently helped down from the scaffolding to the ground, she was aware of what she herself was feeling, quietly, under the swell of the goddess's passionate cries: fear. Simple, human fear.

She stumbled to the door of the temple and leaned against the wall. It was beyond her to leave. She felt she did not have permission.

And then, slowly, the feeling of the goddess's grief and anger faded in her mind, until the screams in her head became audible white noise instead: the sound of rain hammering down on the temple's roof and outside on the cobblestones.

She looked up. The workers were still gathered around her with concerned expressions. She shook her head; though she was still a little dizzy, she actually felt Marina's presence less than she had for weeks. Marina was everywhere—Marina was rampaging through the city—Marina had no reason to focus on one insignificant painter at a moment like this.

"Miss Comete, are you well?"

"I'm all right now," Beatriz said. "I'm leaving. You should too. This rain will go on for a while, and you all should get home. I don't think Marina will care much if her temple is worked on right now. It might even anger her. Maybe one of you should notify the priests, but then you should go home."

"What's wrong?"

"Why is Marina angry?"

"What do you mean?"

"You'll know soon enough," Beatriz said. Her voice sounded calm in her ears. Made sense; she felt numb inside as well.

The workmen crowded around her, questions piling on questions, but they were too respectful to grab hold of her, and she slipped through their midst and out into the street. Rain pelted her, stinging her skin. She had no cloak to protect her, not even her bag to hold over her head as it had been abandoned on top of the scaffolding. She had a smock on over her dress, at least, but within minutes it was soaked through along with the dress itself, which was light and perhaps a little flimsy to accommodate the heat.

She was late heading home already, she knew. She should get home and tell her family what had happened, warn them of the chaos that would ensue over the days and weeks and months to come. But selfishly, she found herself heading in another direction, and twenty minutes later she was standing inside the Inn of the Rising Moon.

The inn's front room, where travelers ate and drank and conversed and watched the dancing shows, was crowded with people, even more so than usual. Many of them probably had come in to escape the rain, and in fact Beatriz overheard more than one group gossiping about it as she pushed her way over to the bar. Some were saying it was un-seasonably harsh, others hoped that it would at least break the heat, and others laughed and said they loved the rain, really, as long as they were safely inside—said it was even better being cooped up with a little company. (Said this with a wink.) She knew that tides would turn in the next few days; soon everyone would be talking about the rain as an omen, everyone would know it for the sign it was. But not yet.

She sat down at the bar and ordered a glass of sangria. It hadn't even been poured for her yet when she felt a touch on her shoulder, and turned to see Vulpa standing over her with a smile.

"Beatriz! I didn't expect you tonight. I wish you'd come sooner. I have to be onstage in just a little while. How do you like my makeup?"

Beatriz liked it. The rouge especially. And she liked how Vulpa's hair was twisted up today—it was twisted off to the side, asymmetrical like a single raised eyebrow. And she liked Vulpa's dress, which seemed to be a new one, golden with hints of green, just a little too short. But then, when had she ever disliked anything about Vulpa's appearance?

"It's lovely. You're lovely," she said. "But I'm not sure you'll get much of a chance to dance tonight. The performances are bound to be cancelled."

Vulpa frowned. "What? Why?"

Beatriz glanced around, made sure no one was listening. The bartender was, though he was trying to hide it. She pulled Vulpa closer and murmured in her ear, "The king has died."

"What?"

"He's dead. I heard from Marina." Well, less heard, more... gathered. "I believe he was killed, though I don't know much. The news will be out soon. Before the night's over, I'm sure."

Vulpa glanced at the others in the inn now, too, brow furrowed. "What do you mean, you heard from Marina?"

"She was screaming. She's very angry now. Can you hear her?"

Rain pounded on the roof of the inn as hard as it had on the roof of the temple.

"Yes," Vulpa said. "I suppose I do." She grabbed Beatriz's hand and pulled her up. "You must be shaken. Let me take you to my room."

"Wait."

"Ah, can't you stay? Did you... why did you come here?"

"I'll stay, a while at least. I thought I'd watch one dance of yours, maybe. Maybe I could go backstage with you until then? Or up to your room, if that's where you're preparing. But I'd like to drink my sangria first. I only just got it."

"Oh, right. Right, have a drink. Maybe it will steady you."

Beatriz hoped so too, but after a sip she put it down. Her stomach was clenching. "All right. Let's go."

"You haven't..."

"Can you lend me a towel or at least a handkerchief? I should dry off."

"You really should. You're getting looks."

She was, indeed, largely looks of disgust or amusement. Vulpa sent a glare at one man who actually didn't look that disgusted but only a bit curious. Beatriz shook her head.

As they headed off to Vulpa's room together, Vulpa muttered in Beatriz's ear, "Is the king really dead?"

"Yes."

"Strange. I thought now that I'd come to the capital, I might see him someday. Maybe in a parade, or if you took me to the palace. Not that there would be any reason to take me to the palace."

Beatriz hardly ever went to the palace, but she would have taken Vulpa there, or anywhere Vulpa wanted to go. That was what she told herself, but she knew, really, that lately she'd hardly even been able to meet Vulpa in her own house. She shook her head. "There will be another king," she said, in some vain, numb attempt at comfort.

"There always is, but King Alejandro's a legend. I always wished I could meet him."

He hadn't been that impressive in person. Over the past few weeks, his presence had mostly just been wearying. But Beatriz remembered she'd found him impressive when they first met, and Ricardo always worshipped him. "He'll be missed," she said softly, and what she whispered, the rain screamed.

* * *

The week that followed was worse than Beatriz had anticipated.

She had not truly experienced the chaos of a regime shift before. When the old king died and Alejandro became king, she had been too young to understand much of what went on, besides which, Don Fernando, worried by certain political conflicts at the time, had sent her and Luis and Lady Gelvira back to their country estate to avoid any involvement. This time around, unfortunately, none of them could leave. Don Fernando, for the same reasons as before; Luis, because he was old enough to count as the new generation that this king's court would likely, eventually, be made of; Beatriz because she was now Marina's oracle and Marina's rage was... evident.

Beatriz had known Marina would not be easily appeased, and she wasn't. The rain continued—thunder, lightning, and showers, with not a speck of sunlight breaking through. The sky was a constant gray, neither blue during the day nor properly, truly dark at night with moonlight diffused among the clouds making it strangely light even when it was pouring. Water levels were rising in the streets, from mere puddles on the evening of Alejandro's death to ankle deep the next day and then deeper and deeper. By the end of a week of constant rain, sometimes heavy as a tidal wave and sometimes lighter but never ceasing, even high ground had a couple inches of water puddled up on it. Lower ground was heavily flooded. The marketplace was closed, and some families had had to leave their homes. Others had moved to the upper floors of their houses, and brought all their furniture and valuables and as much food and drink as possible with them.

And many, of course, left the city. They took it as doomed by Marina's wrath, or simply struck by a spate of political turmoil and poor weather, and they went out to visit family in the country, or—if they were wealthy—returned to other homes in other cities, or, if they had nowhere else to go, simply put their belongings on their back or a donkey's—few in a cart, for the road outside the city, unpaved, was too muddy for wheels. They fled, and took with them more and more of the city's confidence.

Ferrar had descended into panic. The storm was one factor; the king's death a greater factor, especially since the ministry of justice had not released any statement about how he had died, but a number of arrests had been made and it was widely rumored that the death had not been natural. Had he been murdered? Had he been cursed, as the city was now cursed? No one knew, but everyone feared. In the face of this disaster, they turned to anyone who might provide them guidance. Many turned to the new king, who was yet to be crowned but had now arrived in the capital for the first time in his life. They even turned to the princess Leonor, soon to be queen dowager, remembering that the time of the old king, her father, had been a good time.

But there were also those who knew that the new royals, unlike Alejandro, had no particular connection to Marina or to any god, or who simply placed no trust in royalty. And these people, commonfolk and nobles alike, turned to Marina's priests and priestesses, turned, at court, to the minister of rites, Master Galeas, and above all turned to their new and mystical oracle: Beatriz.

Beatriz hated them.

Hate was not an emotion worthy of her, perhaps. It was not undiluted by other feelings, either. She pitied them, for she understood their fear of Marina very well. She feared Marina too. In a certain sense she also respected their religious devotion—this distantly, for she had never been very religious herself, and on finding religion lately she had also found a dread of it—but it also struck her as stupid and pointless, to go to a human to try to appease a goddess when Marina was Marina and would certainly not be moved by someone as unimportant as Beatriz. And so she hated them, especially after the first couple. The first few people to visit the Comete house in an attempt to worm divine insight out of Beatriz were nobles, friends of the family, people she was willing to offer some patience despite her annoyance that even these close acquaintances saw her now as an oracle, which she was not. But after that, as the days went by there were more and more people showing up at their door, many of whom were complete strangers.

Beatriz's savior now was Lady Gelvira. Luis and Don Fernando would have been willing to throw the majority of these visitors out by force, but Lady Gelvira met them with stern, courteous disapproval. "This house is neither a temple nor a court of appeals," she would tell them, "and our ward is neither a priestess nor a performing monkey. Her relationship with the goddess is private, and has nothing to do with the political situation. I'm afraid I must ask you to leave."

And she would stick to these words no matter how the visitors harassed or hassled or begged.

Beatriz, meanwhile, stayed out of the parlor and the foyer as much as possible, and saw few of these visitors face to face. For the most part, she stayed up in her own room or her studio, but a couple of times she snuck out the servants' door into the city, covering body and face with a thick cloak that protected her from both the rain and public recognition. On these days she made her way—by a circuitous route to avoid the most flooded streets—down to the Inn of the Rising Moon to see Vulpa.

The inn had indeed cancelled performances on the night of King Alejandro's murder, once the news of the murder itself got out, but two nights later they had brought the dancing back, though with tamer acts than before. Was this appropriate in a time of national mourning? Perhaps not. But the tension in the inn mirrored the tension throughout the city, and the innkeeper felt the need to at least provide something to alleviate it. Now those so inclined could get stinking drunk and scream praise and insults at the performers, venting their emotions in a relatively harmless manner. The fact that the guests all were getting drunker than usual, and that the drunks tended more towards morose sulking and irate tantrums than cheer, was something that could not be helped. The innkeeper was doing his best.

It was on the third evening of this kind, after Vulpa had already finished her dancing for the night and she and Beatriz had retired to her room with some bread and a bottle of wine to talk and relax, that Vulpa said to Beatriz, "You know, I missed you."

Beatriz swallowed. "I'm sorry I haven't been a very attentive friend. I know I promised to show you the capital, and you don't know many people here."

"It's not that. The city's fine, really. The people at this inn are nice, and I'm doing fine. But I still miss you when you're so busy, just because it's you. I like you being around."

They were sitting on Vulpa's bed, as Vulpa had no chairs in her room, not yet. Beatriz smiled at Vulpa, and was about to apologize again, in a slightly different way, when Vulpa's hand fell on her thigh, a little too high up, and she fell silent.

Vulpa looked at her. "Do you like me, Beatriz?"

There was no right answer to that question—there was one, of course, and in any other situation Beatriz would employ it, but, "You know that things are complicated right now. My vocation is Marina—I can't focus on anything else."

"Do you want to tell me about it?" Vulpa asked. "I'll listen."

"It's... no. Lately it's been different, anyway. She hasn't really spoken to me since the king died."

"Then it's just you in your head."

"Yes. Lately."

"Do you like me?"

"Of course I do, Vulpa, but it's still not a good idea."

Vulpa leaned over and kissed her, and she couldn't help but kiss back. They tasted wine in each other's mouths, and it was strong and sweet. Her hands moved to grip Vulpa's waist, to feel hard muscle under her dress, tense and quivering.

She should have pushed Vulpa away, explained to her why this was a bad idea, how possessive and dangerous Marina could be. Or perhaps told her they could take it slow. Their relationship escalated too fast, it seemed, always: from strangers to painter and model to patient and healer to tentative friends and now to lovers. Such a twisting, fast-evolving love could not be stable, could easily collapse, and while Beatriz had had many lovers before and never much minded the speed a relationship formed or deteriorated, she'd never felt about anyone quite the way she felt about Vulpa. She owed Vulpa her life. She owed Vulpa more than some disastrous fling started at fuck o'clock in the middle of a cursed thunderstorm. But she could not bring herself to push Vulpa away, and when they pulled apart, lazily overwhelmed, she made no more protests. She only ran a hand over Vulpa's hair and said, "I really will paint you someday."

Vulpa laughed breathily. "Oh, Beatriz... you have no idea how annoyed I was when we decided you couldn't."

"Oh? I didn't know."

"I thought maybe we'd never meet again, and if we did it wouldn't be the same. I wouldn't be your model, so I wouldn't really be anything to you."

"I wanted you for more than that, you know, even then. Just didn't have any excuse—and you were seeing Jorge."

"I thought maybe you felt that way. But I didn't really know."

"Now you know."

"Now I know." Vulpa giggled, and kissed Beatriz again, gentler this time.

Outside the rain continued, but it did not intrude in here, into the bedroom, nor did any reprimand make itself known in Beatriz's head. Beatriz allowed herself to hope: Perhaps she was free now. Perhaps this was something she was allowed to have.

22

CHAPTER TWENTY-TWO

The guards who had come when Ricardo screamed for help later considered that they might have—and indeed perhaps should have—killed Ricardo on the spot. In the moment, however, all of them were stunned and confused. Their king was dying of a stab wound and he was askingRicardo why he'd done what he'd done, but his words were nonspecific and, as he continued to speak, even faded into incoherency. Moreover, Ricardo had been the one to call them over in the first place, which seemed to indicate that he wanted to save Alejandro, not kill him. Could he really be the murderer here?

And for that matter—Alejandro couldn't be dead, surely? He was the king of Salandra, celebrated war hero and beloved of the gods. The guards checked his pulse in his neck and wrist, held a hand over his mouth and felt no breath, put a hand on his chest and felt no heartbeat, yet none of this fully convinced them. Sometimes a pulse could be faint or hard to perceive when someone was close to death. There were also stories about people whose hearts stopped who came back to life, sometimes even hours later; none of the guards knew anyone who'd come back to life like this personally, but they all believed it was possible, and if it was possible for anyone, it would surely happen for the king. Fundamentally they all believed Alejandro couldn't really die. So one guard dragged Ricardo off to the palace dungeon to be dealt with later, his fate to be decided by Alejandro when he recovered, while of the other two, one sat at Alejandro's side and put pressure on the wound and tried to shield his face from the rain with his jacket, and the other ran for a doctor.

Ricardo was left in a cell for hours by himself. He wasn't sure how many. He had no way to judge the time—he couldn't even judge by the changing of guards, for guards came in and out suddenly, with exclamations or ominous mutterings, glancing over at his cell but not approaching to him, clearly following no schedule but the changing orders of a catastrophe. Hours and minutes felt much the same. He thought to himself: *the doctor is working hard now to save Alejandro's life. Wounds like these are not easy.* He thought, queasily, of how angry Alejandro would be when he had sufficiently recovered, of what punishment he would hand down. Alejandro had always been fond of Ricardo, but attempted regicide was not something that could be brushed aside. The punishment for such a crime was always death. How could Ricardo have been so foolish? He'd panicked in the moment, thought attacking Alejandro with a knife was the only way to save himself, but even then, he could have surely stabbed some other, less lethal part of his body. A man with half a brain would have stabbed Alejandro's arm or hand to get him to let go, but Ricardo, brainless idiot, had stabbed at his heart. A man with half a brain, for that matter, would never have punched him and started the whole brawl to begin with.

And yet.

And yet it still pricked at him.

"It"—a hard to define "it". There had been nothing wrong with the king suggesting Ricardo meet with the ambassador. He'd wanted

Ricardo to get back to work, to normal life. That wasn't wrong. And strictly speaking, it was the king's prerogative to choose whatever artist he wanted to paint the temple of Marina, since it was his project and for that matter his city, his country. Maybe Ricardo was a little annoyed at that. The project was one he'd worked on for months with the king before he was kidnapped, after all, and he'd never had Alejandro so casually reassign him before. Maybe it reminded him of previous incidents of more minor callousness, incidents he'd brushed aside. But it wasn't really that. Well, it wasn't just that. So what was "it"? Alejandro himself had wondered, had asked Ricardo to explain...

He'd said, at the same time, that he'd treated Ricardo "like family". Well, wasn't that just dandy, Ricardo thought bitterly. If you looked at the way Alejandro treated family, what did that record look like? The kindest, most lenient judge couldn't deny he'd practically exiled Leonor from the capital, left a well-loved princess as a social outcast, not to mention how he'd neglected his wife. That was mere abuse, but if you believed Leonor's claims you would see atrocities. Had Alejandro really murdered his uncle, his aunt, his wife? Ricardo had tried not to believe what Leonor had said. But he'd had to try.

No, that wasn't fair. Ricardo rubbed his head. Alejandro had never treated him badly. He'd spent more time with Ricardo than with either Leonor or his wife—it wasn't Ricardo's place to pick up offended women's grudges. But wasn't it that very favor he'd been shown that got to Ricardo? That he'd been treated so well by Alejandro—thought he meant something to him, even considered the two of them friends, considered himself Alejandro's dear confidant —and maybe Alejandro hadn't cared about him all along, saw him as replaceable, didn't worry at his absence, didn't miss him, didn't think about Ricardo every day the way Ricardo had habitually, almost perforce thought about him. Jealousy, hurt, betrayal. Maybe that was what had pricked at Ricardo.

But that was too dramatic, too poetic, a way to think about "it" too. He hadn't been feeling especially close to Alejandro now or for the past few weeks either. No great affection or intimacy to shock with cruel words (and Alejandro hadn't even been cruel, just thoughtless). So what had it been? Ricardo couldn't say. Insanity. It had been insanity; that was the only way he could explain it.

Insanity. Could he plead that, and beg Alejandro's forgiveness? You couldn't forgive attempted regicide, but if a man were truly insane, perhaps murder wasn't really murder. Alejandro liked to say Beatriz was governed by Marina's will—Ricardo could claim he'd been cursed by some god, or maybe that Alejandro had. "I got that knife I stabbed you with on the festival of Sektos," he might say. "It's the only explanation I can think of, that Sektos took hold of my mind and made me do something I never would have done. Please, you cannot blame a man for following the will of the gods."

...even Alejandro wouldn't believe that bullshit.

All the same, Ricardo tried to formulate excuses to offer Alejandro, come up with phrasing that would render his actions if not acceptable then somehow understandable. He continued thinking this way for some time. He was like the guards, and could not believe Alejandro would not survive, that Alejandro had already been dead by the time he left the garden. Even when a guard came over and called him a murderer and shouted out graphic threats of what kind of death he deserved, he didn't understand that Alejandro really was dead already. Even when the first interrogator came and removed him from the cell, he assumed it was on Alejandro's orders. "Tell the king I'm sorry," he said. "I was insane. I didn't mean to do it. Please, ask him to speak to me or at least to hear me out even if he won't meet with me in person."

The first interrogator only asked him, over and over again, what his reasons had been for what he'd done, who had commanded him to do it or what grudge he'd held. The second interrogator, who came the next day, was the one who officially informed him of Alejandro's death. Ricardo didn't believe him. He thought it was a lie to make him confess to some further sin than everyone knew he'd committed. But the story never changed, and so the knowledge slowly filtered into Ricardo's brain. Alejandro was dead. Ricardo would never be able to make his apologies or offer any explanation. He would never speak to his king, the man who'd owned his complete loyalty and devotion, again.

* * *

The interrogations.

What can be said about a Salandran interrogation?

Stories of them were spread the world over. Certainly Ricardo had known what they entailed long before experiencing them. As a child, his nightmares included images of men hanging from ceilings by their wrists or being stretched out slowly on the rack. Children could only imagine the pain of these things, the distortion of the body. Ricardo as an adult had come to understand better how such things might work on the anatomy, but as he grew and largely encountered no great misfortune, he had grown less afraid of pain, and so in some ways had understood what torture might feel like less than the blindly terrified child he had once been.

Now he came to understand again. The pain was enough, sometimes, to drive away all else: all guilt, all grief, all anguish but the physical. When it let up, and his interrogators left him alone for a while, his thoughts would circle between agony of the body and the mind. Both echoed the same words over and over again—*your fault, your fault, your fault...*

It exhausted him. He could not think straight, even to make sensible answers to the questions the interrogators posed. They were pointless questions anyway.

"Who told you to kill King Alejandro?"

"What was promised to you if you killed King Alejandro?"

"What foreign country do you have ties with?"

"Where did you go while you were out of the capital this summer?"

The first three were nonsensical. The last had an answer, and Ricardo knew, when he had enough of a mind to think, it was a dangerous one. It might have caused Leonor a little trouble if Alejandro had known she kidnapped his favorite artist, but there would be far greater consequences if these people, officials of the Ministry of Justice, found out she had ties with the king's murderer, even if in truth she'd had nothing to do with the murder itself. So Ricardo did not mention Leonor—or at least, he thought he didn't. Her name might have escaped his lips a couple times. But then, so did so many other things. He gave so many answers to these questions posed to him, many of them contradicting, many of them lies. When a session was over, he could barely remember what he'd said or whether it had been anything he said that made it stop or simply concern that he would grow too weak or broken to answer more questions later. What conclusions the interrogators were drawing, he couldn't say.

He had no energy to think about it all logically. He wanted to sleep and was not allowed to sleep.

* * *

The torture didn't make Ricardo hallucinate, but when Leonor de Suelta appeared in front of him, he thought perhaps the hallucinations had finally started. Only the interrogator present, and the guards in the cell, seemed to see Leonor just as well as he did, and in fact deferred to her when she asked them to step aside so that she could sit opposite Ricardo and speak to him without anyone standing too close and distracting them.

"He is a dangerous man, your highness," the interrogator said.

"Deranged. Capable of anything. We don't want to give him a chance to injure you."

"He is in chains, and clearly half dead," Leonor said in a clipped, restrained voice. "But if he were to lunge at me, you are all still here and I'm sure you could protect me. Don't worry yourselves."

The interrogator exchanged a look with the guards, and they all stepped back. A little too readily, Ricardo thought. He felt distantly offended on Leonor's behalf, that she had been taken down here to a wet and dirty dungeon still wearing a fine, gold-embroidered dress that now looked a little damp, as did a cloak she was wearing over it. As did her hair. He felt offended that the guards didn't care enough to prevent her sitting so close to a dangerous prisoner. Then again, guards had done nothing to really protect Alejandro from him either. Maybe no one cared what damage Ricardo did, no matter who he did it to, not enough to stop him. They just wanted to punish him for it. That was all they cared about. As long as Ricardo was in pain, who cared if he committed another murder? Maybe he would kill Leonor. Wasn't some of all this her fault? He would never have been so insane as to kill the king if he'd never met her—he never would even have thought an evil thought about Alejandro—and she'd stolen him away from his commission, and that was really why he'd gotten so mad, wasn't it? Wasn't it all Leonor's fault?

He could feel his lips twisting into an ugly, bloody smile. Leonor looked back at him. Her eyes were glistening. Far too beautiful for this place. He hated her for being better than him. She was a rural outcast, a pariah among nobility, and a petty, kidnapping, possessive, impulsive little bitch. But he was no better than an animal.

"Ricardo Montero," she said. "You have killed my cousin, the king of Salandra. As the future queen dowager and as his family, it is my duty to see you will face justice. Do you understand that?"

No. No, he didn't understand that. He blinked tiredly. Wasn't it enough that he had to adjust to Leonor being here at all? Her words arranged themselves slowly in front of him. Queen dowager. Future queen dowager. Leonor. Mother of a king. Because of Felipe—right, because of Felipe. Alejandro's death made Felipe king, and Leonor queen dowager.

Was that... Felipe was young, very young. He'd likely have a regent. But Leonor? Everyone at court disdained Leonor. She had no influence, no connections. Well, Felipe had bragged she had some, more than Ricardo had really believed. Still, she said "future queen dowager" like it was a title with great weight. What did that imply? Ricardo wanted, for the first time in what felt like years, to know what was going on outside the walls of the dungeon. Leonor awoke the old fire of curiosity in his half-dead bones.

No, he didn't understand.

"I am here to encourage you to confess the truth," Leonor said, looking him in the eyes. "Tell these men—tell me, and tell the world—why you really killed Alejandro. Who or what drove you to the act? A humble painter can't have done it of his own accord. Where did you spend the summer, Montero? On whose behalf did you commit this crime?"

Her eyes were steady on his. Desperate. *She thinks I'll implicate her*, Ricardo thought. *She's begging me not to.* Then, *gods, she thinks I did it for her. She really thinks I did it for love of her, and now she thinks love will keep me silent.*

His response was instinctive. He spat in her face.

The guards were on him in an instant, and on Leonor, pulling her away. As if spit were as deadly a weapon as a knife. Ricardo was laughing. No, maybe he wasn't. He was quivering, anyway, chest heaving, and it was as good a release as laughter, that, although by the look on Leonor's face, she didn't find it, or anything, all that funny.

23

CHAPTER TWENTY-THREE

Ricardo Montero was on Beatriz's mind.

The wrath of Marina over Alejandro's death had laid waste to the city. The shock and anxiety of the people reverberated through it as well. But when Beatriz really thought about Alejandro being dead, thought about him as a person rather than just a king and his death as a person's death rather than simply a catastrophic event, she thought about Ricardo and knew he had to be devastated. Serving Alejandro had been his life, or at least a great portion of it. Alejandro had been his friend, his ruler, often his muse, practically his god. If Alejandro's death had shaken the city to its core, it would have cracked Ricardo to his spine.

Beatriz wanted to know how he was dealing with it, but it would perhaps not be the best idea to go and visit him and try to comfort him and ask him how he was doing. Right now he was angry with her, after all. He'd even been considering appealing to Alejandro to get Beatriz taken off the temple commission, and now Alejandro's death left him with no such recourse. If Beatriz were to visit him now, he might think she was gloating—or worse, empathizing with a grief she had no right to claim. She'd served as Alejandro's favored artist for only a handful of weeks. She'd never known him or loved him as Ricardo had.

Still. Ricardo was her friend, and she felt that if she left it until the new king was crowned and life had calmed down to visit him, the schism between them would only grow deeper, not to mention how few friends Ricardo truly had in the city. So although it would have been easier simply to leave him alone for the time being, she snuck out of her house one (rainy) morning and began the walk down to his house, at a pace that only held the smallest portion of hesitation.

She had imagined the meeting between them might be difficult. Confrontational. She had not realized how difficult it would be to get to his house at all. His neighborhood was situated at the bottom of a slight hill, barely a hill at all, more of a decline. Ricardo often complained about trudging up it into town, but it had never bothered Beatriz much until now. Now, with water gathered in every low part of the city, Beatriz had not yet half descended the hill when the water was a foot and a half deep. She had given up on lifting her skirts long ago, accepting sodden clothing as inevitable, and was willing to accept the water level rising over the top of her high boots (borrowed from Lady Gelvira, who had a wider variety of boots than she did) as well, but it was clear that by the time she reached Ricardo's house, the water would be up to her waist and not entirely safe to walk in—rain was still falling violently, and the way it rushed downhill made a current that would make it easy to slip, besides which she would be unable to see the ground, and there was some debris afloat in the water as well, roof tiles and planks of wood and other miscellanea. Had Beatriz more faith in Marina's patronage, she might have made the attempt anyway, but Marina hadn't spoken to her in days, and it seemed Beatriz was for the moment quite forgotten. Marina might even drown her by accident and not notice until later.

She would have turned back and just gone home, but when she got to the top of the incline again, she found a young boy waiting there. He had what looked like a large, flattish basket with him, tight-woven and layered. As she arrived at the top, he placed it in the water at their feet, and she saw it was in fact a sort of boat. "Trying to get downtown, ma'am?" he asked, with an ingratiating smile. "I'm taking customers anywhere in the city they want to go, even the most difficult sections. Where can I take you?"

She asked his price, which was reasonable, and gave him the address, stepping gingerly into his boat, careful not to capsize it. He took her down the street and around the corner, maneuvering around debris and lamp posts and one fountain that continued to burble slowly and cheerfully in the midst of the downpour. When they reached the Montero house, she saw that there were no lights inside despite the curtains of a couple windows being open, but she had the boy pull up to the door anyhow. She banged on it and called out Ricardo's name, announcing herself, saying she had to speak to him. Nobody came.

"Gone to an inn, ma'am," the boy suggested. "A lot of people have, to escape the flood. I can take you to any inn you want to visit, if you want."

She thanked him but declined. The Inn of the Rising Moon was not in a low area of town, and it was the only other place she wanted to visit that night.

* * *

Seeking out the inn where Ricardo was staying—if he was even still in the city—felt like a step too far for Beatriz, so she decided to let him be. But only a couple days later, a visitor arrived at her own door, though it was not Ricardo. It was Juan.

She thought at first sight that he was bedraggled due to the rain, but realized after a moment that while his hair and clothes and body were indeed soaked, it was more than that affecting his appearance. There was a bruise on his cheek that had gone yellow, and his eyes were red and circled.

The first thing he said to her was, "You have to help my master."

The words did not surprise her. Of course if he was here on her doorstep with despair in his eyes it was not on his own behalf; when had he ever come begging on his own behalf? And Beatriz had still been worrying about Ricardo in the back of her mind for days. Of course he had gotten into more trouble. Staying at an inn—she should never have trusted the comforting words of a stranger. These were tumultuous times, and Ricardo, supporter of the late king, would of course be in the thick of things.

She told Juan to sit down and had tea brought for him. And some bread. He looked like he could use something to eat.

"They're claiming he murdered him," he blurted out, standing in front of the chair Beatriz had told him to sit in, wringing his hands. "He didn't. I swear he didn't. He would never. I don't know who's lying or why or what they have to hide or why they'd choose to frame him of all people, but my master's an honest man. You know that, Miss Comete. And he had so much respect for King Alejandro. He would never have killed him. You know that, don't you?"

"Sit down, Juan," Beatriz said. He was making her nervous. "I'm a little confused. Can you start at the beginning? Where have you and Ricardo been?"

"Prison. For weeks—"

"Weeks? I saw you last week."

"Days, then. I don't know. I was arrested—they came to the house and dragged me out. They would have arrested all the servants, they said, but we don't have servants anymore. They all left. Now I'm actually glad they left, can you imagine? They were angry, though. The soldiers. Wanted more people to target. They dragged me down to the royal prison and ever since then they kept on asking me whether I was involved in the king's murder. They claim my master killed him! Montero! At first I was just stunned but now..." He shook his head. "I don't know who has it out for him now. He never told me where he went when he disappeared. I used to think it might be Valdez, or one of his other rivals, but now I just don't know. None of them would have the reach for this. And the king is really dead. It's insanity."

"That doesn't make any sense. Actual guards arrested you? You were in the actual royal prison?"

"Yes! They've all gone insane with Alejandro gone. I don't know who's in charge now, but he must have some kind of grudge, or... anyway. It's not good." Juan shook his head. "I only got out because Countess Leonor intervened and sent one of her men to have me released. They're claiming there are witnesses and evidence that implicate my master, but there's no evidence against me except association. She couldn't release him, but she could release me."

"Countess Leonor. You mean the crown prince's mother? She's involved in this?"

"The whole damn court seems to be on one side or the other. At least she's trying to help. Most aren't. It's a frame job, but I don't know who they're covering for or how Alejandro really died. Please, Beatriz. You're our only hope here."

"Me?"

Every sentence out of Juan's mouth made less sense to Beatriz, but this last one took the cake. A conspiracy afoot at the royal palace she could believe; dreadful things happening to Ricardo, too. But what on earth was Beatriz supposed to do about any of it?

"Countess Leonor told me," Juan said, leaning forward. "She's talking to everyone now, all the nobles and the officials, people from all the different ministries. Everyone in the city fears the rain is a sign of Marina's displeasure, and the Ministry of Rites won't hold the coronation of Prince Felipe until it stops. But the priests have had no luck with the usual prayers and ceremonies. They're starting to think about other ways to try to appease her now, and tomorrow Minister Galeas will come to visit you—you, Beatriz—and ask you to commune with Marina. You have to speak on my master's behalf and say he's innocent. Marina will want justice too, and you'll have the power to see it rightly done. Just don't forget my master. Please, Beatriz."

Beatriz took Juan's hands and squeezed them. Everything he'd said was insane and frightening, but right now he didn't need to hear about her own confusion. "Juan, I'll do whatever I can for Ricardo. I promise."

"I know. I know you're his friend and will stand by him. It may be difficult, but remember, the countess is on our side—she's a better sort than I'd thought by how everyone talks about her—they may try to confuse you or convince you he's guilty, but you know Montero better than anyone..."

The tea and bread had arrived, and Beatriz cut off Juan's rambling to force him to eat and drink and take some deep breaths. As he did so, she considered the situation as he'd described it. Juan had a tendency to be alarmist, but he usually was accurate about the general details of a problem. If he said Ricardo was in jail, Ricardo was in jail. If he said Ricardo was accused of murder, he was accused of murder. Why this was not public knowledge yet would be harder to say, but perhaps there really was a conspiracy. She didn't know, couldn't know. But if there was, things might even be more dire than Juan thought.

If a minister was coming to see Beatriz, she would speak on Ricardo's behalf, of course. How could she fail to do so? But Juan had an inflated idea of Beatriz's importance, both to the city and to the goddess. Without Marina, she was nothing, and even with Marina, well, Salandra heeded the gods when it suited. Right now Marina had everyone frightened, but some nobles and officials could be pretty tenacious about their ambitions. There might be little Beatriz could do.

She would still try, though. A promise was a promise. She reiterated it many times before sending Juan home, each time growing wearier at its weight and the weight of its very necessity. Why couldn't Ricardo have stayed out of trouble? He used to be a far more safe and sensible man.

* * *

Without Marina, Beatriz was nothing. Still, she would do her best. This was Beatriz's resolution, but the day that followed went nothing like how she had expected.

The next morning, she woke early, even earlier than she had become accustomed to waking for her work at the temple. She found herself dressing in one of her best, most formal gowns, and, with a feeling of purpose, heading for the street, her destination the unfinished temple.

There was blue in her head.

Lady Gelvira stopped her at the door. "You're frightening the servants," she said. "Beatriz. I thought you were done with... this."

"Forgive me, mother," Beatriz said. "The goddess calls me. There's work to do."

Lady Gelvira drew back, lips tight. Beatriz never called her mother, but today the word flowed easily from her lips. She felt that it was only half her speaking, and so it was easy to say things she would normally never dare to say.

"Put on some boots and a cloak, at least," Lady Gelvira said.

Beatriz was wearing neither. She was not even wearing shoes. But the humming in her head would not abide any delay. She dipped her head at Lady Gelvira and walked out the door and straight into the raging storm outside.

The rain drenched her clothes, her hair, her skin. But it was not harsh on her body as she might have expected. Instead, it seemed to caress her. And she did not have to wade through shallow puddles and flooded streets either, not today. The water parted before her, and closed again behind her.

Onlookers—a few braving the street like herself, but most watching from windows—breathed a quiet prayer to Marina: "May the goddess bless us too, and may her wrath be soon appeased." And they all thought to themselves that this woman, if anyone, was the city's hope if it wished to avoid being swallowed up entirely, if it wished the rain to ever end.

At the temple, she was not greeted by the cheerful construction workers she was used to. Unable to continue work in these conditions, they had all gone home. Instead, she was greeted by a couple priests and some courtly officials. Important people. She greeted them all indifferently and went inside.

She had assumed that today Marina wanted her to work on the vault again, but it was not the case. She felt no urge to mount the scaffolding, and instead stood next to it and faced the officials who had followed her in.

"Miss Comete," one of them said (the oldest one, solemnly dressed but not a priest), "how fortuitous to see you here at this hour. We were planning to call you to court today, but this is perhaps a better meeting place. We were hoping you could do something about the current... signs of Marina's displeasure."

Beatriz drew a deep breath. "In myself, I can do nothing. However, I can speak in Marina's name and convey her will to you. Whether you follow it or not will be the decisive factor."

Everyone nodded eagerly. A flurry of words descended on Beatriz, hard to parse, but the gist seemed to be that they indeed wished to comply with whatever she (or Marina through her) might request —and if she could be so kind as to give them an idea now, it would be greatly appreciated.

"To begin with, I'd like to talk to Ricardo Montero, your alleged assassin," she said. "Preferably with a judge present or enough officials to witness the questioning. I believe he'll speak the truth to me."

She wanted to speak further, express her belief in Ricardo's innocence, but though words had flowed easily out of her up to this point, when she tried to speak on his behalf, she found her lips sealed and a tightness in her chest. She fought it, and had begun to say what she wished—"Ri—", but she was interrupted by the old official, who now said, "We will comply with Marina's will."

"You are wise to do so," Beatriz said automatically.

"Would it please you to come see Montero now? Surely haste is a priority."

Yes, Beatriz wanted to say. But that was Marina's will, not hers. She bit her lip, and forced out the words: "Not quite yet. I wish to say a prayer to Marina first, before I go. But in an hour, maybe, I will be ready."

A swell of impatience rocked her, but not too demanding. Marina wanted to get this done with, but she was remembering, now, that Beatriz was her worshipper and favored one, not just her tool. Very well. She would accept obeisance, hear what Beatriz had to say. As long as it didn't take too long.

Beatriz separated from the group and knelt before a statue of Marina that depicted her as a big, curvaceous woman with long, curly hair and closed eyes. It neither enhanced nor lowered her spiritual connection to the goddess, but she could tell Marina appreciated the sign of respect, and it would, she hoped, make the officials leave her alone now that she was done talking to them.

Marina, she prayed silently in her heart, *I am glad you have chosen me for this task. We must see justice done.* She felt the goddess's pleasure, and continued, *We must clear Ricardo's name.*

Rage hit her like a migraine. She dared to take the side of the guilty?

"He can't have done it," she murmured. "He can't have. He's just Ricardo."

"DO NOT SPEAK OF THINGS YOU DO NOT KNOW."

Marina's voice in her head was as loud as it had ever been now, and Beatriz gasped. Cringed. "Milady..."

"RICARDO MONTERO HAS COMMITTED A GREAT CRIME. DO NOT DEFEND HIM."

"No... no, milady, I can't believe that. How could he..."

A boom of blue and black filled her head, and for a moment she couldn't think. When she became aware of herself again, she was on her hands and knees rather than just her knees, and both her arms and legs were shaking. Her vision was blurred with tears of pain and shock. She tried to speak. Her lips twitched soundlessly and her mind could not form properly convincing words.

She knelt there for a long time before she was disturbed, not by an official, but by Countess (Princess? Almost queen dowager now, but not quite yet) Leonor de Suelta. (And when had she gotten here?)

"Miss Comete."

"Countess." Her voice worked again now.

"You recognize me."

"We met once."

"You're Montero's friend."

"Yes," Beatriz said. "I have been for years. And you?" What investment did Leonor have in this case that she would defend a commoner she didn't know, accused of her own cousin's murder?

"I have a high opinion of him, one might say," Leonor said. "I hear you are going to interrogate him. I hope you will consider his case well. Perhaps not all is as it seems. You are his friend..."

Beatriz wanted to assure her that she cared about Ricardo deeply (more than Leonor, most likely) and would do all she could to help him clear his name. What came out of her mouth, however, was, "Would you defend your cousin's murderer, then?"

Marina's words. She had not been guarding herself, and in a moment her self-possession had slipped.

Leonor paled and stiffened even further than before. "No, of course not. Whoever committed this heinous crime should be condemned. I only want to see justice done."

"Do you? You were not fond of Alejandro."

"My cousin and I were not close, but I never wanted him dead, and I too would condemn anyone who killed him. Even Montero."

Beatriz nodded. "Good."

She turned away, and apparently Leonor considered herself dismissed, for she went to fetch her son (Prince Felipe was here? Beatriz really must have been distracted not to notice a crown prince's entrance) and then left the temple. Beatriz sat on her heels a while after that, trying to think, hoping her pose looked something like kneeling and not like exhaustion. At last she heaved herself to her feet and rejoined the officials, who had been waiting all this time. She would see Ricardo, and she and Marina both would speak with him. Surely truth would out.

* * *

The officials presented one condition: that several of them would be present while Beatriz and Ricardo spoke to each other. This way, if Beatriz actually just wanted to help her old friend escape prison or conspire with him in some other way, she would be prevented by the number of witnesses. On the other hand, if Marina wanted to kill Montero without the court's approval, there would be officials there to prevent it.

Beatriz agreed to this condition easily, restlessly. What did she care who was present for the conversation, as long as it came soon? And Marina cared even less—in fact, she approved of witnesses. The more, the better.

When they stepped outside, she found that Don Fernando was waiting there in the temple's foyer. He'd followed her here after hearing from Lady Comete where she'd gone and in what mood. The officials had told him of her intentions. "I will accompany you," he said, in a voice that brooked no dissent. He had not in the past interfered with any of Beatriz's goddess-influenced adventures, and so she was a little surprised, but relieved at the same time. She would have some support there. She already would have a goddess at her back, and it was fundamentally a meeting with a friend, but she hardly felt she could trust either Marina or Ricardo at the moment.

The prison was further from the Comete house than the temple was. Beatriz still walked, and the water still parted. It allowed Lord Fernando to walk freely beside her, too, before splashing closed behind them. They passed a boy on the street who ran behind them for a little bit, enjoying the splash of it like a fountain. Marina would like him, Beatriz thought quietly—but Marina did not listen to her thoughts lately except when addressed, and she was too focused on the call of vengeance to care about a playful boy who loved the water.

The royal prison was beneath the palace, at the same level as the cellar. It was durable: no water had yet leaked in despite all the rain outside, although the air was humid. It was stone, and it was dark. Ricardo had been down here for days. Beatriz felt claustrophobic within seconds.

She would be seeing him soon, Ricardo, and then there would be a chance they could get all this sorted out. But here in the prison, Ricardo's situation, the reality of the crime which he stood accused of, felt too real for her to be optimistic. And Marina was heavy on her shoulders like a thick cloak.

They were led to a small room, which they were informed was the usual interrogation room. There was a small table in the middle of it with two chairs. There were also about officials crammed into the room, looking so deliberately solemn it was more like grumpiness. The prison guard who had escorted them in hurried off to fetch one more extra chair for Don Fernando, so he wouldn't have to hover awkwardly over Beatriz's shoulder. Beatriz herself sat at the table and waited. She only had to wait about ten minutes, maybe fifteen, but it felt like much longer.

Then Ricardo was brought in, with two guards escorting him.

He had only been in prison for a little more than a week, but that much time had been enough to grimly transform him. He was wearing one of his neat, workman's painting outfits, but it was stained brown across the shirt—bloodstains, Beatriz realized with a distant sense of horror—and was overall dirty from being worn for so long without washing or changing. His hair was pulled back with a tie, but tangled, and he'd grown a messy beard and mustache, though neither were very long. There were dark circles under his eyes, and his hands were dirty when he laid them on the table in front of him after sitting down, dirty with plain old dirt and sweat, not with paint as per usual. And his wrists were cuffed.

"Beatriz," he said hoarsely. "I heard it was you. Something to do with Marina? What a farce. Don't involve yourself in this, for goodness' sake."

Beatriz wanted to greet him warmly, wanted to take his head in her hands and check if that was a bruise she saw on his cheek underneath the stubble, to ask him how he was being treated, to tell him she believed in him even if nobody else did. But Marina spoke in her head. *"Let me take over, little one. This is my business."* And Beatriz did not disobey.

Mechanically, she unwrapped the bandage on her hand. Today her scar glowed more brightly blue than ever before, casting its light throughout the room. (Later on Don Fernando would tell her that her eyes had shone the same color in that moment, bright blue and inhuman, and that when she spoke, her voice was like the crashing of the waves.) "Ricardo Montero," she said. "I, Marina, have deigned to come and hear you speak in your defense. You killed my favored one, King Alejandro de Ferrar. Will you offer any excuses? Do you have any defense you can plead when your guilt is evident?"

Ricardo sat back as far in his seat as he could, leaning away from her. "Marina. You. Has my crime been so grave that a goddess will meddle in human affairs now?"

"Alejandro's affairs were always my affairs, as were the affairs of the nation, for he prayed to me for its glory and its protection. He was mine, the man you killed. You were the one who touched what you should not have."

"He was my friend," Ricardo said. "I was wrong. I know it."

"Your friend? To call him your friend is as much a blasphemy as your crime, vermin!"

Ricardo's face twitched. "You are a goddess, but you speak the same way as any of the guards here. The king was as mortal as I." His voice grew distant. "I realized that at last, but not fully, and too late. I wish I could have understood him..."

"Such a thing would have been impossible for scum like you."

Ricardo looked up. "Your words come out of the wrong mouth, goddess."

"You judge my choice of avatar again?"

"My aim has been off lately. I can see now the crime I laid at Beatriz's feet as well as Alejandro's was your doing. I'm sorry for that, my blindness. But you should be sorrier. You have touched what should not have been touched. You've seized the mind of my best friend in the world, stolen the hand of perhaps the best artist in the kingdom. That was something no one should have done. It is too bad. I can punish a king—I can punish my own best friend—but not you." Ricardo laughed. "Still, you came to see me and show me her face. That at least was kind. Thank you."

"I came here to hear you and to condemn you," Marina said through Beatriz's mouth, while Beatriz wanted to sob and to scream but knew she could not, should not even try to wrest back control of herself, not here and not now where all the court officials would back up Marina's judgment, would call for her return. Marina's powers were natural and supernatural both. If she wanted to condemn Ricardo, how was Beatriz to stop it?

"This is all I have to say," Ricardo said softly. "I did kill the king. There is no way for me to argue I didn't. It was a moment of passion, anger, fear, stupidity. I regret it, but only for selfish reasons. I killed him out of anger just as I served him out of love. Were I a logical, objective man, I don't know what I would have thought of him, how I would have seen him. But we are all corrupt and foolish humans, aren't we? I doubt the next king will be any better, in the end."

Beatriz stood up. "You will not live to see the next king. You will be executed before he is crowned." She turned to the officials, who flinched away from the blue light that now was cast upon them. "None of you can disagree with me that this man deserves to die. Judge," she said to one of them,-"will you pronounce his sentence? As for his execution, I will handle it myself. Let me kill him, and I will forgive this country for Alejandro's death. I give you my word—I am a reasonable god, but I will see justice done."

"Guilty," the man said shakily. "Yes, he is clearly guilty. You may do with him what you like."

"Bring him to the temple tomorrow, then, and I will claim his death for myself. I am done here."

She left.

All the way back home, the waters parted in front of Beatriz and closed behind Don Fernando. The rain drove down upon them mercilessly. She felt Marina's grip on her relax only when the door shut behind them at home.

Luis was awaiting her return. Vulpa, too; someone must have summoned her here. Beatriz wanted to throw herself into the arms of one or the other, but even the decision of which to embrace was too difficult. She collapsed in an armchair instead and cried her eyes out.

For a long time she cried and shook without saying anything. At last she said, "It's Ricardo. He's been accused of killing the king. He-he confessed! Marina wants him dead."

"Father said so," Luis said. "He sent word..."

"She wants me to kill him," Beatriz said. In fact she knew exactly how Marina even wanted her to go about it. The image had played out in her mind several times on the walk back, pushed there by Marina like a clinical set of instructions despite being horribly graphic. She knew exactly what Marina would want her to do.

She laughed, and her laugh must have sounded as miserable as Ricardo's. "One death to pardon the whole capital, the whole country. But how can I?"

Vulpa rubbed Beatriz's back.

Now Beatriz could barely sense Marina at all. Marina was outside in the streets, raging with the rain, preparing for her vengeance. Beatriz, her tool, had been put away for the time being. She was not thinking of her.

She looked up at Vulpa. "I have a request."

"Anything, love."

"You said once that if I had drowned in the ocean, and you had found my body, even if my heart had stopped, you would still try to save me. Teach me what you would have done."

Vulpa stiffened. "Beatriz..."

"You're thinking dangerous thoughts," Luis said. "Whatever Marina wants, you can't deny her. She'll kill you."

"There are some things I can't do," Beatriz said. "Denying Marina may be one of them. But killing a friend is another. Don't try to stop me now, brother. Perhaps I can't escape this destiny, but at least face it and do my best to fight."

24

CHAPTER TWENTY-FOUR

In the middle of the night, the night before Ricardo was to be executed, he was brought one final visitor. He expected it might be one of the interrogators who visited more frequently, there to wrap things up, or perhaps a priest, there to tell him what an execution via Marina entailed, but in fact it was an old friend, or rather his old antagonist, Captain Alban.

"I've come on Countess Leonor's behalf," he said.

There were guards outside the door. Captain Alban delivered no secret message, certainly no words of love. He asked Ricardo again why he had done what he did, what allies he had, whether he had any regrets.

To the first, Ricardo had no real answer. To the second, he could only offer denial. To the last: "Regrets? Many. None that should concern your mistress." He smirked, bitterly. Let Leonor make of that what she would.

Captain Alban shook his head. But he didn't press the matter, as indeed he did not push with any of his questions. He, like Leonor, didn't want any real answers; both of them had already decided real answers would be to their detriment. He left less than an hour after his arrival, having said nothing that had not been said before, and Ricardo was at first inclined to see the visit as a goodbye, until he realized the captain had left something on the floor near the door, just hidden enough by shadow and the angle of the door that the guards had not noticed it.

It was a knife.

Ricardo picked it up quietly, staying in the shadow himself. The knife was sheathed, and neither sheath nor knife was very fancy. The sheath was undecorated leather, the knife unpolished metal but—he ran a finger along the unsheathed edge—very sharp. So Captain Alban had left him a gift. Or rather, Leonor had sent him one.

As gifts went, it suited Leonor's personality, and better suited how she saw him. She'd given him a knife once before, after all, the very knife he'd used to kill Alejandro. Did she think he was a good enough fighter to use one knife to beat multiple guards and break out of the royal prison? Not to mention he was locked in right now. Or did she intend for him to use the knife on himself? Had she given it to him as a chance to escape the disgrace of a public execution, to go out on his own terms?

Either way, it was a generous present. Marina had stated she would forgive the capital and indeed the country for the crime of Alejandro's murder if she was allowed to kill Ricardo with her own, or rather Beatriz's, hands. Leonor was risking Felipe's chance at a peaceful, rain-less coronation for Ricardo's sake. Maybe even risking his whole reign. It was more than Ricardo could have expected from her. Nevertheless, he could not accept the opportunity. Killing Alejandro had more than quenched any blood thirst in him, and he could not imagine killing the guards even if he managed to win against them. He had no desire to stain his hands with more blood. As for killing himself... He didn't want to die, but he was tired, and after days of torture, had accepted the execution soon to come. But the hours he had left to live, he would live. He would live for as long as he could, savoring each breath. If Marina wanted him dead, she really would have to kill him.

He hid the knife under some straw in a corner. Hopefully it wouldn't be found until after he was already dead, and it would be no more than a piece of gossip for the guards, and never traced back to Captain Alban or the countess.

Eventually, he got some sleep.

* * *

The guards woke him up early—at least it felt early, it wasn't as if he could see the height of the sun—to prepare him for the grand event of a regicide's execution. He was washed, briskly, though he was not given a fresh set of clothing. Just so he would look somewhat presentable when he died, because he would be dying in front of an audience, and, more importantly, dying in Marina's temple at Marina's hands. The guards didn't want to offend a goddess with his smell.

He was hauled off to the temple in a coach with a roof, so he was barely exposed to the pouring rain. This was for practical purposes —the general populace had heard that the king's murderer was to be executed today and they were gathered outside the prison and along the street, and the guards didn't want to give any angry commoner the chance to kill Ricardo before Marina could. So for a little while at least, he was under the guards' protection. He sat in the coach and listened to the rain pelt against the roof of it, trying its utmost to rip through and get at him. The movement of the coach, jolting on potholes and slipping on wet stones and spraying water every which way, made him sick to his stomach. For a moment his mind strayed to a bouncing cart, a blanket covering his body which he had thought should have been hay. But the next bump in the road brought him back to the present.

When they arrived at the temple, he was escorted out by ten guards. Again he thought they were more here to protect him from the citizens gathered around outside the temple than to prevent him from escaping. Even if he'd brought the knife with him, he couldn't have fought off more than two guards at his best, and he was still weak from his time in prison. He tried to walk into the temple with dignity. At least the sound of the rain mostly drowned out the jeers of the bystanders. He thought he caught a glimpse of Juan in the crowd, but he was hurried inside too quickly to get a good look.

The inside of the temple was a strange mix of austerity and haphazard mess. Beatriz, who was wearing a simple blue dress, was sitting at the front of the temple, right before the statue of Marina, actually on top of the altar, and in front of her on the floor was a large basin of water. Flanking her on either side were various state officials and nobles, including Leonor. All that was very formal. But the temple itself, only half-constructed, was still in disarray. Even the scaffolding for painting the vault was still up, and certain corners still had stone blocks lying beside them, not yet put in place. And there was at least one man present with no official function: Don Fernando, who stood close by Beatriz's side, there only as Beatriz's father.

The guards hauled Ricardo before the altar and Beatriz. Her eyes were glowing again, but Ricardo thought he could see a little of her own emotions coming through—her muscles and the lines of her face were tense, and she looked more anxious than angry. Her voice was low and angry when she spoke, though: "Ricardo Montero, you stand condemned to death for regicide. Do you have any final words? Speak them before these witnesses."

Ricardo would have liked to send a message to his family who lived in the country, or some final advice to Juan. He could not, however, bring himself to go into these things, which to him seemed important, but to all these officials and a goddess would seem like trivialities. Instead, he stared Marina in the eyes and thought things over. Had she worn any other body as her human vessel, he might have spat in her face. Out of respect to Beatriz, he contented himself with saying, "I lived my life as an artist, and did much of my work in the service of King Alejandro. Now I have become..."

He trailed off. At this final moment, he could not say it. "I wish," he said, now mostly to Beatriz, though he doubted Marina or perhaps anyone here would realize it, "I wish I could live another thirty years, paint more paintings and see how the world of art will develop, who will rise and who will fall. Admire more masterpieces. Since I cannot, I hope I can die with dignity, and at least some will remember my work and my name."

Beatriz's face contorted in a way Ricardo had never seen it twist before. He was so preoccupied by this that he barely heard the officials uttering some formalities, and was even startled when Marina spoke again through Beatriz, holding her arms up grandly and saying, "Very well. This man's death is mine, and with it I will forgive the country for Alejandro's murder. Let Salandra be cleansed, and this crime be avenged."

There were still guards holding Ricardo's arms, and his hands were tied behind him. Beatriz's hands grabbed him by the neck and shoved him down to his knees. She pushed his head into the basin, into the water.

Oh, he thought. Of course. He'd assumed it was here for some ritual purpose, perhaps for cleansing—well, Marina had said she did consider this to be a cleansing act. But nothing so sedate or peaceful. Marina wanted him to drown.

He'd told himself he would take death quietly. There was no way out for him. That was fine for a moment or two, except he'd taken a breath before they shoved his head under, and he couldn't bring himself to breathe out and in again. His body knew what would happen, and it wanted to survive. He held his breath, wondering when his lungs would start to burn, until someone, probably a guard, hit his back hard, forcing a gasp and an exhale out of him. He inhaled, and there was the burning after all. Instinctively he began to struggle, pushing back and trying to pull his head up, but both Marina's grasp on his neck and head and the guards' hold of his arms remained firm.

It felt like a long time before the world went black and awareness faded away.

* * *

He did not expect to wake up again.

When he did, he was lying on his back, looking up into Beatriz's eyes. She was leaning over him, and although her eyes were fiercely intent, they were also fully hers—warm brown rather than coldly glowing blue. Her hand still emitted blue light, though, and it spasmed against his chest as she pulled away from him. She had been striking his chest, he realized now, and it hurt, deeper than a bruise.

He coughed, and water came out of his mouth, joining a puddle next to him on the floor. Slowly he sat up. Beatriz helped him, supporting his arm.

There were voices all around them, fearful and angry.

"—cannot simply forgive a man for—"

"Do you want to bring Marina's wrath down on all of us?"

"You may be the goddess's chosen one, but..."

"Ricardo Montero died," Beatriz declared, "which was the agreed punishment. His heart and breathing stopped. I've brought him back to life, which is against no law I know of. You cannot kill a man twice for one crime. If there are to be any consequences, let them rest on me."

She said this without breaking eye contact with Ricardo.

Whether she was speaking to the officials or to Marina herself, Ricardo couldn't have said. Maybe both. Insanity to contradict either. Yet there was no one like Beatriz for audacity. It would have been funny that she dared to do this if it weren't so terrifying. He hadn't wanted or expected anyone to risk themselves for him against a goddess, and now two women in one day, and one of them Beatriz, a simple painter, his brash, idiotic friend. He'd hated her for a little while, but he could never want her to get hurt.

"Beatriz..."

The sound of thunder cracked over the temple. No sound of rain but there was something else outside—a sort of a hissing, rushing sound...

Another woman wormed her way around Beatriz. Leonor. She helped Ricardo to his feet. "Montero should be taken back to the palace or to prison in safety," she said loudly. "His debt has been paid, and the law can't claim the same life twice."

The oldest official present loudly agreed with her, and this seemed enough to sway those gathered into frantic action. Some people scuttled off towards the door, others in other directions. Two guards grabbed Ricardo's arms again and hustled him to the door, following an imperious Leonor. Ricardo looked back and saw Beatriz putting her arms around her father and then shoving her away to follow the crowd.

When they opened the door to the temple, a stream of water rushed in. It hit their shins as hard as a rock, toppling more than one official over. *What is this*, they exclaimed, *what is this?* The water outside previously had not extended all the way up the temple stairs, but now it did—only it was not that the water level had risen, but that the water was now racing up the stairs, uphill, and into the temple.

The guard holding Ricardo's right arm cursed.

"We go forward," Leonor declared. "If Marina wants to attack

Montero or us, she will. Otherwise, Beatriz de Comete has taken the blame for this incident on herself. We should not be here for however Marina chooses to punish her own oracle. She will not be gentle."

"Beatriz," Ricardo said. His voice came out raspy. He tried to turn back, to ask her what the hell she'd done and what she had planned, but he was pulled forward and shoved back into the waiting coach, which soon was in motion, driving him away from the site of his own death.

25

CHAPTER TWENTY-FIVE

When the rain stopped, the capital froze for a moment.

The crowd on the street outside the temple let out a cheer, as did many others around the city, elated that Marina's wrath had passed. She had forgiven the people of Salandra and perhaps would now smile on them again. A new king could be crowned. The world could move on.

Many of the capital's citizens went to their doors and windows to take a look outside, to assure themselves the rain truly had stopped and the clouds were beginning to clear. Their cheer lasted only a few minutes. Then there was a sudden, fierce thunderclap, and before their bewildered eyes, the water in the streets began to move.

The current all over the capital ran with a single mind. It did not run to the low spots of the town, or into the gutters, or out of the city. It ran swiftly over ground both low and high, winding its way up to Marina's temple, where it seeped in the unfinished foundation and flowed straight through the open door.

* * *

In the temple, Beatriz was alone.

The nobles and officials had all fled following the thunderclap and the strange noises outside. She was glad they had taken Ricardo with them and had seemed unlikely to harm him at least for the moment. Don Fernando had gone too, though it had taken some persuasion to get him to do so. Beatriz had told him that her conversation with her goddess was a private matter. Truthfully, she only hoped she could center Marina's wrath on herself. She thought Marina's sense of honor would prevent her going after Ricardo again, but given the chance she might well lash out at bystanders, especially anyone related to Beatriz.

As for Beatriz, Marina's anger didn't frighten her anymore. It wasn't that she wanted to die. But it all felt inevitable. Marina for so long had been controlling her actions, influencing even her emotions and thoughts, and had shown no sign of letting go of that control in the future; would she not eventually claim Beatriz's death for herself too? Beatriz couldn't imagine otherwise. At least this way, Beatriz had done something she herself had wanted, needed to do. She had not let Marina use her hands to kill Ricardo, not in any way that mattered. And now if Marina wanted to kill her, so it would be. She would accept it.

The water was already a foot high in the temple as she approached the scaffolding. She climbed one step up, then another, then another, carefully gripping the wood and watching where she placed her foot. Usually she climbed automatically, in something of a haze, but today, she thought she would fall if she did so. Her body was shaking, and Marina was waiting to pounce on the slightest slip.

"Do you think you can escape me if you climb, little one? That the water cannot reach you? There is nowhere in this temple—nowhere in the world—I cannot reach you."

"I know that," Beatriz said. Her voice sounded calm. How funny.

"There is just something I want to do first. You can drown me then, can't you?"

She climbed up to the top. There were still some of her painting supplies here, left behind when she'd run out a week ago, overcome by Marina's grief and rage. The paint on the pallette had dried out. She laid down more, mixing paint and medium to the colors she wanted. There was a vivid red. A peachy color, more or less like a fair skintone—usually she'd be more particular but today she was in a hurry. A couple of browns. Mundane colors, realistic, a little dirty. More like what she used to use, before the beginning of her divine inspiration.

Below, the water was rising faster than it should have been able to, sloshing higher against on the walls, the scaffolding. She would paint quickly.

She started with the roughest, quickest chalk sketch imaginable on a free space of ceiling. Two figures, a woman and a man. One with her hair loose and wavy, the other with his hair neatly tied back to get it out of the way of his work. She tried to remember the details of her clothing. Ah, but there was no time for precision. Very well. She would start with the faces and work her way down. The clothing was less important.

"How dare you deface my vault with your own petty artwork!"

"You're the one who picked me to paint this ceiling," Beatriz said. "If you regret it, you have no one else to blame but yourself."

The figures were meant to be Vulpa and Ricardo, of course. A last little act of rebellion, and a final work of art, unaffected by Marina's influence on her. (Her scarred hand shook even worse than the rest of her, and she could feel a blue weight on her mind, but she resisted it—this painting was hers and could not be taken from her.) She started with painting Vulpa's face. How high were her eyes again, and how long was her nose? She had a hard time placing them and had to guess at it—the result was not very satisfactory.

She would paint quickly.

She sighed. "I underrate Ricardo. He does a good deal of his work without models, all guesswork. A skill I lack." All her art came from observation—Ricardo would have lectured her on knowing the general forms of anatomy and facial shape well enough to make the woman look, if not precisely like Vulpa, at least like a woman with a little of her soul...

Well, she thought, he would go on making such paintings in the future now. She had ensured that.

As for her, she might not be satisfied with this face, but when she added a little red hair, she thought it was at least like Vulpa enough that if Vulpa looked at the vault later, she would know Beatriz had been thinking of her. That would have to suffice.

"Do you think you can plant your lover on my temple? I will wash this image away and destroy you at the same time."

Ricardo now. Beatriz knew his face a bit better, could depict him more accurately. After all, she had sketched him many times before. They had sketched each other over and over again, lazy afternoon after lazy afternoon when not in reference for some abstract commission. She knew his dark eyes, just how his nose broadened at the tip, the angle of his cheekbones. She smiled as she added a little pink to his thin lips. He always let them get chapped in the winter. This year she wouldn't be around to make fun of him about it, but she knew it would be the same.

Waves crashed against the scaffolding, causing it to shake. The water was halfway up already. There was no way Beatriz would have time to paint the bodies. She would perfect the hair and necklines instead.

"THAT MURDERER. HOW DARE YOU PLACE HIM HERE, AMONG MY CHOSEN ONES."

"He is similar to your chosen ones, isn't he?" Beatriz said. "You raise your chosen ones up like Alejandro lifted Ricardo. Then you kill them or ruin them when they displease you, like you had me murder Ricardo."

"Not murder but justice. He is the sinner."

"Maybe," Beatriz said. "I don't know. I never heard his full version of the story when we went to talk to him. After all, you rather controlled the flow of that conversation." She deepened the shadow on Vulpa's neck. Poor Vulpa had always wanted to see how Beatriz would portray her, but Marina would probably keep her word and wash this painting away. "I could never have killed him. You knew that."

"You should have obeyed me."

"Maybe," Beatriz agreed again. After all, Marina was a goddess. But...

More chiaroscuro, this time on Montero's face, one side of it at least. Make him look half made of light and half buried in shadow. "Ricardo killed someone you loved. But he is someone I love. That's why I'm painting him here on the ceiling, along with all of your chosen ones. I chose Ricardo over you. I'm sorry."

"YOU HAVE MORE IMPUDENCE THAN A MORTAL'S LOT."

Beatriz picked up the chalk again and made a quick sketch next to her two rough paintings. "I'm sorry," she repeated. "I should never have been the one you chose, you know." She'd never loved Marina, only ever feared her and sometimes wanted a taste of her power. Maybe if she'd loved Marina enough, everything else could have felt like simply a gift she was offering; sharing even her mind and body with Marina would have felt like union, or at worst self-sacrifice, rather than corrosion. As it was, nothing she'd given Marina had been entirely willing, not even her death that she was offering now.

She could give one last gift.

"I'll paint the king for you," she said, beginning to lay down the color of his skin. "Here. Try not to wash it away. Or do, if you'd rather have someone else do it. Still, you loved him. He should be here."

"Next to the people you loved more than me? You find that fitting?"

"You loved him more than me, after all," Beatriz said bitterly. She thought of how Marina had tried to make her love Alejandro, how much of her service had been tailored to support their relationship. She dared to be angry at a goddess. "But let's not part on bad terms, shall we?"

Marina was quiet in her mind, not offering either remonstrance nor the slightest hint of inspiration. She painted the king's face, hair, body, clothes... the water rose, but slowly. At last, she set down her brush.

"There," she said. "Now, let us be finished. I think you and I have no more to say to each other. But you'll swallow me up like all those you loved until death nonetheless."

The scaffolding collapsed, and she fell into the water, which had risen almost up to the level of the platform anyway. She didn't try to swim. Let it take her again, as it had that night on the beach. Then Marina had wanted to claim her. Now things were different, but Beatriz still had no way to fight a goddess. Let it be done gracefully, at least.

"Little one," Marina said mournfully, "you never loved me."

Beatriz sighed. Bubbles escaped her nose and mouth.

"Yet I loved you, more dearly than you know. Perhaps you are right, and we never should have been."

Beatriz closed her eyes.

"Very well. As you say, an end to it."

26

CHAPTER TWENTY-SIX

Being a dead man at this point, Ricardo received little news of the outside world and no visitors aside from a couple guards. What he knew was that the new king had been crowned and that the rain had stopped, and he knew the latter more because he'd been outside when it happened than because anyone cared to update him on current events.

The guards offered him frequent speculation on what his own eventual fate would be. "If they know what's best, they'll toss you into the sea to drown you more thoroughly," was the general consensus, but sometimes they came up with more creative ideas about drawing and quartering or burning at the stake. Ricardo ignored them. Having died already, he knew every day of life that remained to him was more than he could really have expected. Still, there was a part of him that dared to hope he might survive all this—Beatriz had done her best to save him from even a goddess's wrath, and the considerable force of Leonor was on his side as well. Perhaps the situation was not entirely unsalvageable.

His hopes were very small, however, and dwindled by the day, until one day, a different guard from the usual showed up in his cell, had his chains removed, and ceremoniously read him an official document written up by the ministry of justice and signed by a couple of different officials for approval. The verdict was this: Inasmuch as Marina had claimed Ricardo's life already, it would be presumptuous beyond belief for Salandra to kill him again, no matter how her execution had misfired. However, allowing a regicide to live peacefully in Salandra would also be a great outrage to all the court and to the general public. Thus, Ricardo was officially exiled. He had a week to leave the country, and the majority of his belongings (here the document went into minutia) were confiscated and now property of the government.

Ricardo was still escorted out of the prison by two guards holding his arms. But when they reached the door, they threw him out and went back inside, leaving him dazed, and free, on the street.

He was not alone. In seconds he was enveloped in an eager embrace by Juan, who apparently had heard he was getting out and had been waiting at the door for him for ages. "Master, you're free at last! Justice finally—I kept on writing to the ministry but no one ever answered me. They almost executed you! You could have died. I was very worried they would do so again, for these cretins clearly have no idea..."

"Executing me would have been just," Ricardo cut in. "I did kill the king, Juan."

"Ah." Juan goggled for a moment. "But—but there must have been circumstances. You'll have to tell me about it later, but first let's get you home. We shouldn't stay more than a day in the capital —we only have a week to leave the country—but there are still some things..."

"We?"

"Yes, you've been exiled, master. They didn't tell you?"

"I've been exiled. But not you, Juan. Surely no one's implicated you in my crimes."

"Oh, no. After the initial questioning they generally forgot I existed, and as I said they wouldn't even answer my letters. But of course I'm coming with you. I've packed up most of my things, but I've only packed a few of yours. I'm not entirely clear on which are now property of the government, even though they read me the edict. You'd better have a look yourself and figure out what you're taking."

"Juan... you should stay in Salandra. My name's been besmirched, and likely yours along with it, but your talent is known well enough. Someone else will take you on as an apprentice, even if it takes a while to find them."

Juan scoffed. "Who else would I want as my master? Every artist in this city is envious of your talent and aspires to be more like you, and that's a fact. No, I'll come with you and finish my training. I was thinking we might go to Efiteria. You've often spoken of the art at their court. Even if they've moved in strange directions and no longer appreciate the classical style as much, it would be interesting to see, and at least they love their artists."

It was not the worst idea. The edict of Ricardo's banishment had not in fact specified where he should go. If he wanted to continue practicing his art, he would have to pick a country that wouldn't hold it against him that he'd committed regicide, and while Efiteria did not in general encourage murder, as a nation it did not greatly like King Alejandro and might in fact congratulate Ricardo for killing him. Hm. Not a bad option, though Ricardo would have to take a while to consider it.

It was a bad idea for Juan to come with him, though. Juan was young, and innocent, and Salandran, and there was no reason for him to ruin his own life like this. Ricardo would have to dissuade him, but first there was a more important matter: "I got little news in prison."

"I can imagine, master. What can I tell you?"

"Beatriz," Ricardo asked, "Is she alive?"

* * *

"Ricardo Montero is here to see you," Inez said. "He says he's been released at last, and he came here first thing to thank you. He's a bit of a wreck, though, not really suitable for visiting. And it's late. I could send him away, miss."

Beatriz pushed herself upright in bed. "Bring him up. I've been wanting to see him. And they say he's been exiled now. I should speak with him while I still can. No, wait, on second thought, I'll come down. I've had more energy today, and I shouldn't greet a guest in bed in my nightclothes."

"You've been sick," Inez said. "It's understandable. Montero should be the last person to criticize you when for his sake..."

"Still, I have my pride. Please indulge me, Inez. Tell him I'll be down in just a few minutes, if he can wait."

"Very well." Inez shut the door perhaps a little harder than she needed to on the way out.

Beatriz sighed, shook her head, and got out of bed. She was in her nightgown. To see Ricardo, there was no need for courtly attire or any makeup, but she at least should wear one of her painter's outfits. Otherwise she'd outrage his sense of decency, and though at this point he might consider himself too indebted to her to mention it, watching him swallow back censure would actually be more painful than getting a scolding.

"Will you help me, Vulpa?" she asked. "I just can't get the hang of changing yet, sorry. Maybe I should have asked Inez to stay."

Vulpa, who was sitting at her bedside, had already stood. "Of course I'll help. Stop apologizing. You can't expect to be able to do everything with one hand yet, can you? Give it time."

Beatriz nodded, and let Vulpa undo the nightgown's buttons.

She had lost her left hand, the one that had borne Marina's mark. They'd found her at the foot of a wrecked heap of scaffolding and other debris, bloody and scratched and soaking wet, when the water drained out of the temple. The Comete family had all been waiting outside—in the closest building with a high enough floor—to fetch her out when the going was clear. They had expected to be fetching a body, but she had still been breathing. But there had been a lot of blood, most of it coming from her left hand, which had been completely crushed by a rock dislodged from the wall. The blood loss had not been fatal, but the hand had needed to be amputated.

Three doctors had been summoned to do the job, the best in the city, the Comete family sparing no expense.

"Did you assist?" Beatriz had asked Vulpa later. (The surgery was a blur of pain to her—she couldn't remember such facts about it.)

"I did not. I have little experience in surgery. Besides, it's not recommended for a doctor to do that kind of emergency treatment for a loved one. They get nervous and make mistakes." Vulpa had ducked her head. "I couldn't have treated you properly. I was a mess."

Beatriz had touched Vulpa with her remaining hand. Teasing, trying to cheer her up, she said, "So you love me, Vulpa, do you?"

"Silly woman. You know I do." Vulpa's eyes were teary. "I thought you would die."

Beatriz had assumed as much herself. She had believed she would never truly escape Marina, and did not fully understand why Marina had let her go. Had it been the remnants of the affection she claimed to feel for Beatriz that moved her to mercy? That didn't seem like her. Or was this rejection—had Marina refused to even take Beatriz in death, casting her away after destroying the mark on her hand that tied them together?

Rejection or mercy: Beatriz could only be grateful.

Even now, even aside from her missing hand, she knew that she was changed, different from the woman she had been at the beginning of the summer—would never fully be the same. But she was alive, and that was good. She would have more time with Vulpa and her family and her art, and that was very good.

While Vulpa had not assisted in the treatment, she'd been around the house a lot ever since, and she did take it on herself to help Beatriz with a lot of everyday tasks she now found difficult. Now she helped Beatriz get into a more modest outfit and walked close by her side, protective, out to the parlor where Ricardo was waiting for her.

Ricardo practically lunged forward when he saw her and pulled her into a hug. Beatriz hugged him back with one arm, arranging the other so that Ricardo's embrace wouldn't squeeze her healing stump, which would be very painful.

"I'm glad to see you well," she told him, though in fact he still looked haggard and dirty and a little bit haunted. But he was free. "I've been very worried about you."

"Beatriz, I'm so sorry. I judged you for something that wasn't your fault, not even slightly. I insulted our friendship, and you saved my life. Please forgive me. You've always known I'm a fool."

"The goddess played with both of us. I don't blame you for anything."

"The goddess... I don't know that she's at fault for the way I acted, how I felt then. But I certainly was not myself. I'm sorry."

Beatriz shook her head. "It's fine. But if you don't let go of me, Luis is going to pull you off any second now."

Ricardo laughed and stepped back, arms shaking as they released her. "Fine. You're right. I'm sorry."

"Sit down. You must be tired."

"I'm all right."

"If you sit down, I can sit down too. And they say I still need plenty of rest. If I'm going to be listening to a long story, I want to be sitting."

"A long story?"

"Well, I was hoping you'd explain where you disappeared to this summer, and how you ended up... well, not that you have to."

Ricardo sighed. "That really is a long story, and not one for a large audience. But if your brother will step away, and your friend here, I'll tell you anything you want to know."

Beatriz smiled over at Luis and Vulpa. "It's all right. We can talk without any supervision. After all, we've been friends for years."

* * *

The temple was a mess.

It had not been wrecked by the water, but some unfinished walls had been damaged, and the smaller statues of sea nymphs and the like had been smashed. The vault had never quite been reached by the waves, and so Beatriz's paintings remained, but towards the center of the circle some paint had been smeared badly enough that you could no longer tell what had been painted there. It appeared to be three figures, but it would have been impossible to say who they were. And then of course there was the collapsed scaffolding, and a certain amount of water damage done to the foundation and to the floor.

The priests of the temple as well as Master Galeas were vehement in saying that the temple should not be simply abandoned or torn down despite it having been a focal point of Marina's rage. After all, if Marina had wished to destroy it in her tantrum, she surely would have. No, it would have to be fixed up, they said. The matter was left under Queen Dowager Leonor's supervision, given that it was not an area where the new king, Felipe had any experience. She agreed with the priests, agreed it was wise to do whatever necessary to ensure Marina's rage would not be directed at Salandra again, and especially not at her son.

The construction workers who had been building the temple previously were easy to hunt down. They had abandoned work for a time, true, but had generally stayed in the city and were willing to go back to work. A few, frightened by recent events, quit, but they were not hard to replace. The difficult thing was finding a new painter to work on the vault. The queen dowager looked through the paintings submitted a couple months ago for the late king's competition, and selected an experienced artist, well esteemed in Ferrar, by the name of Valdez, and he agreed to take up the commission. As there was no increase in rainfall afterwards, general consensus was that Marina approved.

The temple's construction and decoration was completed a few years later, and celebrated with a banquet that was well attended, though the Comete family remained notably absent, and it was said the queen dowager herself had a somewhat distant expression throughout the proceedings, as if her mind was in another place, another time—but then, gossips would say anything, of a queen just as easily as of a painter. Some even said the infamous Ricardo Montero and the scandalous Beatriz de Comete had been good people, misunderstood and poorly used, and everyone knew that couldn't be the case. Better not to listen to that kind of talk.

ABOUT THE AUTHOR

Melody Wiklund is a writer of fantasy and occasionally romance, including the YA novel Eleven Dancing Sisters, published in 2017. In her free time she loves knitting and watching Chinese dramas. Sometimes she draws, more rarely paints. She is a big fan of baroque art, particularly that of Diego Velasquez.

CPSIA information can be obtained
at www.ICGtesting.com
Printed in the USA
BVHW030837070423
661949BV00004B/89